THE WIZARD AND THE WARLORD

THE WARDSTONE TRILOGY BOOK THREE
(Hardcover Edition)

M.R. Mathias

ISBN: 978-1-946187-10-9
2016 Modernized Format Edition
Created in the United States of America
Worldwide Rights

M. R. MATHIAS

This book is a work of fiction. All characters, names, places, and incidents are products of the author's imagination or are used fictitiously. Any resemblance to any actual persons, living or dead, events or locales, is entirely coincidental.

This trilogy is dedicated to anyone who has ever faced addiction or prison time.

You can overcome.

Jack Hoyle is responsible for these amazing 2016 Modernized Edition covers
Find him at www.t-rexstudios.com

Thank you JT, for the formatting help. It was timely.

M. R. MATHIAS

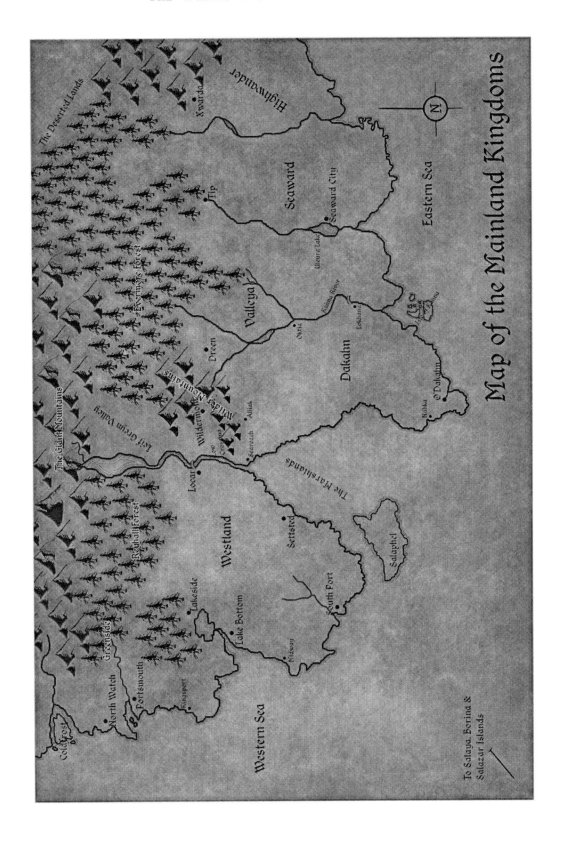

Map of the Mainland Kingdoms

M. R. Mathias

THE WIZARD AND THE WARLORD

Chapter One

"Men are always fighting wars," Telgra's father Dargeon lectured. He was an elf of more than two hundred years. "The humans are never content with what they have, or the world around them. They long for power over each other, so much so that they will lie, cheat, steal, and kill to get it. What is worse is that they will dabble with forces of any nature to give them an advantage."

"Well, what dark nature did they dabble in that caused this wonder to grace our senses?" Telgra asked him.

He laughed at her. They, and a small delegation of their kind, had secretly traveled across the continent from the Evermore Forest and then taken a ship to the Isle of Salaya. Now they were standing atop the island, amid a miniature forest of blooming fiery trees in the late morning of a warm and beautiful day.

"The magic of King Mikahl's sword, Pavreal's sword, was born from the magic of Arbor, my dear." Dargeon put his arm around her and kissed the top of her golden hair lovingly. "It was not a man who caused this blooming love. It was ancient elven magic."

Never in her seventy-two years of life had Telgra questioned her father's wisdom, until that moment. "But father, you prove my point about the humans. Pavreal's sword was forged by dwarven hammers, under the fire of dragons, with the purest of metals that the giants brought us from the mountains. We may have ensorcelled the blade with its power, but on that day, when the sword was made, the races of the light all came together for the good of the world, and all of us in it." She put her hands on her hips, like her mother sometimes did.

He smiled at her with fatherly love.

"Pavreal was a human, Father," she continued. "If it were not for him, our magic would have never been instilled into the blade and would have never caused the fiery trees to bloom. So, therefore, it is humanity who caused this beauty before us. We only had but a small part in it."

Dargeon stood there dumbfounded by her logic. He realized at that moment how much like her mother she was. He decided that the elf who eventually took her hand would most likely be as unlucky as he was blessed.

They made their way back to the monastery's entrance. Some of the monks who tended the mountaintop garden were whispering over a pot of carrot stew.

The elven expedition's second-in-command stepped up. He was an ancient, blue-haired elf named Brevan. He had been speaking to a few of the monks. Telgra smiled at him respectfully. He returned the gesture and then touched her on the shoulder, more or less ignoring Dargeon.

"I think the origin of the fairy trees is more than likely traceable back to the Evermore Forest. After all, that great forest is where the fairy folk have lived for as long as time has been kept."

"I think," Telgra interrupted cautiously, "I think the name fairy tree is misleading. The blooms are bright red and flecked with yellow. It looks like the trees are on fire. I think it's more likely that the ancients called them fiery trees, not fairy trees, and all of us have just lost the inflection over time. The long dormancy of the flowering, and this remote location of the only known grove, possibly caused the name to get misspoken over the years."

Old Brevan narrowed his wispy eyebrows, causing the tips of his ears to push their way out of his long silver-blue hair. "On what do you base this theory?" Looking over her shoulder, he gave a look to the monks who had suddenly gone quiet so that they could listen.

"Master Brevan, it's known that the fae have never been to this island. It's also known that never has one of those trees been anywhere else but this island." Her tone was confident and she spoke with more and more surety as she went on. "It seems obvious to me that if anyone were to call them fairy trees, it would be because of their stunted size. But ask yourself this question: when the humans of this island first saw the trees bloom, did they even know what a fairy was? I've been taught that the fair folk kept to themselves, and still stay hidden from human eyes. Go look for yourself, sirs." She finished with a shy grin at the monks. "In this breeze the sea has gifted us with today, those trees positively look to be ablaze."

Before Brevan could respond, Telgra was lightly skipping out of the open-air hall and down one of the paths that wound through the grove.

"She has a valid point, Brevan," another elf stepped out of the shadows and said matter-of-factly.

Brevan sighed. "Too bright for her own good, I fear," he said while staring aimlessly at the vacant spot where she had just been. After a moment he turned to the human monks and smiled. "Well what do you think of that?"

Later that evening, well after the sun had set, Telgra was standing among the fiery trees, enjoying the thick cinnamon and lavender aroma of their blossoms. Her eyes were looking skyward into the vast openness of the world. She felt like a giant standing in a forest that came up to her shoulders. In the Evermore, the trees reached to staggering heights. Oaks, elms, royal pines and bellow firs all reached hundreds of feet over her head. She figured that an elf standing in this forest would relatively be about a finger's length tall in comparison.

The little girl inside her took over for a while and she began stalking through the trees pretending to be some huge monster, smashing villages and towns under her feet. She worked her way to the southernmost edge of the glade when a horrid smell came to her, carried on the ocean breeze from somewhere to the south. Thankfully, it was a brief sensation. She scrunched up her nose, but paid it little mind. She then started toward a copse that stood separate from the main grove, at the edge of the viewing path that wound its way through the garden.

The sound of crying came to her ears. For a moment the grotesque smell wavered past her again. As she neared the copse she decided that the smell was coming from somewhere very far away. She'd smelled rotting flesh before, when the expedition had come across a long dead mooza in the forest, and again as they crossed the bridge at Tip in an invisible huddle. The humans had been warring there. This smell was very similar. Now, just as it had then, the stink made her want to retch.

She put herself downwind of the separated cluster of fairy trees, and let the savory smell of the flowers fill her nose again. She sat cross-legged and breathed deeply, filling her lungs with the potent scent. It took only seconds to make her feel better.

She was certain that the trees had some magical purpose. There were many medicinal and magical qualities to the petals and buds. She was determined to understand what the purpose of these trees was in the world. When she looked into the sky, a shooting star sped past. She giggled with delight as she lay back and traced its trajectory with an outstretched finger.

A few moments later she slipped into a deep, dreamy sleep.

8

In her dream she was in a forest so great and huge that she felt like a mouse. The ground around her was strewn with leaves the size of blankets and twigs as big as felled trees. Ahead of her, a butterfly the size of a horse, with wings of gold and velvety black, beckoned her to come closer.

She did, though hesitantly.

"Get on my back, Telgra," the butterfly said in a soft, musical voice similar to her mother's. "Let's fly."

"Love to," she heard herself reply as she climbed onto the delicate creature's back. It fluttered into the air and darted to and fro through the monstrous branches of the trees. Higher and higher they went. They passed several little villages of elves who were as small as she was. They had houses made from hollowed-out mushrooms that grew on the giant limbs. The inhabitants waved and smiled as she and her fragile mount fluttered up and past them.

A blackbird darted by, eyeing them hungrily. It started to bank around toward them but ended up spotting something else below. A snake as big as the dragons in the tales her father used to read her lazed along one of the upper branches. Its lime-colored scales were splotched with sunlight. Telgra looked up and saw that the great golden swaths of living light had found a way through the leaves above them. Motes of dust danced through them like cottony flakes of gold.

The butterfly carried them right into one of the rays and immediately Telgra felt the sun warm her skin. The brightness of the Giver's light forced her to look anywhere but up. They fluttered ever upward in tight circles that kept them in the warm, pleasant ray. Soon Telgra saw the tops of the trees below her. Great slab-like leaves flickered on the breeze, each a different shade of green. It all shimmered as she was carried even higher. Below, the mosaic of the leaves seemed to blend into a rolling sea of emerald and teal. A gust of wind buffeted them sideways. Telgra looked up to see that the forest they had just left was surrounded by the white lace of a crashing shoreline. The butterfly, which no longer seemed as big as a horse, fought the wind and turned them into it.

The delicate insect carried them beyond the land. For a very long time only the glistening cobalt expanse of ocean spread out below them. Eventually a mass of land appeared to the south, an island. How big it was she couldn't guess, for she had no true sense of how big or small she herself really was.

As they flew above she saw a dark thing take flight from a clearing in the black forest that covered most of this other island. From somewhere farther away she heard a howling scream. It was followed by the sound of sobbing. Over the menacing island, in a clearing, she saw a circular hole in the earth. Around it, men in robes of bright crimson danced and chanted. As the gusts carried her butterfly haphazardly over the hole she felt a powerful sense of fear. A horrible, rotten smell filled her nostrils and made her stomach roil. She chanced a look down into the depths and froze in terror. A great toothy maw came shooting upward. Behind yellowed teeth, demon-red eyes glowed so brightly that they seemed to outshine the sun. The butterfly tried to turn away, to evade the closing teeth of the fiend coming for them, but it couldn't move fast enough.

Telgra cried out in fear as the fetid mouth of the monster closed down over her. Just as it would have swallowed her, a flash of magical blue light flared and the monster roared out in pain. Telgra looked around to see a man in silver chainmail riding a winged horse made of flame. The man's sword was glowing bright blue. His wavy golden hair fluttered behind him as he swooped back in to attack the beast a second time.

The butterfly was knocked through the air by a scaly limb. Telgra screamed as she began tumbling down toward the open hole. Faster and faster she fell, until the world and all its colors were soaring past in a great blur.

Suddenly, she felt a cold hand patting her gently on her cheek. Her eyes fluttered open and she expected to find herself lying at the edge of the copse of fiery trees, but that's not where she was. A statue of a boy was... was... was doing what? A statue of a boy was patting her face and looking down at her with an expression of deep concern.

"Are you all right, m'lady?" the statue asked.

The deep, grumbly voice of someone low to the ground barked out irritably, "That girl is an elf! She's a fargin elf maiden!"

"Lady," the statue said, with a smile forming on its ever stony face. "Let's get you up now."

Telgra's world spun again. She felt herself falling backward through something. Maybe trees?

"Come, m'lady," a soft, nervous voice spoke.

She fluttered her eyes open again and tensed as the sensation of weightlessness came over her. "Where?" She mumbled the question feebly.

Telgra relaxed when she saw that one of the monks of Salaya had her in his soft, chubby arms. The morning sun was bright, but he was purposely keeping the shadow of his round head in a position to shade her eyes. His smile grew as he felt her fear slide away.

"You fell asleep in the grove, lady," the man carried on. "Your father would turn us all into frogs if we hadn't found you. Oh how the town would talk about that."

"I was dreaming," she said, returning his smile. "The dream was so, so real."

"The trees do that to you, even when they aren't in bloom." The monk's voice grew serious. "I hope they were good dreams."

The look in his eyes piqued Telgra's curiosity. The memory of the fear she'd felt when she looked down into that horrible-smelling pit came to her for an instant.

"What if they were bad dreams?" she asked.

"The dream of the fairy trees helps us to have visions of the future, or glimpses of the present elsewhere." The monk stopped and let Telgra down to her feet. After he looked at her a moment he paled visibly.

"Are the dreams always prophetic?" she asked. "Do they always come to pass?"

"I'm afraid so," the monk replied.

"Then something must be done about the island to the south of here. If it wasn't a vision of the future I saw, then we might already be too late."

Chapter Two

Word that the human's great war had finally come to an end made its way to Salaya by trade ship. The news came the same morning that Telgra had her dream in the grove. This information, the monks explained to the elven delegation, came to the island in the form of sealed scrolls from the High King of men; it wasn't gossip.

The slave master king of Dakahn had been bested, and the tale of the deed was so fantastic that it overshadowed Telgra's dark vision. For days her insistent warnings were dismissed as foolish attempts to draw attention to herself. Other tales of wizards and kings battling the slaver, and of the dragon queen and her acid-spewing wyrm, were told and retold over her. She pleaded with her father to at least look into the matter, but the stories of how the great red dragon that used to guard the seal to the underworld had come to aid High King Mikahl and his wizard were more intriguing. The huge, winged worm had torn down the walls to King Ra'Gren's castle and cleared a road for the High King's armies to march in. Tens of thousands of slaves had been freed. The dwarves had come back to the surface from their underground cities to aid in the battle, too. Telgra's premonitions weren't taken seriously at all.

Her only ally in the matter was the monk who had found her after she'd dreamt. His name was Dostin. Dostin was what the other monks referred to as simpleminded. He was slow, and not always clear with the meanings of his words. He was clumsy and easily pleased or distracted. His pleas to the superiors of his order were taken even less seriously than Telgra's.

Another ship arrived bearing news that the High King was marrying the Princess of Seaward, and that the dwarves had pledged to build a new palace in the new seat of the unified realm of men, a city called Oktin.

After enough badgering, Telgra's father finally conferred with the monks about his daughter's dream. They explained to the elves that dreams in the fairy grove are truly prophetic. Telgra hadn't fallen asleep in the grove. She had been found by the simpleton lying at the edge of the tiny copse. They didn't doubt that she dreamed what she said she did. The dreams of prophecy only visited those who slept in the heart of the grove, and even then the revealing visions only found their way into the sleep of but a small handful.

A full turn of the moon after the ordeal, Telgra was standing near the copse where she'd fallen asleep. She was enjoying the cool, salty air as it swept across her skin. The sun had just recently set and the sky was a brilliant sheet of pastel blue that exploded into a reddish copper band before it disappeared beyond the sea. Stories of the High King's fantastic wedding had made it to the island, too. Telgra found herself envious of young Princess Rosa. The High King had been the one who'd ridden the flaming Pegasus in her dream. Unfounded tales of a hole in the earth similar to the one she saw were being told. Only this hole had been in some Westland castle's bailey yard. Great winged demons had supposedly escaped the hells there. She tried not to think about the dark things. She envisioned herself in a fancy flowing dress of silk and lace standing before an elven hero. Only her hero had no face because a true elven hero hadn't lived for ages. There was Vaegon Willowbrow, the elf who'd helped the High King and the fabled wizard Hyden Hawk. But Vaegon had been killed. His younger brother Dieter was cute, though, she mused. And the Willowbrow family were well-respected hunters.

Her pleasant thoughts were suddenly rocked away when the foul smell hit her full in the face again. She fought back a reflex to gag, and with a determination that only an elven woman can muster, she went to find her father. The smell, this time, wasn't faint. It was thick and horrible.

She was worried, but wanted to show the others that she hadn't been just a silly girl wanting attention, too.

She found her father studying specimens at a well-lit table full of fiery tree deadfall. His yellow eyes, when they met hers, seemed distant, sad. He smiled and the look passed from his amber gaze until he saw her expression.

"Come, Father. This is important," she said simply. She led him out the door of one of the monastery's dimly lit halls. There they rounded up a pair of monks and a younger elf named Corva. His presence among the expedition was solely due to his swordsmanship and archery skills, not his curiosity over rare blooming trees. It didn't matter to Telgra. She wanted him for a witness, nothing more. She led the group hastily up the stairway and walkways.

When they were at the flattened top of the island, standing at the rail near where she had fallen asleep, she faced them all in the southbound wind and stepped back with hands on hips. The young elven guard was already gagging. Her father's face paled and he rankled his nose. The monks said they weren't able to pick up any scent.

"That smell is not a product of my girlish dreaming, Father," she declared, then strode over to the fairy trees at the edge of the path.

Dostin appeared, as did another pair of elves. They were helping the four-hundred-year-old Master Brevan up to the grove.

Seeing her, Dostin eased over to Telgra's side with a warm smile on his round face.

"Hello, Dostin," Telgra smiled up at him with a look of smug satisfaction.

"My lady," he gave a nodding bow of respect. She had told him to dismiss with the formalities when they arrived, but since his brothers and her father were present she didn't chide him for it.

The Giver pulled his magnificent sunset down into the ocean, leaving the sky dark and starlit. The moon was but a faint slip. Her father and the others were engaged in a heated argument and she wasn't interested anymore. She reached across the walking rail and fondled one of the fiery tree flowers. She saw Dostin looking at her strangely.

"What?" she asked.

"I'm sorry for looking, m'lady," he said. He seemed very nervous. She half expected him to say that he had fallen in love with her, but he surprised her.

"It's your eyes." He looked at his feet for a moment then back to her. "After all this time, I'm still not used to them. They look like a wildcat's eyes, or an owl's eyes."

She smirked to hide her relief, then made a strange face, feigning offense.

"Your eyes are strange to me as well, Dostin." She looked back at the fiery trees absently. "When I first saw humans in the town called Dalton, just after we left the Evermore, I thought how similar we were built. Then I saw the eyes of your people and realized I was wrong. Your eyes are like robin eggs, Dostin." She focused more intently on the flower she was stroking and her voice trailed away. "Eggs with sapphires stuck in—" She stopped as she ducked the rail to investigate what had struck her speechless.

The young elven guard, Corva, suddenly pointed skyward and hissed a warning. No one could see anything above at first, then Dargeon gasped. Brevan mumbled a spell and made a flourishing wave of his hand.

"Whatever it is, it can't see us now," the old elf said when he was done.

"What is it?" Dostin asked Telgra. He was craning his neck so far back that he was about to fall over backward.

Telgra was no longer paying attention to the others. Something about the leaves held her captivated.

"I saw something eclipse the stars," Corva said, pointing in the sky while looking to Dargeon for a command.

"A Choska, or maybe a large wyvern," Dargeon said. He glanced at his daughter and his concern over the flying creature evaporated.

She was studying the flowers intensely. She didn't even know creatures had flown over head. Dargeon saw the horrified look on her face. His keen eyes caught the starlit reflection in the tear that ran down her cheek. He hurried to her side, his heart full of fatherly concern.

"What is it, love?" he asked as he hopped lightly over the guardrail.

"Look," she said, putting her chin in her chest and sobbing.

He was appalled. The fairy tree flowers were turning sickly and black before his eyes. He could almost hear the ancient trees crying out in pain. The atrocious smell in the air, or maybe whatever was causing it, was hurting them. He felt an awful pang of guilt as he stroked Telgra's golden hair.

She had warned them, but they had been fools.

"As long as you shit your britches again, Oarly, we'll be all right," Phen said to his dwarven companion. They were in a rowboat fighting the waves just off the rocky shore of the Isle of Kahna. Phen's familiar, a lyna named Spike, lazed in the floorboards. Of the three of them, the porcupine-quill-covered, cat-like creature was the most comfortable at sea. Even so, Phen gently handed the animal up to Captain Biggs, who was standing in the cargo net hanging into the water from the side of the Royal Seawander.

Phen looked like a statue and he could see how his appearance unnerved the captain. How he'd come to appear to be made of marble was another intriguing tale. He didn't just appear to be made of stone, though. He would still be petrified solid if it weren't for the mighty dragon Claret. In truth, his skin was pretty hard. He weighed as much as three full water kegs. The quality of his personal predicament was exactly why he was doing what he was doing.

Oarly had fought Phen's decision to go after the Serpent's Eye emerald from the beginning. Of course, he lost the battle. They, along with Hyden Hawk Skyler and Brady Culvert, had sworn a pact when they found the jewel last spring. Now it was fall, and Brady was dead, killed by a black wyrm, just before the Dragon Queen's wizard took the silver skull. Sir Hyden Hawk had disappeared into the Nethers of Hell, but they knew he was alive. They had no idea how to go about finding him, though, or if he even wanted to be found. That left just he and Oarly who knew about the jewel. Phen chose to go after the emerald while his hardened skin would be an advantage. Soon he was going to embark on a journey deep into the Giant Mountains to find a magical pool that Claret had told him about. The pool's warm spring water supposedly had the power to revive his pigment and return his body to its normal flesh-and-bone state. Oarly protested and pleaded, but due to his pact with the others, he couldn't tell anyone what Phen was planning. He was left with no choice but to come along. Phen knew this was the case. He was smart, a fair mage in his own right, and as confident as they come.

As Phen pulled on the oars, Oarly gave a backward glance at the Royal Seawander. The emerald they were after was in a cave called the Serpent's Eye. It was only possibly to get inside when the tide was low. They'd chosen the moment just right, as it was almost all the way out as they rowed toward the opening.

A huge serpent lived inside. When they'd been to the cavern before, the thing had slithered out of its hole and scared Oarly so bad that he'd soiled himself. Strangely, the creature hadn't killed them, or even attacked them at all. The joke was that the horrible smell of Oarly's shit had scared the thing away. Phen knew that it had left for other reasons, but teasing Oarly was one of his favorite pastimes.

The emerald was guarded by far more than just the serpent, though. It sat atop a pile of gold coins, held aloft on a platter by three life-size skeletons molded from rusty iron. Around the whole monumental display was a shallow moat full of slithery eels with needle teeth that might be poisonous. Phen planned to stroll right through the moat, knowing that their fangs wouldn't be able to penetrate his skin. He also had an elven ring he found on his first visit to the cave. It would let him turn invisible after he snatched the jewel. That part of the plan might not even be necessary, Phen knew. Hyden believed that the iron skeletons might come to life and attack after the jewel was taken, but no one was sure if they would. Up until Phen had been turned into a statue by one of the Dragon Queen's priests, he hadn't been able to imagine an iron rendering of a skeleton coming to life. But now he didn't doubt the possibility at all. If they did animate, though, they would have a hard time attacking him. He planned on putting on his ring and being invisible even before he snatched the emerald.

Phen knew his squat little friend was concerned. He was concerned, too. Noticing the look on Oarly's face, he stopped rowing.

"Stop worrying, Oarly," Phen said, trying to hide the nervousness he felt.

"I don't see it, lad." Oarly shook his head. "I don't see how you can sit in a little boat knowing that if you fell into the water you'd sink like a stone."

Phen cringed. He didn't want to think about it. "Look Oarly, the tide's starting to come back in, so the time for back-stepping has gone. Take a few pulls from that flask and concentrate on being ready to shit your britches."

The dwarf's laugh turned into a low grumble that ended with him cursing under his breath. He did more than take a sip. He emptied the flask and tossed it into the sea. After a moment he pulled another flask from his boot, took a sip, and mumbled a prayer to Doon. "Let us get on with it then," he barked when he was done.

By the time the two were under the rocky ceiling of the entrance and easing into the Serpent's Eye, the dwarf was belligerent. Phen hoped it was true, that dwarves function better drunk, because in moments they would really be past the point of no return. The tide was already rolling back in and closing the entrance behind them.

Phen opened his mouth and went through the motions of breathing, even though he wasn't sure if his body actually drew breath or not. He was thankful that he could see the bottom of the cavern pool through the clear water. He was concerned about Oarly now, though. The dwarf was emptying a third flask while patting around on his person in search of another. When he couldn't find one, he looked over at Phen and shrugged.

Chapter Three

The next night the moon was nowhere to be seen. All nine of the elves were gathered in the heart of the fiery tree grove. Brevan was casting spell after spell, some in hopes of protecting the main grove from the blight that affected the smaller copse, and some to conceal the presence of their activities from the spying eyes that were circling high above. Dargeon had to plead with the leaders of the order of monks to not run to the king of Salaya, or his son, just yet. If the human royalty was notified then the elves would be forced to either reveal their presence, or abandon the fiery trees to their fate. Neither choice was acceptable. Reluctantly, the monks agreed to give the elves some time to work with the trees. They didn't like the idea of keeping the sky-born threat from their king, though. They made that clear.

Once Brevan felt satisfied that his protective spells were in order, he gathered the elves into a circle. It was awkward as they were standing among the trees holding hands with outstretched arms.

The old elven mage, with the help of the others, was about to attempt a powerful casting.

"Where do you want me?" Telgra asked.

"And me?" Corva stepped up.

"The power of the Arbor will burn you both," Brevan warned. "You're far too young for such a casting."

"What little strength they can add might make the difference, Old One," Telgra's father argued for her.

The old elf stopped and stared at her for a moment. His luminous amber orbs were as fierce as anything she'd ever seen. She met his gaze, as did Corva beside her.

"Very well," he snapped.

Telgra was excited, and more than a little afraid. She had only read about high magic or heard tales of it from her instructors back in the Evermore. Her father was a respected mage, but he rarely used his craft. He was an explorer at heart, and he loved nature. He'd been to the Bitter Isles northwest of Coldfrost to observe the great wolves and the ice bears that lived there. He had trudged through the southern marshes cataloging the vast array of amphibians and reptilian life there. He'd even been across the great desert and ridden the humped cullomal beasts through the gorge of fire, where the rare and beautiful tookaskas live.

It amazed Telgra that he'd done all those things, especially since he'd done them without the humans seeing him.

Her father gave her right hand a gentle squeeze. Brevan was on her left. She felt safe enough between the two of them. Poor Corva was between stubborn old Oglav, and Teverall, the expedition's weapon master. Neither of them were particularly powerful magi, but what little craft they did know was needed. If Brevan's worries about the magic affecting them were founded, Telgra thought, Corva would probably find out. She doubted that the foggy old elf would even remember the words to his great spell, though. He hadn't even bothered to acknowledge the fact that she wasn't just a foolish girl trying to get attention. She gave him a glance and a smug look as he started into his casting.

All at once a warm, electric buzz shot through her. It was uncomfortable, yet familiar. Another squeeze of her hand by her father helped slow her breathing and gave comfort. After that she was on her own as the smell of ozone and the tingling kinetic feeling of raw power came sweeping through her. She looked across the circle at Corva, at his wide-eyed, open-mouthed face. She decided that her expression was probably much the same. Then blinding lavender light erupted from her feet and her mind was washed away into a psychedelic swirl of pastel radiance. What happened next, she would never know, but the sound of it was haunting.

At first, she heard the murmur and chant of the four elves who knew what was going on, but then the hissing crackle and the deep resonance of the magical power around her forced all else out of her head. At least until the screaming started.

For a long time she tuned the sound out of her mind, afraid to know what it was that was in so much pain. She felt as if she were stuck deep down in a barrel of honey. There was no up or down, no left or right. She couldn't breathe.

After a short time she realized it was the voices of the trees amplified in her head. They were in agony, some more than others. She heard Brevan's voice distantly as he spoke to them, but she couldn't make out the words. She heard her father as well. She even heard Dostin's shrill whine. His was clear and unmistakable.

"Look, Father Malik," Dostin exclaimed. "The elves are glowing. And the trees are on fire."

The screaming of the trees stopped, and a relative hush descended over the thick buzz of the magic. A sound comparable to a large group all gasping in unison filled her ears. She opened her eyes to look, but was greeted by the same disorienting kaleidoscope of pastel color she had seen with her eyes closed. She was forced to shut them tightly again, lest she began to heave from vertigo.

Dostin's voice rang out in fear. "Oh no," he yelled. "Noooo!" Then he grunted and let out a gurgling scream that caused even the trees to cringe.

"Oh no, my love," Telgra heard her father say sadly, then he let go of her hand.

A soft yell of surprise sounded like it came from old Brevan, but it died away in a gurgling hiss. Scuffling, and then the sound of steel being drawn, came to her ears. Telgra then felt herself being yanked up into the air by something that was causing terrible pain in her shoulders. Blackness crept into the colorful array of her vision and pain replaced the tingle of the magic. She heard her father's desperate cry over the chaos.

"Oh, Telgra, no," he yelled. "Please, no!" His voice was fading, as if he were getting farther away. She could tell by the clipped way he spoke that he was sobbing.

"Put her down!" her father roared. "Put her dow—" The abruptness with which his words ended, and the wet tearing sound that accompanied the instant, echoed through her brain like a thunderclap. Then there was nothing, save for pain. Eventually even that faded into nothingness.

He'd been married for only a few weeks, and already High King Mikahl Collum was fighting desperately to keep his myriad of duties from coming between him and his beautiful bride. His good friend and adviser, Lord Alvin Gregory, was working himself ragged trying to lighten Mikahl's load. Lord Spyra and General Escott were helping as well. This day however, Mikahl had no choice but to leave Queen Rosa's side and see their unexpected guest himself.

Borg, the Southern Guardian of the Giant Mountains, was a personal friend, and Mikahl had no intention of brushing off a chance to see Urp, Oof, and Huffa. The three great wolves had carried Mikahl, Hyden Hawk, and Vaegon the elf out of the Giant Mountains and across the Evermore Forest once. Grrr, the proud and fierce leader of the pack, had sacrificed himself to save Mikahl. The people of the realm unknowingly owed a great debt to that wolf. Had he not saved Mikahl, the demon wizard Pael would have taken the city of Xwarda and used the Wardstone to destroy all that was good.

Why the wolves were here with Borg, instead of at home with King Aldar, Mikahl didn't know. He was glad they came, though. The messenger had arrived breathless and wide-eyed just moments ago with news of the giant's sudden appearance at Dreen's northernmost gate. Very few kingdom folk had ever looked upon a real giant. The half-breed giants who fought alongside the High King in the recent war against Dakahn were as close to a giant as they had seen. Borg was a pure-blooded giant. He stood over fourteen feet tall and was proportionately as human-formed as the next man, save for his huge slab of a forehead.

Lord Gregory had to act quickly to keep General Escott from manning an unnecessary defense against the visitor. Borg was no enemy, but even still, a fifty-man mounted troop was dispatched to escort him through the streets of Dreen to the modest castle the monarchy was residing in while the dwarves built the new palace. Mikahl imagined the wolves were worrying the newly promoted general and the people of the city to death. A demon tore through Dreen only three turns of the moon earlier and destroyed a score of homes and thrice as many people. Borg wasn't nearly as big or as ugly as the demon had been, but he towered over the Red City's low buildings just the same. There was no doubt he was frightening the citizens. It couldn't be helped. Mikahl knew the people would relax after they saw him welcome Borg, though. He smiled as the excitement of the reunion coursed through him.

Mikahl hurried outside to the castle's entry yard, which was really just a glorified horse pen. The knot of armed men forming up outside staggered him.

"Commander Lyle, please get these men out of here," Mikahl ordered.

"But, Your Highness," the man argued carefully. "General Escott said—"

"I don't care what he said," Mikahl snapped. "Borg is my friend, and no more threat to us than a ladybug."

"But the wolves?"

"The wolves are even closer to my heart than the giant is!" Mikahl's voice betrayed displeasure at being argued with over the matter. Already he could see the giant a few streets over, striding quickly closer. A sack holding something the size of a barrel keg was thrown over his shoulder.

"Out of my sight now," Mikahl yelled. "All of you, and if any of you so much as thinks of harming one of those wolves, you'll be pulling the Lord of Lokar's cart around with Ra'Gren!"

Just then, a massive white-furred wolf leapt the wall that surrounded the castle yard and charged full speed at the High King. To their credit, at least a dozen of the archers scattered among the soldiers drew arrows and aimed at the wolves. Luckily for them, no one loosed. Even when the great wolf's huge paws landed on the High King's shoulders and sent him onto his back, they held their arrows. Commander Lyle was suddenly terrified. The shoulder of the wolf that was strolling leisurely past him came up to his chin. His hand went to his sword hilt but stopped when he saw Mikahl fighting away nothing more than slavering tongues and wagging tails. The warning growl of another wolf directed at the archers snapped the commander into action. "Double time it out of here, now," he screamed, and the men started complying.

Within seconds three wolves were crowded over Mikahl, all wagging away excitedly. He spoke loving greetings to them while three other great wolves came over the fence and paced around the yard, watching their pack mates.

The two gatehouse guards looked stupefied. They wouldn't have been able to stop the wolves from getting into the castle yard had they tried their best, and they knew it. Then a gigantic boot, with a wolf-skull for a buckle, stepped down before them. One guard fell to the ground unconscious and the other ran into their weather shelter and shut the door with a bang. It sounded as if he pulled the bolt shut after himself. General Escott and his fifty-man escort were left outside the locked gate, unable to even see inside, much less defend the king if it became necessary.

"King Mikahl," Borg boomed and bowed at his waist politely. "King Aldar sends his regards. The wolves somehow managed to get him to let them come with me."

"Hey, Borg," Mikahl called, trying to sit up. "The bark lizard cloak looks great." Far better than the patchwork goatskin cloak he'd last seen the giant wearing. Borg still wore the menacing-looking wolf skulls on his belt buckle and boot shins, though, and his tree trunk staff looked to have a few new dark, sticky stains on its end.

"Haw," the giant barked out a glum laugh. "It does look good, but it makes me sad when I think about what Loudin lost for bringing the skin to me."

"Aye." Mikahl took a moment to remember his friend and the horrible death he had found in the Giant Mountains.

"I brought you a present," Borg said, dropping the oversize patchwork sack to the ground with a dull thud. A putrid smell roiled through the air. "I'd rather present it to both you and the Lion Lord, if he is around."

Mikahl finally got to his feet, but stayed where he was scratching the three great wolves behind the ears in turn. "It stinks," he observed of the sack, while wondering what was inside it.

"You should be glad you weren't the one carrying it for days and days," the giant chuckled. "And this is from Hyden Skyler." He held forth a scroll that looked tiny in his huge hand.

"Hyden?" Mikahl froze, feeling a sudden wave of hope wash over him. "He's really alive? You've seen him?"

"He is," Borg answered simply. "He told me about the giant you two found in the Dragon Queen's dungeon. I wish you had killed her and her wizards more slowly."

"Aye." Mikahl nodded his agreement as he put the scroll in his pocket for later.

He couldn't remember the name spoken by the emaciated giant they had found. He had it written down, though, and had been planning on making a journey into the Giant Mountains to tell Borg. A pang of guilt came over him. It should have already been done. He dropped his head in shame. "Who was she?" he asked.

"My sister," Borg replied. "You did her honor by avenging her death, Mikahl. I have brought you a small token of my appreciation. Is Lord Gregory here?"

"Aye," Mikahl said. "I'll send for him. My new palace is being built with rooms to accommodate your people. I'm sorry I can't invite you into this one. Would you like some refreshments?"

"A keg of ale will suffice for now," Borg said. "Maybe a boar, or a doe, for later."

Mikahl laughed. "I'll have someone cart something around from the kitchen for you."

He told a steward to fetch Borg a keg and to summon Lord Gregory to the yard, then he jogged the short distance to the kitchen himself. He commanded the cooks to prepare a feast. The head cook looked at him crazily when he told them to roast three full boars instead of just one, but he didn't dare argue with his king. As Mikahl was returning, he heard Borg's booming voice outside. He stepped back around to find Lady Trella and Queen Rosa speaking to Borg from the second story balcony of Lady Trella's apartment. Rosa giggled girlishly and gave Mikahl a wave, and then the two women disappeared back inside the castle.

"Who is Pin, and why does he seek the fountain of Leif Repline?" Borg asked Mikahl when he strode back into the yard. "I think your queen spelled me," the giant continued, "...for I just promised I would look out for this person while he makes his way through our land."

"His name is Phen," Mikahl laughed. "She calls him Pin. He and his dwarven pal, Master Oarly, are fools of the first order. Phen's is a long story which I'll share with you over supper. I've ordered a feast prepared in your honor."

"The whole city of Dreen will want to celebrate once they see the gift I've brought you," Borg boasted.

Just then, Lord Gregory came out of the castle and smiled broadly up at Borg. "Well met, Southern Guardian," the Lion Lord said, using Borg's official title. "I hope my warning about the loosed demon reached your people in time."

Borg nodded and smiled, then picked up the sack he'd brought. He dumped the hideous demon's head out of the bag onto the castle yard, the demon that had recently torn through Dreen. His big face split into a huge grin and the whole pack of great wolves howled out in pride.

Chapter Four

The light that carried through the sea into the Serpent's Eye from outside was fading as the tide rose. Phen cast a spell. A small sphere of light the size of an apple appeared in his open palm then slowly rose and hovered at a point about a foot over his head. He looked around the cavern. Oarly was standing with his feet planted. He was weaving slightly to and fro with the slack bow line of the dinghy held loosely in his hand. Most of his bulbous face was buried in his tangled beard.

"Oarly," Phen said a little loudly. "Tie the line around that stalagmite and let's make ready."

The dwarf jumped at the mention of his name, as if he'd been in a daze, but after a snarl he settled back into his standing stupor. Phen huffed with frustration and then bent down and picked up a loose pebble. He threw it rather hard and it bounced off the side of Oarly's head. The impact sounded like the thump of a ripe melon. Oarly rubbed the spot absently and sneered at Phen. Three heartbeats later the hairy stump took a step back and yelped loudly. "By Doon, lad," Oarly rubbed his head briskly now. "What was that for?"

"You're drunk," Phen returned. "Now tie off the skiff."

"I'm not even close to drunk, lad," Oarly boasted as he finally tied the line. When he stood back up he pulled his axe from his back and puffed his wide chest out. "Now where's this serpent?"

Phen made an expression of pure terror and pointed beyond Oarly into the darkness. "It's... It's right behind you." His voice was trembling with fear.

Oarly looked at him for a long moment and then let out a huff. "Bah! You'll not get this dwarf that easily."

Phen smirked and grabbed a burlap sack out of the boat. Oarly glanced back over his shoulder, just in case.

The natural-formed cave looked much the same as it had the last time they'd been in it. The large, rough chamber had two passages leading up and away from the sea pool that took up nearly half of its rocky bottom.

Phen started down the smaller right-hand tunnel. As soon as he was a dozen paces ahead, Oarly pulled a new flask from his boot and took a deep swig. Phen just laughed at him and carried on. A wave made a loud smacking-sucking sound against the rocks as the tide side seal broke in a wave's valley. Phen laughed because the sound sent Oarly stumbling quickly to catch up with him.

The narrow tunnel was about a hundred paces deep. Phen knelt at the end of it, looking curiously at the ancient skeleton on the floor. It was that of the elf he called Loak, whose ring and journal had helped Phen track down and destroy the Silver Skull of Zorellin.

He thought about all that had led to his being turned into a statue. Only Claret's powerful magic had prevented him from remaining an immobile monument for eternity. He and the dragon had more or less saved the day at the battle of O'Dakahn. Phen achieved his goal of becoming a hero like Hyden Hawk and King Mikahl, though he hated passionately the name he'd earned for himself. He hadn't ever intended to be known to the people of the realm as the Marble Boy. Oarly wouldn't let him forget the title.

Phen couldn't wait to get his pigment back. He hoped that Claret's suspicions about the pool in the Giant Mountains were founded. It was a long and treacherous journey to undertake, and there was no certainty it would help, but it was a risk he was willing to chance. He would do anything to rid himself of the stony skin, and the title Marble Boy, and besides that, he just wanted to be plain old Phen again.

"All right, ease back to where we can see the entry chamber," he said. "Once the serpent slithers out to feed, I'll put on the ring and go get the emerald. Then I'll come back here." He squeezed past Oarly and started back out of the tunnel. "All you have to do is warn me if the serpent returns."

"I'll do more than warn ye, lad," Oarly bragged drunkenly. "I'll have that sea snake on the fire when you get back."

"Aye," Phen laughed. "Fight the beast, if you want to, just be sure and warn me if it returns."

Back near where the tunnel opened onto the main chamber, Phen dropped the contents of his sack out onto the floor. A small bundle of dried meat, a wheel of cheese, and a cord of dried wood spilled out of it. Oarly snatched up the rations while Phen used a flaming finger spell to start the dwarf a fire. Once he was done, he extinguished his magical light. Unlike the dwarves who had returned from the underground cities to aid in the recent battles, who could see as well in the dark as they could in the sun, Oarly had been among the dwarves who'd stayed on the surface and lived in Xwarda. Without the fire's light, or Phen's orb, he wouldn't be able to see at all.

With the fire lit, Phen stood at the mouth of the tunnel, waiting for the serpent to leave.

"Here," Oarly handed Phen a long dagger. "Take this, just in case."

Phen looked at it. It reminded him of the dagger Hyden Hawk had given him before they went into the blue dragon's lair. He took the weapon with a nod of thanks. If he hadn't lost Hyden's dagger on a zard ship, at least a thousand lives could have been saved. He could have run it through the Dragon Queen's heart before she let loose all those demons into the world.

He made to slip this new knife into his belt, but realized that his clothes, and his belt, were as stony as he was. There were only two things on his person that he could remove: Loak's ring, and the medallion that held Claret's dragon tear, and even they looked made from marble.

A scraping sound drew his attention to the other tunnel.

"What is it that I'm supposed to do?" Oarly asked with a blank expression on his face.

Phen turned and looked at him severely. The dwarf grinned devilishly back at him.

Phen shook his head and went through the motions of sucking in a breath. A green phosphorescent glow was wavering at the mouth of the larger tunnel. Soon, the large viper-like head was hovering above the floor as the thing's bulk slid out of the opening. The room was filled with the strange green-tinted glow. The head darted instantly toward the mouth of the smaller tunnel, where Phen stood. Only the fact that the opening was smaller than the thing's skull kept it from snatching Phen up and swallowing him. Its milky, pupil-less eyes narrowed peevishly. A forked tongue shot out and flickered across Phen's face. Oarly was holding his battle axe's blade up over his face to keep his eyes from settling on the creature.

Phen felt the tingling of the dragon tear medallion around his neck. He could see it in the reflection of the serpent's eyes, showering out a fountain of prismatic sparkles. The flickering tongue shot out at the dragon's tear and tasted the air around it. For a long moment the serpent held its head there, as if it were deciding what to do about the intruders. Then it finally eased back. Phen glimpsed the rows of palm-sized suction cups that ran the length of its undulating body as the triangular head moved away. Only when the thing was over the pool did the serpent take its strange gaze off of Phen. When it did, it slithered right into the water and its glow eased quickly out of the cavern and through the now submerged opening. It had to be a hundred paces long from tip to tail. Phen let out the breath he'd been holding and slipped Loak's ring onto his finger.

Immediately, he faded from sight. He glanced at the dagger in his hand to make sure it had vanished too. It had.

He turned to see Oarly still hunched behind his axe blade. As quietly as he could, Phen crept over to the dwarf's side and let out a loud yell. He was rewarded with a new fetid stench. He almost gagged and vomited as he laughed his way across the entry chamber and down the other passage to the serpent's lair. Behind him, Oarly was cursing and swearing, and trying to regain the wits that had been scared out of him.

As Phen walked cautiously down the long, winding tunnel, Oarly braved the water of the main chamber and washed out his britches and small clothes. He'd done the exact same thing last time they were here, only then there had been no fire to dry his things with. He wasted no time wringing the filth out of his garments and hurrying back to the safety of the smaller tunnel. He was glad he'd brought that last flask, for he was shivery and cold. After laying his clothes by the fire, he took a deep swig and sat back with his axe. The stone floor was so cold on his arse, though, that he jumped up. The fire was too small and he was getting cold. After another long pull from the flask, he began hopping and pacing around.

Phen was finding the major flaw in his plan as he neared the darkened serpent pit. He couldn't see. If he cast his magical orb of light, it would hover over his invisible head and throw his shadow. He decided that, up until he snatched the jewel off of its pedestal, it didn't really matter if he was seen. He was immediately thankful for the light. A few more steps would have carried him tumbling down into the shallow pool that ringed the unnaturally formed chamber. He took in the room and felt a deep sense of awe at the beauty of it. Wicked stalactites hung down from the ceiling, dripping water into the pool full of wiggling two- and three-foot miniature serpents. They were identical, save for size, to the one that had just left.

Phen had a theory on why these little serpents stayed so small and guarded the glittery egg-sized emerald, if in fact that was their purpose at all. The water in the moat probably wasn't sea water, and there wasn't any food. They only ate what the larger serpent brought back, so they couldn't grow. He slipped down from the edge of the opening and felt his heavy feet go into the water. He couldn't tell the temperature of the liquid due to of the condition of his nerve endings. He cupped a handful of it, though, and brought it to his mouth. Tentatively he touched his tongue to the water. It wasn't salty, and he decided that he needed to investigate if he could still taste. As he waded across the waist-deep pool to the island of coins and jewels, he studied the metal statues. He didn't notice, when he was there before, the wide, curving swords at their belts, nor the ruby eyes that seemed to follow him. He looked down and saw that the little serpents were furiously snapping and biting at him. If a normal man attempted this, Phen mused, he wouldn't make it across before he was stripped to the bone. Some of them were attaching themselves with their suction cups. He would have to have Oarly burn them off. He was certain that if they escaped into the salty sea water they would grow to be as big as the other one, and he didn't want to be responsible for loosing a bunch of serpents along the coast. There were enough stories already of such beasts attacking ships and wrestling them to the bottom of the sea.

Phen's feet found the base of the mountain of wealth and he started to climb up it. By the time he was standing amid the skeleton guardians, at least a dozen of the little serpents were clinging to him. He took a few calming breaths and decided that the light didn't matter anymore. If he could see the serpents clinging to his invisible skin, then so could anything else. He could burn them off with a flaming finger but he'd just pick up more of them on his way back across the moat.

So much for planning, he thought as he shook his head. He tried to force the jittery excitement and fear from his mind. He needed another way to keep the skeletons off of him after he grabbed the jewel. Phen's confidence always seemed to override his better judgment, but even as he realized this he spoke his next spell, stopping at the last word so that he could loose its effect at the desired moment. Then, without another thought, he grabbed the emerald from the pedestal and gave the nearest skeleton a good shove toward the other two. He stepped back across the moat as quickly as he could. There was no doubt the skeletons were now going to come for him. The one he'd toppled had wriggled and tried to gain its balance on its way over.

The great weight of Phen's body, and the growing number of serpents sucking onto him, was making his crossing slower than he'd hoped. He could hear the coins and jewels sliding into the water as the iron skeletons took up pursuit. Phen felt like he weighed a ton. He was nearly covered with the eel-like things. The added bulk threatened to drag him down, but he pushed himself onward. Finally, just as he felt the thumping tink of one of those curved sword blades across his hardened shoulders, he made it to the other side. He heaved himself up and back-kicked at the cherry-eyed thing. It went sliding back into the moat.

Phen pushed his way into the tunnel floor. Only two of the skeletons were crossing. The other was trying to get its footing on the loose mound of coins. Phen had hoped to have all three of them in the water, but this would have to do.

As the closest skeleton reached up to pull itself into the tunnel, Phen booted it back. He felt the dragon's tear medallion at his neck tingle as its power flowed into his spell. He'd expected it, but the amount in which it magnified his casting was surprising. Slowly at first, the moat's water stilled and clouded as the surface iced over. Within moments it was frozen solid. The eels were trapped in place and the two ice-locked skeletons were thrashing their arms and making silent faces as their eyes burned in anger. The other skeleton started across the ice. It kicked and took two steps, then fell hard as its metal feet lost all traction. Phen dropped to his belly and rolled back and forth across the cavern floor, crushing the dozens of flailing little eels that were stuck to him. Most of them let go, but not all. Without bothering with the last few, he tore off down the tunnel. Oarly and his axe were better suited to deal with the remaining skeleton. The sudden thought came to him that it was still several hours until the tide receded, and that the pool wouldn't stay frozen that whole time. Phen was trying to think, but when he darted into the narrow passage all thoughts left his brain completely. He couldn't fathom what he saw.

Oarly was standing naked from the waist down, tipping a flask back while swinging his free arm round and round for balance. After he gulped his sip, he started humming and dancing a jig.

Chapter Five

Borg was correct. The whole city of Dreen decided to celebrate the death of the demon that had stormed through. Since the head was far too large to post on a pike outside the castle, Borg jammed it down onto the castle's highest flag pole. People all over the city came to see it, and the pure-blooded giant that killed it. During the private feast, which was held in one of the castle's many stableyards, the number of spectators outside the castle walls began to grow. Borg, holding a full-size loaf of fresh baked bread that looked like a dinner roll in his hand, and a wide-necked floor vase full of ale in the other, announced that later he would recount the doing of the deed for them all.

Servants and castle staff spread the word, and by the time the feast was finished there were thousands of people gathered outside the castle. Luckily, General Escott and his troops were at hand to keep the gathering from getting disorderly. Many people were drunk, or trying to get that way, but most were just curious and happy to be hearing something besides the dire news of post-war horrors.

Mikahl made sure the great wolves were fed. Three does, freshly killed by the Royal Huntsmen, were laid out for them. Mikahl didn't want to hear Borg's story; he wanted to read the scroll from Hyden. He took a lantern and the rolled parchment out to where the wolves were. It had been several months since he'd been forced to leave his friend, who'd been deathly ill from hellborn scorpion venom. He'd left Hyden in the depths of the Dragon Queen's dungeon and had thought him dead for a long time.

The oohs, awes, and gasps from the crowd as Borg strode up to the castle's palisade and leaned his elbows on it drew his attention. The giant's warm laugh rumbled through the cool evening air. Mikahl smiled, knowing that the citizens of Dreen were about to be entranced by a wonderful tale. Giants were the very best of storytellers. Mikahl wished the people from Westland could be present too, but most of all he wished King Jarrek's people could hear.

Already the giant's voice was building the tale. Never had so many people gathered in the streets been so eerily quiet. Only the panting of Oof and Urp at Mikahl's side could be heard. He gave them each a pat on the neck then reached down and scratched Huffa behind the ears. Huffa shivered and made a circle. Her toothy maw opened wide into a tongue-curling yawn. The grazing pen they were in was well kept. Mikahl found a workbench under an old gnarled oak and sat down. The great wolves gathered around him, as if he were one of them. Even the wolves he didn't know seemed to accept him as one of the pack.

Once he was comfortable, he broke the seal on the scroll and looked it over. The writing was neat but far from carefully scribed. It made Mikahl laugh. Hyden had grown up in the mountains, illiterate. He was the best archer in the realm, though, and a self-proclaimed master wizard.

Mikahl took a deep breath and began to read:

High King Mikahl Collum,

Mik, I am alive and well, recovering from the poisonous bite of that thing. I am with my people in the mountains, learning from the goddess and preparing for my destiny. I ask that you keep this quiet. A few others will have to be told, as this missive will explain. I know that I can trust you to carry out my requests directly, and efficiently. I will, as soon as I can, return to the kingdoms and grace you with my presence as payment.

Mikahl laughed at that. He knew Hyden wasn't egotistical in the least. The man thought he was a jester, though. Mikahl couldn't help but smile as he read on.

Firstly, the long bow Vaegon gave me is still in the dungeon at Lakeside Castle. Please have it retrieved and given into Phen's care. As you know, it is priceless to me.

Secondly, Talon has found me and I understand the condition he and Phen share. Please inform Phen that I will accompany him into the Giant Mountains to seek the pool Claret told him of. Have Lord Gregory give him directions to my clan's village, and ask Master Oarly to come as a personal favor to me. At your choosing, a small escort should be sent with them as there are still several stray demons about, not to mention the other hazards of the mountains. A few capable swords, and an archer or two should do. If Phen can bring the bow at that time, I would be grateful.

Thirdly, and most importantly, you must be made aware of some things. The thing that used to be my brother is still loose in the planes of hell. It has grown into an enormous power and has assumed the role of Abbadon, the Master Warlord of the hells. He will relentlessly try to find a way into our world. He saw you dispatch Shaella. I believe he will seek vengeance for the death of his love. You aren't in any immediate danger, as there are no open gateways in existence that I know of. The goddess of my people has told me of a device that will allow you and me to banish the Abbadon to a deeper, darker place, where he won't be able to travel the world of man any longer. This artifact lies beyond the Giant Mountains, and after Phen and Talon have been revived in the Leif Repline fountain, we will seek it out. Please choose the party well - no family men, as some of them will not return.

Xwarda must be guarded at all times. The foundation of the city is pure Wardstone, as you know. If the Abbadon, or any of his minions, managed to manipulate that substance, he could breach the barrier between the worlds permanently. This must never be allowed to happen. Queen Willa and General Spyra must be told of the threat as well. Proper defenses must be manned. It may be tomorrow or it may be a dozen years from now, but my brother, the Abbadon, will come. We must be prepared. Below is a list of scrolls and texts I need Phen and Master Oarly to bring to me.

Finally, I do not know what became of the staff Queen Shaella used to communicate with my brother. She held it in her right hand as you took off her head. You must find it and lock it away in a vault, or have Master Amill, or another qualified wizard, spell it powerless. If there is a force that will help the Abbadon find another gateway, or a flaw in the barrier that exists, the Spectral Orb atop that staff is it.

Now all of that is out of the way, I'm happy for you, and pleased that you somehow managed to save Princess Rosa. Tell the Lion Lord that Tylen sends his regards, as do my mother and father. Sadly, my grandfather passed away. Tell Lord Gregory that my Uncle Condlin has assumed the position of Eldest, and that you and your wife are forever welcome here. He asked me to tell you to make sure that the Summer's Day Festival is crowded next year. My people depend on the trade there. Even you could've gotten your name on the Spire this year.

I must close this missive. Borg is growing impatient, and his stinking sack is offending the womenfolk. Once Phen arrives here, I'll have him contact Dreen's mage with a sending. Give my respects to Willa, Jarrek, and the dwarves.

Your friend,

Hyden

Mikahl just stared at the parchment for a long while.

General Spyra was now Lord Spyra. The man was trying to reorganize Westland with the help of Lady Able. Master Wizard Amill had been killed fighting alongside the dwarves at the Battle of O'Dakahn. Hyden Hawk must not have heard.

Borg was well into his second tale. He was now telling the story of how his people once killed a rogue dragon without the aid of magic. Mikahl could hear the giant's booming voice carrying through the otherwise silent night. At his feet the great wolves had fallen asleep, save for Huffa, who kept a watchful eye over the rest. Through all the dire warnings and talk of magical artifacts, Mikahl's mind kept coming back to the same strange fact. Neither Phen nor Master Oarly were at the feast earlier. As he thought about it more, he decided that he hadn't seen either of them for a few days. He began to worry about them. He could only imagine what they were up to.

Oarly saw a glowing ball and three little serpents dangling as if they were trying to swim through the air to get at it. He stopped his advance and looked at the flask in his hand, then back at the scene. Phen's voice startled him so badly that he dropped the container into the fire. When the flames flared from the alcohol he stepped back.

"Oarly," Phen yelled in a panic. "Get your clothes on. No, forget it, get your axe. There's a skeleton coming, and two more back at—"

Oarly's eyes went wide and locked onto something behind what he now realized was the invisible Phen. The boy whirled around and Oarly saw a shiny sword come sinking down at Phen's chest. It hit Phen with a clank and it appeared that the hardness of the boy's condition startled the thing wielding it. Suddenly the skeleton went stumbling backward, the result of an invisible fist, Oarly assumed.

Oarly came charging out of the tunnel with a yelp and bounced off of Phen. The half-naked dwarf went careening off at an odd angle with his axe held high. His battle cry faded into a cry of dismay. It looked as if the axe were too heavy for him and he was having to run to stay under it. He righted himself as Phen pulled Loak's ring off of his finger and became visible again.

Phen didn't know whether to laugh or cringe at the sight of the hairy naked dwarf. The skeleton stepped heavily into a swing of its silvery blade. Oarly met the blow with his axe and cleaved the thing's sword arm completely from its body. Phen felt the wave of relief wash over him. When the skeleton bent down to try to get the sword with its other hand, he strode up to it and kicked it with a heavy marble boot. The skeleton's legs crumbled, and it half fell into the pool. For a long time it thrashed about menacingly, but it was obviously no longer a threat.

"Where are your clothes?" Phen asked.

Oarly looked down and realized that he was naked from the waist down. "Bah!" he growled and stalked off toward the narrow passage.

"There are two more of those skeletons back there," Phen said. "We'd better hurry, before the ice I put them in melts."

"Aye, lad," Oarly said. "If ya hadn't scared me shitless, I wouldn't be needing to get my clothes back on now, would I?"

Phen took a step back. He didn't think he'd ever seen Oarly so mad before. He had to fight to hold in his mirth.

"Look," he said, holding up the egg-sized emerald for the dwarf to see.

Oarly looked at it, gave a nod, then continued his tirade. "We got buckets full of jewels left over from that blasted dragon's lair. I got scars from getting that treasure. What good is one more jewel, lad? I just don't understand."

"This one is magic. You played like you were dying in that lair, Oarly. You made me cry when I thought you'd died." Phen turned toward the larger tunnel. He could hear the skeletons' loud, scraping approach. "If I made you shit yer britches a dozen times, we still wouldn't be even."

Oarly's anger vanished. He even barked out a laugh. He knew he'd made the boy cry like a babe. He pulled his boots on and grabbed the flask he'd dropped. Most of it had indeed spilled onto the fire. He still drained the last few drops.

"All right, lad, let's see what you've stirred up, then."

Together they charged off into the larger cavern. One of the skeletons had pulled itself in two, and the torso was trying to drag itself along the floor by its arms. Seeing that, Oarly gave it a wide berth. Phen took a long stride and planted his heavy foot on its rib cage. The thing rattled and then grew still. Phen leaned down for a closer look at its jeweled eyes. The rubies looked like onyx pebbles now that the power in them had been extinguished.

"You don't even need me, Marble Boy," Oarly chuckled. "That blade that slashed across your body didn't even scratch your robe."

"Stop calling me Marble Boy," Phen yelled. He hated that. He hated that he sounded like a little child in a play yard over it, too. "I won't be Marble Boy for long, Oarly. You can wager on that."

"Awww, lad, you just don't know," the dwarf replied, pointing down at the serpent-covered third skeleton lying still at the bottom of the moat. Somehow the little eel-like creatures had survived the freeze. They wiggled and squirmed through the melting slush as if nothing had happened. "You will be Marble Boy forever." Oarly laughed heartily and clasped Phen around the waist in a brotherly hug. "As long as you live, you're doomed to be remembered as the boy made of marble who rode the red dragon and saved us at the Battle of O'Dakahn. Only if you somehow manage to magic yourself into a king, or a god, can you shake such a nickname."

Just then a loud splash erupted from behind them in the entry cavern. Both of them turned and started quickly back toward it. If it was the serpent then they were possibly trapped between it and all the little ones in the pool. As they ran, Phen gave the emerald to Oarly and fumbled for Loak's ring. It was hard to get it back off of the medallion chain and onto his finger while holding the dagger. He almost dropped it. Finally he put the dagger between his teeth and slipped on the ring.

The opening of the big tunnel wasn't blocked off yet, but they could see that the entry cavern was filled with the slithering green glow of the serpent.

"I'll look," Phen said.

"Extinguish your light, fool," Oarly hissed. "It'll see you, if it hasn't already."

"Oh." Phen had forgotten about the light spell entirely.

Suddenly the place went dark save for the continuously moving glow that radiated off of the serpent. Phen eased down to the big cavern and looked. The serpent was in front of the smaller tunnel, intently flicking its tongue as far as it could reach. Phen felt the jewel on the medallion around his neck begin to tingle and knew instantly that the serpent would sense it.

"Out of the tunnel now, Oarly," he yelled. "Stay against the wall. We can't let it trap us inside."

The great head of the serpent lunged at Phen's fountaining jewel, its huge, toothy maw opening wide as it came. Phen realized then that being invisible before this sinuous monster did absolutely no good, but by the time the thought finished in his head, he was covered in a cloud of fresh fishy smell, and the serpent's mouth was closing down over him.

"For Doooon!" he heard Oarly scream, but Phen was yanked off his feet and the world turned into a dark, spinning frenzy.

The Wizard and the Warlord

Chapter Six

Telgra's eyes fluttered open. The puffy clouds she saw in the sky weren't twirling about crazily anymore. In a panic, she glanced around. There were no shiny-armored kings riding winged horses of flame. There were no talking statues trying to greet her. There was only Dostin and Corva and the open sea. She lay back for a moment and felt relief, but then the memory of the great spell, and the horrible sounds she'd heard, came flooding back into her mind like a torrent.

"Where is my father?" she yelled, trying to sit up again.

"Give her another sip please, Dostin," Corva said. "I'd do it myself but—"

Telgra saw the nuances of the look on Corva's elven face and the wounds on Dostin's. She felt a deep ache in her shoulder. Not sure that she was ready to hear the answer to her question, she sipped from the flask Dostin offered. After a moment, she slipped back into a dreamy sleep.

When she woke, the starry sky wasn't bobbing and weaving. She looked around and saw that she was in a camp. Waist-high grass teaming with noisy insects surrounded a trampled-down circle, blocking her view of what was beyond the immediate area. A pale blue flame flickered in the center of the encampment. It gave out little warmth, but its soft light was welcome.

A snore from a few feet away was coming from the plump, round-faced monk. Telgra stretched but immediately regretted it. Her shoulder was sore. She inspected it and found a trio of ugly purple scars that had recently been healed by elven magic. The way the ache still throbbed deep inside her body, she knew the wound had to have been healed more than once.

Inspecting the area, she found most of a single sail dinghy jutting up into the sky over the grass nearby. She vaguely remembered being at sea in it. By the way it swayed and rocked, she knew it was sitting in water. Her nose told her that the water around her was brackish. The whole area smelled musty, like half-rotted vegetation.

A loud splash exploded through the night. It came from not too far away. A grunting, huffing noise, like someone running, more splashing, and then the distinct sound of an elven bow loosing arrows quickly. Without knowing she'd done it, Telgra scooted herself precariously close to Dostin. She was tempted to wake him. A deep-rooted fear was taking hold of her. It wasn't the fear of the moment. She was a capable mage and forester. She was more than able to defend herself against most any man or beast. It was the fear of what had happened to the fiery tree grove, to her father, Brevan, and the other elves. It was the fear of the reason she was sitting in a marsh camp that was far, far away from the Isle of Salaya.

Corva was approaching now, she could tell. He was dragging with him whatever it was he had killed.

"Don't get it so close to the camp," she said into the night.

"Yes m'lady."

It baffled her as to why males always felt the urge to display their kills. In the elven towns of the Evermore Forest the hunters felt obligated to show off the prey they had tracked and killed. Maybe it was to impress their mates, or to feel superior, or maybe it was just to let people know who had supplied the food. Corva would have brought the carcass right into camp, she knew, but this was no village in the Evermore. The scent of fresh blood and gore might attract something they couldn't handle. Besides, she would rather not know what she ate out here.

A few moments later Corva returned, carrying a fat, bloody chunk of meat. He gave Telgra a forced smile, and then with a wave of his hand caused the soft blue flames of the fire to flare yellow and red. He carefully cut strips of the flesh and arranged them on the rocks around the flames. Within moments the savory smell of roasting meat filled the air.

"What happened?" Telgra asked. She hugged her knees to her chest, readying herself for the answer.

"Like you, lady," Corva started, looking at her sadly, "I was overwhelmed by Brevan's great spell. When I came to my senses, they were—they were…" he looked away.

"I'm no sapling that needs sheltering, Corva," she said. "Out with it."

"We were set upon by those dark things. Wyvern I think, by the way the bodies were corroded." He looked at her, unashamed of the tears that were trailing down his cheeks. "A larger creature, a Choska maybe, grabbed hold of you. Your father, Brevan, and most of the monks that were outside were killed." He looked at Dostin sleeping soundly beside them. "Dostin found you. You'd fallen a good distance and were in bad shape. He prayed over you for a very long time, keeping you alive. After he brought you back to the monastery, it took several attempts to stabilize your body."

Tears streamed freely down his face now, and had she not been drawn up into such a tight ball, Telgra's trembling might have been violent.

"Why are we out here?" she asked.

"The King of Salaya sent men up the mountain, many men, to investigate the attack and to protect the monastery. We managed to—" he sobbed and looked grateful when Telgra uncurled herself and moved to his side. "We were not to be seen by the kingdom folk. Those were our orders. So I helped the monks quickly bury them."

He hugged her close, trying not to get any of the sticky blood from his hands on her. She sobbed and shuddered into his chest as he continued.

"The monks gave us the little craft," he said. "Dostin, I think, came without his brothers' permission, but he did so because of his loyalty to you."

For a long while they were silent, then the wind kicked up and sent a whiff of the now charring meat into their faces. Telgra relaxed her grip around Corva and let him tend the food. While he was turning the meat she asked, "What of the fiery trees?"

"Those that were inside the spell circle are alive and thriving." He dropped his head. "The rest of them withered to their deaths."

"We have to get home and organize a party to do something." She sniffled and tried to gather herself.

"I wish it were that easy," he said. "The Queen Mother will not allow us to interfere or interact with the kingdom people. She will say that this is a human problem, and that the humans should deal with it."

"The fiery trees, and those dark things that killed our people…neither are humans," she replied.

"I agree," Corva said. "But I don't think the Queen Mother will. You know her heart better than any other. She may listen to her daughter, but we still have to get ourselves all the way back to the Evermore before we can even begin to try to convince her."

"That may take too long, I fear," she said, standing. She took in a deep breath. "I will have to go to this High King Mikahl for help."

"We cannot disobey the Queen Mother," Corva argued. "We are not to meddle with the humans at all."

"Dostin is a human," she said. "And I'm ordering you to do this, so the responsibility of it falls on me. I'll deal with my mother."

"Yes, m'lady." Corva handed her an arrow with a piece of cooked meat speared on its tip. She saw that his gaze was full of respect. But deeper in his eyes she saw a want for vengeance. The feeling that the decision she had just made might determine his fate made her uneasy, but she didn't let it stifle her resolve.

The next morning they set out for the human city of O'Dakahn. The port there was the closest to Oktin, where the High King was supposedly having his new palace built. Princess Telgra, heiress to the ruling seat of the entire race of elves, had made up her mind.

Late that afternoon, while they were skirting the marsh delta of the eastern branch of the Leif Greyn River, the sky began to darken. Within minutes the wind had gone from slightly breezy to a savage, blasting gust. The boat was forced away from the marshes and soon darkness overcame them. All sight of land was lost. Wild, jagged lightning bolts split the sky and thunder exploded as rain began to pour down. The waves grew from three- and four-foot rollers into huge, breaking beasts that threatened to crush the boat with every swell. The sky was so black that even the elves' keen eyes couldn't see more than a few feet ahead of them.

"Hold on," Corva yelled as a wave broke over them with terrible force. It felt like the boat was under a great waterfall for a moment, but then the sensation passed.

"Princess Telgra, Dostin," Corva yelled. "Bail out the water. Another wave is—" He bit back his words as lightning struck a few feet away. In its brilliant flash he saw that Dostin was no longer in the boat. Telgra saw too and immediately began scanning the water.

"Broaaash!" the monk bellowed as he broke the surface and gasped for air. "Haaaaalp meee!"

"Give me the end of that rope," Telgra ordered.

Corva froze. He wasn't about to let his princess risk her life for a human monk. He would do it. He reached down to grab the line at his feet, but found it already uncoiling. He looked up just in time to see Telgra leaping over the side into the stormy sea. A few moments passed before another flash of lightning revealed her paddling deftly beside the flailing monk.

She tied the rope around Dostin then waved back at the boat. "Pull!" she yelled. "Corva! Pull us in!"

Another wave crashed over the craft. The rope slipped from Corva's hands and he was forced to cling to the sides or be thrown overboard. When the boat smacked back down into the sea he was battered about the hull, but managed to grab the rope again. With all his might he hauled them in, heave after heave, until finally he saw Dostin's terrified eyes through the darkness. It took all the strength Corva had left in him to drag the monk up into the boat. Though about to give out, he turned back to pull Telgra in, but was overcome with dread. She wasn't there. A distant lightning flash confirmed it. Nowhere could she be seen.

"Telgra!" he screamed at the top of his lungs. He turned to the other side of the boat and yelled again, "Princess Telgra!"

When the next lightning struck he peered into the night as far as his keen vision could see. He cast a light spell but the storm suffocated its illumination like a shroud. For long hours, and to no avail, Corva fought the storm and called for his princess, while all around the boat the storm raged relentlessly.

Phen felt like he was being rolled down a rocky hill inside a barrel keg. Luckily his hard skin kept the serpent's teeth from piercing into him. Through his terror, he was worried that one of his legs might be broken off as they were hanging out of the creature's maw. With all the determination he had, he used Oarly's dagger to stab at the inside of the serpent's mouth. Already he was coated in slimy blood. It was the awful fishy smell of the creature's breath that threatened to render him helpless, though. He had to fight not to be consumed by a fit of gagging heaves, something he wasn't sure his body could handle. He hoped Oarly would hurry and save him. The idea that the half-drunken dwarf couldn't manage the task never even crossed his mind.

Oarly's battle cry echoed around the chamber as the serpent reared its head up and tried to chug Phen down its throat. Oarly, inebriated or not, wasn't about to let that happen. He was far too fond of the lad to allow it. He darted out from the wall and ran right up under the serpent, then took a massive hacking swing at the beast's neck. He felt the axe bite deep and had to roll back against his momentum to pull the blade free.

The monster hissed through its half-open maw, spraying blood in a mist across the cavern wall. Oarly shuddered, hoping it wasn't Phen's blood. With a roar, he brought the axe back around and finished his chop. A piece of the serpent's neck, a chunk shaped like a wedge of fruit, fell to the floor. Oarly had to run under the creature's head as it turned to attack him. He saw Phen's legs hanging out of its mouth. They were drenched in blood. He went into a rage at the sight and tore into the serpent's side with a berserker's frenzy. His axe went back and forth, slicing deep gouges into the foul-smelling monster. Suddenly the thing lurched and sprayed a gout of blood across the cavern. Then it wormed sideways and pressed Oarly tight against the wall with its side. In a fury of its own it dropped Phen into the sea pool with a plop then turned its attention on its attacker.

Oarly froze in wide-eyed terror as the beast held its big viper-like head up over him. A long, flickering, black tongue preceded the rank fishy spray of slimy, bloody breath.

"Bah, your breath smells like a fish-house trash barrel," Oarly spat through his fear. Then he closed his eyes and said a prayer. "Doon save me from this foul creature. I uh, uh, uh..."

Phen righted himself. Thankfully he'd landed in the part of the pool that was only waist deep. He immediately saw Oarly's predicament and charged up out of the water, racing through the words of the first spell that came to mind. He put his hands out above the serpent's scaly body as a lightning bolt erupted through them. He felt the dragon's tear at his neck once again add its power to the flow. For a long moment, he heard Oarly sputter with the jolts. "Uh, uh, uh, uh..."

Phen stepped up even closer, while beneath his hands the serpent took the brunt of the damage. No sooner had the spell ended than the creature darted its head into the larger of the tunnels and began squirming down the passage as quickly as it could.

Oarly fell away from the wall, still jittering from the power of the spell. His mop of hair was smoking slightly, and he howled out wildly. The serpent was almost down the shaft when Oarly rolled up like an acrobat and brought his axe down. He cleaved what was remaining in the main cavern from the beast's tail.

"Haw," Oarly said, pointing to the seven feet of glowing serpent curling and uncurling on the cavern floor. "I cut the fargin serpent in half, I did!"

Phen cast his light spell, and Oarly looked at him crazily. Both of them were drenched in disgusting spew.

"Aye." Phen cringed at his wild-looking friend. He wasn't about to argue with that. "Now let us be on our way before the other half comes back. The tide turned a while ago. I think I can wade us out of here."

Oarly hurried over to the boat and untied it. He climbed in, looking at the large tunnel with a mixture of fear and bravado on his gore-covered face. A few moments later they were working their way out of the Serpent's Eye cavern. Around them a storm was raging violently. It was all Phen could do to climb the rocky shore and tumble himself into the boat. His great weight kept the craft glued to the sea as gale force winds carried them into the darkness. It wasn't long before all memories of the serpent and the emerald were cast aside so they could concentrate on the one thing they had to do to keep Phen from sinking to the bottom of the sea. Frantically, they bailed and bailed and bailed.

When that was done they bailed some more.

M. R. MATHIAS

Chapter Seven

Phen woke to an insistent tugging at his leg. He sat up quickly, looked down at it and was overcome with terror. A fair-size snapper, probably twelve feet from nose to tail, was gnawing on his marbled foot. He flung himself back, and with his other boot stomped the creature right in its snout. It let out a breathy gasp of surprise and darted away with a splash.

Phen crab-walked backward until he was no longer half in, half out of the water. Instinctively, he checked to see if Hyden Hawk's medallion was still around his neck. It was.

He was surrounded by high grass. Rising to his feet he saw he was in a sea of the stuff. Some of the grass was swaying oddly, as if it were rooted in water. The green carpet went on and on in all directions as far as he could see. The grass was high enough that finding Oarly might be a problem. He began calling out for the dwarf as he started working his way around the mostly invisible water line.

When he paused to catch his breath, Phen looked at the scratches the snapper's powerful jaws had gouged down his legs. They didn't hurt. His nerve endings were deadened. He couldn't really define the way he felt. He was weary, heavy, and he was mostly hungry, but he wasn't complaining now. Had he still been of flesh and bone his leg would be a ruin.

Phen remembered he and Oarly clinging to the dinghy, riding a huge wave right into the marshes. He hoped Oarly was on this same rise of land because he didn't want to go wading through the treacherous swamp looking for his friend. To punctuate that thought, Phen stepped forward and sank to his knee in soft, sucking mud. He wasn't light enough to be traipsing around this sort of terrain. He did well to keep from panicking as he slowly worried his leg free. As he did, a new idea came to him.

He worked his way back to where he'd awakened. He began pulling up clumps of the long marsh grass. After stomping down a broad area, he made a pile in the middle. He used his fire finger spell to light the bundle. It took a while for the green grass to catch, but when it did, it sent up a roiling cloud of smoke. After gathering enough grass to keep the beacon rising into the air for a while, he sat down and made himself comfortable. Occasionally he called out for the dwarf, but he didn't get excited and wear his voice out. Oarly was as well trained as any ranger, and if anyone could survive out here, it was him. The dwarf probably couldn't see three feet around him in that tall marsh grass though, Phen thought with a laugh. He heaped some more grass onto the fire so that the smoke pillar rising into the still air became unmistakable. Confident now that his friend had something he could see to guide him, Phen lay back and closed his eyes.

Oarly woke to total darkness and a terrible throbbing in his hip. He wiggled the rock that was digging into him into a more comfortable position, then he closed his eyes again. No sense stumbling around in the dark, he grumbled to himself. Besides, his head was pounding from all the cheap brandy he'd stolen from the Royal Seawander.

The next time he woke he was sweltering hot. It was still dark outside, but he felt like he was suffocating. He raised himself up and something banged into his head. He dropped back down to the ground in a crouch. He was wide awake now. His heart was hammering through his chest like a forge hammer. Glancing around in the darkness, he saw a sliver of light a few feet away. It was the strangest thing he'd ever seen, a bright greenish-brown line barely a hair's breadth wide. He studied it for a long time before realization came to him. He was glad he was alone. Hyden Hawk and Phen would never let him live this episode down.

With a huff he stood up and pushed the upside-down dinghy off of him. The air wasn't much cooler out from under the boat, but it was fresh, and the sun was shining brightly. He dropped the dinghy back on the ground and rubbed his head where he'd knotted it against the floorboards.

The smell of something burning was strong in the air, but he wasn't tall enough to see over the grass that surrounded him. Without hesitation, he climbed up onto the bottom of the little rowboat and peered around. He glanced at the sun to get a sense of direction and two things came to his attention right away. The pillar of smoke rising out of the trampled-down clearing was about a quarter-mile away to the south. He was sure it was Phen, but a bit to the west of that, and not so far away from the fire, was another trampled-down area. He wasn't sure what it was about that spot that drew his attention, but it did. He studied its position in relation to the smoke and started off.

It took about ten feet of struggling through the thick grass for him to pull his axe off of his back and begin swinging it ahead of him. It was tiresome labor, but he was sure it would make it easier to find the boat later. Besides that, he told himself, he needed to sweat the drink from his blood. He had no brandy to put back in him, and until he worked the poison from his body, he knew he would be miserable.

About halfway between the dinghy and the source of the smoke, something huge and brown shot across his path. It was moving toward the other trampled place he'd seen. He figured it might be a snapper's nest. Or maybe it was a swamp dactyl's nest and the snapper was just going for the eggs. He remembered that marsh and swamp creatures liked to laze in the heat of the day. He'd never actually been in the marshes, save for that trip up the Leif Greyn on a pirate ship with Lord Gregory and Lady Trella. The idea that the flattened grass he was seeing was actually a big creature creeping up on Phen came to him and he quickened his pace.

"Oarly!" Phen's voice called out.

"I'm coming, lad," Oarly called back with relief. "Stay put now."

Phen stood and quickly spotted the line of Oarly's travel through the grass. A moment later the wild-looking, breathless dwarf came stumbling into the clearing.

"Something big is in the grass, yon way, about a stone's throw." Oarly pointed. "Might be trouble."

"Get your wind back and then we will go see about it," Phen said. "There's water right over there. I can't drink any, so I didn't check to see if it was fresh." He pointed to where the low-lying land fell away into the shore. "I tried to look for you, but I sank in the mud." He indicated his dark-caked legs.

"Bah," Oarly exclaimed. "Water's probably brackish. You did right to start a fire. Let's check that place before I get too comfortable."

"Aye," Phen said, letting Oarly lead the way. "You didn't by chance see the boat, did you?"

"I spent the night guarding it, lad." Oarly thumped his chest. "The fargin boat is safe and sound."

Phen saw the human body before Oarly did, and pushed his way past the dwarf to get at it. Just as he started into the clearing, a big mud-brown lizard came out of the grass hissing and grunting. Its teeth were bared to defend its meal. Phen was in no mood to tussle with the creature. He thought he'd seen the body twitch, the chest rise and fall. He didn't even bother with a spell; he just raised his white, shiny arms up high, let out a roar, and started toward the thing. The lizard hesitated a moment, then tore off through the grass. Oarly chased after it, howling and cursing.

Phen went to the figure and was surprised to see that it was a young girl. She was muddy and haggard, but breathing. He shook her gently and her eyes fluttered into a squint.

"Are you all right, m'lady?" he asked.

Her eyes shot open in surprise and alarm swept across her face. Oarly was traipsing back up, and when she saw him both of them froze.

"That girl's an elf," he said incredulously. "She's a fargin elf maiden."

"Come, m'lady," Phen said, trying to calm her with a smile. "Let's get up now."

The fact that he appeared to be carved from stone came to him, reflected in her wild yellow eyes. He was overcome with embarrassment. Had he been his normal flesh and bone self, he would've glowed cherry with it.

"Relax, girl," Oarly said gruffly. "He's not a threat, or a monster; he's just Marble Boy."

Phen shot a look at the dwarf that was both pleading and menacing at the same time.

"I dreamed of you," she said softly. Her hand came up and brushed across Phen's stony cheek. He regretted not feeling the touch.

"See there, Phen," Oarly said. "It proves my point. Not only are you destined to be known as Marble Boy throughout the kingdom, but even elf maidens are dreaming of you."

"I never believed them when they said that dwarves were rude and impolite," the elf girl said with a scrunched nose. "But I see I should have listened to my teachers better."

"How did you come to be here?" Phen asked, ignoring Oarly's dumbfounded expression.

"Bah," Oarly growled. "She would have been lizard food if it weren't for me, and now she is calling me names. I say we leave her, Phen."

"I'm sorry, sir dwarf, if I offended you," the girl said. "But you were calling your companion names, and I thought you needed a dose of your own medicine."

"Never mind him,"Phen said with a grin. "He's just an unemployed jester."

"I thank you both," she shivered. "I don't quite remember what happened to me, but I thank you both for coming to my aid."

"Let's get her to yon fire," Oarly said a little more softly.

Phen helped the elven girl to her feet and Oarly chopped them a wide path with his axe.

"You're a long way from home, lady," Oarly said as they came to the clearing where Phen's fire was still smoldering. "The Evermore Forest might as well be on the other side of the world from here."

"Where is here?" she asked.

"See that tiny black fang shape jutting up to the north?" Oarly stood on tiptoe and pointed until she and Phen both sighted it. "That's Dragon Tooth Spire. We're somewhere near the sea edge of the Great Marsh."

"I just don't know." She clenched her fists at her side and pouted like a little girl. "I remember a big black-skinned creature clawing me." She shrugged her shoulder out of her blouse uninhibitedly to show them the scars. "I remember men dancing and chanting around a hole in the earth on some island far below me. Then I was in the sea in a storm. I— I…" She hugged herself again and sobbed. "I can't even remember my own name." Her sob turned into a wailing shudder and she crumpled to the ground and began to bawl.

Phen looked at Oarly and the dwarf just shrugged and started down the trail he had come from in the first place.

"I'm going after the boat," he called back over his shoulder.

Phen reflected on what the girl had said. A memory of priests dancing around a hole in the earth in a Westland castle garden while demons and worse things crawled forth into the world came to him. "Were these men around the hole wearing red robes?"

"How did you know?" she asked with enough surprise in her voice to stifle her crying.

"One of those red-robed priests turned me into this." He gestured at his marble-colored body.

"Oh." She looked more closely at him. He tried not to be embarrassed as she took him in. When he was transformed he'd been wearing a hooded mage's robe. Now it was stone like the rest of him. It was impossible to see where his garments ended and he began. He hoped she didn't ask him how he went to the bathroom, because he didn't. He was relieved when she smiled politely at him.

"Are you sure it was an island?" Phen asked with growing concern.

"Yes." She heaved out a sigh. "Though seen from high above. I was in the sky." She looked as if she expected him not to believe her, but he just nodded.

"Borina, most likely," Phen reasoned. "The priests of Kraw helped the Dragon Queen summon forth Gerard—uh... the Dark Lord or whatever you want to call it. Can you remember anything else?"

"I remember trees that weren't aflame, but were on fire."

Phen grunted and scratched at his hardened chin. He'd recently heard a similar description of trees from someone, but he couldn't remember who.

"If we can get out of here, we will escort you to the High King. He will know what to do."

Phen stood and looked toward the southwest, where many, many miles away the island of Borina sat with a few other little atolls. "If those red-robed fools have opened up another gateway there's no telling what has crawled up into the world."

He stood there for a long moment, contemplating, then he turned back to the elven girl. "I can tell that your shoulder was magically healed. Do you remember any—" His voice trailed away. She was curled up into herself, lying like a babe and sleeping.

Phen sat down, closed his eyes, and sought out his familiar, Spike. The lyna cat responded to his magical probing quickly. Through their link Phen had the lyna seek out Captain Biggs at the helm of the Royal Seawander. They had established a few signals with the captain before leaving the ship. There was nothing that would explain to the captain that they were hundreds of miles southwest of the Serpent's Eye at the edge of the Leif Greyn River Delta, but he could let them know they were alive.

After having Spike pester him long enough, the captain realized what was happening. "Where are they?" Biggs asked the lyna excitedly. He looked haggard. No doubt they had been searching since the storm passed. Phen knew the captain of Queen Willa's royal vessel wouldn't want to return to tell the High King that he'd lost two of the realm's greatest heroes on a lark.

Phen felt for the man. He and Oarly had more or less bribed him into this. Now that he had Captain Biggs's attention, he thought about how he could say what he wanted to say through his familiar. He got the captain to follow the lyna down into the Royal Compartment where Phen and Oarly were quartered. There was a map of the southern coast spread out on the booth table. Spike hopped up onto it and began trying to unroll it further westward. The captain watched stupidly for a moment, but after Spike pushed a paperweight off the table Biggs suddenly got it and helped the strange animal unfurl the rest of the parchment.

Phen had to struggle to see through Spike's eyes in the dimly lit cabin, but he managed to make out the coastline on the map. He had Spike indicate the marshland west of O'Dakahn, the area labeled Leif Greyn Delta.

"You drifted past O'Dakahn, then?" Biggs asked.

Spike paused and nodded his quill-covered feline head.

Phen tried to be more creative and had Spike trace the shape of the letters S M O K E, but that only served to confuse the exhausted-looking captain. Finally, Spike, on his own, darted up to the unlit lantern and began thumping on it with his tail. A few minutes later Biggs finally said he understood that they would light a fire for him to use to locate them. He said he felt stupid talking out loud to the little feline, but he did it anyway.

Biggs told the lyna that it would be midmorning before he could get the ship that far west. Phen wished he could talk back to the captain through Spike, but that just wasn't possible.

Sometime later the grunting, huffing sound of Oarly's return came to Phen's ears. He stood to see what all the commotion was about. Oarly had dragged the dinghy the entire quarter mile across the grass by himself.

"What did you do that for?" Phen asked him.

"So we'll have a way to leave this blasted lizard den, boy!"

"You should have said that's what you intended to do, Oarly," Phen said matter-of-factly. "Captain Biggs is on his way. I imagine they will row the cargo skiff right up to our fire."

"Bah," Oarly plopped down and scowled.

Chapter Eight

"Are the instances related?" King Mikahl asked the Lion Lord.

The great wolves and Borg had left Dreen the day before. They were headed to Castlemont to try and spread some hope for the people there. The giant admitted that he was supposed to spy on the breed giants of Lokar for his king, as well. The joyful reunion was over and Mikahl was now in a private council chamber dealing with the current issues of the realm.

"It's hard to say," Lord Gregory answered. "The men in Southport were on one of Glendar's three ships. They admitted as much, but they deserted when Glendar's ship sank. They came to Westland to look after their families. The odd connection is that they said the ship sank off of the Valleyan Coast near Crags, but the more obvious commonality is that all of them, especially the two skeletons the Valleyan fishermen netted, should be dead, but aren't."

The room was silent for a while. High King Mikahl, Lord Gregory, Cresson the castle mage, and General Escott were sitting around an oak table in the modest room. The small chamber was annexed from Dreen's throne room. They all agreed that a matter such as this one should be discussed in private. There was no reason to alarm the people with tales of walking dead men, even if they were true.

They'd just learned that a few weeks earlier a fisherman from the Valleyan village of Crags caught up two human skeletons in his nets. The skeletons had writhed and twisted and tried to get free of the tangle of ropes, but the quick deckhands worked swiftly enough to secure them. The skeletons were now in an iron cage. The fisherman captain mounted the cage on a horsedrawn wagon and was now dragging the spectacle from town to town making a fortune in copper pieces from the common folk. Queen Rosa's mother, who still ruled over Seaward, had sent the scroll.

It said that the captain was there in Seaward City, saying that one of the skeletons was actually that of King Glendar.

The other incident was a little more disturbing. Outside of Westland's main trade center, Southport, two other men who had fought with Glendar and Pael were alive when they shouldn't be. They had been working the lumber trade, felling trees that would be shipped to the builders of Salazar. A miscut caused a towering pine to come crashing down on them. One man's ribcage was crushed; the other had a branch speared completely through his guts. The incident happened days ago, yet both men were still speaking and alert. Even as their dead flesh was beginning to rot and fall away, they weren't dying as they should be.

"Pael's entire army was undead by the time he reached Xwarda," Mikahl said. "I suppose some of the men, those on the ships who weren't dead yet, had already been spelled to become as such."

"So then we have three hundred of these— these things, running around?" General Escott asked, with more than a little alarm showing in his voice.

"One of the ships sank, so the number is more likely nearer two hundred," said King Mikahl.

"Your Highness," Cresson said, indicating that he would like to speak. Dreen's Castle Mage smoothed his black robes nervously, waiting for Mikahl to respond.

"Cresson, it isn't necessary to ask me permission to speak when we are in private counsel," Mikahl laughed good-naturedly. "As a matter of fact, when we are not in the throne room, or formal court, you are hereby commanded to speak your mind to me, without asking permission to do so. Your respect is appreciated, but you would not be here if your opinions weren't wanted."

"Thank you, Highness," Cresson said. He stood as he continued speaking. "The idea that some hundred souls are trapped under the sea is disturbing to me. The fact is that they will live as undead beings for eternity, or until their skulls are separated from their spines, or your blade draws in their souls and sends them where the gods will. The same goes for the men whom Pael spelled that still live. They will never truly die. This could turn into a serious problem at some point. There's a spell, though, that the late Master Targon taught me a few years ago when I studied under him in Xwarda. The spell would reveal to me if a person was under this type of necromancy." He paused, wrapped his hand around his long black goatee and stroked it slowly. "I think that if we can identify those men who were spelled by Pael while they still truly live, then we can counter their individual curses somehow. Master Sholt surely knows these spells as well."

"What are you going to do, Cresson," General Escott asked, "walk around the realm casting a spell on folks as you pass? Those men could be scattered about anywhere."

"The two men in Southport would know some of the others who were on the ships," Lord Gregory interjected. "From there we could start compiling a list."

"Aye," Mikahl said. "Lady Able has a firm grasp on things in Westland. I think General— I mean Lord Spyra, might be able to handle this sort of thing."

"Agreed," Lord Gregory nodded. "Spyra could use the distraction, I'm certain. The loss of his wife left him empty."

"Aye." Mikahl nodded. He was pleased to have Lord Gregory's input. It was always sound.

"Excuse me, Your Highness," Cresson said with a strange expression coming over his face as he hurried out of the chamber.

"Strange one, he is," General Escott said after the door closed behind the mage. "I don't much like the idea of magic, or those who study it. It's unnerving, especially in battle."

"He's all right," Mikahl said. "You should've met the castle wizard we had to put up with." He shared a look with Lord Gregory.

"What was his name?"

"It was Pael," Lord Gregory said with a halfhearted chuckle. "I'm sure most people think you're a little strange as well, General." He grinned and slapped Escott on the shoulder. "What with that tattoo-covered head and all."

The general's eyes narrowed and his face bunched up into a scowl. "It's an Ultura tradition to be inked with your Spirit Chivon once you pass your rite of passage."

"Aye, but on your head?" King Mikahl cringed at the idea of it. Loudin had been inked as well, but in those days Mikahl lacked the confidence to ask about more than a man such as Loudin offered. "Doesn't it hurt?"

"It's more than my head—"

The general's answer was cut off by Cresson returning. The mage looked distraught as he hurried to get himself standing before King Mikahl.

"Your Highness," he began. "Master Wizard Sholt has relayed a message. It originates from Prince Raspaar of Salaya. The monks have come under attack by dark winged creatures. These things were described as hellspawned beasts and baby dragons. I assume them to be wyvern due to that description, and the description of the wounds they found on the deceased. One of the dying monks told the prince that evil was brewing in the south. The minds there that Master Sholt trusts agreed that he had to mean from the Isle of Borina. It's the only land south of Salaya."

"Borina," Lord Gregory said. "That's where the red priests are from."

"Maybe they have the staff you're after," General Escott suggested.

"I saw a priest fleeing Westland in the sky, on that black wyrm, not long after I killed the bitch." Mikahl put his face in his hands and growled. "I should have known he'd taken the staff as soon as Sholt told me it wasn't anywhere at Lakeside."

"The Salayans are asking for your aid in taking military action against Borina." Cresson continued. "The creatures destroyed most of something called the Grove. Sholt didn't know what that was, but he said Salaya's only mage was a novice at best, and wasn't worth questioning."

"Yes," Mikahl looked at Lord Gregory for confirmation.

The Lion Lord nodded in the affirmative. The look on his face was anything but kind.

"Make a sending to Sholt," Mikahl commanded hotly. "Explain to him I am personally going to Salaya to attend to this matter. If he is able, have the prince ready his forces to sail this night, if it is possible. Ask them to meet me on Borina. Tell Sholt of your idea to identify those that Pael put under his spell, as well."

As soon as Cresson left to do as he was bidden, Mikahl ordered General Escott to send Commander Lyle and two dozen men to pick up the fisherman who was displaying the skeletons he'd caught in his nets. Only after the general was gone, and he was alone with Lord Gregory, did he speak of Hyden's dire warning about the staff.

"I have to destroy it," Mikahl said. "Hyden said it could be used to open another gateway."

"I'll keep the search for Phen and Master Oarly going while you're away, Mik," Lord Gregory said. "The two of them will turn up soon, I'm sure of it."

"Aye." Mikahl smiled through his anger. "It's not like Phen can hide himself very well."

"He still got that ring," Lord Gregory reminded him. "But don't worry, I'll find them. You see to the other problem, and see what you can do for the fairy trees. Lady Trella would die if she knew they were harmed."

"Aye." Mikahl understood. He remembered the brief bit of romance the Lion Lord and Lady Trella had shared atop the mountain that sheltered the grove.

Mikahl didn't waste any time. He pulled on a shirt of gleaming chain mail and made his way up through the castle to the sitting room where his wife, Queen Rosa, and Lady Trella, along with half a dozen ladies and little girls congregated daily. He knocked politely, and then strode into the room. Lady Trella scowled at him for not waiting for a response, but when he told Queen Rosa that he was leaving for a few days, Lady Trella let the look slip from her face.

After a long, passionate kiss that caused even the littlest of the girls to gasp and stare dreamily, he strode out onto the balcony, drew his sword, Ironspike, and let it fill him. He took a deep breath as the great symphony of its magic came rushing into his head. He found the melody for the bright horse and called it forth. All at once a brilliant flaming pegasus appeared beside him. With only a glance behind at the wide-eyed faces of the women, he climbed onto its back and held on as it leapt into the air.

Within minutes the Red City was far below and behind him. He felt exhilarated and anxious for battle as he went streaking southward toward.

Prince Raspaar of Salaya was the king of the island in every aspect save title. His father had turned over all aspects of governing the kingdom after the prince had cleverly made them wealthy beyond imagining. When King Glendar marched his army out of Westland to attack the east, nearly every able horse of the kingdom was commandeered and brought with them. Weeks later, when the Dragon Queen and her lizard-man army crawled out of the marshlands and took Westland for their own, she had the only land bridge to the east destroyed. The men and women left in Westland still had fields to plow, and carriages to pull, and a hundred other reasons to need horses. The prince began shipping Valleyan horses to Westland. He made a fortune for his little kingdom, and in the process he set up offices there. His people spied on the Dragon Queen for Mikahl and ultimately one of his ships carried Hyden Hawk and the High King into the land secretly so they could rescue Princess Rosa. It was during that rescue that the High King killed the Dragon Queen. Prince Raspaar and King Mikahl were not close by any means, but they trusted each other. The Prince was sure that his summons for aid in the matter of the Borinian demons would be answered. So sure, that he sent a pair of ships carrying half of his small army to the Island of Borina before he even received the High King's response.

By the time King Mikahl arrived, more than forty Salayan soldiers and a dozen red-robed priests had been killed. Several of the acolytes and novices confirmed this. Worse was that the high priest had gotten away with the staff. And even worse than that were the bodies of the thirteen virgin girls murdered in a ceremony to reanimate the sewn-together body of the Dragon Queen. The corpses, both old and new, lay rotting in the clearing, filling the air with the horrible stench of death.

The High King was angry beyond words with what he found. He spent long hours interrogating the survivors about where the high priest might have fled, but none of them would say. The senior priest who would have actually known had been cut down by Prince Raspaar's men. Mikahl wasn't too worried about the tales of the reanimated Dragon Queen. He was more concerned with getting the staff away from the absconded priest of Kraw.

"What should we do with all these red robes?" Prince Raspaar asked Mikahl later.

They were back on Salaya looking at the strange circle of fairy trees that refused to die.

"Borina is not part of my kingdom," Mikahl said. "Nor is Salaya. I would punish the novices severely, but let the families of those thirteen girls decide the fate of the priests."

"It won't be pretty."

"Nor will it bring those girls back to their mothers," Mikahl said flatly. "I have to worry about this rogue priest now. I have to get that staff away from him, and if he has somehow managed to revive that bitch queen, then there is a whole new keg of worms to deal with."

"This staff is dangerous, then?" Prince Raspaar asked.

"Aye." Was all Mikahl could think to say.

Chapter Nine

Captain Biggs, like most of the men on his crew, couldn't get over the elven girl's wild yellow eyes. Their stares, when she first came aboard, made her uncomfortable, so she stayed below deck for the short journey to O'Dakahn.

Once they were tied to the dock, Oarly sent a deckhand into the city to procure fresh clothes for the girl. He asked for a hooded cloak, so that she could hide her elven features, and even spent several golden coins to hire a carriage to carry them to Kander Keep. They planned to catch a river boat that would carry them all the way upstream to the fork. From there it was only a half-day's ride to Dreen.

The whole journey would take four or five days, depending on how strong the current was versus the strength of the water mage. The Kahna River was as unpredictable as a witch's mood. Phen and Oarly explained all of this to the elven girl, who still couldn't remember her own name. When they were done, she recounted the one thing she could remember, which was the strange ceremony performed by priests wearing red robes as she looked down from the sky.

Phen, feeling foolish for doing so, made a sending to Cresson. If the girl had really seen what she said, then the High King would need to know.

Cresson's response to the elven girl's claim surprised Phen.

"The High King has already gone to Borina to deal with the matter. There is also a standing order for you and Master Oarly to report to Lord Gregory immediately."

"What is that about?" Phen asked the distant mage.

"I don't know, Phen. A giant named Borg came to Dreen. A real giant, with a pack of great wolves. I overheard him talking to King Mikahl. The giant gave him a scroll from Sir Hyden Hawk himself. The next day, the High King made the order for you to report here immediately." Cresson paused only to catch his breath. "They found some undead men, left over from Pael's army. I am readying to travel to Westland to aid Lord Spyra in tracking them down."

Phen had quit listening when he heard Hyden's name. When Cresson finally stopped speaking, Phen said, "Tell Lord Gregory that we are leaving O'Dakahn this moment. We will sleep along the way. And Cresson—" Phen paused to see if the castle mage was paying attention. "Don't tell anyone, other than Lord Gregory or the High King, about the elven girl. Do you understand?"

Cresson seemed displeased at having to keep his mouth shut, but he agreed. After a brief parting courtesy, Phen ended the sending.

He was so excited to get back, he didn't bother to put a cloak over himself as he followed Oarly and the robed elven girl off the ship. Without a care, he strolled down the dock to their carriage. When they saw him, the people of O'Dakahn, hundreds of them, stopped what they were doing and stared. Heads bowed in respect, some even took a knee.

"What is that all about?" the elf asked Oarly from under her hood.

"Marble Boy here rode a dragon into this city and freed these people from Ra'Gren's slavery."

"King Mikahl, King Jarrek, and even you were there, Oarly," Phen replied. "I didn't do anything by myself. All I mostly did was hang onto Claret."

Oarly stopped them midway down the plank-walk. "No, lad." Oarly's voice was serious and held much reverence. "You and Claret saved all of us. We were about to be crushed by the Dakaneese soldiers, and those slimy skeeks outside the city wall."

"I barely knew what was happening," Phen argued as he herded them back into motion. "Claret did it all."

Oarly leaned over and whispered to the elf, "He's being modest because he likes you, I think."

Once again, Phen found himself feeling the urge to blush, but his stony flesh wouldn't allow it. He found that he wished he'd remembered to put on boots, gloves, and a cloak, so that he wouldn't attract so much attention, too. Now the people on the streets were staring at him, and would until they were well out of the city. He was thankful that Oarly had gotten a covered carriage for them to travel in. The eyes of so many made him feel uncomfortable and strange. He was certain that if he didn't appear as a marble-skinned freak, his heroic status would draw far less attention.

"At least the way out of the city will be clear," Oarly said, as if Phen's discomfort pleased him. "They always part the sea of people for Marble Boy to pass through."

"You're abominable," the elven girl said, moving from Oarly's side of the coach to Phen's as the boy got in. "I think he is just jealous." She hooked her arm in Phen's. "Not only are you taller and more handsome than the dwarf, you don't smell like a wine-soaked goat."

Even Oarly had to laugh at that one, but when the laughter died down, and the two sitting across from him were looking at the overcrowded cesspool of humanity that was O'Dakahn, he sniffed at himself to see if he really stank. Nearly gagging, he decided he would take a bath at Kander Keep. In the meantime, he decided he would do what he always did. He pulled a flask from his boot and proceeded to get drunk.

King Mikahl noticed a strange look in the eyes of one of the monks as he spoke to Prince Raspaar. When he mentioned that an elven girl had been found in the marshes, a girl who had supposedly seen the red-robed priests and the dark creatures they had released, a certain monk looked at his feet and hurried away. Mikahl didn't make a scene. Instead, he approached the monk later, when the man was in his private quarters.

"Tell me what you know of the elven girl," Mikahl said. "Our conversation will be in confidence, for there are far worse creatures, and more dark things liable to come calling, if I cannot put a stop to this."

The monk took a long time contemplating his response. "She is safe, then?" he asked.

"She is in good hands, and in the process of being escorted to the city of Dreen."

"Dreen sits at the edge of the Evermore Forest, no?"

"Yes," Mikahl replied impatiently. "Now tell me what you know of her."

"I cannot betray her confidence, but I can tell you the rest." The monk glanced at a long, black, hanging tapestry with the symbol of a tree emblazoned on it, and mumbled a short prayer. "Only because I feel it in my heart that your intentions are true and have your word that this conversation will be kept in confidence, will I speak to you." He smiled somberly. "After all, King Mikahl, you and your sword started all of this.

"A few months ago, nine elves came here to study the blooming fairy trees. They traveled in secret across your lands. The elven girl's name is Lady Telgra. I stress Lady as her title, for she is older than you and I both, though she appears to be half as young as either of us. She had a premonition, a dream while she slept among the trees. Your mage recounted the vision to you true, save for the fact that she didn't see this happening physically; she saw it in a vision. She also knew that the stench of death wafting on the wind from Borina was making the trees ill. The elves cast a powerful protective spell. The circle of trees you see that are still thriving is the very circle their bodies made when the spell was cast. The wyverns came, and there was something bigger, too. Lady Telgra and an elven guard were the only two who survived. She was badly wounded, and both elves refused to let the kingdom folk know that they were here. The guard helped us bury the other elves and then left the island on a small boat." He paused and seemed overcome with sadness. "No others were found with her?"

"No," Mikahl answered. It burned his blood to a boil that the elves were so foolish. They had been this way about helping to fight Pael's undead army. At Vaegon's burial, they were too high and mighty to stand with Hyden Hawk and him while one of the bravest beings to ever lived was put into the earth. If he had been told immediately after the attack, he would have been able to face down the high priest and gain possession of the staff, but the elves were too good to call for the help of men.

"I only ask about more survivors because one of our monks, a simpleton named Dostin, was seen leaving with the two elves. I had hoped to learn that all three had survived the storm."

"Why would they take a human with them, if they didn't want the humans to know they were ever here?" Mikahl asked.

"Dostin and Lady Telgra became friends while the elves were on Salaya." The monk shrugged. "I can't answer that question. Already I fear I may have betrayed the trust of the elves."

"No," Mikahl corrected. "You did what was wise, and I appreciate your candor."

Mikahl had no idea what all of it meant. He couldn't believe that a race whose people lived for hundreds and hundreds of years could be so ignorant and arrogant. He finally had to force it all out of his mind as he rode his flaming bright horse over the Isle of Borina again. He spent long hours flying low, searching for any symbols in the earth, or any other sign of an open portal. He was relieved to find none, but the relief only lasted until he realized that no one knew where the high priest had gone. That meant that no one had any idea where he might try to breach the barrier to the Nethers.

After a while he forced even that out of his mind and began to wonder about Phen. How that boy and the dwarf wound up finding the elven girl in the marshes he would never know. He didn't relish telling Hyden Hawk that the staff was still missing, and that instead of answers, he would be returning with more questions. He felt as if he had somehow failed his old friend.

As he left the island behind for the journey back to Dreen, he began trying to reason out where the high priest might try to hide.

Who would possibly welcome him? It was only after he had passed the blue of the ocean and was flying over the dingy brown expanse of the marshes that it came to him.

"Two men, one very large, but with feet small for his size, and the other man short and wide, were here with her," Corva said, studying the trampled-down mud and grass where Phen had built his fire in the marshes.

"How do you know all of that, Corva?" Dostin asked slowly with eyes full of both skepticism and wonder. His expression seemed to teeter between belief and total disbelief of the elf's findings.

"Footprints, Dostin," Corva said. "Come with me." He led them down the trampled and hacked trail that went where Telgra had washed ashore.

"See there." Corva pointed to the obvious boot heel marks in the soft earth. "See how the steps are really close together."

Dostin nodded as he studied them intensely.

"They are close together because the man in those boots had very short legs." Corva pointed to a more widely spaced set of tracks. "See how deep those prints are? It's because the man who made them is extremely heavy, or maybe he is wearing armor. I doubt it's protective gear, though. Armor out here will get you killed faster than it will help you."

"Why?" Dostin asked, completely forgetting his lesson on tracking.

Corva chuckled. It had been like this the whole two days since the storm. Dostin was scared for Lady Telgra and trying to keep his mind occupied. Corva found answering the monk's silly questions helped him to stay focused, so he did his best to not get frustrated.

"Because the weight of armor will sink you in the mud," Corva said as he knelt down to study the depression where Telgra had lain. "If you fell in the water, you would drown because you couldn't get out of the stuff."

"Oh," Dostin huffed. "So you think she is all right?"

"When you asked me that this morning I was stretching the truth when I said yes, but from what I have seen here, she was found by two men and was taken from this rise in a flat boat. They probably went to a bigger vessel, maybe-" He tensed, straining to listen.

Dostin saw his sudden jerk to attention and tried to listen as well. "What is it?" he whispered.

"Down now!" Corva hissed, indicating for Dostin to get on his belly.

Corva swiftly and silently put an arrow to the string. He squatted down so that his head was just below the top of the marsh grass. What he was hearing, he could not say, but he was sure that something large was quickly coming toward them.

Dostin tensed. It was clear he heard it now, too. Corva was ready to shush him when the monk started to ask what it was.

Corva's heart hammered in his chest as the sound of speech came to his keen ears. The language wasn't one he had ever heard before. It wasn't even close to human. It was broken with hisses and gurgling growls. He chanced a peek up over the grass and was disheartened to see a huge, four-legged lizard with several armed lizard-men riding its back. They were headed right for the sailboat that had carried Dostin and him to the rise. If he'd been alone, he could have fled easily, but a glance down at Dostin made him cringe. The monk wasn't nearly fast enough, or smart enough, to survive out in this type of terrain for very long. That meant Corva had to fight, at least until he and Dostin could get back on the boat and away.

"I'm going to draw them after me, Dostin," he whispered. "When they start chasing me, go straight to the boat and push off. I'll swim out and join you. You got that?"

"What are they?"

"They are Zard-men," Corva answered. "They are just two-legged lizards. If one of them tries to stop you, bash him in the snout."

"I wish I had my staff," Dostin said. "Father Blegish always says I'm the best with the staff."

"I'm sure you are, Dostin," Corva said with a forced smile. "Now wait just a moment after I'm away and then go straight to the boat."

Dostin nodded and rose to all fours so that he could take off quickly.

Corva darted straight through the thickest part of the grass. He made sure to make plenty of noise as he went. As he hoped, the Zard turned their lizard mount and started after his obvious trail.

Dostin broke. He ran as fast as his plump, middle-aged body would carry him. He got to the boat, and with a mighty heave, he pushed it out into the still water. Once he was underway, he stood and began searching for Corva.

A few moments later he spied the elf swimming toward him and smiled as he saw how well Corva could move through the water, almost like a snake. It wasn't until he reached down to help his companion into the craft that he saw it wasn't Corva. It was one of the Zard-men.

Fist-sized bulbous eyes, as black as pitch, transfixed him while the thing pulled itself up into the boat. Dostin was so afraid that he couldn't even bring himself to scream.

M. R. Mathias

Chapter Ten

Sir Hyden Hawk Skyler charged over the snow-covered precipice and dove headlong into a slide down into the icy valley. The angry shagmar beast was right on his heels. Its huge teeth snapped so close behind him that Hyden felt the impact of their clacking together. The over-hairy mammoth bear tried to slide like Hyden had, but its big forelegs splayed out before it, and its weight dug into the mushy snow, scooping up a small hill that helped grind it to a halt.

Hyden was glad for the distance he gained. The thing had gotten too close for his comfort. When he slowed his descent and took to his feet again he somehow busted the leather strap that had been holding his long black hair out of his face. He nearly clothes-lined himself on a branch as he charged down the slope into the trees. The angry mountain creature behind him was already back on the chase. Hyden cursed. He kept having to brush the mess of his hair out of his face as he ducked under branches and leapt over shrubs and deadfall.

The unmistakable shriek of his hawkling familiar pierced the forest from nearby.

"Yeah, I know that was close," Hyden answered as he ran. He slowed his pace a bit, knowing that the density of the trees would slow the shagmar enough that he could get his second wind. He still had a long way to go.

The hawkling's flight was slow and ungainly. Seeing this made Hyden think about Phen. Both Talon and the boy had been petrified. It was a wonder that the bird could even fly, weighing three times what it should. Luckily, only Talon's body was affected, not his feathers. They were bleached of their normal golden brown color, though. Spotting Talon in the snow caps was nearly impossible.

Hyden wondered how well Phen was getting around. Thank the goddess that he'd had the presence of mind to call Claret before making Phen take the dragon tear medallion. If it hadn't been for the old dragon, both bird and boy would be completely statuesque. The last time he'd seen Phen was just before he leapt onto Gerard's malformed body and dragged him back into the Nethers of hell. Phen had been about to destroy the Silver Skull of Zorellin, which amazingly he did. How he managed to get himself and Talon turned into statues, not even the hawkling could convey. According to Talon, Phen had already been invisible when it happened.

Hyden glanced back over his shoulder and saw that the shagmar was still coming. He picked up his pace again and pushed his hair back out of his face.

He had no doubt that Phen would come bearing the news that the staff hadn't been retrieved. Hyden had felt its power being used recently, and not for good. Since he had put on the ring he took from his malformed brother, he now understood a wealth of things he hadn't before. The amount of magical power he could command now still amazed him. The mysteries of the world unraveled before his eyes, and his senses were keener than those of any creature alive. If he concentrated on the source of it, he could even feel magic being used by others thousands of miles away.

Suddenly he felt the shagmar closing on him rapidly, and from a new direction. It was flattening trees and shrubs alike as it came bearing down. Hyden did the only thing he could to avoid the huge beast's devastating course. He stopped. It went barreling past where he would have been and howled in frustration. He didn't stick around. Hyden bolted full speed ahead, darting and dodging obstacles and fighting his blasted hair as he went. The thing had passed by so close that he smelled its raw, musky scent. It reminded him strangely of this dwarven friend Oarly.

Hyden focused his concentration on what was before him as he ran out of the trees into the rocky streamed at the bottom of the valley. In the spring and early summer the wide lower part of the valley would be underwater, but it was fall now and only a meandering channel flowed through the rocks.

The shagmar let out a savage roar as it gained the relatively clear stretch of washed-out valley bottom.

Talon fluttered down across Hyden's path, calling and chirping his concern.

"I am hurrying," Hyden yelled back at the bird. "Go slow him down if you're that worried."

The hawkling banked away and started into a shrieking dive. He crossed the shagmar's path just a few feet ahead of the beast, letting out a piercing call as he went. The shagmar faltered its step and nearly went tumbling headlong across the rocky riverbed, but it didn't stop. Two heartbeats later, it was back in stride and only a few dozen feet further behind Hyden.

With his mind, Hyden thanked the hawkling. A critical moment of his madman dash was coming up, and the few feet of separation might make all the difference in the world. The valley narrowed ahead into a V-shaped gulch. There was just enough room on each side of the waterflow for Hyden to run without getting wet. The shagmar wasn't so lucky. It came down the corridor splashing torrents of spray that slowed it even more.

Hyden glanced back. He was only thirty paces ahead of the beast and just starting to pull away. His breath was running out and his lungs burned with the icy high-mountain air. The shagmar roared and showed its fangs. Hyden almost fell face first into the rocks. The beast, with its wide bearish snout and raging eyes, looked remarkably like Gerard had in the Nethers. Talon shrieked into Hyden's brain, pulling his attention back from the moment.

"Aye," Hyden said out loud, as well as in his mind. "Signal Tylen and Little Con so they'll be ready below."

With a caw of agreement, Talon soared ahead and disappeared from view.

Hyden studied the terrain. The trick was making the shagmar think he was running ahead, when in fact he had stopped. It was either that, or let the huge mongoloid bear get so close that he could feel its breath on his neck. Hyden didn't like that idea. Already he'd been close enough to hear its gnashing teeth and smell its filthy fur. He didn't want one of those arm-sized claws near enough to snag him up. He let the creature get within twenty paces just to make sure it couldn't slow itself and tear him to shreds. The thing was so big that he could feel its thundering foot falls shake the earth behind him.

He focused on the white-scarred boulder ahead of him, and charged onward as fast as he could until he got there. Beyond the marked stone the river bed fell away a few feet. He leapt down onto the ledge, passing the boulder, and in four strides went from a full run to a hopping walk. He almost didn't stop in time to keep from going over. When he turned, he found the shagmar leaping in midair at him. It was all he could do to dive up under the monster as it came down with all its forward momentum. The impact of the creature broke the slab from the cliff. Beyond was nothing but a two-hundred-foot sheer drop of waterfall. Hyden couldn't even scrabble up to get a handhold before the whole shelf went sliding over. He could only shake his head. The shagmar's momentum had carried it out past the broken flat of granite that Hyden was now riding into a fall.

The idea of leading the shagmar to the cliff-drop was clever. The creatures had the uncanny ability to leap great distances, like across rivers or narrow canyons, but this one had nowhere to go and no purchase from which to leap. The shelf wasn't supposed to break away, though.

Hyden pushed himself up and away from the falling chunk of rock. He spread his arms out wide as if they were wings. A hundred times he had felt the sensation of flight by putting himself in Talon's mind and feeling what the hawkling sensed. Naturally, he spread his wings to fly; only

Hyden didn't have wings, nor could he defy gravity with his arms. The thing with Talon was only sensory. He realized this about halfway down when he saw the shagmar smash a crater below him.

Half a dozen of his cousins came out of nowhere to run their spears into the beast to make sure it was dead. All of them, save for Tylen, were looking up at Hyden as he came plummeting toward them.

Hyden had no idea what to do, so he let his mind tear through what he had learned about the ring. At the moment, it was all a confused jumble. Talon screeched by, seemingly panicked, too, but the bird was repeating the same call over and over again. Finally, just as the slab of granite exploded below him, Hyden figured out what the hawkling was trying to tell him to levitate.

He tucked and flipped and forced his feet to aim downward and then cast the spell. His fall slowed and he came to a hover just feet from the ground. The timing of the maneuver could not have been pulled off any more smoothly if he had done it on purpose. Once he realized that he was safe, he stepped down onto the earth, then slumped on a chunk of stone and let his hammering heart slow down.

"That was fantastic," Little Condlin said as he charged across the twenty or so feet that separated Hyden and the scattered pieces of the granite slab.

"It's a shame you didn't harvest hawkling eggs with us this year," Tylen said. He had harvested twelve eggs this past season, which was a new record for the clan, and he was proud of it. "You could climb up on the cliffs all day and night and just jump back down."

"We didn't make squat with the harvest this year," one of the approaching boys said. "But that was great, Hyden, even though you got lucky when Talon saved you."

"Talon!" Hyden sat up. His chest was still heaving from his grueling run. "I'm a great wizard, Shalloo, don't you know?" Hyden was in fact a dismal apprentice mage at best, at least until he'd gone into the Nethers and taken back the ring from Gerard. Ever since he'd bested the truly legendary wizard Dahg Mahn's trials and entered his tower, he liked to joke that he was a wizard of the highest order. The jest had more to do with the hundreds of dead magi and masters of magic that had failed Dahg Mahn's trials before him. The answer to Dahg Mahn's riddle had been so simple to Hyden that it baffled him that so many wizards had failed at the cost of their lives. The simplicity was what had beaten them. They over-thought the riddle; they tried farfetched logic and just couldn't get it.

"I saw you at the end, Hyden Hawk," Shalloo was saying with a knowing expression on his face. "You probably filled your britches."

Talon fluttered down and landed on Shalloo's shoulder. The bird cawed out his agreement.

"He did look scared," Tylen agreed. "But nevertheless we will be eating shagmar steaks long into the winter because of Hyden's daring."

"It's a good thing, too, because Summer's Day was almost empty this time," Little Condlin said. "We couldn't buy, barter, or even steal the supplies we needed for the year."

"I told you," Hyden said as he stood. His breathing was getting back to normal. "Next year will be even better, and the keep moss will stop the eggs you harvested this year from hatching, so it will be twice as good then."

"Are you going to keep the shagmar fur, or sell it?" another of his young cousins asked.

"I haven't thought about it."

"It's yours by right," Tylen said. "You baited the shagmar over the falls, after all."

"I baited the falls over the falls as well," Hyden joked. "I'll think about it on the way back to the village." As he spoke, he felt the sudden sense of alarm welling up inside him. "Excuse me," he said abruptly as he stomped off into the trees, leaving his cousins looking at each other with scrunched-up faces.

"Probably going to clean out his britches," he heard Shalloo joke behind him.

"Come on, let's get this thing skinned and cut down into quarters," Tylen said.

It was the staff again causing the dark feelings in Hyden's soul. It was unmistakable. And he could tell that it was no small doing either. He felt it sharply and knew without a shadow of a doubt that the staff was being used for something horrible. The more he concentrated on it, the more the feeling of dread came over him. He wasn't sure what to do about it, if he could do anything at all. Maybe it was just meant to be for he and the beast his brother had become to fight.

No, he decided. He didn't want to face Gerard again. That thing was not his brother anymore. There was nothing he could do at the moment other than hope that whatever dark magic was being attempted would fail.

Chapter Eleven

Queen Shaella, for all intents and purposes, was a zombie. Her brain, and all the twisted knowledge and memory it held, was wiped away during the preservation ceremony the priest named Eopeck held on her body. Physically, the resurrection worked perfectly. Not even a scar remained where he reattached her head. The spell worked so well that the noticeable bald patch over the Dragon Queen's ear, where Claret had once licked her with dragon's fire, was healed. So was the pink dagger scar that once ran down her face like a tear streak. With the full head of dark, wavy hair, and the life essence of the thirteen virgins coursing through her body, she looked like a girl of fifteen, save for her voluptuous womanly figure. Even the devout priest found his eyes lingering too long on his mindless, yet exotically beautiful, creation. It took him long hours of explanation, and many ember-eyed glares from the Choska demon that had deemed itself her protecter, to convince the Zard forces that she was really Queen Shaella. She could barely speak complete sentences, so she could not convince them herself. Eopeck explained that she was still in the process of healing, and that several more ceremonies needed to be performed before she could be back to herself. It was a lie, but convincing the Zard turned out to be as easy as feeding a starving dog. The lizard-men desperately needed a leader. Queen Shaella had literally taken them out of the swamp and led them to a somewhat civilized existence in Westland. They clearly wanted some of that back.

Some of the Zard who had pledged fealty to King Mikahl remained in Westland, but very few. The rest were now spread across the marshes in large clusters, trying to recreate the life they'd found in Westland. The trees that grew in the deep swamps were not sturdy and were unsuitable for building with. The land itself was soft and unpredictable. The Zard were frustrated and somewhat scared. The return of their queen was welcome, and Eopeck and his Choska demon were ultimately recognized as saviors to the Zard cause. Eopeck was the one who revived their queen, after all. The Zard wanted Shaella back to herself. They had no problems helping the priest prepare for the next ceremony.

The ritual he had planned would let the Abbadon, Kraw as the priests called him, back into the world without breaching the boundary or opening a gateway. He was going to fill Shaella's empty core with the Abbadon's soul. All Eopeck needed to do it had unexpectedly washed up on the edge of the marshes, saving him and the Zard a long and dangerous campaign into the Evermore to take some elven blood.

Not much—just a drop or two of the magical liquid was all that was needed.

Out on the islands, the Choska had almost delivered the rare life nectar, but Salaya's magical trees had befuddled the hellspawn and foiled the attempt. The wyvern were so mentally affected that they attacked and killed the very folk they were sent to capture alive. Until the Zard patrol came across the monk and the elven man struggling by the sea, Eopeck thought he would have to try to nab an elf from the forest.

Destiny, he decided, was on his side. It was meant to be that the king of the hells would find a way into the world. If not, the sea storm wouldn't have washed one of the elves right into their hands.

Eopeck smiled at the thought as he watched the sunset. In only a few hours he would help the master into Shaella's body, and from there, they would find a way to breach the boundary. Soon, the whole of the hells would empty into the world of men and wreak terrible havoc.

Just as the Abbadon had commanded Shaella to do things through the spectoral staff, he now commanded Eopeck. The master told him to shave Shaella's head. Eopeck had no clue why he was doing this; it wasn't necessary to the ceremony. He dared not voice any question concerning the matter, though. He was sure the dark one had his reasons.

The symbol of transference was carved into a wooden altar that the Zard had made out of a long dead cypress trunk. The area had been cleared, and all other preparations made.

Torches set on tall poles in the circle around the makeshift altar were lit as darkness overtook the marshlands. The myriad sounds, from creatures both large and small, that Eopeck heard out in this horrible place, never ceased to amaze him. He wasn't afraid, though. The Choska demon was circling in the sky, guarding the illuminated circle from any creatures that might be drawn in by the light. The Zard had warned him of snappers big enough to swallow a man whole. After all the recent battles, and the bodies that found their way into the river, the beasts lusted for man flesh. They had grown to enormous sizes feeding on the corpses. The light, and the scent of man, would surely draw them. The Choska, though, was far more deadly than any snapper. At least that's what Eopeck told himself.

The Zardess that shaved Queen Shaella's head escorted her, naked and glistening wet, into the circle of flames. Even hairless, the sight of her made Eopeck's loins burn. Her full breasts and the perfect curve of her hip were undeniable to his eyes. It was no wonder Kraw's host had loved this woman when he was alive. She was so captivating that he had to fight to keep his mind on the task at hand.

A glance at the moon told him that it was time. Another Zardess joined the first, and they led Shaella over to the cypress altar. Eopeck strode out of the circle to the cage that held the heavily beaten elf and his foolish monk companion. With a grin full of malice he jabbed his dagger into the elf's arm and squeezed dark blue blood into a fluted silver goblet.

"You will pay for this," Corva whispered through his broken teeth. "I swear it."

"I may pay for it, elf," Eopeck snarled back through his dark, pointed beard. "But it won't be this night."

King Mikahl saw the Choska circling over the ring of torches and had no choice but to land the bright horse a good distance away. The pegasus, due to its magical flaming nature, glowed brightly, making a stealthy approach at night virtually impossible. Ironspike's own pale bluish glow was a little easier to hide. He had learned a trick from Phen, of all people. A long, thick, velvet sock slipped over the blade kept it from being seen while it was drawn, at least until he grew angry. Then, the white-hot blaze of the razored steel responding to his mood would burn the concealing material away. He wasn't angry at the moment. He was too busy trying to creep up on the circle of torches. Through Ironspike's magical symphony, he shielded himself and camouflaged his movements as best as possible. He wished he had Phen's ring, or at least someone with him to draw the attention of all the Zard lingering out beyond the reach of the torchlight.

As if the gods were granting his wish, a monstrous splash came from the far side of the ceremony grounds. Instantly, the Zard and the Choska began moving that way. Seeing his chance, Mikahl ran in a half crouch toward the torchlit area. A block-shaped structure cast the only available shadow for him to hide behind. When he got closer he saw that the structure was an elevated crate-like cage with two men huddled inside. A wheelless horse wagon is what Mikahl decided it was, and now he saw it had pontoons lashed to the frame. The prisoners were kept off the marsh floor, above the water, so that the snakes and other crawly things wouldn't devour them before they served their purpose. They were surely sacrifices, just as the bald woman lying on the altar was. There was another huge splash, followed by a demonic roar, and the hissing speech of several Zard-men came from across the way. The noise continued as whatever had come too close to the light was violently subdued. Mikahl used the moment to get right under the cart. The quiet rasp of a short repeating prayer came to his ears.

"Can you hear me?" Mikahl whispered. He noticed that one of the men in the cage was intently watching the red-robed priest and his strange ceremony. The other was a monk. The woman on the altar drank from a silver goblet, and now the priest was moving the glowing staff back and forth over her body while chanting. A symbol on the wooden altar was glowing where its shallowly-carved groove had been filled with blue liquid. Mikahl's voice almost made the man yell out, it startled him so much.

"Are you injured?" Mikahl asked quickly.

"Very," the startled prisoner answered, glancing at the monk curiously.

The monk's prayer was so simple. "Come save us, Lord, save us so we can find Telgra." Over and over again he kept repeating the mantra. Corva looked at Mikahl sadly. "Too injured to fight, or even walk away from here."

"Can you fight when you are healthy?" Mikahl asked. "Are you trained?"

Beyond them in the firelight, the priest carried on like a madman.

"I'm trained," Corva answered. "But my friend is just a holy man from Salaya."

"I'm going to touch you with my blade. Don't be alarmed. It will heal you, hopefully enough to flee. Mikahl took a deep breath, trying to think. "Follow the shadow of this cage. Keep on going. The marsh is shallow enough for a long way. I have to get that staff away from that priest."

"Come on then," Corva said, shaking Dostin out of his prayer. "Be ready to run, my friend."

"When I draw this cover from my blade, I will be revealed, so move quickly," Mikahl told them.

With a flourish he pulled the sock off of Ironspike. Its soft blue glow filled the immediate area and startled away a fifteen-foot snapper that had crept up out of the high grass. Immediately Mikahl touched the flat of the blade to Dostin's hand. Magic pulsed into the monk. Almost instantly he was alert and rubbing at his arms with unabashed awe on his face.

Hissing shouts erupted from nearby.

"Now you," Mikahl said. "Hurry."

"I'll take the priest," Corva said as he touched Ironspike. "You go for the staff."

The power of the pulse that shot into this one was so violent it even jolted Mikahl. The high king stood stunned for a moment from the shock. He suddenly realized that Corva wasn't human.

"Elven blood, elven magic," Corva explained simply.

Mikahl cut through the wrist-thick wooden poles as if they were butter.

"Run, Dostin," Corva urged. He started toward the wide-eyed priest at a dead run, narrowly ducking a spear thrown by a Zard-man as he went.

Mikahl didn't wait around either. He charged toward the priest as well. His only concern at the moment was the staff. Even as a hot scarlet ray streaked out of it at him, he ran full speed toward it. The magical shield Ironspike provided absorbed the brunt of the blast. Mikahl didn't even miss a step.

Eopeck was so close to finishing the ceremony that the intrusion cut off the final words of his prayer. Had he not recognized Ironspike's glow he might have finished instead of turning, but he was wise enough to know that the High King couldn't be disregarded. He sent a sizzling kinetic blast at Mikahl and swept the staff like a club at the charging elf. The impact of the spectral orb on the elf's skull caused the most unexpected thing to happen. The powerful crystal orb exploded, shattering into several pieces. Eopeck, in his sudden realization of terror, cried out the last words of his prayer as the power of the orb dissipated into the night. The staff fell from Eopeck's grasp; the elf's momentum carried his unconscious weight to Eopeck and both went tumbling over the wooden altar. Three bodies went flailing in a tangle right out of the torchlit circle.

Mikahl caught the staff in his left hand before it even hit the muddy ground. He whirled back toward the Zard-men pursuing him and swung Ironspike wildly. The Zard nearest him fell in two bloody pieces and the one behind it decided to launch his pike instead of getting into the range of Mikahl's blade. It missed.

Beyond the Zard, Mikahl saw the damnedest thing. The chubby, balding monk had taken up one of the cage poles and was clobbering a trio of Zard swordsmen. Chunks of meat and scale flew everywhere as the staff-like weapon spun and struck true again and again. A fist-sized black eye caved in, and then a clatter of teeth sprayed out with a mist of blood.

So much for the monk being incapable, Mikahl thought.

A woman's cry, a scream full of sheer terror, from behind him caused Mikahl's attention to turn. He whirled around just in time to see the red-robed priest being dragged out of the torchlight by a huge snapper. The look in the man's eyes and his pain-filled yells brought a smile to Mikahl's face.

From not very far away in the darkness a demon's howl split the night. The sound was accompanied by a woman's gasping and gurgling. Mikahl knew it was the Choska demon. He charged over to defend the unconscious elf. He knew the sound of the demon well. A Choska had killed Grrr in the Evermore Forest. The same Choska had later killed Vaegon in the Battle of Xwarda. It had nearly killed Mikahl, too.

Mikahl saw that the wound on the elf's head wasn't fatal. He had the staff that Hyden Hawk asked him to get, and the fargin priest was nothing but snapper scat now.

He glanced at the monk. The man seemed to be enjoying the damage he was doing to the skeeks. The monk's tongue was poking out of his mouth in stern concentration as he pounded and jabbed and cracked away at the now leery Zard-men ringed around him.

Satisfied that he'd accomplished what he had to do, Mikahl unleashed a thunder clap from Ironspike's blade. It was so loud that it sent the Zard, the snappers, and even the Choska demon fleeing into the night like startled curs. Even the monk bolted into the swamp away from terrifying sound.

THE WIZARD AND THE WARLORD

Chapter Twelve

Even after three days of comfortable, semi-quiet traveling, the elven girl still couldn't remember her name. Try as she might she just couldn't remember anything about herself. It just wasn't there.

Any unease she'd felt traveling with Phen and Oarly was evaporated by the pair's antics and generosity. She'd learned that Oarly's bitter attitude was more sarcastic jesting than actual ill will. Phen, she could tell, was smart and very humble. Even if she had no personal memory, she still knew how rare it was to have ridden and spoken with a dragon. The fact that he had snuck onboard a Zard ship using an ancient elven ring to help save a princess amazed her. She had to needle the details out of Phen and endure Oarly's constant jibes, but she managed to hear most of the story. As they rode upstream in the crowded riverboat cabin Oarly told her about Phen's next great journey to find the mysterious Leif Repline fountain.

"Leif Repline," she said excitedly, not knowing how she knew the translation. "...means life replenish. Maybe if I go with you, the fountain will restore my memory."

"Aye, it just may," Phen agreed. Any reason to spend more time with the beautiful elven maiden was fine with him. Besides that, he told himself, she was probably right. The fountain would very likely restore her memory.

Noticing Phen's attraction to the elf, Oarly had pulled the boy aside one day and gave him a friendly warning.

"Don't let your thing get hard over her now, lad," Oarly said, as deadpanned as he could manage. "It might break off. Then you'll be in a real fix."

Since then, Phen had tried to keep his thoughts about the elf from drifting too far. Oarly's little warning, though, only made it all the harder to avoid thinking of her in that context. Phen still hadn't figured out if Oarly had been jesting or not. Either way, there was too much at stake to be taking chances. He found himself trying to associate her sweet scent, and the golden glint of the sunlight on her hair, with something repulsive, like the smell of the serpent, or visions of a half-naked Oarly fighting the iron skeletons in the cave. Spike was no help in the matter. The lyna cat spent more time with the elven girl than he did with Phen. She knew all the right places to scratch his ears, and did so fondly.

"So I can go on this journey with you?" she asked carefully. "I'll not be a bother."

"Can you do anything?" Oarly asked. "We won't be riding in carriages, or traveling in boats. The Giant Mountains are as harsh as it gets, especially since winter is moving in. We won't be riding much, either. Can you hunt, or wield a sword? Can you handle the rough of the wild?"

"I'm an excellent archer," she blurted out defensively. Then she giggled happily, realizing that she just remembered something about herself.

Oarly's winking nod assured her that he had planned the tricky questions all along.

Phen's smirk showed plainly that he thought Oarly was full of it. "Yes, you can come along," Phen answered her question. "But we need a name for you. Since our Master Dwarf is so smart, let's see if he can drag you into blurting out your name."

"I'll do it too, lad," Oarly boasted. "Just you wait and see."

"I almost had it," she said with an exasperated huff. "I can't stand this not knowing."

"Just make up a name for now," Oarly suggested. "What do you want your name to be?"

"Oh, I don't know," she said with a contemplative frown. Her feral yellow eyes made her look angry as she thought about it.

"How about Karee?" Phen asked. "That was my mother's name. At least that was the name the ladies at the orphanage told me."

"Karee," she sounded it out, tasting the way it felt on her lips. A smile spread across her face. "Karee it is."

"Bah!" Oarly exclaimed. "That's about as elven as Oarly Shardsworth."

"Karee is a beautiful name," she said. "And I like it. From now on, call me Karee."

"Lady Karee," Phen corrected. Her mannerisms and intellect spoke of nobility. Phen saw it even if she and Oarly didn't.

"No, Phen, just Karee for now," she told him.

"The idea of the exercise was for her to decide what she wanted to be called, lad," Oarly grumbled. "You challenged me to get her to reveal her name and then you ruined my plan." He got to his feet and scowled through his hairy face. "I'm going out to get some air."

"Thank the gods," Phen joked. "You are a miserable companion when you are sober. I can't believe there wasn't a drop of drink to be found anywhere in Oktin when we stopped over."

"That's what happens when a few hundred dwarfs start building a palace." Oarly looked back and grunted as he exited the cabin. He paused at the door and had to fight to suppress his smile. "Remember what I told ya, lad," he warned. "Don't let it break off now."

"Break off?" Karee asked, looking at Phen with a curious expression.

"Nevermind him," Phen sighed. He took a breath, trying to focus his mind on the feel of Master Sholt's wand smacking across his knuckles in class.

"What's wrong, Phen?" Karee asked. "You don't look like you want me to go on your quest with you."

"I'd rather you than Oarly, any day," he laughed. "Of course you can come along, but since Dreen is so close to the Evermore forest, wouldn't you rather go see your people?" Phen shrugged. "Surely someone is worried about you. Your mother and father, a friend. We might be long months in returning from the Leif Repline fountain."

At the mention of her father, she felt hollow for a moment. For a fleeting instant she knew, but something swept in and filled that void before the memory could manifest itself into a true reflection of the past.

Phen noticed the sudden blank expression and the vacant, almost fearful look in Karee's wild yellow eyes. He put his hand over hers and squeezed gently. His touch, as cold and hard as it was, put a bright smile on her face. It must have been a contagious smile because he found himself grinning back at her stupidly. Spike broke the moment by leaping onto the bench where Oarly had been sitting.

Phen was as pleased as he was surprised when she didn't let go of his hand and purposely used her free hand to scratch behind the prickly lyna's ears.

"I would rather go back to my people knowing who I am," she said absently, after a time. "I have a feeling that this is all happening to me for a reason." She forgot Spike and put her other hand over Phen's so that he now had both of her hands in his. He wished he could feel her touch more specifically.

"I had a vision of you finding me." She scrunched up her face, searching for an explanation. "I know that much in my heart, so I will follow the course I am on and see where it leads me." She sighed and rolled her shoulders. "But, as you said, someone might be worried about me. I don't even know that my family is from the Evermore Forest, but surely someone there would know of a missing elven woman. Is there a way I could get a written message to the elves when we get to Dreen?"

Phen didn't think that the term elven woman described her very well. She appeared far too young to be considered a woman grown, but he understood the desire to be accepted by one's peers. "Of course," he told her. "We can send a rider or two to Vaegon's Glade. They can leave your message there. Your people will find it."

Again she felt the tremor of memory as Phen spoke. Vaegon—the name seemed vaguely familiar to her, but she didn't know who he was, or why she recognized the name.

"Who is Vaegon?" she asked before the thought left her.

"He was a friend of Hyden Hawk and King Mikahl," Phen said reverently. "The only elf who concerned himself with helping stop the demon wizard from using Xwarda's powerful bedrock to destroy the world. Lord Gregory said it was because Hyden saved his life the year before last at the Summer's Day festival, but both Hyden and Mikahl said that it was more than that. They think of Vaegon as a hero of the realm. He died fighting a Choska on the wall in Xwarda."

The stirring in her mind continued, but never centered on anything. The idea that only one of her people would stand up against such an evil foe seemed to block out the rest of it. For a long time she chewed on her cheek and thought.

Phen found his adolescent mind wandering in the wrong direction again, so he busied his mind with the thoughts of the Leif Repline and of hopefully getting to see Hyden Hawk soon. Oarly broke the silence this time when he stormed into the little cabin. The dwarf seemed uplifted by his stint of the air above.

"You love birds need to get ready," Oarly said excitedly. "The fork is in view, and the rumor is that there's plenty of wine, so don't dally."

It was midday before Corva slipped back into consciousness. Dostin had carried him a long way through the swamp following King Mikahl. Mikahl didn't remember Dostin from his short stay on the Isle of Salaya, but Dostin remembered the High King and his legendary sword. He wanted to ask a thousand questions but was too nervous and overburdened with Corva's weight to get them out of his mind. By the time they stopped, the monk was so out of breath that he couldn't talk.

"This is a deep enough channel to be reached by river boat," Mikahl told the monk. He couldn't believe that the man had carried his elven friend through the night. It was a valiant accomplishment. The monk hadn't so much as complained. As a matter of fact, Mikahl was sure that Dostin hadn't even grunted or made a sound at all.

After Corva was laid in a comfortable looking position, King Mikahl gave Dostin back his makeshift staff and used Ironspike to start a fire. "Watch over him. I'm going on to Low Crossing. Wait here."

"Are you coming back?" Dostin asked fearfully. He suddenly blushed and took a knee. "Your Highness," he added.

"A boat will be along for the two of you soon. I'll see to it personally. Just keep putting grass on the fire so they can make out the smoke." Mikahl gave his best reassuring smile. He started to say something about the monk kneeling, but was too exhausted. For a long while he just watched Dostin. "Get up, my friend," he finally said after he realized that Dostin wasn't going to get up until he told him to. "If you want to meet up with the elven girl, she will be in Dreen in a day or two. You are welcome to stay at the castle there, both of you. You helped the realm with your bravery and skill. I am in your debt."

"You saved us from the priest's cage, so we are even," Dostin replied without thinking about it. "How do you know about Telgra? Do you know the short man and the heavy one who are helping her?"

It took Mikahl a moment to figure out that the monk was talking about Phen and Oarly. "How could you know about them?" he asked.

"Corva saw the tracks and told me it was a big, heavy man with little feet and a really short man who helped her into a boat."

"Corva is an excellent tracker then," Mikahl nodded. "That's exactly what happened. She is on her way to Dreen with two of my most trusted friends. Should I give her a message? I will see her later this day."

Dostin scratched his head and thought about it. "Tell her to wait for us in Dreen. Corva and I will come along as soon as we can." He glanced at Corva. "Is he going to be all right?"

"Aye," Mikahl nodded. "He'll come around. I will tell your friend Telgra to wait for you. If you stay put until a boat gets here, you should be safe. Tell Corva I said thank you for his help and that he is welcome anywhere in my kingdom, as are you, mighty Dostin."

Mikahl laughed at his choice of words. The brave monk was mighty.

He looked at the sky. The sun was starting up into the day with vigor. "I'm off, my friend," he said. He checked to make sure that the broken Spectral Staff was still lashed to his back, then he drew Ironspike. At once, the bright horse appeared under him, and in a single rising leap he was off.

He flew straight to Low Crossing and ordered a boat to be immediately sent to pick up Dostin and Corva. "Treat them like royalty and escort them directly to King Jarrek," Mikahl ordered. "Tell him to have the monk and the elf escorted to Dreen as soon as possible."

The boat captain gave a head bow and promised to comply with his orders. After that, Mikahl was on his way to Dreen where his young queen waited.

"Where are we?" Corva asked after he fluttered his eyes open and saw that they weren't near the ceremony grounds and it was broad daylight. His head had a throbbing, egg-sized lump on it. His fingers discovered how tender it was when they found it.

"Oh, hello, Corva," Dostin grinned happily at the elf. "We're waiting on a river boat right now. Telgra is on her way to Dreen, and we are supposed to see King Jarrek for help getting there. The High King says that we get to stay at his castle. He says that he owes us for helping him."

"Shhh," Corva hissed with a half grin on his face. Dostin's voice made his head hurt worse. He'd always wanted to see the great city of Castlemont. The elves who had seen it all agreed that it was a wonder to behold. The idea that he was about to betray his Queen Mother, though, wasn't lost on him. He decided that even she had to agree that if Telgra was in Dreen, he had to go get her.

Dostin loaded grass on the fire. The pillar of smoke it created was reassuring, but the amount of insects and strange noises around them kept them uneasy. When the old river boat finally arrived, they both found they couldn't wait to get on it.

THE WIZARD AND THE WARLORD

Chapter Thirteen

Phen was too heavy to ride a horse so they had to take a horse-drawn wagon from Fork to Dreen. The only wagon available had just been used to haul a load of fruit to the docks at Fork. The bed was sticky and pungent and was drawing insects. Luckily, the farmer put Phen on the bench seat in the middle. He drove his two-horse team from Phen's left, and Karee road under her hood on Phen's right. Oarly was too drunk to mind the bed of the cart.

Phen offered to pay the farmer handsomely for the trip, but the man wouldn't hear him.

"It's my pleasure to give Marble Boy and his companions a ride," the farmer replied proudly. "My boy Brendley was sacked at Seareach by those Dakaneese bastards. A ride is the least I can do for you, sir."

During a rough section of road about halfway through their journey, they were jostled to and fro dramatically. The driver looked back over his shoulder to the wagon bed and cringed. Nervously, he nudged Phen, who followed the farmer's pointing finger with his eyes.

Phen burst out laughing at what he saw. The farmer visibly relaxed and continued urging the horses along.

Oarly was out cold. Phen couldn't contain his mirth as the jolting motion of the wagon tossed the dwarf around. Oarly's hair, beard, and every inch of his clothing was matted with sticky fruit juice and bits of leaves and debris. A swarm of bright yellow bees hovered around him like a cloud.

Karee chuckled quietly when she saw. "At least he won't smell like a goat now." She gave Phen's cold hand a squeeze.

"Aye," Phen replied. "We might have to shave him to get all of that out of his hair."

They arrived at the low, but seemingly endless, red block wall that surrounded the city of Dreen. It was just after dark, but the gate guards let them in with no questions. Once they recognized Phen, they all saluted. Karee watched with sleepy eyes as they rode past street after street of low built one- and two-story red brick structures. She asked through a yawn why they were built so far apart.

"See the fences between the homes? During the day, those pens are full of horses and cattle. Some still are." Phen pointed at a large yard full of cows. "The whole city's commerce is based on horse flesh. It's probably the biggest city in the realm, but it has far fewer people than Xwarda or Seaward City." Phen looked at Karee to see if she was still listening, and found her nodding into sleep against his stony shoulder. He hadn't even felt her lean against him. A few long hours later, they finally reached the castle's palisade wall. By then Phen was fighting sleep as well.

The fatherly look of concern on Lord Gregory's face when he quietly escorted Karee into the castle was overpowering.

"Phen, you should never leave without telling someone where you're going or what you're about," the Lion Lord scolded. The man's gaze made Phen feel a visceral sort of fear. "Now let us take in this elven girl who has caused such a stir."

Phen looked at Lord Gregory inquisitively. "How did you know I was traveling with an elven girl?"

"The same way I know that master Oarly is going to sleep in the hay barn until we can get all that muck washed off of him."

Karee chuckled at that then peeled back her hood.

Lord Gregory had traveled, for a time, with the elf Vaegon and had attended many a Summer's Day festival where the elves dominated the archery competition. He was still taken aback by the wild look of the girl.

"Lord Gregory, may I present Lady Karee," Phen said in a somewhat official manner. "Lady Karee, this is the famous brawler, Lord Gregory. He's also known as Lord Lion, or the Lion Lord."

"That's enough, Phen," Lord Gregory said. "I was told that her name is Lady Telgra."

"It is!" Telgra exclaimed with a happy clap. "I'm sure of it." Her tired gaze evaporated and her look became serious. "Who told you about me?"

"The High King returned from the Isle of Salaya earlier this evening. He would have greeted you himself, but he is already in his bed chamber." Lord Gregory looked at Phen and grinned. "After relieving the high priest of his life, he was exhausted."

Phen started to say something, but Telgra cut him off. "But how does he know my name?"

"She can't remember anything about herself," Phen explained. Phen was a little disappointed, but it wasn't the fact that she would not be going by the name Karee now. It was the news that King Mikahl had killed the priest who had turned him into a statue. That man could have reversed the spell on him. It was a last-resort hope that he had been holding on to, just in case the Leif Repline fountain didn't restore him. Now it wasn't even a possibility. At least the bastard could do no more harm.

"…told the High King about you," Lord Gregory was explaining to Telgra. "A monk named Dostin and an elf named Corva. Both helped the High King kill the priest and regain possession of the staff he was using to wreak havoc. Dostin sent word with King Mikahl for you to wait here for them."

"That is six days away at best," Phen told her.

"How soon are you leaving for the Leif Repline?" she asked.

"I'm not certain." Phen looked at Lord Gregory. He knew he and Oarly had been ordered to report because of Hyden Hawk's message, but he didn't know why yet, or what the message was. Suddenly, it was all that mattered to him. Hyden Hawk was his closest friend, as close as a brother to him. His change of demeanor must have shown, for Lord Gregory clasped him on the shoulder and chuckled.

"King Mikahl will speak with you in the morning regarding your journey. I will speak with you more after that."

"I'm going with Phen," Telgra said a little more forcefully than she had intended to. "The Leif Repline might help me remember who I am."

Phen put a hand on her shoulder to calm her.

"No one will try to stop you," Lord Gregory assured her. "But if you go with Phen, you'll likely miss your friends."

"Then I will miss them," she said matter-of-factly. "I don't remember them. I want to know who I am without people who claim to know me asserting their influence."

Lord Gregory thought about that a moment then gave her a nod. He didn't tell her that her friends would not be told where she had gone if she went. The location of the Skyler Clan village wouldn't be handed out to them no matter what. Instead, he smiled kindly and urged them toward the castle.

"Queen Rosa wanted to greet you personally, but she and the king have retired, like I said. I'll escort you to my wife, lady. She will help you find a bed and someone to tend your needs. Phen, you must rest and be ready to attend council in the morning."

THE WIZARD AND THE WARLORD

The Lion Lord led Telgra up the stairway. About halfway up, he paused and turned back to Phen. "I already had stablemaster Wade gather up Oarly."

Phen started toward the kitchen but remembered that he couldn't eat or drink. He couldn't really sleep, either, not physically. He ended up in his small downstairs room, where he washed himself with a wet cloth, then laid back in his bed and let his mind drift.

He thought about Karee, or Telgra, the beautiful elven maid who was a good archer and had dreamed about him once. He found, though, that wondering what Hyden Hawk had to say in his letter dominated his thoughts. He missed his friend. For a long time he'd thought Hyden dead, but after the High King's wedding, a mysterious gift from the Skyler Clan gave them all hope.

Phen laughed. Hyden was such a horrible spell caster, yet the things the man accomplished without so much as trying to use magic at all were spectacular. Hyden always joked, in a self-mocking sort of way, that he was a great wizard, when in actuality he was. Not the sort of flashing smoke and lightning type of mage, like Pael, but a wizard of a far grander scale. Once, with only a suggestion, Phen saw Hyden start a series of events that led to thousands of Wildermont slaves being freed.

Hyden had also tricked the Dragon Queen out of her first dragon and then set it free from the magical collar that bound it. Claret had helped defeat Pael, and then recently saved Phen and carried him into O'Dakahn and destroyed the Dakaneese army. All of that, just because Hyden Hawk once helped her.

Phen was still thinking about all of it when a knock came to his door. He got up, opened it, and was surprised to see people bustling about in the corridor beyond the dark-haired, long-bearded Cresson.

"The High King awaits you," Cresson said with a sheepish grin. "They are in the council hall. You can break your fast there."

"No, Cresson, I can't," Phen said with an ironic smile. "I haven't eaten in months."

Cresson nodded and walked away. Phen followed him to the council chamber and was surprised to see Queen Rosa and Lady Telgra leaving the room giggling.

"Oh, Pin," Queen Rosa said. "She is a delight."

"You've never told me all the things you did for your queen while she was a hostage," Telgra said with clear admiration showing on her elven face. "You really are a hero."

"The best hero in all the lands," Queen Rosa said with a kiss on his cheek.

When Phen finally was inside the room, he found he was hiding his face as if he were blushing.

"As your friend, Phen, I'll say this," the High King said after the door was closed and bolted. "It is good to see you back safely. Later, I want to hear your tale. Master Oarly has already told me some of it, but he couldn't tell all due to some sort of oath he said you'd sworn."

"Where is he?" Phen asked. A sharp look from General Escott reminded him with whom he was speaking. Phen just shrugged back at the man. Mikahl had said they were speaking as friends, not as a king and subject.

Mikahl laughed. "He's at the pump house being sprayed down. While I was going through my morning routine, he came stumbling out of the hay barn. I almost killed him because he looked like some kind of wild creature."

"Aye," Phen chuckled. "What of Hyden's letter?"

A few sets of eyes fell on Cresson then, but the mage's expression stayed blank.

Lord Gregory harrumphed at the High King.

"We will get to that." Mikahl's tone had changed. "Now Phen, as your king, I will say this. You are an important and integral part of this kingdom. Disappearing without notice is inexcusable. A note to me saying that you were departing and couldn't be specific would have saved us all, especially Queen Rosa, a whole lot of needless worry."

Phen waited for more scolding, but it didn't come. Instead, Mikahl pulled out a scroll and read Hyden's letter to them. By the time he was done, Phen was head over heels with excitement. He couldn't believe that Hyden Hawk was going to go with him to the Leif Repline fountain. He should have known, because Talon would need the restorative powers as much as he did. He wasn't very thrilled about having a four-man military escort, but at least King Mikahl agreed that Telgra could go with him.

Just when Phen decided that things couldn't get any better, he was told that the party would leave on the morrow. By the gods, he had a lot to do. Gathering the books Hyden wanted, and his own texts, would take hours. Mikahl made it clear that they would stay at the Skyler village for the roughest winter months. The High King explained that it was far too late in the year to try to go all the way to the fountain before spring.

After the meeting was concluded, Phen found Oarly by the barn, still fighting a persistent bee and picking leaves and twigs from his tangled hair.

"Give me the emerald," Phen said.

"Emerald?" Oarly's expression went completely blank.

Phen could tell that something was amiss. "The emerald we took from the Serpent's Eye cavern. I gave it to you before that blasted thing tried to eat me. Remember?"

"I… uh… I sort of remember," Oarly stammered. "I thought I gave it back to you once we was in the boat."

"There was a storm raging down on us when we got back into the boat. I have no pockets, Oarly. I know you didn't give it back after we washed up in the marshes." Phen's anger was plain.

Oarly realized what had happened then. He took two steps back, to get himself out of Phen's range. "What do you need it for right now, lad? We're about to go on another quest."

"I'm going to have it mounted on a staff while we are gone," Phen explained. "It should be ready for me when we get back. It is a rare and powerful magical gem, you know."

"You will have to wait until we get back," Oarly said, taking another step away.

"Until we get back?" Phen took a step toward the dwarf.

"I thought it was a rock poking in my leg back in that marsh where we washed up."

Oarly bolted away as fast as his short legs could carry him. Looking back over his shoulder he called, "I pulled it out of my pocket and left it there." By then, he was moving at a short-legged dead run toward the safety of the castle gate.

The Wizard and the Warlord

Chapter Fourteen

Phen was forced to spend a good part of the morning mapping and notating directions to where Oarly had left the emerald. He decided that the dwarf was impossible. Hopefully the magical jewel would still be there in the mud when he had the chance to go back after it. His mind was alive with other thoughts, though. The idea that they were going to cross all the way out of the Giant Mountains into unknown lands was wildly exciting. Hyden's letter said that there was something there that would banish the hellspawn forever. That also meant this journey might take a very long time.

According to Phen's best calculations, based on the various maps he'd studied, it would take them more than three months to cross the mountains. The jagged peaks and bitter cold were inhospitable at best. Not to mention the numerous legendary creatures that supposedly lived in the depths of the range—mammoth shagmars, unfriendly ice dragons, and the mystic and deadly dread wolves were just a few of the monsters they might encounter. Plus there were mountain trolls, orcs, and night stalkers. There were also razor-toothed snow worms, fog wraiths, and all the creatures he had studied under Master Amill and Master Sholt back in Xwarda. There were countless tales of adventurous groups of men, just like their own, that had gone off into the depths of the mountains never to return. These stories had been told over campfires for thousands of years. Even the giants, whose entire kingdom was within the range, didn't go to some of the deeper places.

By the time Phen had finished making his maps, and collecting his and Hyden's texts, he had a pile too big for him to carry. He had to find King Mikahl and see if they could take a wagon to Hyden's village. With cold weather gear, rope, supplies and weapons, and the huge pile of books, they would need twenty pack horses if they couldn't.

Oarly was coming out of the council chamber as Phen approached. The dwarf put up both hands, palms out in a show of supplication. "I'm sorry about the emerald, lad," he said gruffly. "I truly am."

"It's all right, Oarly." Phen gave a sincere smile. "It's just a trinket, in the scheme of things. You're my friend, and we can find it when we get back from this journey."

Oarly stood there as if waiting for a "but" or a punchline, but none came.

Oarly felt horrible, even ashamed at his carelessness. "It just goes to show you, lad," Oarly said with a grave nod, "we dwarves do stupid things when we are sober."

"Aye," Phen laughed. "You'll need a dozen pack horses to carry enough drink to keep you drunk on this trip. We will be in the mountains all winter and then some."

"I know it, lad," Oarly grunted. "That's why I was speaking to the High King. We will need a wagon cart or two to haul our stuff to the clan village."

Phen smiled. Oarly was on his toes this morning. Either that, or the long run along the castle he'd made fleeing Phen earlier had cleared his head.

"What did he say?" Phen asked.

"Wagons can go all the way up into the foothills." Oarly grinned. "We can get them as close as a day's hike. I figured two wagons, and we can leave the escort to watch them while we make a few trips unloading."

"Aye," Phen agreed. "Better yet, let the escort do the unloading. I still have to get with Lord Gregory and find out where the village is."

"You must not have heard." Oarly was glad to be giving Phen some news that would cheer him. "The Lion Lord is going with us, at least to the Skyler village. Hyden's folk brought him back from the dead, they say. He wants to thank them and give them gifts and such."

"That's eight people," Phen said, smiling despite his concerns. "Any more men and we might as well armor up and tote a war banner."

Oarly laughed. "Are you going in?"

At Phen's nod, the dwarf pushed the door open and followed Marble Boy. Since Lord Gregory was there with the High King, Cresson, and the general, Oarly thought that Phen might be able to work out some more of the details that needed tending before they left.

Mikahl was speaking to Cresson as if he were someone else. Oarly recognized the mage's blank look. He was in the middle of a sending spell. The idea of the magic made him shiver. After each phrase the High King spoke, Cresson repeated the words as if he were translating. A moment later Cresson would repeat what someone else replied to another mage in some distant place. The whole idea of it was as perplexing as it was disturbing. Oarly supposed that it wasn't that much different from the resonating stones that dwarves used to communicate underground, but even those were foreign to him. Oarly took a sip of the flask on his hip and then started listening.

"…we welcome General Escott and the added protection the alliance force will give us, Your Highness," Cresson repeated the words of someone else in a droll monotone. "Though I don't see Xwarda as susceptible as Sir Hyden Hawk does. Nevertheless, his warnings will not go unheeded. His wisdom cannot be questioned. Our city would have fallen if not for him. All access to the Wardstone is being monitored relentlessly and the ship builders and other tradesmen who require pieces of it are being sifted as well as can be without questioning their honor or offending them." Cresson paused and looked up at the High King expectantly.

"Tell Queen Willa that the general will be leaving Dreen in a matter of days with his troop. She should expect them in a few weeks. Tell Dugak that Master Oarly will not be able to join the group going underground this winter, he regrets, but duty has called him elsewhere. Assure Dugak and General Diamondeen that he is not on another bender; he is serving the realm.

"I will be departing with Queen Rosa to Westland soon. I want to spend the winter there. I haven't been home, for any length of time, since my father died. Lord Gregory and Lady Trella will be in charge here, though the Lion Lord is leaving on a short journey on the morrow. I will have Master Sholt cast a sending when we arrive at Lakeside Castle. We miss you, Willa. Tell Starkle and Lady Andra we miss them, too." Mikahl waited for Cresson to look up and then nodded that he was done speaking.

A few moments passed, then Cresson looked up. "Queen Willa says that she loves you as well," the mage relayed. "Don't go too hard on Phen, he's just a boy. Master Oarly, though, knows better than to abscond without notice. We will prepare for the general's arrival. If you happen to see King Jarrek, tell him to hurry back to Xwarda, at least for a visit." Cresson looked up and appeared to be relieved that he had gotten through all of that. "That's all she said, Highness."

"I'm sure you're tired, Cresson," the High King said. "Queen Willa will go on and on if we let her. You're excused for now. I will send someone for you, if need arises."

"Thank you," Cresson said as he bowed himself out of the room.

"General Escott, you're excused from council until you've returned from Xwarda. I will want weekly reports sent via Master Sholt throughout the winter."

"And I expect the same through Cresson," Lord Gregory added.

The general nodded his understanding and followed Cresson out the door.

The Wizard and the Warlord

Once the door was bolted behind them, Lord Gregory laughed. "I still can't believe I used to think Queen Willa was an old witch." He shook his head. "It just goes to show how powerful rumors can be in shaping our views of the world."

Feeling the informal mood take over the room, Phen finally spoke. "The rumor's power was intensified by the fact that, for a couple of generations, Highwander and Westland had no direct communication."

"I'm glad your brain wasn't turned to stone." Mikahl grinned at Phen. "You're too fargin smart for us to do without."

"Aye," Lord Gregory agreed. "I can see why Hyden likes you so much. It's his attachment to Master Oarly that I can't figure out."

"It's me ability to adapt to any situation, and the way I can ignore the feeble wit of you Westland folk that he likes," Oarly shot back with hands on hips.

"Hey," King Mikahl said to the dwarf, "I'm a Westlander too, ya know."

"My point exactly," Oarly deadpanned.

Lord Gregory laughed out heartily.

"How long do you think we will be holed up in Hyden's village?" asked Phen.

"At least eight weeks," Mikahl answered. "If it were me, I would stay in one of those rabbit holes until spring."

"Rabbit holes?" Oarly asked.

"Hyden's people live in underground burrows that the giants made thousands of years ago," Lord Gregory said.

"Well, at least they have good taste," Oarly grunted his appreciation.

King Mikahl wrapped his arms around his shoulders and shivered. "It gets so blasted cold in those mountains that even the pack horses will have to be kept underground."

"No wonder Hyden wanted me to bring so many books," Phen chuckled.

"That reminds me," Mikahl said as he strode over to the map table and retrieved a long leather bundle. "This is for you to deliver to Hyden. It's the bow Vaegon gave him. You will never even begin to understand how much this means to Hyden. Guard it with your life." The look in the High King's eyes made Phen shiver.

"And don't sit on it, lad," Oarly said. "You'll surely snap it in half if you do."

"Another thing you should know," Lord Gregory said. "The Skyler Clan doesn't really like elves that much. Lady Telgra might not enjoy spending months cooped up with them."

Mikahl nodded agreement with the Lion Lord. "For that matter, she might not care to go on with your group after she has restored her memory in the pond you're going to visit." He set his gaze on Phen again. "You should let her know the full extent of what she's getting into. As valiant and helpful as her companions were to me, they won't be told where she's going, either. The location of the Skyler Clan's village is to remain secret at all costs."

Phen nodded that he understood, and he did. As attractive as she was to him, he was still of an age where the excitement of the upcoming journey was more powerful than his budding male urges. At least that was the case when she wasn't in sight.

"I better talk to her," Oarly said as seriously as he could manage. "Phen here is smitten by her beauty. He might get a little too excited and break off his magic wand."

High King Mikahl and the Lion Lord shared a look then simultaneously burst into laughter as they realized what the dwarf was insinuating.

Phen sighed and scowled at them. Suddenly an idea came to him. It was hard to cast the spell without laughing or giving himself away, but he managed to do it unnoticed.

69

Phen pointed at a tangle of Oarly's hair. "What is that?" he asked.

Oarly heard a buzzing sound where the boy was pointing and his laughter stopped immediately. He pulled at a wad of his hair and walked a full circle, craning his neck, trying to look at it. He resembled a dog chasing his own tail.

Phen gave Mikahl and the Lion Lord a wink as he grabbed Vaegon's bow and quickly eased out of the room.

"What is it?" Oarly yelped as he danced in a circle. "Where did Phen go?" All of a sudden a half-dozen angry bees came out of the tangle and began swarming around his head. The dwarf began skipping and hopping and swatting like a madman, trying to bat them away.

"That's not funny, lad!" Oarly raged. "They're… they're… they're fargin stinging me, Phen!" he cried out in a voice that was a full octave higher than normal. He flailed his arms and ran around the council chamber, hopping and spinning.

"Back to the pump house," Lord Gregory ordered through his guffaws.

"Or jump in one of the troughs," High King Mikahl added with a slap of his knee. Then to Lord Gregory, Mikahl said, "I bet a gold piece that the dwarf doesn't make fun of Phen's magic wand again."

THE WIZARD AND THE WARLORD

Chapter Fifteen

Phen let Oarly suffer his swarm of magic bees until after he had eaten his midday meal. Luckily, the welts and stings disappeared along with the rest of the illusion. Phen reveled in how potent his spells had become, especially with the dragon tear medallion aiding him. A simple illusion had not only caused Oarly pain, it had caused his skin to react by swelling and turning plum red. It seemed to Phen that while the spell was in effect, it was really more than an illusion. He vowed to experiment with those types of spells on the journey.

That afternoon, he and Oarly, along with Lord Gregory and Lady Telgra, inspected the three wagons that were still being loaded.

"It will take years to get through the mountains with all this stuff," Telgra said, shaking her head in disbelief. "I've got a pack and a saddlebag worth of stuff that Queen Rosa and Lady Trella loaned me. That's all I'm taking." She turned to Phen. "What is all of this for?"

Phen found Oarly and Lord Gregory staring at him for an answer as well. He hadn't talked to her yet. The loading of the wagons had distracted him.

"Walk with me, my lady," Phen said, offering her his arm. "There are a few things you should know before you commit to this quest."

"I would say so, if you are planning on dragging all this over the mountains." She hooked her arm in his and they started away. They walked to a quiet place outside the barn where the wagons were staged. The fall breeze was cool, yet the sun was bright. They stopped in the small strip of shade that ran alongside the main structure.

Phen looked at her. "We are going to spend the harsh winter months with the Skyler Clan. They are the people who…"

"They are the ones who climb the sacred cliffs for hawkling eggs," she said over him.

"Aye," Phen touched her chin and pulled her gaze to meet his. "What else do you remember?"

"Nothing about myself. So all of that stuff is to get us through winter then?"

"Yes, it is, but I have to tell you more." Phen smiled awkwardly. No matter how hard he tried, the idea that this beautiful elven girl was staring at a petrified freak made out of marble wouldn't escape the back of his mind. "We're not stopping at the Leif Repline fountain… I mean… we are…" he shook his head and grabbed the bridge of his nose. "We're stopping there, but once we're done at the fountain pool, we're continuing on. A friend of mine, Hyden Hawk, is in the clan village we're going to lay over at. He is a great wizard. He is going with us to the fountain. His familiar, the hawkling named Talon that I told you of, shares the same affliction as me."

"You told me about Talon on the boat," Telgra said. "Where are we going after the Leif Repline?"

"On the far side of the mountains there is an artifact, or an enchanted weapon, or something that Hyden says can be used to seal away the demons and the Dark Lord for good."

"Those lands aren't even on your maps and yet you're going there after some magical thing?"

"Yes." He shrugged, showing that it was out of his control. "I only found out early this morning. I was supposed to tell you sooner, but I got caught up with Oarly and packing."

"You told me that Vaegon was the one elf who helped the kingdom of men against the demons." She stood proudly and her wild eyes flared as she spoke. "Now there is another. I will go on this quest into the unknown with you."

"But what if after you get your memory back you don't want to continue?" Phen asked with concern. "We won't be able to escort you home. You could be an elven princess or something."

"That's silly, Phen." She giggled at the idea of it. "I won't change my mind. You have my word. And if I do, I will suffer my decision on my own."

"All right," Phen nodded. His happiness was plainly visible by the huge grin on his stony face.

"What are we going to do in your friend's village all winter, Phen?" she asked with a grin as wide as his. Her eyes met his and she put her arm around him.

Phen found that he suddenly needed to be thinking about something else.

"The lad is in a fix," said Oarly to Lord Gregory. "I can see it plain. Humans and elves aren't meant to be attracted to each other, yet I see she is as smitten as he is."

"Phen doesn't really appear to be human anymore, though," Lord Gregory replied. "And you have to admit, she is beautiful."

"She's probably a hundred years older than him," Oarly grumbled. "The boy will get his heart broken."

"We all do, sooner or later."

Oarly looked at the Lion Lord and realized it was the truth of it. He nodded and changed the subject. "So the horses that we use to pull the wagons will act as our pack horses next spring then?"

"Aye." Lord Gregory was glad to be back to business. "You'll have twelve horses available when you leave in the spring. I don't know if you'll use them all or not. Hyden's cousins, Tylen, Shalloo, or even Little Con, might want to go with you. It will be good if they do because they have experience in the heights and can hunt and scout for the group."

"It's too large a group already, I think," Oarly said. "We'll attract too much attention. The smaller predators will flee us, but the larger ones will see us as a threat or a meal."

"Don't let me find out that you are afraid of the mist monster," Lord Gregory chuckled. "All those tales of ice dragons and dread wolves are just campfire stories."

"They're more than stories, man," Oarly argued. "Those tales came from happenings. Embellished maybe, but I bet my boot flask they aren't just made up."

"No, they are not," Phen said as he and Telgra returned. "There are razor-toothed snow worms, gargantuan shagmar bears, and giant mountain-trolls up there. There's a hundred other things as well."

"What in the fargin hells is a snow worm, lad?" Oarly asked with concern showing plainly on his face.

"They burrow through the snow and snatch you under as you're walking along," Telgra said, with hand animations adding to the effect of her words. "Shloop!" she sounded loudly, making a falling-through-the-surface motion. "Just like that, you're gone."

Phen and Lord Gregory both laughed at the wide-eyed look on Oarly's face.

"You should be on the training yard watching the High King, lady," Lord Gregory said after a moment.

"Why?" Telgra asked.

"He is choosing your escorts today. It is amusing. It seems that all the men who are capable of managing a wagon and a four-horse team aren't capable of wielding a sword."

"The wagon drivers can return with you and the empty wagons," Phen said.

"Aye," Lord Gregory agreed. "That's what I told him."

"By Doon, there's going to be a hundred men on this trek before nightfall." Oarly stormed off toward the horse pen where Mikahl was practicing.

"I'm going to speak with Queen Rosa and the ladies," Telgra said. "Finding guards is men's work."

"I'll escort you," Lord Gregory said. He was still grinning over Oarly's discomfort from the snow worms. "I need a word with Lady Trella anyway."

"I guess I will go with Oarly," Phen said reluctantly. He'd actually hoped to spend some more time with Telgra. He'd have plenty of time with her soon enough, he told himself. Thinking about Oarly's warnings, he decided he would probably have too much time with her.

After a half hour of sparring with the wagon drivers, Mikahl decided that Lord Gregory was right. He had already chosen two archers and was now watching several matches on the yard to see who he would choose as swordsmen. He liked the youngster named Jicks. He was originally from Wildermont and had been held as a slave in Dakahn for a time. Jicks was only sixteen or seventeen years old, but that was close to Phen's age. Mikahl liked the way Jicks improved during every session, and the way he strove relentlessly to prove himself.

His second choice, Mikahl decided, would be someone with battle experience and years under his belt. Mikahl felt sure that with Oarly's proficiency with the axe and hammer and his ranger skills, along with Phen's magic, two archers, and Jicks's sword, the group would be able to handle any trouble. Hyden's ability as an archer was second to none, but he tended to take wild risks. A man with a cool head, a sure blade, and the reasoning of many years in the field is what Mikahl wanted to add. Lord Gregory would be perfect for the job, but he wouldn't dare take the Lion Lord away from Lady Trella for more than a few days. He himself needed the Lion Lord's wisdom to manage the realm far too much to do without him anyway.

"I like Jinx," Phen said as he stepped up.

"It's Jicks, and he is in," Mikahl replied, not looking away from the training yard. "Phen, go over to that group of archers and tell them that on my command they are to start loosing on the men sparring." Mikahl scratched his chin. "Tell them to send high arcing lobbers, and use target tips. Remind them that we don't want a bunch of injuries."

Phen nodded that he understood the command. "What are you up to, Mikahl?" he asked, knowing that any use of title was forbidden on the practice yard.

Out here, a stable boy could whip the High King, or any ranked solider, without worry of retaliation. If he had the skill. Mikahl was extraordinary with his blade, though. The best swordsman in the realm could barely last five minutes with him. And that was without Ironspike. If Mikahl used his magical blade, the fight was over before it got started. Phen admired the fact that even now, as High King, Mikahl went through a vigorous ritual each and every morning. His dedication was admirable.

"I want to find out who of the lot is calm under fire," Mikahl answered Phen's question with a grin. "Besides that, Oarly is out there."

A moment later, Mikahl called out, "Attack! We're under attack!"

As arrows came raining down around the combatants, some men dove for cover while some scrambled about. Oarly went streaking straight for a weapons rack to grab up an axe, which impressed both Phen and the High King. Jicks took up a defensive position in front of his king and ignored the falling arrows.

Mikahl scanned the yard and the chaos that had taken it over. He saw his man standing with his sword still clenched in his fists. The man was looking at the archers angrily with his wooden shield over his head to protect himself. His opponent had run off.

The man was at that age where gray starts to streak the hair over a man's ears and the rest of it starts to thin out. Not as old as Mikahl would have preferred, but old enough to command his own respect from Oarly and Hyden. Mikahl was even more pleased to see sergeant stripes on the man as he strode over to him.

Phen called the archers off, and after he saw who the king was moving to speak to, he jogged over to Jicks and introduced himself properly. Phen liked the fact that Jicks was from Wildermont. Brady Culvert, who had gone on a different quest with him and Oarly had been from there as well. King Jarrek made sure all of his soldiers were competantly trained. The two younger men eased close enough to hear what Mikahl was saying to the sergeant.

"So, you're from Highwander then?" Mikahl asked, seeing the insignia on the his leather protective gear.

"I am," the sergeant said. It was clear that he had a hard time keeping himself from adding a "Your Highness" or at least a "sir" to his answer. "I fought those stinking corpses both days, first at the west gate, then again at the breach near Whitten Loch."

"Aye," Mikahl nodded, respectfully noticing the scars around the man's mouth. During the battle of Xwarda, the west gate was where the demon wizard's undead army came through into the city. It was one of the bloodiest, most gruesome battles ever fought.

"What's your name, Sergeant?"

"Welch. Buxter Welch."

"Are you married, Lieutenant Welch?" Mikahl asked.

"It's Sergeant, Highness," the man corrected kindly. "My wife died in the battle, along with my unborn son."

Mikahl clasped Buxter on the shoulder. "It's Lieutenant Welch now, even if you don't choose to go on the quest."

Lieutenant Buxter Welch smiled a smile filled with broken teeth. It appeared that at one time he had taken a sword hilt or a mace to the face. "I wouldn't have been out here fooling with these youngsters if I didn't want to go, my king."

Mikahl laughed. "You're going to hold rank over the rest of the escort. Jicks here is your main blade." Mikahl gave the young swordsman and Phen a hard look that told them both what he thought about their eavesdropping. "Come, I'll introduce you to the archers."

Once they were away from Phen and Jicks, Mikahl continued speaking. "Phen, Master Oarly, and especially Sir Hyden Hawk, are not under your command, but you are not under theirs. I expect you to respect Sir Hyden Hawk's wishes, but I also expect you to draw on your experience and speak your mind with them openly. They'll risk their lives for the most trivial things if you don't remind them what they are about. I need you to be the voice of reason among them. Now, let's go find those archers."

Later that evening, after dinner, Lady Trella spoke to Telgra quietly in the ladies' sitting room. Queen Rosa was there, as well as a few of the younger ladies in attendance. Trella had hoped for something more private, but didn't want to offend Queen Rosa. Trella was also certain that Rosa would love to comment because the topic of this conversation was going to be her hero, Pin. Lord Gregory had brought several things to his wife's attention in hopes that she would speak to the elven girl. It was awkward, but she agreed there was reason for concern. Phen was well loved and no one wanted to see him hurt, or pulled too far from his studies.

"He adores you, you know," Lady Trella said, getting to her point delicately. "He doesn't understand the differences between elves and humans. At least his urges won't allow him to see reason."

"I adore him as well, my lady," Telgra admitted. "I suppose I hadn't paid any mind to those things either. When I'm with Phen, I forget that I'm an elf. I can't quite explain it."

"You'll live to be a few hundred years old, the gods be willing," Lady Trella said. "If he's lucky, he might live to be eighty. Are you ready to watch him grow old, and are you willing to force him to watch you stay young while he withers?"

"Oh, my lady." Telgra wiped away a stray tear. Nervously, she scratched Spike behind his prickly ears as Trella's revelations hit home. "I don't ever want to hurt Phen. It feels so right when I'm with him. What should I do?"

"Follow your heart," Queen Rosa said. "Pin is very special to me, but I see plainly your love for him. To deny him that now is as wrong as to hurt him later. You must choose."

"Very well put, Your Highness," Trella said.

"I'm not even sure he likes me in that way," Telgra said, biting at her bottom lip. "He gets quiet and distant when we are together; it's as if he is thinking of something else entirely."

"Oh that." Lady Trella gave a blushing grin. "It seems our dastardly dwarf has put something in Phen's head. It's awkward, but my husband explained it to me today when expressing his concern about your feelings." She was blushing and had to look away before she could continue. "It's about his manhood…"

As she told her, the shrill giggles and shocked gasps that came from the ladies' sitting room could be heard echoing through the whole castle.

Unknown to anyone, Phen had been listening to the entire conversation through his link with his lyna familiar. Spike was in Telgra's lap. If he could have blushed, he was sure he would have glowed in the dark with embarrassment.

Chapter Sixteen

Commander Lyle was intrigued by what he was hearing about the caged skeletons he was trying to track down.

"They try to talk to you," a potter on the streets of Seaward City said.

"One of them reached out from the cage and made to touch me," an old woman told him.

"They're downright unnatural," said another.

"Nothing but empty eyes and clacking jaws," a blacksmith said as he wiped sweat from his face. "It's probably just a trick with wires."

If the people of Seaward City hadn't been so welcoming to the commander and the two dozen men riding with him under the High King's banner, he might have been angry that the old fisherman had moved on. He found it hard to be upset at anything when the people in the street were treating him and his men like heroes. Bakers passed them fresh bread and pastries as they rode by. A leathersmith even gave Commander Lyle a set of studded gauntlets as they passed.

The city itself was spectacular, with its icy blue marble public buildings and large, wooded parks. The darker gray stone towers at the corners of the block wall that surrounded the city gave it a surreal appearance, for they glowed turquoise in the sunlight. The rooftops looked like poured molten gold. Some of the structures inside the walls were made of whitewashed wood, but they were clean and well kept. Occasionally a magnificent building formed of Jenkata glass blocks stood out from the rest. Queen Rachel's palace wasn't as big as Commander Lyle would have thought it to be, but its seven spires were impossibly tall and built of the same powdery blue stone as the city buildings. He was sad, as were his men, when they had to leave the hospitality of Seaward behind. The fisherman had taken his cage to the Highwander city of Weir.

The commander figured that the man was planning on making his way up through the eastern coastal cities. By all accounts he had made at least a keg full of coppers in Seaward City.

Commander Lyle didn't feel like he had to hurry across Seward, but he did so because his king would wish him to. Weir was big enough to keep the spectacle for at least a week. Even still, as the ferry boat carried the group across the Pixie River into Highwander, he found that he couldn't wait to see the skeletons.

The ferry wasn't large enough to carry all of his company across at once, so he posted four men to stand at the boathouse to wait on the next ferry and took ten men with him into the city.

There was no heroes' welcome in Weir. The procession of armored men riding under the High King's banner barely merited the attention of the Highwander folk. They weren't disrespectful; they yielded the way to the commander and his men, but the people were oddly incurious about why they were there.

"It's a true seaport," Lyle's second in command, Sergeant Tolbar, said to him. "They see folk from Westland, Dakahn, and the islands regularly."

"But we just left Seaward City a few days ago and it's a massive port," Lyle argued. "Don't they see the same people there?"

"It's on the freshwater side of Ultura Lake. Most sea craft from farther east unload here. The goods then move along the coast and up the Southron River to Seaward City by way of local barges."

Commander Lyle pondered this as they made their way through the large, dirty city of Weir. The fisherman and his attraction weren't hard to find, but it wasn't easy to get up close to the small pavilion tent that had been erected over the wagon cage. Already a crowd of more than a hundred people was gathered in the alley where the man was set up. The distraught woman who told them where to go also said there were three skeletons now, not two. This baffled the commander, as well as Sergeant Tolbar, but didn't distract them from their duty.

"I think, Sergeant," the commander said as they sat atop their horses, observing the growing crowd, "I think that we should find the city guard and explain what we're about. With this many people, things could get messy rather quickly."

"Yes, sir," the sergeant replied. "What should I tell them? Will we wait for the rest of our men?"

The commander studied the crowd for a while before answering. "Post four men here before you go. They are not to do anything other than make sure the wagon cage stays put. I'll find the captain of the guard myself." He forced a smile through the sudden strange feeling that had come over him. Whether it was the idea of finally seeing the undead creatures, or something else, he felt that something here wasn't right. "Why don't you work on finding shelter and food for all of us. Two nights should be sufficient. I don't want us to be spread out either."

He spurred his horse around and pointed to a pair of his men, indicating that they should follow him.

"Once you've secured a place to put up for the night," he called over to the sergeant, "set up a rotation for this post. I want to know if this wagon cage moves so much as a finger's breadth."

Lord Spyra looked at the list of names in his hand. There were only seven. Worse was the fact that the two lumberjacks who should be dead, but weren't, were losing the ability to speak. It was hard enough dealing with the stench of them. The one whose ribcage had been crushed was virtually a skeleton now. The other wasn't far from it. The last words he had spoken were something to the effect of, "Kill me." The other had nodded his maggot-ridden head.

Only two of the men on the list were supposedly in Northern Westland. Another was last known to be in the city of Curve on Salaphel Island working another lumber tract. The rest had joined Dakaneese mercenary companies, or pirate crews, before the recent war and hadn't been seen since.

Already Spyra had sent men after the two in the north. He was in Southport, and Curve was only a day and a half away. He was going there himself. Since Salaphel was under Westland jurisdiction, he didn't feel the need to take a military detachment with him, but he did bring a pair of his liege men to aid him if they were forced to give chase.

The superintendent at the Salaphel lumber tract welcomed Lord Spyra into a big log structure and generously offered his table to him and his men. Spyra indicated for his men to sit and did so himself. The table was long enough to seat forty men, and the torchlit room was open. The high, log-raftered ceiling was spacious but heavy with pitch smoke from the torches on the walls. No one knew why Spyra was there, so there was no need for posturing or trying to conceal his motives. The poor superintendent was clearly worried that he had done something wrong, or maybe he thought one of his men was guilty of a crime. Often the men wanted by one city guard or another for illegal acts ended up working the mills. Rarely did a lord come to visit, and never for social reasons. Lord Ellrich used to frequent the islands in the spring to enjoy the abundance of grottel that were rousted out of their forest nests as the undergrowth was cleared out before harvest. The huge lord could eat a dozen of them in a single sitting. The superintendent was hoping that a table full of the fat, meaty creatures would keep him in Lord Spyra's good graces.

"Sir," Spyra said, trying to use a comforting tone. "Could you invite a certain worker of yours to dinner?"

"They come and go, my lord," the superintendent said guardedly. "Is this man in some sort of trouble?"

"Not in the way you might think. He has committed no crime. As a matter of fact, I would just like to ask him a few questions."

"Give me his name, my lord, and I will make sure he is at the table this eve." The superintendent scratched his chin curiously. "You're sure he's not a wanted man?"

"No," Spyra answered. "Believe me, after the man hears what I have to say, he will be thankful I spoke with him."

The superintendent became a little nervous after Spyra gave him the name, but he repeated it to an assistant and told him which foreman the man worked under before sending him off to fetch him. Spyra sent his two men with the superintendent's assistant just as a precaution. The superintendent disappeared into the kitchen and conferred with his cooks about the night's meal, then returned and took a seat across from Lord Spyra.

"Can you tell me what this is about?" the superintendent asked.

Spyra saw no harm in telling the man, even though he felt foolish speaking of such things as wizards, spells, and living dead men.

"Some Westland men, who were fighting under King Glendar, sailed out of O'Dakahn. For whatever reason, they've become scattered about the realm. No doubt they believe themselves to be thought of as Westland deserters." Spyra saw the superintendent swallow hard and wondered why the man was getting so worried. "Those men actually did the right thing by deserting Glendar. High King Mikahl wishes to thank them."

"So they're not in trouble, these men?"

"Not at all." Spyra felt that he might just have found more than he'd hoped to. "In fact, the High King has declared that all they have to do is swear fealty to him to be fully absolved of the deed, but…"

"I knew there was a 'but'. There's always more to it," the superintendent said. "What more is there? A penance for the Crown of a year's labor, or a hefty fine to fatten the coffers?"

"You're getting ahead of yourself," Lord Spyra snapped. He was a big, formidable man who had spent his whole life in the Highwander military. He wasn't used to being questioned, and frankly didn't like it very much. He took a few moments and tried to remember the fact that he was a lord now and not a general. "Let me finish next time, before you go running off at the mouth, man." He pierced the superintendent with his eyes and went on. "Those men were bespelled. All of them. The men on those ships with Glendar won't die, even when they should." Spyra stood and started pacing with his hands clasped behind his back. The idea of the undead, and the man before him, had him on the verge of anger. "Those who still have a beating heart can be saved from the horrible fate that awaits them. Many of them have already met a terrible end."

"My lord." The superintendent's relief was palpable. "I apologize for interrupting you. We have seen the effects you speak of out here. Several, perhaps thirty, of our men were on those ships. There were more, but we had to burn them after they started rotting away. Only after their bones were charred to ash did they stay dead."

"Well then, we have just made a great step to fulfilling the High King's orders," Lord Spyra said with a smile that showed he was holding no ill will, and that his irritation had passed. "I was ordered to question these men and compile a list of all who were on those ships. I have to find out who was burned and who else is missing, but a wizard named Sholt will come and do whatever it is he does to remove the enchantment Pael put on them. They can kneel to me and say the words of fealty to King Mikahl after dinner. That will make them free men again."

"That will be good for them, my lord," the superintendent said, "but I will lose more than a few of them when they learn that they are free to go home and such." He stood and wiped his brow. "It's good to know we wasn't in the wrong by burning those that wouldn't stay dead either." He looked up, his eyes focusing on something far beyond the roof of the cabin. "It wasn't easy."

It took Spyra a moment to realize that the man was praying. He waited until the prayer was done before offering a suggestion.

"Why don't you have them all rounded up after dinner. Tell them what it's all about. I have to ask them who else was on those ships and then go track those men down."

Later that evening, thirty-two men were absolved of their desertion. By morning, Lord Spyra's list had grown to more than a hundred names, only eighteen of whom were known to be dead. His next stop was going to be a little trickier. More than half the men on the new list were working out of the New Westland settlement on the Isle of Salazar, where those lords and merchants who had escaped the Dragon Queen had settled. Most of them were working aboard ships. Finding them all wasn't going to be easy.

Spyra decided that he had to go back to Southport and take a ship to Salazar from there. For this trek he would need at least a handful of men. Salazar wasn't part of Westland, or even under the rule of High King Mikahl. Finding cooperation there wasn't guaranteed.

He wanted to go back to Southport anyway. He figured he should at least grant the two skeletons being held there their last wishes. He didn't relish the idea of it, but once that was done he would separate their skulls and end them.

With an anguished wail and a torrent of tears, Queen Rosa said goodbye to Phen and the others. They were standing in the starlit courtyard outside the red brick castle. The queen was only emotional over Phen, though. It amazed King Mikahl how much she cared for the boy. The small comfort he gave her while she was a prisoner of the Dragon Queen had bonded them for life.

Lady Trella wasn't much better with her goodbyes. She didn't wail and moan, but she wouldn't let go of Lord Gregory for a long time.

"I'm only going to be gone for a few weeks, my love," he told her.

"You told me that once before and I spent an entire year thinking you were dead."

"Aye." He squeezed her closer to him. "That won't happen again. If it wasn't for the Skyler Clan, I would never have been able to come and find you, though. I owe them a great deal." He kissed her lips. "You're welcome to come along."

"No, Rosa needs me to help her prepare for Westland, and there are huge lists of things that she has to handle when she gets there. She doesn't know our customs. Besides that, the skeeks destroyed Lake Bottom, and I'm sure Lady Able needs help at Lakeside."

"I'll be back soon, my love," he told her again. "There and back again, I swear it. I'll only stay for a few days."

"What is this? No tears or hugs or kisses for me?" Oarly asked the High King with a smirk on his face.

"Master Oarly, I promise you that when you return from this adventure you will be awarded land, title, and a healthy chest for all you've given up for this realm." Mikahl grinned broadly. "But if you want a kiss, you'd better find it elsewhere."

"I'd rather kiss your horse than you, King Mikahl. But I'd rather kiss a bottle of brandy than either of you."

Lady Telgra hugged Queen Rosa, then Lady Trella in turn. Her eyes seemed to glow in the predawn darkness. They were full of excitement and sadness, and more than a little uncertainty.

Jicks said goodbye to his mother. His father had died last year when Pael and Glendar sacked Castlemont. The High King shook his hand, which was no small thing to a common soldier. Mikahl went on to assure him that his mother would be well cared for while they were gone.

One of the archers was saying goodbye to a girl who was as loud as Queen Rosa. It was clear that she didn't want to see her man go.

The other archer was a loner, like Lieutenant Welch. The two of them stood watching over the scene.

From somewhere in the darkness, the order to load up was called. A few moments later three overcrowded wagons, pulled by four horses each, rolled out of Dreen's north gate. They were headed toward adventure.

Chapter Seventeen

Commander Lyle was on the verge of smacking the fat, dimwitted city guard captain who sat across from him. The office was furnished opulently with polished teakpanels, ensconced brass lanterns, and thick, padded leather chairs. The space was decorated far beyond the means of the man sitting on the other side of his huge, glossy-topped desk. He was obviously on the take, and it perturbed Commander Lyle quite badly. Worse, the man was actually refusing to give him aid, which meant he was refusing to act on an order given by the High King. The man kept reading and rereading the document Commander Lyle had given him, but incomprehension, or maybe disbelief that it was actually from the king, is all that showed on his round face.

"I'll have to check with Queen Willa," the man finally said. "I'll send a rider in the morning. It's already past the dinner hour. Too late to send one tonight."

"Queen Willa lives in Xwarda, man," Lyle said. "It will take a rider five days to get there and five days to get back. What difference does it make if it is dinner time when he leaves?"

The captain of the city guards scratched his head absently and handed the scroll back to Commander Lyle. "By the time a man readied his horse and prepared himself for such a ride, it would be dark. And it will take at least eight days to get to Xwarda, because my messengers do not travel at night. There are bandits and far worse dangers roaming the hills of Highwander. This isn't Westland farm land."

"Listen, Captain!" Lyle stood and roared while pointing a finger. "I don't know what your game is, but this is an order from the High King." He smacked the rolled parchment across the desk. "The High King reigns over Queen Willa. His order cannot be reversed, or be questioned by you, or even Her Majesty."

The man's confused look of dismay made Commander Lyle's blood reach the boiling point. He was sure the veins in his neck were standing out like cords as he began to shout. In the background, beyond the rushing of the blood in his ears, he thought he heard footsteps scrambling outside the door.

"If you do not comply with my granted authority, I'll have you arrested for dereliction of duty or insubordination. Better yet, if you think to defy me, I'll do away with all the rank and rigmarole and just whip your fat ass."

"Lieutenant!" the guard captain yelled, his face white with fear. "Arrest this man!"

The door to the office burst open and several armed men came in, though all of them except one looked to be as afraid of Commander Lyle as their captain was. Surely everyone outside the door had heard the conversation.

Commander Lyle drew his sword, and in a pair of heartbeats positioned himself behind the captain with his blade against the man's fleshy neck. "Call them off, fool," Lyle ordered. "I've fought dragons and demons and Dakaneese sellswords. I didn't do it so some lazy scoundrel like you could pilfer the coffers and grow fat. We will send word to Queen Willa and the High King, just like you suggested, but it will be an inquiry into how you can afford to work in such luxury while half the people in the realm are fighting desperately to rebuild a simple place to call home."

The lieutenant of Weir's city guard, a short, wiry man with a very long mustache, seemed to think that was funny. After he finished laughing, he told his men to put away their weapons. Hesitantly, they did.

He picked the scroll up from the captains' desk and read a few lines. "I think you'd better cooperate with this one."

"I will," the terrified captain blubbered. "I swear it. Just get him off of me."

"It's too late for that, man," Commander Lyle said to the lieutenant. "I don't know who you are, but unless you're ready to back up the document you hold, you should mind your business."

"There's no need for violence here, Commander," the lieutenant said through a wide, delighted grin. "Our corrupt friend can be put in a cell until your charges are rendered, but there's no need to take off his head."

The captain whimpered at that, and the lieutenant's smile widened. Lyle realized then that the lieutenant was really enjoying this. Maybe he was tired of the captain's treachery. He probably didn't have the rank to do anything about it. Lyle knew that meant someone was empowering the captain, or he had some strong swords in his pocket.

"By all rights I would be justified to pike this traitor's head at the city gate." He returned the lieutenant's grin so he knew he wasn't really going to do it.

Just then, a man who towered over the lieutenant stepped through the door and pushed him aside. This man was armored in well-worn studded leather, and by the scars on his face and arms he looked to have seen his share of battles. He held a loaded crossbow in one muscled arm, and it was aimed at Commander Lyle.

"Shoot him," the captain said, not realizing that the crossbow was also aimed at him. "Shoot him now, before…" his words were cut off by the feel of Lyle's blade slicing into his neck. "Nooo, please," the captain managed.

"It's not very wise to order the death of the man whose blade is at your throat, Captain," Lyle said with a glare at the man whose arrow might kill him if the trigger was pulled. He could tell by the look on the lieutenant's face that the situation no longer amused him. His hand was on his sword hilt, but the hesitation in the gesture was obvious.

"I hope you're not in Weir alone, Commander," the lieutenant warned.

"I'm not alone. As a matter of fact, there's my man Petar now."

The man with the crossbow grinned. His expression showed that he wasn't about to fall for that old trick. His grin disappeared, and the bolt from his crossbow loosed wildly and hit his captain in the shoulder, when Petar cracked him in the head with the hilt of his sword.

The captain gave out a painful yelp and Commander Lyle cursed at Petar for causing the man to fire at him. "By the gods, man, you could have waited until he was pointing that thing somewhere else."

"Sorry, Commander." Petar grinned.

The lieutenant sighed loudly and plopped down in one of the fine leather chairs that sat on either side of the office door. "Well I hope you have enough men to take Lord Vidian out, because that was his son your man just thumped."

"Who is Lord Vidian?" Commander Lyle asked. He didn't wait for an answer. "I have the entire armies of Westland, Dakahn, Wildermont, Seaward, Valleya, and even Highwander on my side, man. What are these people thinking? King Mikahl will come through here and clip all their heads if they think to defy his authority."

"You might have to inform Lord Vidian about all that. Your wars never made it to Weir, and Lord Vidian has been leeching the city for as long as he's been alive. His family owns the barges, the warehouses, and most of the people you see strutting about."

Commander Lyle grabbed the four inches of arrow protruding out of the whimpering captain's shoulder and pulled it sideways. The captain screamed and followed in the direction he was being pulled. A moment later, Lyle was sitting at the captain's desk. He was no fool. He thought he knew exactly how to handle this mess.

"Petar, bind his hands please." Commander Lyle rifled through the desk until he found a parchment and quill. He quickly scribbled out a few paragraphs. "Lieutenant, will you take this traitor out of my sight. I was sent here to deal with an entirely different mess. Petar, you stay here. I need a word with you."

As soon as they were alone, the commander had Petar close and bolt the door. He scribed out two more scrolls identical to the first.

"Is Markeen still outside?" he asked his man.

"Yes, sir," Petar answered. "He's out front with our horses."

"Take these. Keep them hidden. One is to be ridden to Queen Willa in Xwarda. One is for Queen Rachel in Seaward. The other should be taken back to Dreen, to the High King, but by way of Tip, not by crossing back over the Pixie River this far south." The commander stood and indicated which parchment went where.

"Go now, and put our men on the road immediately. Give them each an extra horse, and here," he took out several silver coins from his pouch. "Give them each enough to eat and maintain their mounts. Tell them they must hurry, though. There's about to be a shit storm in Weir. Once the riders are off, have all of our men meet me in the alley where the skeletons are being displayed."

"Yes, sir," Petar answered.

"Be careful," Lyle said as the man left the office. He glanced down at Lord Vidian's son lying unconscious on the floor and shook his head. Quickly, before he followed Petar out, he wrote a few paragraphs on another scroll and carried it visibly in his hand as he exited the building.

Even at this late hour there were a lot of people about. Almost all of them glanced at him as he passed. No doubt they had seen the captain tied up and bleeding as he was escorted to the local cell house, or at least they had heard the rumors. None of them could know why, but surely the gossipers had come up with a dozen reasons why he was there. Even as he and Markeen rode through the streets toward the alley, people gawked and pointed with unsure expressions on their faces. He hoped he could take the wagon cage and get out of town, but if he couldn't, he wanted to make sure his three messengers got well away.

He wasn't sure if what he had in mind was the right thing to do or not, but he was certain he had to follow his orders. He hoped that a disruptive confrontation with the crowd as they commandeered the wagon cart would distract this Lord Vidian's men long enough. The lieutenant would be on his own, Lyle knew, and he didn't like it. There would be severe repercussions for laughing while the fat captain's life was in jeopardy. Lyle figured that once he and his men were gone, the captain would be released and would seek revenge. He tried not to worry about it for the moment. King Mikahl or Queen Willa would send someone to deal with the errant lord soon enough. Lyle had plenty on his platter with getting the skeleton cage into his possession and moving toward Valleya. It was dark, and the alley was even more crowded by the time he and his men got into position. He sent Markeen to buy some torches and was now giving orders as they were unbundled and passed out.

"Use your horses to force through the crowd," the commander ordered. "Be sure not to trample anybody."

"What about us?" one of the three men who had given up their horses to the messengers asked.

"Once we commandeer the wagon cage, you'll drive it." Commander Lyle pointed as he answered. "Two of you get crossbows and guard the driver until we're clear of the city. Once we're away we'll figure something else out."

"Is the fisherman going to put up a fight?" a man asked.

"I doubt he will, but there may be trouble from the city guard, so have your weapons ready." Lyle took a breath and gave the order to light the torches. A moment later he forced his destrier into the crowd and began shouting out commands as if a dragon were about to attack.

"Get back!" he yelled. "Go home. Clear the way. By the order of the High King, move away from the cage!"

His men began repeating the commands, and in only a few short moments the people were shouting their outrage. The well-trained Valleyan war horses didn't flinch; instead they began shouldering the people back is if they were in a battle. Most of the crowd figured out that they needed to get back, but few of them went very far. They wanted to see the confrontation that was surely about to take place.

"By order of the High King, get back, clear the way," Lyle repeated.

"Go home, people. This is none of your concern," Sergeant Tolbar added from not too far away.

"What's all this about?" screamed a small, weathered-looking man from the flap of the pavilion tent. A few people in the dispersing crowd echoed the demand to know why they were being herded away from the spectacle.

"Are you the man who owns this wagon?" Commander Lyle asked over the murmurs of the people who remained.

"I am," the old fisherman said with his chin held out. "What of it? You got no right to stop me displaying my catch."

"By order of the High King you are to pack up and turn your wagon cage over to us." Commander Lyle shrugged at the man sympathetically. "King Mikahl wants to see these skeletons firsthand, and truthfully, so do I."

"You can see them for two coppers a man. The High King can afford to pay me, too." The fisherman made a face. "I was only charging a copper, but the Lord of Weir put a tax on me." Saying this seemed to remind the fisherman of something. He took up a defensive posture in front of the pavilion flap beside a huge man holding a double-bladed axe. "What right does the High King have to interfere with a free man and his honest business?"

Commander Lyle looked at the axe man. One of Lord Vidian's employees? Probably posted there to make sure the fisherman didn't stiff them on the tax. He shook his head. "You are advertising that one of the skeletons is King Glendar. Is that correct?"

"It's true," the fisherman said with his hands on his hips. "Look behind you. You are costing me and the Lord of Weir our wages. Now be off."

"I don't care who we're costing money," Lyle said. "If the mighty Lord of Weir needs these hundred coppers so badly, then he needs to find better advisors. A hundred coppers wouldn't feed the captain of the city guard for a day." Lyle swung down off his horse and drew his sword. With a few confident strides he took up a challenging position in front of the axe man, who moved to defend himself.

"King Glendar was the High King's half-brother, you buffoon," Lyle informed them with wild, battle-eager eyes. "The man has every right to keep you from displaying his royal family as if they were a bearded lady or a three-legged elf. If you don't want your skeleton lying among the others in that cage, step aside now."

The Wizard and the Warlord

For a few intense seconds Sergeant Tolbar thought he would have to loose his crossbow on the man with the axe, maybe even the fisherman, but a commanding voice from above them broke into the power of the moment.

"There's no need for any of that, Commander. Give me the report you wrote for the High King and I'll order the wagon into your custody."

"No tricks?" Commander Lyle asked with an inward grin of relief.

Lord Vidian didn't seem to be all that much. An imposing figure to the common folk maybe; he was well built, with long, silver-gray hair. He had intense eyes and a calm, controlling demeanor. He wore a plush suede cloak over his silk blouse and kidskin pants.

"I'm only here for the cage and the contents," Lyle said a little nervously. "The rest of it is none of my business." He took the scroll he had carried out of the office, held it up and lit it with a torch. It burned away in his hand.

From above, Lord Vidian nodded to his men that a deal had been struck. It didn't take long to clear the grounds after that. The fisherman looked sullen, especially when Commander Lyle and his men began ogling the unnerving sight in his cage.

The skeletons turned their eyeless heads as if they could somehow observe what was going on. They didn't seem pleased to be there, but they didn't look to have the strength to escape.

"We heard there were three of them now," Lyle said as he flinched away from a grasping, bony hand. Inside the cage, yellowed teeth clacked together.

"Don't know nothing 'bout more than these two," the fisherman replied a little too quickly, and gave a fearful glance at his wagon.

Commander Lyle was sure he was lying, but only sighed and ordered his men to prepare to roll out. His orders were to get the cage and the two skeletons in it. He would amend his report to warn of the third skeleton they had heard about. He felt lucky to accomplish what he had without getting himself or his men killed.

Around midnight they, along with the fisherman and his wagon, were moving north out of Weir's city gate. The ferry didn't run in darkness, and the commander wanted to be away from the inhospitable city as quickly as possible. He knew there was a bridge into Seaward in the city called Xway. It was just a short distance up the Pixie River. He figured they could be out of Highwander altogether by midday on the morrow. Only then would he and his men be allowed to rest.

It wasn't a great surprise when a group of hooded bandits swarmed them just before dawn. River road bandits were common, and Lyle's men were trained to deal with them. What was surprising was that they didn't fall or stop when they were hit by the crossbow bolts fired at them. What really shocked the commander was when the leader of the group pulled back his hood revealing that he was nothing more than a living skeleton himself.

M. R. Mathias

THE WIZARD AND THE WARLORD

Chapter Eighteen

The evening Lord Spyra returned to Southport, Master Wizard Sholt was waiting for him in the royal apartments.

It was unsettling for Spyra when he tried to conceive the nature of magic. It bothered him that the wizard could seemingly read his mind. Spyra had just been contemplating how to get word swiftly to Sholt and then he opened the door to the apartment and Sholt was there. Spyra didn't want to think about how the wizard had gotten there so swiftly either. He thought in military terms. His mind worked in offensive and defensive mode, whichever one was appropriate for the situation. He could never get himself out of defensive mode when he was around any sort of mage. Sholt was a slightly different case because the two of them were both from Highwander. Both had sat on the council with Queen Willa in Xwarda as well. They had fought Pael side by side. There was a bond of trust between the two men which allowed Spyra to confer with Sholt as if they were true friends, and maybe, Spyra decided, they really were.

It seemed fitting to the one-time general that the two of them were still chasing down and snuffing out the last tendrils of Pael's destructive rampage. Lord Spyra tried his best to keep himself on equal footing with the master wizard as they spoke.

"Lord Spyra." Sholt bowed respectfully. He was of middle age, though with wizards you never really knew. He wore a white, high-collared robe. The hem, collar, and belled sleeves of the garment displayed an intricate pattern of black and gold lions and swords. The man's long, dark hair and closely trimmed mustache and beard framed his thin face and gave his deep-set eyes an almost menacing cast. The hard look evaporated when he smiled, though, which was what he was doing when he saw Lord Spyra wave off his bow with a look that showed it was unnecessary.

"Master Wizard, we've known each other far too long for that ceremonious crap," Spyra smiled back. "Can I offer you some refreshment, some food?"

"No, General," Sholt replied. He intentionally used Spyra's old title, as he often did, out of respect. "I've been here a full day, so I'm settled. I came to test a remedy for the problem these men are facing."

"How would you test something of that sort?" Spyra asked curiously. "If you remove the spell or enchantment from one of the inflicted men, wouldn't you only know if it worked if you killed him and made sure he stayed dead?"

Sholt chuckled. "Well that would work, but since I can cast a seeing spell to let me know if a man has been ensorcelled, we don't have to kill them. If my remedy works, after a while the man wouldn't appear to be under Pael's spell anymore."

Spyra pinched the bridge of his nose and tried not to get mixed up. "You're telling me that you're going to cast a spell, or whatever it is that you do, on one of these men. Then, if your spell works, when you cast another spell to see if they've been spelled, then you'll see that they haven't been spelled at all?" He shook his head and knew that he appeared baffled.

Sholt laughed out loud this time, but not mockingly. "I think you've got it, General," he said. "It's not necessary for you to understand. We can start by trying it on the two who are still..." He steepled his fingers in front of his chest searching for the word he wanted. "...lingering," he finished.

"If it works on them, those two will just die?"

"Correct."

"Without pain, I hope," Spyra mumbled. "They were afraid to cooperate when they were falling apart. I've fought in the trenches and seen the most grievous of wounds. I've seen them days after they were inflicted, but I don't think anything has ever gotten to me like seeing those two rot away before my eyes." He stood and indicated the door that led out to the street. "Both of them want to pass on, Master Wizard. When they could still speak, they told me so."

"Then I think we should oblige them." Sholt's expression was grave. "I observed them for a while yesterday. I hope I didn't offend them. It's hard to think of them as once being human and alive in their current state."

"I understand," Spyra said as they exited the apartment into the cobbled street.

They were in the most prestigious section of Southport. The autumn evening was chill, and the light fog left a slick sheen on everything so that the flickering of the many lantern flames danced on a million reflective surfaces. The street was relatively empty; only a few people could be seen moving about the city. A couple spoke quietly above them from a balcony as Spyra and Sholt passed by. A lute playing a lighthearted melody could be heard in the distance.

"It makes me feel like a monster to keep them in a cell," Spyra said as they neared the constable's office.

As far as cells go it was far from your typical rock square with steel-barred doors. The constable's office, in this part of Southport, was clean and well kept. The cells were used primarily for drunken merchants, or noble folk who became a temporary threat to themselves or those around them. The occasional thief or murderer had occupied one of the large, furnished chambers. But not often.

When they entered the constable's office, which was connected to the prison by a long hallway, the stench of rotted flesh hit them like a hammer blow.

"Hold on, my lord," the constable called from across the street. "I had to take a breather. It fargin stinks so badly in there I can hardly stand it."

Spyra noticed that the sign over the establishment the constable was leaving read, The Axe Master's Lodge. It was a private drinkery for the many merchants who'd made their gold off of the lumbering industry, one way or another. He could see that the constable had had more than a few sips of stout by the man's gait as he closed the distance between them. With two rotting dead men who weren't quite dead in the rooms inside, who could blame him?

"You'll be getting rid of them soon," the constable said as he opened the door for the other two.

"Very soon," Spyra assured him. "As a matter of fact, why don't you go round up a man or two and a wagon to haul them out to the gravediggers."

"With pleasure, my lord," the constable replied and then scurried off.

The two undead men were in their shared cell. The one with the crushed ribcage was lying in a thick, congealed pool of muck on the bed. The other sat in a chair with his skull laid across his folded, nearly skeletal, arms at the small table in the middle of the cell.

"The master wizard here has come to help you pass on," Spyra said awkwardly. "He will remove the enchantment on you so that Pael's evil taint won't follow you to the grave."

The one at the table stood, stumbled, and then caught himself. A piece of loose yellow-green stuff splatted on the floor below him, and a half-dozen maggots fell out of his eye and nose holes as he began pointing and trying to speak from a ruined throat. He stopped after a moment and slumped back down in defeat.

"Can you write?" Master Sholt asked. Suddenly the skull rose up and nodded affirmatively.

Just as suddenly, an ink pot, a quill, and a curling piece of parchment appeared on the table before the rotting corpse. It was slow and awkward, but eventually the thing began to scribble out what he wanted to say. After a few long moments, during which Spyra thought he might vomit from the thick smell of the place, the undead man stood and brought the page over to the bars.

Sholt took it and read aloud.

"Kill us. Kill us so he will stop calling us to him. What?" Sholt asked. "Who's calling you, and where do they want you to go?"

The undead man reached out, took the parchment, and went back to the table. Already a clean piece of paper awaited him. Seeing it, he let the first fall to the floor. He leaned over, wrote a few words, and gave the new page to Sholt.

The Warlord is calling us. He wants us to go that way. Please make me die.

Sholt looked up and saw where the man was pointing.

"That's east," Spyra observed. Oraphel and Southport were the only two places immediately east, he thought. Beyond that there were only the marsh lands, but beyond the marshes was Dakahn.

The undead man pulled his finger across where his throat had once been and glared with empty sockets at the master wizard. It was the unmistakable sign of a man slicing his neck. In this case, it was an undead thing begging for true death.

Sholt nodded his understanding. "You must leave us now, general," he said. "Outside the building, preferably."

Spyra left and went across the road to the Axe Master's Lodge. Hopefully, as a lord of the realm, he could get a drink in the private establishment. He needed one.

Sholt emptied a pouch of silvery dust on the floor and then poured a flask of virgin water onto it. He chanted the words to a spell, and a bright, crackling lavender flame flared from the pile. Smoke divided into two equal wavering streams and made its way through the bars. For a long while nothing else happened, then suddenly the fire faded and both of the bodies collapsed. Sholt cast another spell and was relieved to learn that Pael's taint lingered here no longer.

His spell-weary mind was racing with the implications of what the undead had written, but he tried not to think of them. He left the constable's office and went straight across the way to join Spyra. If they wouldn't serve him, he decided that he would cast a charm spell on them all. They didn't so much as question Lord Spyra or Sholt. They seemed to know what the men were about. In fact, the barman sat a full flagon of his most potent brandy wine in front of each of them and then went about his business.

After shaking off his initial shock, Commander Lyle charged his destrier at the nearest robed skeletons. It was dark but a pair of torches had been kept aflame on the wagon, so there was some visibility, but not much.

His horse reared up and lashed out with its powerful hooves. The skeleton had apparently expected a different sort of attack, like a sword swing or a passing stab. It was caught off guard when the destrier didn't charge past him. The first hoof went into its ribcage, and when the horse came down it crushed the whole skeleton to the ground. The other hoof struck the skull and shattered it with a splintering pop.

Sergeant Tolbar called out a couple of orders after seeing his commander engage the unnerving enemy. Soon, the sound of steel on steel, and steel on bone, rang out. Some of the skeletons had loose-fitting shirts of mail under their cloaks; others had old leather pieces, unmatched and ill-fitting, strapped to their tissueless frames. Most of them had short swords that they seemed to wield effectively, but a few of them had deadly crossbows.

It appeared that maybe twenty of the skeletons were ringed around the group, but with only two torches and a ground full of long, dancing shadows, it was hard to tell.

Petar, following the sergeant's order, spurred his horse and formed up with a few other men around the wagon cage. The two kingdom men on the bench fired their crossbows, reloaded, and fired again as quickly as they could. They didn't know that they were doing absolutely no damage to the undead. The bolts went right through, or rattled away, deflected by the bony forms of their targets.

A man screamed as an enemy crossbow bolt caught him in the neck. Hot blood sprayed from the wound in pulses.

Suddenly, the light from another torch flared. The man who ignited it threw it up and out from the wagon in a flickering arc that lit up the whole area as it passed through.

Commander Lyle saw that there were only a dozen or so of the skeleton warriors close at hand. A larger number of robed figures appeared to be further out from the group, but he couldn't trust his eyes. He fought stroke for stroke with one of the things. Finally, the skeleton jabbed its sword into Lyle's horse, running its bloody blade right up to the hilt. As Lyle tried to dismount without getting crushed, he saw the same skeleton pick up another sword, and thrust it into Sergeant Tolbar's back. It left the blade inside the man and then ran away into the darkness.

Sergeant Tolbar screamed out in pain and valiantly fought the thing before him. He didn't last long, though. A moment later he slumped out of the saddle and was hacked to death before he hit the ground.

Out of nowhere, a deep, rumbling roar erupted just as the sound of galloping hoof beats came from behind them. Commander Lyle darted his eyes around, searching for the source of the sound. To his shock, he found it when a dark four-legged thing as big as a horse darted into the light and leapt on a pair of his men. Its wicked maw found one man and its bulky weight carried the other and both horses to the ground in a writhing heap. The man who wasn't in the creature's mouth began screaming in pain and fear. Lyle could see that one of his legs was bent at a grotesque angle and partly pinned under a motionless horse.

The thing, whatever it was, and the other man, were already gone.

Lyle took a bolt to the side then. Having caught in his chain mail, the arrow only grazed him. He stumbled out of the way just as a handful of riders passed through the torch light, howling and screaming, and hammering their shields like wild men.

Another torch went spinning through the air, revealing a handful of city guardsmen from Weir. Their horses were terrified as the riders went waving their swords around among the undead.

At the edge of the light, both Petar and Commander Lyle saw the retreating group of skeletal men and the large, hairy back of the creature that was dragging their man's torso away with it.

"Run me through," Sergeant Tolbar yelled through clenched teeth from the ground. His body was a ruin lying in the middle of the torchlit scene. How he was still alive was beyond reasoning. "Kill me, man. Come on, do it," he begged the stupefied man looking down at him.

Petar climbed from his horse and ran to the sergeant. A glance told him that the wounds were fatal. He didn't hesitate when he pushed his blade tip through Tolbar's throat, but he did mumble a prayer.

"Well met, Lieutenant," Commander Lyle said gruffly to the only man he recognized.

"I couldn't stay around Weir after what happened," the wiry man said, pulling on his long mustache. His expression was tense and confused as he glanced around the bloody body-strewn road. "But by the gods, Commander, it looks like I might have done better there than out here with you."

One of the men sitting on the wagon fell forward into the horses. The horses mistook it for the command to go and started ahead. They stopped after only a few feet when the wagon wheel wouldn't roll over a man's arrow-ridden corpse.

"I think they were after their friends," Commander Lyle said with a sigh of frustration. "They're gone."

The lieutenant rode around to the far side of the wagon and looked around. "Maybe," he said as he gracefully leapt from his horse and bent down to retrieve something from the ground. "They killed the fisherman." He stood back up holding the leather satchel that had been strapped around the fisherman's shoulder.

The lieutenant reached inside it and pulled out a golden crown encrusted with enough jewels to buy a castle.

"Maybe that really was Glendar's skeleton, Commander," the lieutenant said, seeing the Westland lion head etched into the circlet's front-plate.

He led his horse back around to the other side of the wagon cage and passed it up to the commander.

"It has to be authentic," Lyle said, more to himself than to anybody. The magnificent craftsmanship and the large, glittering emeralds in the piece were definitely fit for a king.

"Eight men dead, Commander," Petar reported. It didn't appear that the skeletons were coming back. "There are two wounded, but not grievously."

"Thank you, Petar," Lyle said. "See to them." He put the crown in the saddlebag of a riderless horse and studied the scene.

"I think our orders dictate that we chase them down," Lyle reasoned aloud. "Set up a perimeter watch and make a bonfire. In the morning we'll bury the dead." He turned to the former lieutenant and the men he'd brought with him. "Will you be joining us?"

"I do believe it best. We've lost our old employment," the lieutenant said. "My name is Mordon Garret, and we are at your service."

Chapter Nineteen

Corva wanted to be mad at Dostin for slowing him down, but he couldn't. The monk was as determined as he was to catch up with Telgra. Dostin hadn't asked for food, or rest, and he didn't complain when Corva pressed them on through the passes well after dark. Sometimes Dostin pushed the elf. King Jarrek had given them each a horse, and a pack horse for them to share. Corva didn't ride, though. He loped alongside Dostin's mount and gave the horses a run for it. Ironically, it was Corva's haste that caused them to pass right by the quest party encampment in the night.

Both Corva and Dostin saw the bonfire, and the guards. The overloaded wagons looked like they were part of a trade caravan. A single loud snoring, like that of a huge ox or maybe a stud bull, cut through the night. By dawn it was too far behind them to even wonder about. They had no idea that Telgra was coming through the pass toward northern Wildermont. When Corva and Dostin left King Jarrek three days ago, it was assumed she was waiting for them at the red castle in Dreen.

Corva had been mystified to tears by all the destruction they'd seen. It was baffling to think that one wizard could have done so much damage. It was also frightening to think that the Queen Mother had refused to aid King Mikahl and Hyden Hawk, even after Vaegon had pleaded their cause to her. It was true, he realized, that by stopping the demon wizard Pael from manipulating the Wardstone, Mikahl, Hyden, and Vaegon had saved all the races of the realm, including the elves. He was more than a little ashamed when the well loved and respected Wolf King told the whole of the tale. King Jarrek had fought with Vaegon and the others on the walls and in the streets of Xwarda. Had they not just witnessed firsthand High King Mikahl's bright horse and the power of his sword, they might not have believed the fantastical story. It was hard enough to believe that Pael had tapped the power of demons and leveled the entire city of Castlemont. To think that King Mikahl had eventually cut off the wizard's head after a grueling two-day duel of magical forces was unfathomable.

Corva planned on having a long talk with Telgra. His hope was to influence her to start chipping away at her mother's policy of not involving themselves in human affairs. Obviously, the Queen Mother, her advisors, and the many members of elven society had no idea how close they had come to being annihilated. Corva had to find Telgra first, though, and then hope that she would listen to him. She had an open mind, but if she was anything, she was headstrong.

"I need food," Dostin said weakly as they topped a low-backed ridge of shelved stone. The sun was high overhead but the breeze was cold. Corva decided that the horses needed a break as well.

"Let's get down there into the valley," Corva pointed. "There's less wind, and still some green grass for the horses."

Dostin didn't answer; he just heeled his mount down the slope into the multicolored valley below. The trees that still had leaves shivered red and gold and brown in the wind. The monk was glad to find Corva had spoken true. In the valley bottom he found a place in the sun out of the wind and climbed off of his horse with a groan. He took three painful steps and his legs wobbled out from under him.

Corva laughed and took the reins of Dostin's mounts. He hobbled the horses in a wide patch of grass and went about removing the saddles. He sat the packs by the exhausted monk and rummaged through them until he found some food. They ate bread and cheese and dried salted meat, then drank watered wine from a flask. Dostin fell asleep and Corva sat back and listened to the birds calling over the rustling of the leaves.

He must have slept, too, for when he opened his eyes again he and Dostin were no longer in the sun. Evening was approaching. Reluctantly he woke the monk, and after they ate and drank some more, Dostin gingerly climbed back onto his horse.

Thoughts of seeing the elven princess safe and sound overrode any soreness either of them felt. If they kept their pace, in two days they would be in Dreen. With that in mind, they worked their way up and out of the valley and in total silence kept traveling through the darkness of the night.

The first day had been pleasant for the quest party. The second only slightly less so, but by the third night they were all on edge. The hard board seats hammered at their arses as the wagons worked through the rough mountain road. The four guardsmen rode horses unattached to the wagons and were the envy of the rest of the group. Telgra chose to jog most of the time, which frustrated Phen because he couldn't keep pace with her, or even the wagons. Overloaded as they were, the four-horse teams had little trouble pulling them along at a brisk pace.

Unbelievably, the nights were worse than the days. Oarly's persistent and extremely loud snoring carried on from the time he fell asleep until he woke. And waking him during the night was impossible. Luckily, the dwarf was up just before dawn every morning by himself. Only then did anyone else get a chance to sleep. The group had unconsciously been leaving camp later in the mornings and traveling longer into the night, so that they could steal those few hours of sleep as the sun rose. Everyone in the group, save for Phen and Oarly, was red-eyed and cranky at best.

Phen wasn't as affected by the almost scary sounds of the dwarf's snores. He'd gotten used to it during the long months they'd traveled together. That didn't stop him from conspiring with Jicks to help the others get at least one full night's sleep, though.

It was the night after Corva and Dostin had passed them almost unnoticed. Lieutenant Welch spotted them and watched them from afar with a nocked bow in his hand. He was ready to drop either one of them if they ventured too close. No one else paid them any mind.

Phen told the lieutenant of his and Jicks's plan for the dwarf. The lieutenant didn't agree with the foolishness, but he knew that the rest of the crew needed a good night's sleep. Even Lord Gregory pitched in by toasting the might of Doon a dozen times as they ate their rations at the fire.

Telgra said she wanted no part of it. Phen thought that she actually felt sorry for Oarly.

When Oarly passed out drunk and began to snore, Jicks picked him up by the legs and Phen took his arms. The two boys carried him a good way up the valley side. Oarly snored the whole way and never so much as batted an eye as they hauled him along. They laid him out on a flat shelf of rock and then crept away. The horrible sound of his slumber, they figured, would keep anything wild away from him.

"If not the sound, then his smell will keep him safe," Phen said.

By the time the two boys were back in camp, the others were sleeping soundly. Only the lieutenant who had drawn first watch with one of the archers was awake. Even Telgra, who had protested the trickery vehemently, was asleep.

Later, when Jicks and the other archer were on watch, the youngster found that, without Oarly's constant snoring to keep him awake, his eyes kept sliding closed. Sleep eventually overcame him. Luckily for the group, the archer stayed alert and the night passed uneventfully.

Oarly woke to a warm, moist smell that was as out of place as the low, rumbling growl he could hear. He opened his eyes to find a curious mountain cat in his face. It wasn't nearly as frightening as the sea serpent or the dragons he'd been face to face with of late, so he managed to stay calm. Seeing Oarly's eyes move, the cat's hackles stood on end and it reared back to pounce. It bared its teeth, and its growl became insistent.

Oarly's first thought was that the others were in danger, but as he felt his hip for his utility dagger, he came to the conclusion that he wasn't in the camp anymore. The cat was easily as big as he was, and it was pouncing to attack. Oarly's dagger wasn't there. He rolled quickly to the side and found himself in thin air. As he fell, he saw that he was high up the valley slope, above the camp. His heart was in his throat when he hit the rocky ground half a second later. He'd only fallen a few feet. The cat bounded off of the shelf where he had just been and leapt down at him as he rolled through the undergrowth to the valley bottom.

Oarly managed to roll to his feet, stop himself, and turn to meet the beast head on. The cat got a good claw in and opened the dwarf's shoulder, but Oarly muscled it down and sank his teeth into its nose. In a wild fit of utter terror, the wildcat wiggled and scrabbled and tried to get free. In the process, it sliced Oarly to ribbons with its razor claws. Oarly finally roared and twisted at the wildcat's neck until it snapped in his grasp.

After a moment, he rolled off the dead animal and inspected himself. He wasn't dying, but by Doon he had a dozen long, bleeding furrows torn through his chest and thighs. He made a mental reminder to relentlessly pursue his revenge for those who were responsible for this jest. He didn't consider it anything more than that. He would much rather be shredded by a wildcat than endure a day of feeling the effects of squat weed.

Oarly got to his feet, grabbed the dead beast by the scruff of the neck, and dragged it into the camp. He was pleased to find everyone, except for the wide-eyed, open-mouthed archer, sound asleep. The poor archer didn't even try to protect Jicks or Phen. The sight of the bloody dwarf dragging the mountain cat was enough to leave him awestruck.

Jicks, who should have been awake, was Oarly's first victim. He knew Jicks would have helped Phen. He was the only one with nards enough to buck Welch. Oarly had been expecting the two of them to pull something. He threw the mountain cat on the sleeping boy and then leapt on top of the pile, keeping the wild animal's head in Jicks face while he screamed out in terror. The camp came alive then. Only Lord Gregory's sharp eye kept the waking archer from loosing arrows on the hairy, bloody thing on top of Jicks.

"Phen, you're in for a horribly long trip," Oarly yelled. "Remember the cinder pepper? You will beg for that kind of pain."

"By the gods, Master Oarly, you need attention," Lieutenant Welch said, trying to calm the wild-looking dwarf.

"No, sir," Oarly yelled, holding the wildcat's carcass over his head. "This here wildcat needs the attention. How did you do it, lad?" Oarly asked Phen, blowing bloody spittle from his mouth as he spoke. "Did your blasted little lyna tell the mountain cat to get me? How did you do it? Tell me lad. Tell me how you did it?"

"I didn't have a wild animal attack you," Phen said defensively. "We only took you up there because you were snoring so loudly at night."

"All right then, lad, don't tell me how you did it." Oarly threw the wildcat back on top of Jicks. "It was a good trick, I'll grant ya. But of all of these people, you know the revenge I'll be exacting on you. It's a matter of pride now."

Everyone in the group was speechless. None of them, not even Phen, who knew Oarly better than anyone in the realm, could imagine the dwarf killing the wildcat with his bare hands. And to believe that he thought it was all some elaborate jest was baffling.

Phen mumbled another apology about the wildcat, but Oarly wasn't trying to hear it. Telgra glared at Phen until he was shamed.

"Come, Master Oarly," Telgra said sweetly. "We need to tend your wounds. Let these fools clean your kill and make our morning meal."

Oarly looked at her stupidly for a moment, then down at himself. He was dripping blood from the slices in his skin and breathing quite heavily. "I need me flask, Lady Telgra," he said in a calmer tone.

"Of course you do." She gave Phen a look that pierced him deeply. "Phen will fetch it, won't you, Phen?"

"Yes, ma'am," Phen said, looking at his marble-colored boots.

Jicks was sitting up now, wiping the tears from his face. It wasn't clear what had scared him more, the wildcat, or the wild-eyed dwarf. Either would be terrifying to wake up to.

"If you're done crying like a babe," the lieutenant said, "then you can explain to me how Master Oarly got close enough to you to scare you to tears. You were on watch duty, boy."

Jicks flushed bright scarlet and looked away.

"It's my fault, lieutenant," Phen insisted. "I talked him into helping me trick Oarly."

"That has nothing to do with the fact that Jicks was sleeping on his watch," the lieutenant said. "He put every single one of us at risk, and I'm not about to let him forget it."

"Latrine duty for the duration of this quest is a start," Lord Gregory said. "I fell asleep on watch duty once, Jicks. My captain had me shoveling horse shit out of every stable he could find for a year." The Lion Lord smiled, seeing that Jicks understood the magnitude of his mistake. "I'm sure Lieutenant Welch will come up with a comparable punishment for you. As for Master Oarly's mishap, I think that we are all to blame for that. I just hate to think about how he will get us back. According to the High King, Oarly is one of the most ruthless tricksters in the realm."

"Aye," Phen agreed. "I'm sort of afraid of him now."

Chapter Twenty

The thirty-two wood cutters, mill workers, and loaders who had deserted Glendar's army and wound up on the Isle of Salpahel congregated around the large table of the company cabin. Master Wizard Sholt had already prepared his spell and dusted the table with a silvery powder reagent that was required to make it work. The gathering men were nervous. Lord Spyra banged a goblet on the table, loudly drawing everyone's attention. The large, imposing form of the former general standing beside the wizard helped bring about a sudden hush.

"In a moment, Sholt here will relieve you of the curse that you're under, but I have a question I want to ask first." Spyra began pacing back and forth as if he were about to make a pre-battle speech to encourage his troops. "Have any of you had an urge to go east? Or have any of you heard voices in your head?" He paused in his stride to listen for an answer. "I know nobody wants to sound like a raver, but this is important. Speak up now, and be honest." He stopped and clasped his hands behind his back and surveyed the men. None of them said a word, but none of them looked away either. He sighed with relief. "Very well then," he finished with a nod. He opened an arm to the wizard, indicating for him to take over, then made his way outside the cabin.

A few moments later the light of the afternoon sun was challenged momentarily by a surge of bright lavender light. A collective gasp from inside the building coincided with the flash. Lord Spyra shivered involuntarily. The idea of being spelled with magic, even in order to be rid of a curse, was enough to make him cringe.

He was glad the living men who had fallen under Pael's enchantment were not being called by the Dark One. He had learned his men were tracking some of the others across Westland in a southeasterly direction, and not on a known road. After comparing the reports and looking at a map, he had come to the conclusion that they were all being called to the Dragon Tooth Spire.

With Master Sholt's help, Spyra planned to send a message to High King Mikahl explaining his findings and informing him of the trip to the Isle of Salazar he and Master Sholt were about to undertake. His orders were to track down the men who had been affected and, with Master Sholt's help, do what could be done to cure them. His orders were not to chase after rotting undead skeletons who claimed to hear voices, even though his military mind told him that it was of concern.

Men were starting to filter out of the company cabin. Some stopped to thank Spyra, and others questioned him about their freedom.

"You're as free as any man," Spyra assured them.

The superintendent, knowing that at least half of the men were as good as gone, was talking about improvements he was planning for the operation. Spyra gave him a shrug that said it wasn't his fault, then turned and went back inside to check on Sholt. The wizard was slumped at the head of the table. Spyra knew that curing all those men at once had drained him. He sat down beside his old friend, willing to wait while he slept.

Commander Lyle studied the trail that the skeletons and their beast had made when they fled. The tracks led them north to Xway but disappeared there. Lyle picked up the trail again west of the bridge. After some intense questioning, they learned that no one in Xway had seen anything out of the ordinary. The bridge guard and the toll man hadn't allowed a group of hooded men, certainly no skeletons, across the bridge, yet the trail resumed on the other side of the Pixie River and continued straight west through the countryside. After following for two full days on horseback, Commander Lyle knew that they should have come upon anyone who was traveling on foot.

Already Commander Lyle could see Seaward City a good day's ride to the west and slightly north of the trail. He was confused and unable to figure out how the skeletons were covering ground on foot faster than his trackers were on horseback.

Lieutenant Garret didn't have much to offer on the matter. He stated that there was no bridge across the Southron River within a hundred miles of Seaward City. Its flow was considerably stronger and wider than the Pixie River, which the skeletons might have been able to wade across. That wasn't possible here. Garret suggested being prepared to fight when they closed on the river bank. He was fairly sure that no ferryman would haul the group they were pursuing across, and if one did, he would remember them plainly.

As the day wore on and the direction of the trail didn't vary, Commander Lyle took the lieutenant's advice and ordered the men to prepare for action. It was only a matter of hours before they came upon the river. The terrain was lightly hilly and not suitable for an ambush, but the commander was fully aware that there were forces far greater than normal involved here. He didn't want his men caught off guard. They were following living skeletons, after all.

Things grew tense as the sun began to get low in the sky and the smell of the river filled the air. The shallow valley offered a few places where a group could hide, but they saw nothing other than the sparse trail. The tracks led right up to the river's edge, then disappeared.

"Did they go in?" Commander Lyle asked his trackers.

"Must have," one answered with a perplexed look on his face.

"There's no indication that they went up river toward Seaward City or the other way, neither," the other tracker added.

"It's easily five miles north to the closest ferry," the lieutenant said.

"I'm guessing we'll pick the trail up across the river, unless the fargin bastards washed back out to sea."

"The fisherman caught the two he kept in the cage off of the coast of Crags," one of the men said.

"Have two men ride upriver and get us a barge," Commander Lyle ordered. "Make sure there is a water mage aboard. We will want to cross and be able to move up and down the other shoreline until we pick up the trail."

"Maybe those two litch yard ghouls washed out of the river into the man's nets," Lieutenant Garret said.

A long silence passed as they watched two men ride up the river bank to fetch them a boat.

"Maybe he didn't catch them in his nets at all," Commander Lyle finally said.

Her mind was not her own, that was certain. The Abbadon, the thing Gerard had become, had a firm grip on her since the red priest cried out the last word of his spell. It was no easy task getting her through the marshes that night, fleeing the High King and avoiding the hungry snappers that seemed to be everywhere. Eventually, a small Zard craft had picked her up. Using the knowledge of the Dragon Queen's memories, the Warlord of Hell recalled his lover's past and took command of her. Through Shaella's body, he called the marsh creatures in from near and far. With her hands, he raised the lightning star banner for them once again. He had the Zard set up a command post in a little known lava-bubble cave that was formed at the base of the Dragon Spire.

The Abbadon was powerful beyond reason, but he was still trapped in the empty Nethers. With Shaella under his command, though, he could tear open a breach large enough to free all the dark demons and devils trapped below with him. Together they could take back the world from which they had been banished. He knew he had to restrain himself, though. The demon Shokin had used Pael to break free. They had failed because of haste and power lust. Gerard himself had been blinded by his own love for Shaella. If he hadn't been weak, King Mikahl couldn't have taken her head. Gerard's brother Hyden had played a large part in that. Shaella was his again now, but she was no longer Shaella. She was only a vessel, a body for him to occupy. She had no way to resist him, no will of her own.

The Abbadon knew he couldn't just march her across the land to Xwarda and tear open a breach, though he was tempted. He had to plan, use the newfound peace in the realm, and the upcoming winter, to his advantage. He would let them find comfort and grow lax in the cold months ahead. He'd already had Queen Shaella order her Zard to start pirating ships. Gold could buy sell-swords. Sell-swords could spy on the state of things across the land. When the time was right, he would send Shaella to Xwarda and, through her, he would use the power of the Wardstone to destroy the barrier between his world and the world of men. He would not fail. He would get his revenge on the High King he had loved so much. He would tear his brother to pieces for taking his ring. He would lead an army of demons and devils and hell-spawned beasts across the land to devour everything in their path.

"Another bone man has come to your call, mastress," a Zard said to her. The Abbadon hissed as the idea of thinking like Shaella, as a woman, came naturally to his consciousness. Outside the torchlit cavern that she'd taken over, a half-rotten being stood, awaiting her orders.

"Take him to the boiling pot first, Szlan," the Dark Lord said through Shaella. Her perceptions were his at the moment, and the smell of the decaying man, however sweet to his nostrils, was foul to hers. For the time being, he appeased her senses. Boiling the meat from the skeletons remedied this, and the gore that came from them kept the snappers and the carrion from the immediate area.

To the Warlord, the undead were a nuisance. He hadn't yet found a good use for them. His call to those of the dark had been intended to bring in the few demons and lesser hell-spawn that had already escaped the Nethers. Some had come to him. Others were on their way to the dragon's tooth to do his bidding. The skelatons were completely unexpected.

The larger creatures weren't allowed to travel at will. Only night time flights from one uninhabited place to another were allowed. The last thing the Warlord needed was to draw attention to Queen Shaella's empty body and the growing army of Zard returning to her service.

Gerard wasn't worried about being attacked there. It would be next to impossible to come at the Dragon Spire through the marshes. Too many Zard were alert for just that sort of approach. This was their terrain, and a handful of the lizard-men could destroy a full regiment of men out here in a matter of moments. It was the High King and his magical pegasus, and Hyden and his blasted hawkling that he had to worry about.

Shaella had once been a capable sorceress, but now that her mind was mush, she couldn't cast a simple cantrip. Through her, the Warlord could do some magic, but if confronted, even an inexperienced mage would be able to kill his host. This would destroy the link the red priest had created between her and their Abbadon, Kraw. They secured a defense and stayed hidden until the time to leave for Xwarda became the priority. Making sure the way to Xwarda would be clear of obstacles was also on the agenda. Gerard figured it might be as simple as mounting Shaella on the back of the Choska demon and flying her there. That decision wouldn't be made until after he had his spies tell him all the little ways that peace time had taken the realm off its guard. Remaining undiscovered was the most important thing for them to do at the moment. If they could manage that, it was just a matter of time until he could finally be free.

Chapter Twenty-One

The next few days, for the quest party, passed by relatively quiet and uneventfull. Oarly shared a wagon bench with Lady Telgra, and the two of them spent the days conversing quietly. Phen spent his days trying to read while bouncing along, and his evenings helping Jicks dig the latrine pit outside the camp. The young swordsman hadn't so much as blinked during his watch since being reprimanded. Both Lord Gregory and Lieutenant Welch spent time with him explaining the importance of duty and the toll it sometimes took on a man. They also told him of the rewards that come to those who bite down and bear the heavy load that superiors sometimes pile on their men. Phen listened, too. He was determined to share Jicks's punishment, even if it hadn't been imposed on him.

Both boys kept a wary eye out for Oarly. Phen told Jicks how Oarly once faked his own death just to prank Phen. The dwarf was ruthless. The torturous hell he had put Sir Hyden Hawk through with the cinder pepper was downright evil. Neither of the boys looked forward to what the dwarf was no doubt planning for them. The look on Oarly's face when they happened to catch each other's gaze was mischievous and full of malice.

The dwarf didn't act out of the ordinary, though. As a matter of fact, the night after the incident with the wildcat, while everyone was at the campfire, Oarly spent a long time sincerely congratulating Phen and Jicks on their prank. No matter how much Phen denied having anything to do with the wildcat, Oarly refused to believe him. On the surface, everything seemed to be as it always had been. Phen, though, was deeply disturbed by Oarly's pledge of revenge, and by the bright red slashes across his body. The feelings were intensified by jealousy. Telgra had spent all of her time with Oarly as of late. Her smile seemed forced, and she hadn't allowed herself to be alone with Phen, even for a moment, not since Oarly was mauled.

She and the dwarf carried on like old friends. Phen couldn't see any physical attraction between them, but that didn't help clear the confusion and conflicting feelings that clouded his mind.

The small caravan came out of the Wilder Mountains into the northernmost reaches of Castlemont. The road here leveled out as it carried them through the parts of King Jarrek's land that hadn't been totally destroyed. They didn't linger. Their first destination was still a long way north.

The morning they crossed the Everflow River at High Crossing into the Leif Greyn River basin, Telgra left Oarly and squeezed in the bench seat next to Phen. A wave of relief washed over him, yet he felt a nagging hesitation. This could be the start of Oarly's revenge, a voice told him. Telgra's smile and easy demeanor soon evaporated those thoughts, though, and hand in hand they chatted excitedly about seeing the Great Monolith called Summer's Day Spire. Both of them were disheartened to learn that, though they might be able to see it most of the afternoon, they wouldn't arrive at its base until afternoon of the following day.

As the day wore on, the breeze coming down off the Giant Mountains looming to the north grew chill.

Telgra giggled and pulled her cloak tighter around her shoulders as Oarly's complaints rang back from the wagon ahead of them. Phen wished he could put his arm around her and pull her close to warm her, but he couldn't. His stony skin was as cold as the air around them. Telgra didn't complain. She wiggled closer to him. The two of them watched as the smooth black spike before them grew taller and taller.

That night at the fire, Oarly asked Lord Gregory about the brawl he had won a few years back. The Lion Lord had gotten his name carved into the base of the great monolith beside the other champions of the realm. Lord Gregory waived the question away with the shake of his head, saying that it was nothing, but everyone knew better. The Lion Lord was famous throughout the kingdom.

"I was there," Lieutenant Welch said, reaching for Oarly's flask. "I lost a handful of coins that night, I did." He paused to take a sip of the liquor, wincing at its bite, then handed the container back to the dwarf. "The Valleyan Stallion, they called him. They said he could lift a horse, and by the gods he looked like he could. Then there was Lord Gregory, the Lion of the West. Just like now, he didn't look like much."

This drew a chuckle from the group. They were all crowded around the bonfire for warmth and listening dutifully. All eyes were either on the lieutenant, or the subject of his tale.

"I bet on the Valleyan because he'd destroyed his opponents in the preliminary rounds. Our Lion Lord looked like a swollen lump by the time he won his way to the brawl. There were thousands gathered 'round the fighting circle, screaming out wagers, and carrying on like savages. When they announced the fighters, they called out Lord Lion first. Once I saw the look in his eyes, I knew I had lost my coin."

"He was hungry that night, and determined, and though he wasn't bulging with muscle like the Valleyan, he was veined and ropy. He moved like a big cat.

"When the battle began, the Stallion charged in, swinging his huge roundhouse blows. One caught the Lion Lord and sent him to a knee."

"Aye," Lord Gregory chimed in, rubbing at the side of his head reflectivity. "It felt like getting hit by an anvil."

"I thought it was over with," Lieutenant Welch continued, with arm reached out toward Oarly. "But the Lion Lord leapt back up and kicked the big bastard in the chin. After that, it was blow for bloody blow." He leaned over and snatched the flask from the dwarf's hand, since Oarly wasn't paying attention. After a long sip, Welch eyed the dwarf and then took another. "They went down in a tangle then, the both of 'em." He passed the flask back to Oarly, who was staring back at him now. "They rolled around and grappled for a terribly long time, each getting a shot in here and there. The crowd was on the verge of exploding, but then, all of a sudden, the Valleyan was sitting on the Lion's chest with a bloody grin on his face. He pulled back an arm the size of a tree limb and the whole crowd gasped in horror. The blow would have surely caved in Lord Lion's skull, but that's when our Westlander made his move. He bucked his legs up behind the Stallion's back and scissored them around the man's drawn arm. The Lion bucked again and rolled over underneath him..."

A knot of wood popped in the fire, sending up a fountain of tiny orange sparks. Telgra eased slightly closer to Phen, who was captivated by the lieutenant's story.

"The arm went back even farther as the huge Valleyan was pulled sideways and there was a grinding snap and a scream as his shoulder came undone.

"You'd think that would have been the end of it, but it wasn't. Lord Gregory rolled to his feet and staggered around while the Stallion roared and tugged at his dislocated arm."

"I couldn't believe it," Lord Gregory said. "The man should have been down. I felt his arm break. I don't think I've ever been that afraid of anyone in my life. He just looked at me and ground his teeth as he snapped his arm back into place."

"It showed on your face," Welch chuckled. "You looked like you might bolt away from the circle."

"Believe me, I thought about it."

"Don't believe him," said the lieutenant. "Our Lion is too modest. When that big, scary, blood-covered Valleyan charged him, Lord Gregory jumped up and did a spinning thing. When his back fist hit that sucker, he froze in his tracks then slowly toppled over like a felled tree. The Valleyan stayed in the dirt that time. The Red Wolf soldiers guarding the circle had to protect him from being trampled."

"The next day, my hand was the size my head should have been." Lord Gregory smiled at the memory of the glory and the pain. "My head was the size of a pumpkin."

"Will we be able to stop and see your name on the Spire?" Lady Telgra asked.

"Aye," Lord Gregory answered. "Maybe seeing the names of the elven archery champions carved there will help you remember something."

"Isn't that where Hyden met Vaegon?" Phen asked.

"Aye," Lord Gregory nodded. "The two of them were in the middle of the championship round when the Dragon Queen—she wasn't the Dragon Queen then, just Pael's daughter, and one evil bitch—she started the battle that broke the Dragon Pact. They never finished the competition."

"Hyden told me that Vaegon was winning when the battle started," Phen said.

"Aye, but Hyden made the most impossible shot and saved Vaegon's life."

Lord Gregory strolled over to Oarly and reached for the dwarf's flask. Oarly passed it up, but it was empty. Lord Gregory threw it at him with a snarl. Oarly laughed and feigned offense, but quickly pulled another full flask out of his boot. Lord Gregory took a pull from it. Phen noted that the look on his face was intense. The Lion Lord had been poisoned, beaten within inches of his life, and then dropped from a great height by some terrible dark beast.

"Hyden shot an arrow out of the air right before it sunk into Vaegon," Lord Gregory told them. "Then the two of them saved me from Pael's poison."

"The squat weed," Oarly barked with a laugh. "Vaegon gave you the squat weed to get the poison out of you."

Lord Gregory chuckled with the others, but it wasn't a very fond memory. "The elf swam the Leif Greyn River in the night to get it from the Reyhall Forest, where it grows."

"Will there be a festival next year?" Jicks asked from his watch post at the edge of camp.

"There should be a Summer's Day festival for the ages next year," Lord Gregory said. "But you won't find me brawling anymore. The last one nearly killed me."

"You could win the brawl, Marble Boy." Oarly cackled drunkenly at his own revelation. "By Doon, we could make a fortune. No man could so much as bruise ye."

"I read that, before your people went underground, the giants used to have a competition, too," Phen said, with a flare of annoyance showing in his tone. "They called it dwarf tossing. The giants would throw a dwarf as far out into the swell as they could. Now that your folk have returned, maybe I could get with Borg. You two would make a great team."

"Bah!" Oarly swatted at the boy then rose and made his way to his bed roll. He muttered under his breath, "No giant'll be tossin' this dwarf like a tater sack."

Everyone laughed, but within moments the camp, and the surrounding valley, was filled with the sound of Oarly's snoring.

One of the wagon drivers threw a couple of pieces of deadfall on the fire and stirred it to a roar. The cold of the coming season, and the breeze coming from the mountains, made the night bitter to everyone, save for Phen. The clear sky was reflected on the still surface of the reservoir the river formed. Phen sat with Telgra and enjoyed the beauty of the night. It didn't take long for the others to turn in. Phen looked down to see that Telgra had fallen asleep against him. He gently woke her and helped her to her bed roll. He put one of his blankets over her, since he didn't need it.

Jicks was on watch with the lieutenant, and Phen would have normally sat with them for a while, but tonight his mind was full. Lord Gregory's great brawl, and Hyden and Vaegon competing on the archery range, filled his thoughts. Ages and ages of champions had competed against one another here so that the victor could have his name carved on the Spire for people to see for all time.

Phen woke from his light sleep to see that the sun was coming up. Oarly had just crawled out of his bed roll, Phen knew without looking. It was the sudden lack of his friend's snoring that had woken him. He was feeling less and less intimidated by the dwarf as each day passed. They were the best of friends, and the unsettling image of the bloody dwarf throwing around a dangerous animal that he had killed with his bare hands had lost its edge.

He wished that Oarly would believe him when he said that he had nothing to do with the wildcat. He found Oarly and they spent the morning chatting and speculating about the Spire, Hyden's village, and the long, treacherous journey beyond that. Apparently, Oarly didn't like the cold, and Phen didn't have the heart to tell him that up in the Giant Mountains, even in the summer, it was ten times as cold as it was right now.

According to Lord Gregory, not this night, but the next, they would leave the wagons behind and make the half-day's ride up into the foothills to the Skyler Clan's village. Oarly seemed more intrigued by the clan folk's underground rabbit holes than the chance to see the great Spire.

For Phen, the morning wore on as slowly as any he'd ever endured, but finally the base of the towering black triangular Spire came into view. It was awe inspiring, and the entire group was silent as they approached it.

Each of the three faces of the Spire's base was about a dozen paces wide at the ground. It rose up hundreds of feet, tapering inward slightly as it went, forming a perfect needle-like spike.

Phen walked around it, scanning the hundreds upon hundreds of names carved carefully into the faces. The most recent names were just above eye level, and the space between them and the ground was filled with the names of champions. Phen noticed that the lower names were strange, and some were even carved in the old language. He observed that for many years, possibly centuries, the names had been carved in fancy script. From waist-high to the present, the names had been rendered in plain, simple lettering.

"Dwarves carved those," Oarly boasted, pointing at the fancy work. "The lettering is too clean and complicated for even the elves to manage."

Phen nodded. Oarly was probably right. Dwarves did stone work far better than any other race. They came around one side of the Spire to find Jicks, Lieutenant Welch, Lady Telgra, and a few others eyeing Lord Gregory's name. Phen saw it and then eyed the Lion Lord. Pride radiated from the man like heat from the sun.

For many years Phen saw that there was a member of the Skyler Clan listed as the archery champion, but for the last two dozen festivals the names were all elven. Telgra studied those intently, but no sign of recognition showed on her face.

"If they had a competition for who could sink in the mud the fastest, you could be on there too, Phen," Oarly laughed as he took a pull from his flask.

Phen pointed to a place only a few feet off the ground. "Look Oarly," he exclaimed. "Tection Shardsworth, thrown forty-two paces clear by Draran."

"No," Oarly said, peering closely at the inscription.

Phen wondered if Tection was one of Oarly's relatives. Shardsworth wasn't a very common name in the dwarven history books.

Oarly huffed with a curious, yet prideful look on his face. He scratched his head and looked Phen in the eye. "How do you think they land, lad?" he asked seriously.

Phen shrugged. "Does it matter?"

Chapter Twenty-Two

Commander Lyle wasn't pleased to be on the verge of heading back to Dreen empty-handed. He was sure that the High King wouldn't be happy with his failure. After crossing the Southron River, they hadn't seen a trace of the skeleton crew or their strange beasts. They spent a whole day going up and down the far shore and searched for another day in the village of Crags, questioning the folks about the fisherman and his initial catch. Then, just to be thorough, the commander had them search the rocky terrain around the village for any sign of the undead. There was nothing. It was like the skeletons they had been following just walked straight into the river and never came out.

Lieutenant Garret suggested that the skeletons had boarded a barge similar to the one they had used to cross the river. It made sense, but this mystery barge hadn't been found. Nor was there a single witness who might have seen it.

Commander Lyle was certain that a barge was a possibility, but the lay of the land made it highly unlikely for a barge to pass by unseen.

At night, a barge with a capable water mage might have been able to land somewhere along the vast shore of Ultura Lake. Searching the shoreline of such a massive body of water would be next to impossible. It could be, Lyle decided, that the skeletons were going back in the direction from which they had come. Leading the commander's group to the edge of the Southron River, then backtracking, didn't seem likely for them to do, either. The idea that these things were intelligent enough to lose a trained pursuer was frightening.

As they rode into the town of Lake Port, failing King Mikahl was eating at Commander Lyle's pride. He had to make a decision soon. Searching fruitlessly would only delay him from explaining what had happened. He was sure that failing to report an attack upon kingdom men by armed skeletons was some sort of dereliction of his duty. High King Mikahl should know everything that happened. Commander Lyle just couldn't bring himself to give up the search yet.

After securing enough rations for the men and horses to last another week, Lyle found a merchant who had a detailed map of Valleya. While his men ate a hot meal of beef stew and freshly baked bread at a nearby inn, he studied it. After asking several questions about the surrounding areas, Commander Lyle made his decision. He had Petar choose four men to accompany him and ordered the other five to ride to Dreen. He gave Petar a written account of what had happened. It included a list of the dead and explained that Lieutenant Garret and six of Weir's city guard had joined his company.

"Ride to Southron, then head straight north to Kastia Valley," Commander Lyle told Petar. "Stay on the roads and make as much time as you can."

"Yes, sir," Petar answered.

Commander Lyle dismissed him to his duties and then ordered lieutenant Garret to take four men and go a few miles west out of Lake Port, and then work his way north to the town of Southron looking for any signs of the skeletons' trail. The commander and the rest of the company would travel the road and the shoreline north and do the same.

"Don't scout at night," the commander said. "Study the terrain and scout for tracks till the light runs out and then make your camp. We should meet up at the north side of the lake, in Southron City, by tomorrow evening."

"What if we find a trail?" Lieutenant Garret asked.

"Follow it," the commander answered. "Use caution, and leave us a trail to find. If we don't see you in Southron by the morning after next, we will come search you out. Do you really think you will find anything?"

Lieutenant Garret smiled and gave a shrug. "In just the last few days, far stranger things have happened."

"Yes they have," Commander Lyle agreed with a grimace. "If we find a trail, I'll send a pair of riders out to find you." He looked at his remaining men and then back at the lieutenant. "Make your trail obvious."

"Yes, sir," the Weir city guardsman replied. Without hesitation, he found his horse and started rounding up the men he would take with him.

The next night they met up in the lively trading town of Southron. Neither group saw anything to indicate that the skeletons had passed through. Reluctantly, Commander Lyle gave up the search. The next morning, as they started out for Kastia Valley, the whole group seemed defeated.

Commander Lyle reasoned that, when he reported his failure to the High King, at least it wouldn't be a surprise. The message he sent with Petar would break the news for him. It was a small consolation, for he had to face the families of the eight men who had been killed under his command. That, he felt, was far worse than facing King Mikahl's disappointment. The fact that he couldn't report a success, that those men had died in vain, was the worst of it. Commander Lyle wasn't looking forward to his return to the red city.

Three long days later, the commander entered the castle gates followed by his men, and the seven others from Weir. He sent them all to the stables to tend the needs of their mounts while waiting to see if they had new orders, or if they were to be dismissed to their regular duty. Lieutenant Garret would be interviewed by the king himself, since Lord Gregory was afield; that much he knew. Most likely the others would be questioned before they were added to the High King's roll.

Lyle entered the castle and noticed immediately that something was happening. Servants and ladies hurried about with strained looks on their faces. Some were carrying bundles and boxes in their arms. He saw Cresson and got his attention. The mage came over, stroking his long goatee beard and informed the commander that the king and queen would be departing for Westland on the morrow. The whole place was in an uproar trying to prepare for the departure.

"I must see him," Commander Lyle said urgently.

"Go wait in the council hall," Cresson told him. "The High King is in the throne room trying to explain to someone why he can't tell them where someone else is without betraying a trust. He will probably be glad for the interruption."

Cresson entered the throne room and gave a wave of apology for intruding on Corva and Dostin's inquiry. He whispered in Mikahl's ear and then stepped away.

"I'm sorry, there's urgent business forming," the High King said. "I've already told you all I can. Lord Gregory may be able to tell you more when he returns, but I cannot." The king excused himself and followed Cresson.

Commander Lyle was pacing back and forth nervously when Cresson and the High King came into the council hall. He was surprised to see the expression on King Mikahl's face.

"Commander," the High King smiled. "It amazes me that you could get a wagon cage with two living skeletons in it inside the castle gates without making even the slightest of a stir. I figured the rumormongers would have carried us the tale as soon as you entered the city."

Commander Lyle blanched. Had Petar not delivered his report? Suddenly he was very worried for the young soldier. The concern must have shown on his face.

"What is it?" King Mikahl asked. His smile had faded.

"I sent a man with a message." He put a hand on the back of a chair to steady himself. "He should have arrived yesterday at the absolute latest."

"We received your message about the suspect activities going on in Weir." King Mikahl looked to Cresson for confirmation. Cresson nodded. "Obviously that is not the report you are referring to."

Commander Lyle stepped around and collapsed into the chair. "No, Your Highness, I suppose I should tell you everything."

King Mikahl nodded as he took a seat at the head of the council table. Cresson peeked out the door and waited there as the commander began. After a moment, a tray of refreshments was brought. Cresson took it from the servant and placed it within both the king's and the commander's reach. Over an hour later, Mikahl rubbed at his stubbled chin with unhidden concern showing on his face.

"Cresson, get the kingdom map," King Mikahl said. "The big one. Commander, I want you to show me exactly where you encountered these things, and the trail that you were able to follow."

Cresson scurried away and quickly returned with a huge map that showed the realm from Westland to Highwander. "The commander located the bridge that crossed the Pixie River and the Highwander town of Xway." He indicated a straight line from there to just south of Seaward City.

"Mark the line please, Cresson," King Mikahl said.

The mage traced the commander's route with his own finger. A faint red line remained visible on the parchment where the digit passed.

Mikahl studied the direction of the mark for a moment. "Now make a line that leaves South Port in Westland going due east into the marshes. Then make a line going southeast from the town of Riverbend in northern Westland." The High King looked at Commander Lyle for a moment, clearly focused on his thoughts. His eyes brightened. "Extend all three marks until they intercept."

They watched with growing concern as the marks came together.

"It seems that General... Lord Spyra, rather, was correct in his assumption," Cresson observed. "The lines all lead to the Dragon Tooth Spire."

"Somehow, something from the hells is calling these undead skeletons to the Spire." Mikahl shook his head. "I suspect that your man Petar was either killed, or he found a trail to follow. Either way, I think the answer to this threat lies at the Fang."

High King Mikahl suddenly remembered something from the ceremony he, the elf Corva, and the mighty monk had interrupted. The sacrifice. The girl had just vanished. No, he decided, she was just a body the priest was going to sacrifice. Why else had her body been shaved of all its hair? The odds of her escaping the snapper-filled marshland were so slim that Mikahl let that train of thought go. The ceremony had been far to the north of the Dragon Spire. He remembered that the great seal Pavreal had made in the dragon's lair up there had been the point where Pael had breached the Nethers and let loose the power of Shokin. It was that same power that turned all those men into undead skeletons in the first place. It was possible that some lingering magical effect was drawing them there. Or maybe one of the demons still running loose was rooted into the lair and calling them. Either way, something had to be done about it before the situation was out of hand.

It still left the question of what happened to their man Petar. Mikahl knew the young man from the training yard. He was no slouch with the blade and had the kind of self-discipline off the field that commanded the respect of his superiors. There was no reason to believe that Petar would abandon his orders. However, Mikahl could see him going off half-riled, trying to take down the things that had attacked their party and killed his friends.

"Cresson, I want you to cast a sending to every wizard, mage, and marsh witch from O'Dakahn all the way to Pearsh," Mikahl said, running his finger up the eastern bank of the Leif Greyn River delta on the map. "Petar and his four men are to be sought out and intercepted. If they are alive, I don't want them going off into the marshes alone. I want men from O'Dakahn to search the edge of the marsh for any sign of man or beast that shouldn't be there. I want our people in Strond, Oktin, and Lokahn questioned to find out if Petar and his men crossed the Kahan river. I want every man in the realm on the lookout for those skeletons, too. They attacked a large group of men under my banner. I doubt they will hesitate to attack a village full of innocents, or a trade caravan." He turned to Commander Lyle. "Tell this Lieutenant Garret I want him and the men from Weir to ride directly to Xwarda. Queen Willa will take their statements. I think a dozen-man escort should do. Tell him that, once this mess with Lord Vidian has been settled, Queen Willa or I will see to his next posting personally." He took a deep breath and indicated for Cresson to begin with his sendings. The mage studied the map for a few more moments then moved to a corner of the room and began chanting and moving his hands about quietly.

"Commander Lyle, I want you to pick out a small group who can track and travel fast. Five or six men at the most. Backtrack from here and search for the place where Petar left the road. You told them to mark their trail obviously. I'm sure he did so."

Commander Lyle stood and gave a curt bow.

"I will be leaving for Westland on the morrow, Commander," the High King said. "Until Lord Gregory returns from his current endeavor you will report to me directly through Cresson. Do not move to attack these undead things. If you find nothing between here and the last place you saw Petar, return immediately and Cresson will give you my commands."

Commander Lyle nodded again and performed a smart about-face, then left the room to carry out his orders. King Mikahl went to the closet in the council hall where he kept some personal items and fumbled through them. He waited until Cresson was between spells before he spoke. "I'm going to investigate the Dragon's Tooth," he said as he pulled a shirt of chain mail over his head. He refastened his swordbelt at his waist over the armor and went to draw the blade.

"What should I tell the Queen?" Cresson asked with a look bordering on fear coming over him. "The two of you are due to leave in the morning."

"If I'm not back, she is to leave without me. There is a small army escorting our carriage. She will be safe."

Cresson made a sour face. "It's not her safety that is in question. It's the foul mood she will be in when she learns of this."

Mikahl let out a long sigh, knowing the truth of it. "I will go speak with her." He smiled at the way relief washed visibly over the mage's expression. "You have enough to do without having to deal with the wrath of the High Queen as well."

As Mikahl strode toward the door he wondered why flying off to the Dragon Spire to confront some unknown enemy alone didn't frighten him, yet going to tell his wife that he might not be there when she left for Westland in the morning unnerved him to no end.

Chapter Twenty-Three

Corva was just about to reveal to King Mikahl that Telgra was the daughter of the elven Queen Mother, but the human mage interrupted him. He'd refrained from telling the High King this in their first two meetings because of the fact that the knowledge, once made public, could bring about terrible repercussions to the elven kingdom. Corva was certain that King Mikahl had a good heart and had no intention of bringing harm to the elves, but there were the rest of the courtiers there and the strange mage as well. He tried to speak to the High King alone, but the castle was always a flurry of activity. The High King barely seemed to have time to breathe. If a not so honorable person learned of Telgra's identity, she could be captured and ransomed or worse. With such leverage, a few humans might be able to turn the wrath of the Queen Mother against whomever they desired.

Telgra was the heir to the entire elven kingdom, and the position was one that no other elf could ever fill. More than an inherited title, the line of Queen Mothers had a special bond with the earth and the forest that no other could obtain. They were deeply connected to the Heart of Arbor. Telgra's powers, as she matured, would become incomprehensible to even the most learned elf. The current Queen Mother would not hesitate to make war on all mankind to protect her lineage. Thus Corva kept his tongue. He would have told the High King in private, but now the long-bearded mage was saying that King Mikahl was going, and that he would not be returning until winter was over.

The hospitality of the red castle had been extended to Corva and Dostin indefinitely. They could stay and wait in relative luxury for Lord Gregory to return. Dostin said he'd met the Lion Lord last summer when the man and his wife had visited the Isle of Salaya. It was on that very trip that the High King accidentally caused the fairy trees to bloom with his sword.

By using his keen senses, Corva managed to ascertain that Telgra was ultimately on a quest to the Leif Repline fountain. They were supposedly spending the winter months in some place so secretive that no one would reveal its location. She was traveling with a dwarf and a boy who'd been curiously spelled to stone.

There was an elven fable about the magical fountain and the creature that guarded it from abuse, but Corva couldn't remember it. All he could recall was that the place was deep in the treacherous Giant Mountains and that the beast hadn't sounded all that terrible by its description. The journey was no doubt dangerous. He felt that he had to find her and talk some sense into her. He couldn't imagine what she was thinking.

King Mikahl was being so tight-lipped about her that Corva had to respect his resolve. The king's explanation that he would be breaking his word to someone if he revealed where they were spending the winter was completely understandable. Corva had made similar promises in his life. He was frustrated beyond reason. Cresson said that she might have sent a message into the Evermore to be left at Vaegon's Glade, but the mage wasn't certain, and no one could say what the missive said. The question was, would Lord Gregory, upon his return, tell them where the others were spending the winter? Corva concluded that, if he couldn't find out where Telgra was holing up, he would have no choice but to return to the Evermore Forest and face the Queen Mother with what he knew.

The idea of adventuring through the dangerous mountains with a dwarf, a person made of stone, and the legendary wizard Hyden Hawk intrigued him enough that he was envious of Telgra. If he found her before winter was over, and saw that she was reasonably safe, he could see himself going along on such a quest. Only if she was safe.

After waiting in the throne room for an hour, then finding out from the mage that the High King was no longer in Dreen, Corva decided that there was still a lot he could accomplish. There were stablemen who could be questioned, wagon loaders, guardsmen, and gate keepers. All of them were seemingly befuddled by his appearance. He could use that. Someone had to know where they had gone.

Dostin had stood patiently beside him throughout the morning session of the High King's court without complaint. Corva had become attached to the monk's loyalty. With a warm smile and a pat on Dostin's back, he suggested that the two of them find something to eat and a private place to talk. Corva found that Dostin's simple outlook on things often helped him make decisions. Dostin would no doubt again ask him a dozen different questions pertaining to why no one would tell them where Telgra had gone. Corva would answer. Dostin would ask more questions, and in the process of answering them, either Corva would find a new idea to help find a solution, or the solution would be there in one of Dostin's simplistic queries.

They found a servant and asked if there was food available and if there was a place they could sit and talk quietly. The man showed them to a dimly torchlit hall used mostly for the staff. The weathered wooden table seated ten and had dirty plates and bowls piled upon it. The servant quickly tidied an area and hung a lantern on the wall nearby. He scurried away after telling them that he would return soon with some food and wine.

The two spoke while they ate, mostly Corva answering Dostin's questions. Several members of the castle staff stopped in to take away dishes or clean the table and floor. It became clear that they were trying to get a glimpse of an elf without being obvious.

No sooner did they finish their meal than Lady Trella backed into the room as if she were trying to flee someone. She pulled the door to and stood there for a long moment, peering out of the crack. When she turned, she yelped out in fright. She hadn't seen the two sitting there watching her.

"I'm so sorry," she said, blushing brightly and trying to avoid the elf's gaze. "I hope I didn't intrude. I um… I was uh…"

"Hello, my lady," Dostin said. He half stood and bowed his head. "You aren't bothering us at all."

"Are you all right?" Corva asked, standing. "Is someone after you?"

"No… no…" She blushed even more and gave Dostin a girlish wave. "The truth is, I'm hiding from Queen Rosa." She giggled uneasily. "She is driving me mad with her preparations for Westland. And now that King Mikahl has suddenly left she has become a terror."

"Come, sit." Corva indicated an open seat at the table. "Join us. We were just discussing our predicament. You're not intruding."

"Thank you." She smiled a little easier. "I sometimes hide in here when I want to get away from the silliness of the younger girls."

"My lady, you are barely a child yourself," Corva said with all the sincerity of a hundred-and-twenty-five-year-old elf.

"No, she's not," Dostin said stupidly. "She's probably thirty-five summers old."

Lady Trella beamed at the both of them. She was in fact nearing her forty-fifth summer. Lord Gregory, Rosa, and the younger girls always told her how youthful she appeared. She'd always thought they did so to make her feel better. These two had no reason to exaggerate. She was suddenly at ease and her smile was brilliant. "You're too kind," she replied.

"Because Corva is an old elf, over a hundred, he thinks all of us humans are little children," Dostin said to her conspiratorially. "If you ask me, he is the one who looks like a child."

Corva just smiled and shook his head. He reminded himself to explain to Dostin later that, when speaking to women, elven or human, you weren't supposed to cheapen the compliments others gave them. He doubted Dostin understood the concept of a compliment. The monk spoke entirely from the heart. When he said something nice about someone it wasn't because he was trying to make them feel better. It was because it was the truth, as he saw it.

"They say all elves look young," Lady Trella said to Dostin with a grin. Suddenly something passed through her eyes and her face changed to one full of concern.

"I was told that the fairy trees were destroyed," she said. "Is it true?"

"Not all of them, my lady," Dostin answered with an almost blank expression on his round face. Her sudden change of emotion must have confused the monk. "The elves saved some of them."

"Far too few," said Corva. "Hopefully, soon my people will be able to help the grove restore itself to its former glory. But that might take centuries."

"One of my fondest memories is from that grove," she said. "I'm sorry to have interrupted your conversation with my silliness. I think I will leave you two to finish your discussion."

"My lady," Dostin started. "Will your Lord Gregory tell us where Lady Telgra is spending the winter? We have to find her. It's important."

"And urgent," Corva added with a look of appreciation at the monk.

"Only he or King Mikahl could tell you the exact location of the Skyler Clan village," Lady Trella told them. "All I know is that it's in the foothills of the Giant Mountains somewhere north of the Summer's Day Spire."

"Thank you, my lady," Corva said. He stood and bowed. "You don't know how much you've helped ease my mind about our Lady Telgra. Just knowing she's safe and in good hands is a great comfort."

"Well then, I'll leave you two," she said.

Dostin called out, "Good day, my lady," and Lady Trella paused by the door.

She turned and smiled at him broadly. "If you need any provisions, just ask the stablemen," she said. "I will give him the word to get what you need."

"Your kindness will be remembered, my lady," Corva said, bowing to her again.

Dostin stood awkwardly and bowed as well.

"Are we going to the Spire to find Lord Gregory?" Dostin asked.

"Yes, we are," Corva said, feeling the relief of knowing that he could now find Telgra sweep over him.

"What if he won't tell us where she is?" the monk asked.

"Then we will just wander the foothills until we find the Skyler Clan village," Corva answered, thinking, but not saying, that they would wander down the tracks that the caravan left behind.

"What if the giants find us?" Dostin asked. "I heard a story that a giant guard roams the edge of the mountains and eats the people who trespass there."

"I'm not worried about the giants, Dostin," Corva said.

"Why not?" the monk asked, as if not being afraid of a giant were absurd.

"I'm not afraid because elves don't taste good." Corva laughed at Dostin's expression, but a moment later Dostin said something that made his mirth vanish.

"There are ice dragons and trolls in the mountains, too, Corva." Dostin scratched his chin. "I heard that they love to eat elves." The statement wouldn't have bothered Corva so much had it not been completely true.

It had been decided by Lieutenant Welch that he and the other three members of the king's guard were to escort the quest party to the safety of the clan village. They'd then return to start hauling the supplies from where they had to leave the wagons. The six riders moved slowly, because Phen and Telgra were walking.

Lord Gregory was pleased to be returning to the calm and peaceful place where life had been slowly restored to him. He'd woken there after being unconscious for months. He'd had to relearn how to walk and ride, and it had been no easy road to travel. Only the deep love he felt for his Lady Trella, and the urging of the Skyler Clan members, had kept him striving.

Phen felt as if he were returning to a place he had visited a dozen times. He hadn't actually been to the clan village, but Hyden Hawk had told him hundreds of stories about the place. He was anxious to meet the cousins too. They all had a story about them.

Oarly was drunk and trying desperately to stay on the back of his horse. His short, stubby legs weren't long enough to straddle the animal, so he was forever teetering and tottering on the verge of falling to the ground. Every so often he would throw an arm out wildly and let loose a string of curses. Jicks, Phen, and even Lady Telgra were stifling giggles as they watched him. Two of the braver guards were discussing a wager over when the dwarf would hit the ground.

The hills were scattered with color. The wind was brisk and rattled the golden-brown and red leaves from the trees. The pines and firs were still green and filled the air with a pleasant aroma. The trail wasn't bad for the riders, or the horses. The slow pace helped, as well. They made much noise as they passed, scaring away most of the wildlife, but in the distance the birds sang out, and once a pair of hearty deer shot off from a stream, waving their white tails like warning flags.

"It's fargin cold," Oarly yelled, then gave out a yelp as his feet shot over his head. He nearly flipped out of the saddle backward, but somehow managed to hang on. Everybody, including the normally serious Lieutenant Welch, had a good laugh.

"No, Oarly," Lord Gregory said brightly. "Soon you will be begging for days like this."

"I'm going back with ye, Lord Lion," Oarly snapped. "We dwarves wasn't meant to be out in this frigid climate."

"You're welcome to winter in Dreen, master dwarf," Lord Gregory said. "You're welcome to winter anywhere in the kingdom, as far as that goes."

"Aye, but… ut… ut," Oarly bounced up and landed on his side in the saddle somehow. For a long moment, both of his legs stuck out one way while his flailing arms shot out the other.

"By the gods, Oarly," Phen laughed hysterically, "how did you manage to stay on?"

Lord Gregory had to stop his horse, he was laughing so hard.

"Bah," Oarly yelled as he righted himself in the saddle yet again. "By Doon, what I'd give for a cave incher, or even a little mule."

"What's a cave incher?" Jicks asked.

"It's what dwarves pee with," Phen said.

Telgra blushed furiously and whacked Phen on the shoulder. Immediately, she yelped, feeling her hand smart as it found Phen's stony flesh.

Everyone was laughing then; not even the guards were paying attention. That's when a hairy beast shot out of the rocks and leapt with a wild, cackling growl, taking Oarly right out of his saddle.

Oarly screamed in terror as he crashed to the ground under the awful-smelling creature. "Ughhh! Get it off!"

Everyone else could see the pair of human legs sticking out of the ugly, but dead, creature's hair-covered skull. Lieutenant Welch, Jicks, and two guards were off their horses with swords drawn, and one of the archers was ready to loose. Phen had to dart his horse in front of the bowman. The other archer's horse had bolted in fear.

From above them, a few dozen young men, all looking quite similar with their long black hair, tan skin, and crude leather clothing, appeared out of nowhere. They were all laughing.

Just then, the screeching caw of a hawkling filled the air. Talon, his feathers as white as Phen's skin, swept by them. The bird circled sharply and came flapping down onto Phen's head. After folding his wings in and pumping out his chest proudly, the bird looked at Telgra and cooed.

"By Doon, get it off me," Oarly was yelling. "It's fargin got me!"

A younger version of Hyden Hawk wiggled his way out of the shagmar skull and hopped up to his feet. He looked around at all the tense faces nervously. When his eyes found Lord Gregory, he grinned broadly, showing a row of bright white teeth.

"Well met, Little Con," Lord Gregory laughed. "You might want to clear off a ways. That dwarf is dangerous when he is agitated."

The boy glanced at Oarly, who was finding his way out from under the huge shagmar skull. Little Con grimaced, then bolted up the nearest hillside.

The tension evaporated and everybody quit laughing, save for one. Up on the hill, a lone voice was guffawing madly. Phen turned to see Hyden Skyler huddled up in the grass, holding his stomach. After a few moments of this, Oarly shouted out indignantly. "It's over, man! You fargin got me. It's not that funny anymore."

"No, Oarly, it's not you," Hyden said, pushing his long black hair out of his face with one hand as he pointed with the other. "It's not you I'm laughing at anymore." Hyden struggled to his feet while still holding his stomach. "This is the first time I've gotten to see Marble Boy."

"That's not funny, Hyden," Phen yelled. And again, everybody, even Lady Telgra, had to chuckle.

M. R. MATHIAS

Chapter Twenty-Four

High King Mikahl felt the chill of the approaching winter as he flew on the back of the bright horse. The magical pegasus carried him over the brown farm lands of central Dakahn, then out over the deep emerald triangle of the marshes. Queen Rosa hadn't been happy about him leaving on some dangerous errand on the day of their departure, but he'd come anyway.

"Westland is your homeland, Mikahl," she said. "If we were going to Seaward to winter with my people, would you like it if I ran off and left you to travel alone?"

No I wouldn't, he told himself. "There is a threat to the realm, my love," he told her. "I have to go."

"No, you don't!" she yelled. "You have thousands of soldiers, six kingdoms' worth at your command. You should send them to investigate and handle the threat. This is what they are for."

What she said made sense to Mikahl. He'd been raised a squire, and he depended heavily on people like Lord Gregory, King Jarrek, and Queen Willa to help him make his decisions, but none of them were at hand for this one.

"I'm the only one who can get there in a few hours. I'm the one with the power of Ironspike at my command. Please try to understand."

"I understand that if you don't stay around long enough to make an heir, the sword will be useless for the future generations of men." She began to cry then. As other emotions overcame her anger she sobbed. "If you die, the whole realm will lose the protective power of the sword. And beyond that, I will miss you so terribly. I can't… can't…" Her voice was lost in her tears.

Mikahl waited until her sorrow subsided. "Love and duty do not mix well," she said as she wiped away her tears. Then she kissed him goodbye and went about preparing for the departure as if the whole scene hadn't just taken place.

Mikahl was left feeling small. He saw the dark, fang-shaped spire rising up out of the jungly swamp and refocused his attention. He had to bank south to keep it in front of him. It rose about four hundred feet above the soupy mess of shallow swampland. A few mud islands supported the thicker groves of some tall, willowy trees, and a vast plethora of reptilian, amphibian, and avian life forms.

From the north or south, the "dragon's fang" appeared to be about eighty paces wide at its base. It tapered up to a perfect point and had a slight curve to it, so that it truly did resemble some sort of fang. The history books said it was once a mountain that used to spit fire and flaming rocks into the air, but time and the powerful flow of the Leif Greyn River wore it down to what it was now. From the east or west, Mikahl thought it looked like a shark's fin cutting through the swamp. There was a giant worm hole about midway up that went completely through the fin. Inside the worm hole, Mikahl knew it opened up into a cavern. Claret used to live there, before Hyden set her free.

Mikahl figured that a Choska, or a pack of hellcats, had moved in, or maybe a marsh witch had gotten hold of some old spell books and was dabbling with forces that were drawing the skeletons in. He also decided that Rosa was right. He shouldn't risk his life until the protection of Ironspike's magic was guaranteed to reach beyond his life. He decided he would only investigate, and then make a decision about what needed to be done. A few breed giants with their dragon guns could take out a Choska demon without the aid of magic. Add a capable mage and a few hundred men with well-equipped marsh boats and they should be able to easily handle the mess. There was no need to risk his life fighting the realm's battles by himself. Rosa's comments about the future of the land had sunk in. If he died, there would be no one of Pavreal's bloodline left to ignite Ironspike's power.

As the Dragon Tooth Spire loomed larger before him, he was thinking about spending the winter at Lakeside Castle with Queen Rosa, trying to make an heir. The sudden burst of a flock of dactyls taking flight startled him. The big birds had a ten-foot wingspan and razor-sharp beaks as long as a man's forearm. These were smaller than most dactyls, but there were hundreds of them. A great cloud of thumping wings exploded out from the nooks and crannies near the lower part of the black rock formation. He was forced to go around them in an arcing loop so that he came at the worm hole from the side. He'd never seen so many birds at once, and he suddenly realized the damage that a flock could achieve if they acted in concert. Without a thought, he drew Ironspike and called forth all the shields that its power could generate.

He was surprised when he guided the bright horse into one side of the opening. The cavern beyond was relatively empty—just old bones as big as he was littered the place. Pieces left from Claret's many meals, he figured. He wondered how the dragon had stayed sane living in the jagged black cavern for so many centuries. He imagined the diet of snappers, geka lizards, and other marsh creatures had grown old as well.

The bright horse faded away as Mikahl stepped around and over the loose scree to the opposite mouth of the wormhole. He looked down. The dragon couldn't have ever gone hungry, he decided. Even with his average human eyes he could see at least four huge snappers floating like logs in the grassy pools below. He also spied a camp. A Zard camp. At first this alarmed him, but then he realized that the Zard had to have gone somewhere when Bzorch and his breed giants ran them out of Westland. There looked to be about a dozen of them going about everyday things, like cooking and building. They weren't planning to march back into Westland, that was clear.

He went back to the other side of the wormhole and scanned the marshes below; more snappers lying in the evening sun, a few more Zard, two of them stalking something with spears, or maybe gigs. Then Mikahl saw two Zard-men hauling what looked to be a struggling, half-rotted man toward a huge, boiling cauldron.

This was interesting.

Mikahl watched as they forced the undead man into the boiling pot. They held him under the water for a long time with long, paddle-like tools. A few moments later a clean skeleton crawled forth, free of rotting flesh and tattered clothes.

Alarms began to go off in Mikahl's head.

The skeleton was standing there looking at its bony body and legs as if it had just put on a new style of clothing. Suddenly, a large figure, easily twice the size of a big man, stepped out of a tangled patch of willowy trees. The thing looked to be made of moss. Mikahl had to suppress the smile that forced its way through his concern. It was a swamp troll. He'd been told stories of them a hundred times while sitting around the fires and table boards at Settsted Stronghold. He'd traveled its dozen outposts many times as the king's squire. He'd never once believed the fabled creatures existed, yet here came one, and it didn't look pleased.

The swamp troll strode up to the freshly boiled skeleton and, with a savage blow, battered the undead thing to pieces. The two Zard-men who were attending the boiling pot retreated and were now hiding in a thick patch of marsh grass. Mikahl watched from above as the swamp troll took the skeleton's skull and roughly pulled the dangling spinal bones away from it. It then walked over to the boiling pot, sniffed and let out a curious-sounding roar. A moment later it turned and walked right over the skeleton's rib cage, crushing it to splinters. The swamp troll went back into the trees and continued until it was lost in the deep green hues of its environment.

120

THE WIZARD AND THE WARLORD

Mikahl didn't know what to make of it. It didn't look like the skeletons that were coming this way were faring very well when they got here. Something told him there was more to this, but he didn't see an immediate threat. If he flew back to Dreen now, he could get there in plenty of time to leave with his wife, which would make her extremely happy. He had enough time and daylight remaining that, if he left now, he could also make a pass up the length of Dakahn to look for Petar and the pack of skeletons that had assaulted Commander Lyle. He wasn't about to forget the attack on his men.

He decided he would order a more thorough investigation once he and the queen were in Castlemont. A few breed giants, a hundred men with marsh boats, water mages, and a capable wizard or two should be able to manage. He figured that he should probably send some breed giants with their dragon gun crews to help guard Xwarda's wall, as well. He knew for certain that there was at least one Choska demon loose, and no telling how many hellcats and wyvern had escaped the Nethers. He had promised Hyden that he would make sure Xwarda was prepared for an attack. He would keep that promise whether he saw a threat or not.

He called forth the bright horse again and rode it out of the dragon's lair. The dactyls were still swarming around the base of the fang, but he paid them no mind. He did notice that a few of them followed him out of the marshlands, but they peeled off and disappeared once Dakahn was below him. The boldness of the swamp birds gave him pause. He decided that maybe a dozen breed and three hundred men might be more fitting to investigate the Dragon's Fang up close. He also decided that he should set up a permanent patrol out of Settsted. With what the Zard had accomplished under Shaella before, it would be foolish not to do so. He decided that the same should be done along Dakahn's marsh border. The organization of the patrols would give him something to do over the long winter months.

He thought about how to initiate his new plan as he flew across Dakahn, searching below for any sign of Petar or the skeleton crew. Twice he thought he saw something, but when he circled lower the first time, it had only been a group of men on horseback traveling from Oktin to Archa. The second time had been a group of night hunters outside of Svorn. Mikahl accidentally scared the pack of swamp swine that they were after. He felt bad for ruining their hunt.

It was late and he decided that he was doing no good. A few long hours later, just as the sun was beginning to rise, he was back in Dreen, landing the bright horse on the balcony of the royal bedchamber. He entertained thoughts of trying to produce an heir that very morning, but Queen Rosa apparently wasn't so concerned about that issue anymore. No sooner did he wake her than she was rattling off a list of things for him to do. About halfway through, he decided that he might have been better staying out in the swamp.

The soul of Gerard, the Abbadon, Warlord of the Nethers, now resided in Shaella's resurrected body. Her shaved head reared back in manic laughter. The swamp troll couldn't have had better timing. The Warlord had given the order for the Zard to go about their business, or hide in the swamp grass when the dactyls had first called out their alarm. They had seen the bright horse coming from miles away. What was left of Gerard decided that if they attacked the High King, even if they managed to kill him and seize the all-powerful blade he possessed, the repercussions would be insurmountable. He wasn't ready to defend against a full attack from vengeful kingdom men. It was better to hide and wait out the winter while growing stronger and gaining numbers.

The swamp troll had been badgering the skeletons for days. It was widely known that the moss-covered creatures were fixated with skulls. It was sheer coincidence that this one decided to attack the boiling pot while King Mikahl watched from above. It never occurred to the Warlord that all of the skeletons and decomposing undead coming to his summons would lead anyone to his location, but he knew now. He had been so concerned with concealing the movements of the demons and larger things that he had completely overlooked the pesky skeletons. Now that the High King was aware of them, he had to do something. His first inclination was to pulverize their bodies and give their skulls to the swamp troll. Then a better idea occurred to him. If he sent them on a mission, one that would lead them to their destruction, the High King would think the threat had passed.

He decided it should be O'Dakahn. It was the largest city in the realm, and the closest to the swamp.

If Shaella's mind hadn't been so barren, he might have been able to do this himself with a simple spell and a flick of her wrist. Instead, he had to order the Choska to command the skeletons. The Warlord hated to risk the creature, though. If it met an ill end leading the skeletons into O'Dakahn, it wouldn't be able to carry him, in Shaella's body, into Xwarda when the time came. After weighing the options, he decided that drawing the attention of the High King away from his location was more important than anything else. Shaella's body was light enough that a hellcat, or even a hearty wyvern could carry her. He summoned the Choska and instructed it to find a place at the marsh's edge near the village of Nahka and summon the skeletons. Even with help from the Zard, it would take a week or more for the them to traverse the swamp and get there, but other undead from across the realm might come too.

"In ten days, take the undead you've gathered and attack O'Dakahn," the Warlord commanded through Shaella's body. "Use whatever is necessary and available to get into the city. Lead the skeletons to their doom and be careful to save yourself." The Warlord ran Shaella's hand through the stubbly hair on her head. "Return to me once this deed is done, and make sure you're not followed when you come."

Chapter Twenty-Five

Hyden Hawk Skyler finally got hold of himself. He jogged down from the hill he was on and reached out to shake Lord Gregory's hand. He gave Oarly and Phen big hugs in turn.

"Sorry, Phen," he said, holding back a laugh. "But it is funny."

"I didn't laugh at you when Oarly had you shitting fire," Phen shot back harshly, but the way he hugged Hyden gave little room to doubt the love he felt for him.

"Aye," Hyden said, losing his grin for an instant. "Who is she?"

"This is the Lady Telgra," Phen said, feeling rude for not making the introduction already. "Lady Telgra, this is Sir Hyden Hawk Skyler."

"Just Hyden, lady," he replied, with a slightly strained look on his hawkish face. He was about to ask why she was here. His people had no love for the elves. He personally had no problem with them. One of the bravest beings he'd ever known was an elf. Phen saved him from asking the awkward question, though.

"Telgra has lost her memory." Phen took her hand as he spoke. "She needs the Leif Repline fountain as badly as Talon and I do."

Hyden immediately noticed the way Phen spoke of her. After a glance at Lord Gregory, and a quick seeing spell that no one noticed, he bowed to her with a smile.

"You may have to suffer my people's dislike of your race," he said honestly. "But you are safe here among us. We won't harm you."

She batted her wild yellow eyes at him nervously and forced a smile. "Thank you."

"You could have gotten that boy killed, Sir Hyden Hawk," Lieutenant Welch said nervously.

"Oh, I doubt it," Hyden grinned. "You and the boy reacted quickly enough, but not that quickly. A real attack on this group at that moment would have ended all of you, save for Phen and Oarly." Hyden glanced again at Telgra then added, "The lady, and the Lion, would have probably made it, too."

"What?" the lieutenant snapped, looking at Lord Gregory for support.

The Lion Lord just shrugged.

"My blade could have easily been in that boy's flesh. It would have, had I not seen it was a boy and not some wild creature."

"I'm not trying to offend you…" Hyden looked at the man's collar to see what rank he held. "…Lieutenant. I'm just telling you the facts. Your whole party was surrounded by my clansfolk. If we had meant you harm, you would have been porcupined before your sword came free."

Lieutenant Welch's face turned red, but he gave a curt nod. "Point taken," he said. "Still, even with arrows in me, your man could have felt my blade, had I not seen two horsehide boots sticking out of that hairy thing."

Hyden extended the man's sword to him hilt first, as if he were reaching to shake the lieutenant's hand. "Hyden Skyler," he introduced himself.

"Lieutenant Buxter Welch," the lieutenant replied. He reached his hand toward Hyden and saw that his sword was being handed back to him. Lieutenant Welch froze in dismay. It was clear he didn't understand why he didn't have his own sword anymore.

"I assure you, Lieutenant Welch, my cousin was safe from your blade."

"Wow!" Phen said. "How did you do that, Hyden?"

"It's a variation of that spell that sent Oarly's boot off into the Nethers," he said. "You'll be surprised at what I've learned. Watch this."

A cloud of roiling smoke and a shower of sparks enveloped Hyden. The display was accompanied by a loud, crackling pop. When the smoke cleared, the space where Hyden had been was empty.

Two of the horses whinnied in surprise. Phen turned at the tap on his shoulder and found Hyden Hawk standing behind him, grinning ear to ear.

"You've got to teach me that," Phen said excitedly. After a moment he blurted out proudly, "Me and Oarly went back into the Serpent's Eye. We got the emerald out of the sea cave, but Oarly lost it in the marshes."

Hyden glared at Oarly. "By the Goddess, Phen, why would you let Oarly carry the Earth Stone?"

Oarly looked at the two of them and waved them off. "Bah!" he grunted, and stalked over to where Lord Gregory was speaking to one of Hyden's cousins.

"No pockets," Phen said, patting the stony robe that covered his body. "I mapped where he left it, at least."

"You still have my medallion, I see," Hyden said.

"Do you want it back?"

"Not yet," Hyden answered seriously. "I think that, since you had it on when you were petrified, you should wear it until you go into the fountain pool." He gave Phen a pat on the shoulder and stepped away.

"Shaloo, Little Con," Hyden called out. "Round everybody up. There are three wagons to unload back at the edge of the basin."

Hyden turned to Lieutenant Welch. "All they need is one of your men to lead them to the wagons. They'll pack the stuff back."

"They'll need some horses too," Lieutenant Welch said. "The dwarf has kegs, and Phen has trunks full of books."

"There are several trunks full of gifts, as well," Lord Gregory called from where he and Tylen were standing. "Tell the boys not to peek."

"I'll go with them, Hyden," Tylen said. Tylen was on the council of elders now, and the boys would obey him with no question. Hyden smiled. "Don't you be peeking, either, Tylen," he joked.

After they'd gone, Lord Gregory led his horse over to the others. "Lady Telgra," he said, "you should probably stay close to me when we get to the village. The clansfolk know me and will accept your presence more easily if you are seen with someone they trust."

"Yes, Lord Lion," she answered, looking nervous.

"How could you know that we brought three wagons?" Lieutenant Welch asked Hyden.

"I've watched your approach since you stopped at the Summer's Day Spire," he replied.

From above, Talon gave out a loud, shrieking call of explanation. The sound of his familiar reminded Hyden of something and he began searching the ground all around them. With alarm in his voice he asked, "Phen, where is Spike?"

"He's in an aerated trunk on one of the wagons," Phen sighed. "Oarly killed a wildcat on the road and Spike still wants to exact feline revenge or something. I didn't have a choice."

"You should have put Oarly in the trunk," Hyden said with a shake of his head.

"Phen and that fargin lad Jicks toted me off into the hills while I was sleeping, then they set a wildcat on me," Oarly said.

"Was he snoring?" Hyden grinned at Phen and the boy laughed.

"It's not funny, Hyden." Oarly strode up and pointed at the sky accusingly. "That fargin wildcat nearly killed me."

Hyden laughed at his friends as he spun away. "Come on," he called back over his shoulder. "We're still a good ways off."

He led them through a series of shallow valleys, then over a rocky ridge that was high enough for them to see the vast expanse of gray and white that was the Giant Mountains. A blast of icy wind whipped at them as they started down the other side. No one said a word. The sharpness and cloud-shrouded emptiness of the mountain range they would be crossing in the spring left them awestruck. All of them found that they were intimidated.

"Bah!" Oarly grumbled as he scurried deftly around a large pile of broken rock. "It's fargin cold as a witch's nipples."

"You sound like Mikahl," Hyden laughed. "Excuse me... I mean High King Mikahl. He whined like a hungry coyote about how cold it was the whole way on our journey to meet King Aldar."

"That's why he's the king and you're not," Oarly barked. "He's got enough sense to know when it's cold outside."

"You'll live, Oarly," Hyden said. "I've got shagmar cloaks waiting for all of you at the village. There should be a big kettle of stew on, as well."

"A flask of stout and a bowl of steamy stew." Oarly gazed dreamily at the sky as he spoke. "What more could a dwarf ask for?"

"You could ask for a hot, scented bath," Phen said with a chuckle. "Or maybe clothes that don't smell like goat piss, or a trim of that shrub on your head. There are still scales from the serpent tangled in your hair and probably more than one of those fruit bees."

Oarly stared at Phen while he hurried up to Hyden's side. "I cut that blasted serpent in half," Oarly said. "You should have seen the front end slither down into its hole."

"He cut off the tip of its tail," Phen laughed.

Oarly stopped and turned, his face red with anger. "Now listen here, lad, I'll not be the butt of all your jokes on this fargin journey. I cut right through that serpent with me axe. You seen it. I'm getting tired of... of..." Oarly stopped. There was a loud buzzing in his hair. "Don't do it, lad!" he warned, but it was too late. Already a cloud of angry bees were swarming out and stinging the dwarf.

"Ah... Phen... stop it, lad..." Oarly yelped as he skipped around and batted at the angry insects. "Help me, Hyden, it fargin stings."

"After the tricks you played on all of us?" Hyden laughed hysterically as Oarly spun and whirled his arms around. "How could you dare complain or ask me for help?"

Phen stopped laughing long enough to end the spell.

"Bah!" Oarly growled when the bees disappeared. He went stalking away from them.

"Are they always like little boys?" Telgra asked Lord Gregory.

"Aye, they are," he answered through his grin.

"I see I'm in for a long journey," Lieutenant Welch commented. "I'll have to learn to ignore them so I can stay alert."

"I promise you, Lieutenant," the Lion Lord said with a look that showed he meant it, "when there are teeth and steel clashing around you, and the blood is flying, there is no better company to be in. From what the High King has told me, they will be jesting in the heat of it."

The lieutenant looked at the imposing mountain range ahead of them. "Out there, in all of that, I don't think there will be much to laugh about." He spoke more to himself than anybody else. "Fools of the highest order, that's what King Mikahl called them."

"Exactly," Lord Gregory said.

"Did you bring my bow, Phen?" Hyden asked.

"Aye. King Mikahl went after it himself. It's in the hard case along with the texts you requested."

"Did you find the ones I wanted?"

"And then some." Phen replied.

Hyden waited until Lord Gregory was talking to Lady Telgra, then asked Phen softly, "Do her people know where she is?"

"No. She wrote a message and I sent riders to leave it in Vaegon's Glade. It said that she was well." Phen shrugged. "She doesn't know who she is, Hyden. She didn't even know who to send the message to."

"To the Queen Mother, I'd guess," Hyden mused aloud.

"How would you know?"

"Who else would you send a message to, if you were an elf and you didn't know who you were?"

"Aye," Phen agreed.

"Thank the goddess that Old Condlin took the place of Eldest," Hyden said. "If my father had been chosen, then Telgra would be in for a long winter." After a moment, Hyden changed the subject.

"Lord Gregory," he called back over his shoulder. He had stopped on another ridge. This one was smoother and covered with clumps of green grass still fighting to survive, despite the coming season. Beyond them lay a shallow, rounded valley where more patches of the persistent foliage defied winter. When Lord Gregory, Lady Telgra, and the lieutenant caught up, Hyden pointed down into the valley. "Lord Lion, do you remember this place?"

"Is it where the hellcat set upon us and took Vaegon's eye?"

"No," Hyden forced a smile. "That valley is half a mile away." He looked at the Lion Lord and then the others. "This is where you landed when you fell from its claws, after it carried you off."

"By Doon," Oarly said from behind them. "Set a hellcat on me and see what happens to it."

"Aye." Lord Gregory smiled down at the dwarf. "I wish you'd been there, Master Oarly. Vaegon lost an eye, and I nearly lost my life."

"You did lose your life, to hear my mother speak of it," said Hyden. "She told me you were a swollen lump until midwinter."

The Lion Lord nodded. "I owe your family much."

"They are excited to see you again," Hyden said. "My grandfather thought highly of you. My father, too. They say that the heart of a true lion beats in your chest."

"Enough already," Oarly cut in. "Enough reminiscing. Let's get some of that stew."

For once, no one argued with him.

Another blast of wind hit them. This time it didn't seem to pass. For a long while, as Hyden led them in and around the foothills, it pushed at their faces and hissed across the roughening terrain.

"Look, Phen," Telgra yipped with delight. "It's snowing."

Phen looked up to see that it was. Tiny flakes were blowing at them on the wind.

"Just what we need," Oarly grumbled.

"You haven't seen anything yet, Oarly," Hyden laughed. "We'll see ten feet of it before winter is over."

"TEN FEET!" the dwarf exclaimed. He looked from face to face to see if Hyden was teasing him or not. It was clear that he wished he was being jested with again. "I'll be riding on Phen's shoulders if we're going to be out in that kind of mess."

"That's too close to the surface, Oarly," said Phen. "That's where the snow worms will be hunting."

"Bah!" Oarly said, still waiting for someone to crack a smile and reveal the joke. No one did.

"I'll be in one of them rabbit holes your folk live in, Hyden," Oarly said. "I'll not be roaming around in the snow."

"When the snow is ten feet deep, we tunnel through it to get from burrow to burrow. You'll see."

"What about the snow worms?"

"You cut a giant sea serpent in half, Oarly. What is so scary about some snow worms?"

Oarly didn't answer, but his scowl was priceless.

They rounded another set of hills, topped a rise, and then started down into a deep, bowl-shaped valley. They were halfway through it when Lieutenant Welch realized they were already in the well-hidden village of the Skyler Clan. Phen saw it plainly on the man's face.

Only a tiny gray trickle of smoke spiraling up into the sky from a hilltop, and a concealed tunnel-way, could be detected.

Everyone was startled when a man and woman, both near to Lord Gregory's age, came right out of a hillside and started toward them. After that, dozens of faces began to peer out from hidden shafts and crannies. Phen was surprised to see so many dozens of people there, and all of them with the same long, dark hair and tan skin as Hyden Hawk. Even the girls looked the same.

"An elf?" Harrap Skyler scowled as he took Lord Gregory's hand.

"Be kind, father," Hyden said, showing a little unease.

"Yes, Harrap, be kind," Hyden's mother told her mate. "If you act like an old goat, I'll have Hyden turn you into one."

The tense moment passed. "So far so good," Hyden muttered to Phen.

Phen realized that he had never once seen Hyden show such open uncertainty until that moment. He pondered the idea as the snow falling around them changed from a light dust into fat fluffy flakes. In just a matter of minutes the entire valley was covered in a thick blanket of white.

Chapter Twenty-Six

Lord Gregory took Hyden's room in the family burrow. Hyden, Phen, Oarly, Telgra, and Lieutenant Welch shared a larger burrow, one usually reserved for livestock. The three men under Lieutenant Welch bunked in the burrow that Borg had once turned into a stable cavern for the horses.

The underground burrows were roomy enough. The walls and ceilings were generally stone slabs formed into square structures, buried by the giants aeons ago. The burrow the companions were sharing had four rooms and a long, covered entry tunnel. The central room was furnished with a carved wooden table and chairs, and a divan made from lashed-together deadfall, cushioned with stuffed goatskin pillows. The other three rooms were for sleeping. Each had a soft, wood frame bed and a small table along with a shelved cubby to store personal items.

Telgra was given her own room. Phen and Hyden shared, as did Oarly and the lieutenant. The main room sported a hearth, and the fire served to warm the other rooms. Smoke was vented through a shaft at the highest corner of the ceiling. There were no windows, but the walls of the main room were carved into a leafy, vine-strewn pattern, which had been worn to near obscurity over the centuries.

Oarly spent a long time admiring the work that one of his ancestors had obviously done. No giant or elf could work stone that well. He drank several toasts to the quality of the craftsmanship.

When the time came, Hyden used Lord Gregory's farewell as an excuse to get himself, the Lion Lord, and the Eldest alone. He had something of the utmost importance to tell them, but for the three days that his friends were in the village it had been impossible to get the two men away from everyone else.

First, it was the gifts. It took a whole day for the clansfolk to open the thoughtful presents the Lion Lord had brought them. No one had been left out. Every man, woman, and child received something from him and Lady Trella: dolls, wooden blocks, letter boards, toy swords, jewelry, farming implements, leather goods, cloth, and even a few bottles of expensive liquor. It was clear that Lord Gregory had spent a fortune.

That first day, Hyden had given up trying to isolate his uncle and the Westlander. He was thankful that his people were too occupied to worry about Lady Telgra's presence. The whole snow-covered valley was alive with clacking sword fights and giggling glee.

The second day, Hyden got caught up with the companions in a discussion about the route they should take, the supplies they would need, and the matter of packing the gear for their trek through the Giant Mountains. The ideas and concerns kept him preoccupied throughout the day. Later in the evening, Phen and Oarly approached him, worrying over his unease. Hyden assured them that it had nothing to do with them.

The third day, Hyden finally herded Lord Gregory into his Uncle Condlin's burrow. Condlin's boys, Tylen and Little Con, and their mother said their goodbyes and thank yous to the Lion Lord. Hyden showed them his agitation, and thankfully they excused themselves. Finally, Hyden sighed and gathered both men's attention by getting to the point of his distress.

"She is the daughter of the Queen Mother," he blurted out to their blank expressions.

"Who is?" Lord Gregory asked.

"The Lady Telgra," Hyden answered. "I cast a seeing spell on her. One day she will be the leader of all elven kind."

"By the goddess, she must be moved to a private burrow and treated as her station dictates." Hyden openly showed his surprise when the Eldest said this. His Uncle Condlin went on. "Just because we have issue with the feral creatures, we can't just treat her like common folk."

Hyden couldn't help but smile at his uncle's reaction. Maybe there was hope for his people yet. "She doesn't know who she is," Hyden reminded them. "Besides that, my father would start a ruckus if any elf were treated better than a clansman."

The Eldest nodded his agreement. "But what do we do?"

"There are other people looking for her, Hyden," Lord Gregory said. "Another elf, and a Salayan monk who were in her party. They were separated in a storm. Phen and Oarly washed up on the same chunk of marshland she did." The Lion Lord went on to explain what he knew about the situation.

"We don't do anything," Hyden finally said. "She's going with us to restore her memory. My concern is that her mother, the Queen Mother, has to be aware that she is alive and well. Phen sent word to the elves from Dreen." Hyden looked at Lord Gregory with a sympathetic grimace on his face. "No doubt a delegation of elves will soon visit the red city, looking for her."

"She has made it clear that she doesn't want to deal with her people until she has been to the Leif Repline fountain," Lord Gregory said. "It will be a delicate situation. The Queen Mother won't be happy. I don't think Mikahl will allow me to betray Lady Telgra's trust."

"Why not just tell her who she really is, Hyden?" the Eldest asked.

"It's not my place," Hyden answered simply. "She said she didn't want to know until her whole memory was restored. I only told you because, as the Eldest of this clan, you should know who is in your village and under your protection. I honestly think that her going on this quest will help the future relationship between men and elves tremendously."

"Only if she survives," Lord Gregory said. "If she were to die while questing with humans, it might easily start a war."

"I cannot deny her a place on this quest," Hyden said. Then to his uncle, "Even if we have to spend the winter elsewhere." His voice told them both he was firm in his decision.

"Have you sought the advice of the goddess on this matter?"

"I have," Hyden nodded. "As should you."

"I have no problem with the situation," Lord Gregory offered. "But the other elf and the monk will be in Dreen when I return. What do I tell them? Not long after, a delegation from the Evermore will come as well. I've heard that older elves can divine things from men with their magic."

"I will consult with the White Goddess, Hyden," Condlin said after a long moment of thought. His expression showed that he didn't want to say what he was about to say next. "But unless there is some great revelation as to why I should put our people at risk while betraying the Queen Mother, then I am afraid you and your friends might have to winter somewhere else."

"I understand, Eldest," Hyden said. "I will make preparations to leave here as quickly as possible. I hope that a day or two more of Skyler hospitality will be extended so that we may leave fully prepared."

"Aye, Hyden," Condlin said. "Make careful and complete preparations; do not rush into the winter."

"Where will you go?" Lord Gregory asked.

"If I don't tell you, my friend, then you don't have to feel as if you're being untruthful or withholding from the elves when they question you."

"Nor will they be able to divine the information from you," the Eldest said. "You won't be forced to lie to King Mikahl either."

"You're sharp as a blade, Hyden Hawk," Lord Gregory laughed. "I have an idea where you will go, and I approve."

"I won't have to lie to the elves when I send Tylen into the Evermore to tell the Queen Mother that I have seen her daughter and that she is well," the Eldest said.

"Why contact them at all?" Hyden asked.

"If you ever have children, Hyden," the Eldest started prophetically, "you'll understand. The Queen Mother is a parent, and no parent should have to wonder about her child's safety. It's just a matter of respect."

"Telgra's more than a hundred years old, but it couldn't hurt relations between our clan and the elves." Hyden shrugged. "At least wait until we are well away." He remembered watching Condlin carry a travois with his dying son on it for days. This was just after another of the man's children had fallen to his death. If anyone alive understood the grim realities of parenting, it was Condlin Skyler.

The Eldest smiled. "I hope you know that I would never do anything to hinder you, Hyden. If I didn't know that you had a hundred other places to spend the winter, I might find a way to temper my brother's hatred for the elves and keep all of you here."

Hyden saw the love in his uncle's eyes, and the sincerity. "I couldn't put you in that position." Then to Lord Gregory, Hyden said, "It was grand seeing you again, Lord Lion. Give Mikahl and Rosa my best. King Jarrek and Queen Willa, as well. I'm afraid I'm going to be far too busy to see you off. I'm sure Phen and Oarly will want to say goodbye, though."

"I was hoping to get away without having to see those two again," Lord Gregory joked. "I don't envy you."

Condlin poured a round of brandy wine for himself and Lord Gregory as Hyden left.

Hyden found he was relieved. All he had to do now was find an excuse for the sudden change of plans that didn't offend Lady Telgra. He was sure King Aldar would shelter them through the harsher months of the winter. Finding Borg, though, would be the trick. He wouldn't hole the party up while searching for the giant. He would lead them to the cavern where he, Mikahl, Vaegon, and Loudin had taken shelter once before. If they couldn't find Borg, they could ride the bitter weather out there.

Lord Gregory left later that afternoon. Phen handled the goodbye well, but Oarly was drunk and became over emotional. Lieutenant Welch and Jicks had to pry the dwarf off of the Lion Lord. The clansfolk had a good laugh at the scene. A trail of little black-haired swordsmen followed the Lion out of the valley, but after he disappeared over the other side of the ridge, the children returned.

Two days later, the quest party, looking like a line of wild-haired two-legged creatures leading a train of horses, eased out of the snow-bleached valley as the sun filled the sky with a peachy light.

Hyden's excuse for the change of plans was simple. He said that if they could get to the fabled city of Afdeon before the winter trapped them, then they were that much closer to the restorative fountain when spring came. Neither Phen nor Lieutenant Welch wholeheartedly believed the story, it was clear, but Hyden was glad that no one questioned him over the matter.

The shagmar cloaks were warm, but still Oarly complained. Spike rode in a deep, fur-lined pocket Phen had sewn into his. The few days spent trapped in the aereated trunk had quelled the lyna's desire to get at the dwarf. Talon searched ahead of them for signs of trouble, and Hyden spoke some words that would hopefully find their way to the ears of the giants' Southern Guardian by way of bird or beast.

The first leg of the quest was finally underway. An elven princess, an ornery dwarf, and six men leading ten heavily-loaded horses headed north into the Giant Mountains.

Hyden hoped they could find Borg before the weather turned nasty. A little snowfall was nothing in the foothills. Once they were in the heart of the range they would either find Borg and gain the shelter of Afdeon or be forced to ride out the winter huddled in a cave, like the ancients. Hyden hoped it wouldn't come to that. He had to remind himself that he had newfound power to use, the power of the ring he had taken from what was left of Gerard in the Nethers. The many ways he might use magic to find Borg, or even the hidden city, made the odds next to impossible for them to be stuck for the winter. It was with that optimism that he began thinking of other ways to contact the giant while he led his friends into one of the most treacherous places in the realm.

Lord Gregory made it back to the wagons. Each had only a single horse to pull it now, but they were empty, so it was a manageable task. The three drivers were also soldiers, men King Mikahl had picked from the ranks because of their ability to drive the wagons. There was no perceived threat between the foothills and Dreen, but with demons still loose in the world, the High King made it clear that he wasn't taking any chances.

Lord Gregory chose to ride in his saddle. The hard board seats weren't very kind to his old body. The weather lessened the further south they went. When the tall, needle-like spire came into view ahead of them it was the afternoon of the second day. The snow was so light that it wasn't even noticeable, but an icy mist had blanketed the Leif Greyn Valley. Visibility was limited as they moved through it, and they were almost to the base of the spire before they saw Corva and Dostin standing there nervously.

Lord Gregory dismounted and strode over to the face of the monolith, where his name was carved. He hadn't met them yet, but he knew without a doubt who they were.

"She is important to our people, my lord," Corva said. "Far more important than I can explain."

"She doesn't want to be bothered at this time," Lord Gregory told them. "I know who Princess Telgra is. The problem is that they have already moved on from where I left them. Even if I wanted to, I couldn't tell you where they have gone."

"The Queen Mother won't understand the kingdom's lack of cooperation in finding her daughter," Corva explained. "I do not know how that will affect our already shaky relationship."

"Your queen should understand lack of cooperation extremely well." Lord Gregory's tone had a bit of bite to it. "The princess is safe, I can promise you that. Men from the village where we parted ways are already on their way into the Evermore. That is all I can say."

"Is your name really on there?" Dostin asked stupidly.

"Yes, it is." Lord Gregory pointed to the script. "Here."

Dostin eased up close and squinted at the carved letters. He spoke aloud as he read. "Lord Alvin Gregory, Lord of the West, victorious over Sir Willmont Baylor of Valleya in the Brawl."

"The princess was under my protection," Corva said to Lord Gregory with the proper amount of respect in his voice. "If you don't tell me, I'll just follow your tracks to where you came from. It is my duty."

Lord Gregory nodded and shook his head. The elf's sincerity, and good intent, was radiating from him. "You'd better hurry along then," he said evenly. "It's snowing in the foothills."

Corva nodded then unexpectedly extended his hand up to the Lion Lord. "Thank you, my lord. Come now, Dostin, we must make time."

Lord Gregory watched after them, but after only a moment they were lost in the icy mist. He wasn't certain he wanted to know what would happen when the monk and the elf entered the clan village. The snow wasn't deep enough to obscure his trail completely. If the elf could track at all, he would find the Skylers. If the two of them managed to survive that, then maybe they could find Hyden and the others. He decided that it wouldn't be a bad thing if that happened. What King Mikahl had said about the monk's fighting ability, and the elf's determination to carry out his duty, meant they could probably help Phen and the others succeed.

Lord Gregory also found that he didn't want to think about what would happen if the quest failed. If Princess Telgra didn't return with her memory, or worse, didn't return at all, then the friction between the humans and the elves would surely turn volatile.

M. R. Mathias

Chapter Twenty-Seven

King Mikahl sat jostling in the opulently decorated royal carriage. Queen Rosa and her attendant, a girl named Allysan, sat across from him, giggling and pointing out the window at the soldiers surrounding them. Their three-hour-long discussion of a green dress they were going to make had numbed his mind completely. The huge procession was far slower than anyone had hoped it to be. They had been traveling five days and were just now coming out of the Wilder Mountains into Castlemont. Mikahl wanted desperately to be riding Windfoot out in the open, away from the silly women, their shrill outbursts, and their whispery secrets.

Once they were inside the thick canvas pavilion tent that was erected for them each night, Rosa became his world, and he hers. During the day, though, he felt as if he were being tortured. Rosa had begun rigorously working on creating an heir when they were alone, but during the day she was so prim and proper, and sometimes downright silly, that he couldn't stand it. He was hoping that King Jarrek would appear soon so that he could excuse himself from her company without offense and get some air.

The queen's mirth slowly faded to silence as the edge of Pael's destruction came into view. She had seen Castlemont after its destruction, but it never ceased to be overwhelming. Even with thousands of men, dwarves, and a few dozen breed giants working nonstop to rebuild the wreckage, the magnitude of devastation was chilling.

Mikahl chose not to look. He wanted to see the reconstruction and the new bridge at Locar. He wanted to find hope in Wildermont. Out here in the outskirts there was little of it.

Allysan pointed out of the window at something. As Queen Rosa wiped a stray tear from her cheek a smile spread across her beautiful face. It was such a wonderful smile that Mikahl was forced to look to find what caused it.

Up on a gently rolling hillside, a pair of very young boys were running along a fence line, skipping and pointing down at the royal procession as they went. Another boy was ahead of them. This one appeared a little older and was shooing sheep out of the way so they could keep up. Higher up the hill, a woman stood before a cottage, smiling and waving down at them. Smoke rolled up from the chimney and clothes whipped in the breeze along the line where they had been pinned. Mikahl noticed that there was no man in sight, and that the stack of chopped wood beside the house was nearly exhausted.

He glanced ahead of them. The next property was a ruin. It had been larger, probably once a lord's manor by the looks of the jagged pile of rubble and charred timbers. Mikahl could imagine Pael's army, actually Glendar's army, occupying the place while their troops marched past toward Dreen. They'd probably torched the place. Once the beams were burned through, it had crumbled. Out here, Pael hadn't bothered to wreak havoc personally. This destruction was from the Westland men Glendar had recruited. Mikahl could see some of Pael's magical destruction further ahead, though. From the procession's vantage point in the hills, a good view of Castlemont Proper spread out before them. It looked as if a mountainous foot had just stepped down out of the clouds and crushed everything under it. A long line of leveled terrain lay where one of the gigantic towers had fallen.

Mikahl was about to pull his eyes away when he noticed a clump of buildings rising up out of the mess. They were new, and even from the distance, he could see the majestic quality of the dwarves' construction: arched entryways, high, peaked corner towers, and steep tiled roofs decorated the cluster of two- and three-story constructions. A single tower rose up over them proudly.

Upon further inspection, Mikahl saw other buildings at various stages of completion scattered about the city.

He found himself feeling better about things. Rosa must have noticed his shift in mood because she reached over and squeezed his hand. He glanced at her and felt himself flooded with love. She was silly at times, but at others she was quite astonishing, both as a woman, and as a friend. Considering their marriage was brought about over a political need, he knew that he could not have done better. It was rare in such unions to find that both people could love each other.

Mikahl gave her a sparkling smile. He knew how lucky he was to have her, even if she sometimes drove him crazy.

"Oh look, Mik," she said, following Allysan's pointing finger. "It's King Jarrek. He has called up a formal greeting party to escort us to his castle."

Mikahl grinned. He hadn't seen Jarrek in a few months and was anxious to be in the company of his old friend. "My lady," Mikahl said through his grin, "King Jarrek's castle is only a pile of rocks. They will probably escort us to an outlying stronghold within the city's wall."

"We can stay at our pavilion, for all I'm concerned," Rosa said with a blush. "Lately, it's become one of my more favorite places to be."

Allysan giggled and whispered something, causing Rosa to giggle as well. Mikahl found his cheeks blooming with heat too. He was never more thankful than when the carriage came to a stop and one of the commanders knocked politely on the door.

"High King Mikahl, King Jarrek has invited Your Highness to join him," the man said after the door had been opened. "If it pleases, he would like to give you a personal tour of the progress. Your horse has been readied. I'm to apologize to my lady, for the roads in most areas are not suitable for the carriage."

Mikahl looked at his wife askance.

"Go on, Mikahl." She smiled. "I'll see you soon enough."

"Thank you, Rosa," he said as he hurried out to find Windfoot.

A few hours later, he and King Jarrek rode side by side through the heart of Castlemont. The score of men escorting them were spread out so that the two could speak privately.

"Under Diamondeen, the dwarves have done wonders," Jarrek was saying. "They are using blocks and materials from the destroyed buildings to construct the newer ones. It saves us from having to haul so much debris out of the city."

"Who will be their next king?" Mikahl asked. The former king of the dwarves had died fighting to free Jarrek's people from Ra'Gren's slavery. The dwarves, newly returned to the realm, had gravitated toward Castlemont and Oktin, where their service as stone workers was needed most. King Mikahl hadn't received much news about them in Dreen, for King Jarrek was as busy as a man could be.

"It's hard to say," Jarrek answered. "It's something that will be done below in one of the underground cities. I'm sure they will choose well, though."

"How has our Lord Bzorch been faring?"

King Jarrek barked out a laugh. "You should see the new bridge. Well, you will see it when you cross it in the morning. He is a fair enough bridge master and I don't think any other breed giant in the pack could keep the rest under control as well as he does." Jarrek cringed. "I would sure hate to be Ra'Gren."

"He's still alive?"

"Oh yes." King Jarrek made an elaborate circular gesture with his arm. "When he and the remaining overlords aren't pulling Bzorch around in his cart, the Lord of Locar has them chained to a giant gear wheel that turns the dwarves' millstones."

"Do you think we are wrong torturing Ra'Gren that way?" Mikahl asked. "It seems sometimes that we are no better than him by doing so."

"No, sir." Jarrek's voice was stern. "Ra'Gren and his overlords enslaved tens of thousands, and killed thousands of innocents, just to entertain themselves." The Red Wolf's tone grew heated as he spoke. "If they were to live a thousand years smoldering on a bed of hot coals, they wouldn't have suffered enough."

It was King Jarrek's turn to enquire then, and the two men spoke for a long time about Queen Willa, Queen Rosa, and plans for the realm. Mikahl told him of Hyden's quest and the progress at Oktin. That night King Jarrek held a feast in their honor and once again swore his fealty to High King Mikahl and the might of Ironspike.

Mikahl had told him of his concerns about the marshes and the threats the Zard might pose. After the main course was devoured, the Red Wolf announced that men would be sent immediately into Dakahn to help organize a marsh patrol similar to Westland's.

Rumors of a riverboat full of Wildermont steel being pirated on its way down to O'Dakahn took on a new light. Mikahl's proposed marsh patrol would make it all but impossible for pirates to thrive along either channel of the Leif Greyn River. The nobles and the other folk in attendance at the feast were excited about the news. Such protection from thievery would benefit every merchant, smith, and bargeman in the realm. Soon that talk died away. A lute-playing bard, accompanied by a harpist, filled the hall with bright, uplifting song. Most of the gatherers moved to the courtyard where the musicians were joined by a large, hairless woman's angelic voice. Even though it was cold enough to see one's breath, a blanket of hope and promise warmed the hearts of all.

The next afternoon, after sleeping as late as possible, Mikahl received word from King Jarrek that he would be busy in the city and regretted not being able to see him off. The Red Wolf did promise to visit him in Westland soon. It was common knowledge that King Jarrek spent his days out in the rubble and dust hauling debris or stacking stone blocks with the other laborers. He was one with his people, and since Pael had torn the heart out of his kingdom, he sweated, strained, and even bled the love back into his land. Mikahl admired his resolve. Like Hyden and Phen, he was one of the realm's greatest heroes. King Mikahl felt lucky to know him.

Locar was only an hour's ride from Castlemont on horseback, but with the huge escort of soldiers and the seven-wagon train, it took most of the morning to get there. Bzorch, the Lord of Locar, waited on the Westland side of the newly repaired span. He was huge and imposing sitting in his wagon cart behind a team of well-muscled, but broken-looking, men.

Mikahl had grown frustrated and exited the royal carriage to inspect the bridge from his horse. Only one lane was complete, but another would be done by winter. The dwarves and breed giants were using the old columns that jutted up out of the Leif Greyn River to build them all, but they were using newly mined granite out of the Wilder Mountains to add onto them. Mikahl estimated that it would be spring, and spring again, before the entire five-lane bridge was restored to its former magnificence.

As Mikahl approached Bzorch, the breed giant climbed out of his cart and took a knee. Seeing that he was still nearly at eye level with Mikahl, even though he was still mounted, Bzorch lowered his head even more. Mikahl couldn't help but note the amount of respect the alpha breed was showing him. Their relationship was held civil by the thinnest of strands. Bzorch had led breed giants against Westlanders and against Mikahl's father, King Balton, at Coldfrost. Mikahl had been there, but only as a squire. The Dragon Queen had given him his title, but Bzorch betrayed her in order to do what was best for his people. The breed giant and his huge crossbow-like dragon guns had helped win the day at the Battle of O'Dakahn.

"Lord Bzorch," Mikahl said, seeing that King Ra'Gren and his once fat overlords looked healthy in the chains that held them to Bzorch's cart. Mikahl smiled at something he remembered Jarrek saying earlier.

"Well met, Lord of Locar," Mikahl said as Bzorch stood up.

Windfoot whinnied and pranced nervously back. Bzorch, easily ten feet tall and as wide as a set of double doors, grinned down at his king. He wore no shirt, only horsehide britches and shin-high boots. Studded leather gauntlets strained around his meaty forearms, and one of his serving-tray sized pectoral muscles jumped as he spread an arm out in invitation.

"Welcome home, High King Mikahl," he boomed. "We have been awaiting your return most anxiously."

Ra'Gren, once the wealthiest king in the realm, snorted a laugh of disgust from his place at the front of the wagon harness.

Even to Mikahl, Bzorch's words sounded strange. Not so many years ago the breed giants had feasted on the flesh of men and women under his father's protection. Mikahl realized, though, that Bzorch had probably practiced the words all morning. He looked away and his eyes met Ra'Gren's. Before he could stop himself, he hacked up a wad of phlegm and spat it into the dirt.

"You've done well with the bridge, Lord Bzorch." He held Ra'Grens gaze as he spoke. "You should fatten up your wagon team and make them into a stew."

Ra'Gren paled and looked away. Bzorch laughed low and loud. "I would have eaten the bastards long ago, King Mikahl, but there's no one left in the realm despicable enough to replace them."

Mikahl nodded agreement, but in the back of his mind he was thinking about Lord Vidian, the tyrant from Weir. He was quite sure that Queen Willa would amend the man's punishment and send him to Locar.

"I've got orders for some of your men," Mikahl said as he reined Windfoot out of the way of the royal procession that was just now filing its way across the bridge. "I would like a dozen of your dragon gunners, with ropemen and whatever else they need to operate. I would have them in Xwarda before full winter sets in. Queen Willa and General Escott will assign them from there. Pick a few of your folk, the more civil of them, to establish an embassy there. Once that's done, a rotation can be set so that no one has to stay for too long."

Bzorch's smile looked more like a snarl but his eyes showed that he was pleased his people were needed in such a way. "I can have them moving in two days' time."

"Good." Mikahl nodded. The awkward tension between them was beginning to ease. "Also, the Zard and a Choska may be stirring up trouble at the Dragon's Tooth Spire." Mikahl noticed the breed giant's grin growing broader on his ape-like face. "I'll be sending a few hundred men on barges to investigate. I would like it if you could send a handful of your less civil kin, and a few dragon guns with them, as well."

"If it pleases you, King Mikahl," Bzorch said joyfully. "I would lead them myself. I hate the Zard."

"I will leave that decision up to you, Lord Bzorch," Mikahl smiled. "The soldiers and barges will be in Settsted in a fortnight. I want the area around the Dragon Spire thoroughly investigated and anything you perceive as a threat eliminated."

Mikahl found that he felt sorry for anything Bzorch got his hands on. A seriously sharp-looking fang, as long as Mikahl's little finger, was jutting menacingly over the breed giant's upper lip as he strode away.

When Mikahl rejoined his wife in the royal carriage he was feeling better than he had since King Aldar told him he was King Balton's son. For the first time in his reign, he felt that all was at peace. Nothing so dire or dangerous that it couldn't be contained was threatening them, and hope was as plentiful as the leaves falling from the autumn trees. Even the people of Wildermont were bustling with purpose. The horrors of the past few years were all but forgotten as the people of his kingdom looked toward the future.

He smiled at his beautiful wife. Queen Rosa smiled back at him. He found the idea of spending the entire winter in Westland trying to make an heir as appealing as anything he could imagine.

M. R. MATHIAS

The Wizard and the Warlord

Chapter Twenty-Eight

The white ram heard Hyden Hawk's words from the blackbird, who had heard the words from one of the otters in the valley. Since the ram could traverse the mountain peaks with relative ease, and speed across the hills at will, the curved-horned beast took it upon himself to carry the words all the way to the Southern Guardian. For two days, the ram leapt across the rocky precipices and eased around the sheer cliffs on its way toward Borg. The animals knew the circuitous route the giant used to cover the part of the mountains he guarded for his king.

The smaller creatures had to know where Borg traveled. Sometimes he shared the company of King Aldar's great wolves. They were servants of the Giant Kingdom, but they were predators as well. Knowing this, the white ram was hesitant to linger along Borg's trail. He didn't want to become dinner for one of the huge beasts. He found a snow owl sitting in an ice-laden fir tree and headed to tell her Hyden Hawk's words. He hoped she would hang around until Borg passed. The scent of great wolves was heavy in the air and his instinct wouldn't allow him to linger.

"Wise owl," the white ram said in a way that only animals could understand.

"What is it, curved-horn?" she asked, twisting her gray-flecked head at an odd angle to look down at him. "You're far away from the rocky heights you call home." The owl's coin-sized amber eyes snapped open and shut.

"I have words for the giant man, Borg."

"Who… who… who spoke these words?" the owl asked.

"Hyden Hawk spoke them."

The owl nodded. "They must be important words."

"They are," the ram replied, prancing nervously in place. The scent of wolf was strong, and the ram couldn't help the way it made him feel. "Will you hear these words and speak them to the giant when he passes?"

"Who… who?" The owl fluttered down to a lower branch on the fir tree, sending a shower of collected snow cascading down onto the icy ground.

"The giant," the ram answered, wondering if the owl had really been asking.

"I know who… who?" the owl said. "Tell me the words and I'll tell the giant."

"Hyden Hawk's herd is moving north to the Cairn of Loudin. He wishes Borg to join them, and aid them."

"Who?" the owl said.

"Who what?" the ram said in frustration. "Hyden's herd is moving north toward the Cairn of Loudin. He wishes Borg to join them and aid them."

"I heard you the first time," the owl said defensively.

"Then why did you ask, 'who?'" the ram growled just before charging the trunk of the tree and butting it with his horns. An explosion of snow and ice came piling down on top of him.

The owl fluttered back up to her original perch and chuckled. The ram shivered the snow off of himself and stepped back so he could see the owl again.

"I am an owl," the bird said informatively. "I say 'who' because it is my nature, just like it is yours to butt heads or even trees when you get frustrated."

"Will you give Borg the message?" the ram finally asked.

"Who?" the owl said.

The ram started to grow angry again, but stopped himself. Instead, he snorted and bounded off into the trees.

The owl laughed at the hard-headed animal again before taking to the air. Owls were wise, and this one knew exactly what part of the trail Borg was traveling. The owl also knew instinctually that any message from nature's human counterpart was of the utmost importance. She wasted no time. Before the sun went down, the Southern Guardian was in the owl's sight.

Sadly, Petar and his four companion's bodies were found mauled and covered by a blanket of carrion birds. They were in a copse of trees outside Kastia Valley. Commander Lyle had returned to Dreen with more orders, but the High King hadn't left any for him. Cresson suggested that he take his trackers and ride to O'Dakahn to help search for the mysterious skeleton crews.

Several Dakaneese troops had patrolled the banks of the Leif Greyn River as King Mikahl ordered. Skeletal footprints were found between Owask and Svion. Now the marsh witches and magi who catered to the superstitious sailors and bargemen along the river were saying that some dark evil was growing out in the swamp near Nahka.

Cresson thought that Commander Lyle should be the one in charge of investigating these things, but already a man from O'Dakahn had been placed in position. The commander's experience outside of Xway made him the most informed man in the realm on the matter. Cresson was so confident in that reasoning that he made a sending to O'Dakahn telling them that once Commander Lyle arrived, he would take charge. He gave Lyle papers, resupplied his men, and assigned him more than the coin necessary to establish an office in Nahka.

Gerard's—the Warlord's—orders for the Choska had been vague. The bat-like demon had to ensure that all the skeletons that answered his summons were destroyed during the attack on O'Dakahn. Being a demon, the Choska fed on terror and pain as much as actual food. It decided that it could create quite a meal for itself if it planned well. With its evil magic, the Choska enlisted the aid of a dabbling sorcerer in Nahka. The man bartered the goods the skeletons pirated, and brought them back swords, hooded robes, and torches.

The city of O'Dakahn was vast and wild. Though sections of the wealthy metropolis were well guarded and protected from the unsavory, most of the massive port was considered a cesspool of raw human nature. Pungent tobaccos and herbal potions of the most stimulating nature could be found, sexual fantasies were bought and sold, and a wager could be placed on almost anything at any time of the day or night. It wasn't hard for the four dozen hooded skeletons to get into the underbelly of O'Dakahn where the streets stayed crowded through the night, and even the city guards tended to look away.

The gatehouse that led from this rough and tumbled part of O'Dakahn to the mercantile district stayed closed and barred at night. It was manned by reputable guardsmen, the incorruptible sort who hoped to rise in the ranks by protecting the merchants and lesser nobles who resided beyond their post. The gate guards were well trained and stayed in practice with their weapons by drilling responses to ways in which their posts might be compromised. As often as they went through these rigorous defensive maneuvers, none of them could defend what was coming this night.

The Choska demon swept down out of the darkened sky and sent a series of streaking crimson rays into the gate. The heavy planked doors didn't explode apart, but they burst into flames that were so hot the hinges and metal bands that held them together began to glow cherry red. Slowly, the metalwork grew malleable and dripped away, causing sparks to fountain up as the hot drips hit the cool hardpack.

THE WIZARD AND THE WARLORD

Dogs barked in fear and anger. The guards sounded the alarm as the ember-eyed demon came back around. Crossbows thrummed and arrows shot forth, some striking the Choska as it came on again. The arrows did little more than enrage the thick-skinned creature. It let out a shrieking cry that dropped men to their knees. The clank of weapons hitting the cobbles echoed, as hands were pressed protectively over their ears.

Huge, clawed feet latched on top of the gate and tore the planks away from the melting metal. Then from out of the shadows, the robed skeletons came swarming. In a matter of seconds, the guards were overrun.

Torches flared to life, lit from the burning gates, and like maddened fireflies, small bands of undead spread out through the streets, shattering glass and setting curtains and thatch aflame. Soon a dressmaker's shop was so consumed in fire that a whole portion of the city was illuminated. Another shop burst into flames down the way, and in the distance, as the sound of clanging steel rang out, a horrible scream cut through the night.

The Choska demon circled high above, shrieking and reveling as the horror and shock of O'Dakahn's residents wafted up into the night. Soon the ample city guard would be diverted from another part of the city to come and rescue the merchants, but until then the Choska basked in the horrific glory of the people's terror.

To further the mayhem, the Choska swept by low a few times, rupturing eardrums and spreading panic with its horrible, piercing call. It watched as guardsmen came rushing in from several different places. They held their lanterns high and their swords flashed brightly. One by one the skeletons were cut down and trampled apart by city men.

The Choska lingered, savoring the pain of the burned and wounded, the terror of the orphaned and widowed. The uncertainty of the futureless, whose livelihoods had just been destroyed, was like sweet nectar to the hell-born beast. As dawn approached, the Choska fled the city, sated and successful in carrying out the Abbadon's command. It winged its way westward toward the Dragon Spire to tell the Warlord of its success. The Dark One would be pleased, and the Choska would no doubt be rewarded, maybe even with a more substantial meal of Zard flesh, one that it could peel from a living morsel, or even a thrashing geka. Gloating in its success, the Choska decided that it wouldn't wait for the Abbadon's reward. Swooping down over the village of Nahka, it spied a herdsman rounding up his goats in the dawn light.

The man never even saw the demon drop down on him, but his scream was no less harrowing because he couldn't identify his attacker. Several people in the village saw him torn apart by the giant, bat-like fiend; they also watched the Choska wing away, heading due west. Everyone, even the children in Nahka, knew what lay due west. After all, a dragon had lived there for the last three centuries.

The same morning, High King Mikahl and Queen Rosa rode atop their carriage, on the parade bench, into the sizable Westland city of Crossington. All around them people yelled and cheered. The cobbled streets were packed, mostly with elderly folk and women. Wild packs of children ran around, too. It was clear that everyone in Westland was relieved to have one of King Balton's sons, a rightful heir to the Westland crown, back on the throne.

Mikahl was exhilarated. In his youth he had spent many a day in Crossington. It wasn't his actual home, but it was so close and so familiar that he was beside himself. The entire skyline of northern Westland's main trading center was filled with fluttering golden lions. Green and gold wavered on the chilly breeze everywhere. It was inspiring.

Rosa waved and smiled at hundreds and hundreds of little girls, whose fathers and lives had been ravaged away by war. The smiles on some of their faces looked to be the first ones they had made in quite some time.

Crossington, it seemed, had been affected more than any other place by the Zard occupation, save for Lakeside Castle. The people were starving for familiar leadership. With Mikahl came a sense of security.

Even after they were back inside the carriage with Crossington behind them, Mikahl's blood was tingling. The only feelings he could compare the sensation to were Ironspike's symphony and Queen Rosa's bed. His true home was ahead of them, the castle where he had been born and raised. Mikahl had worked for the kingdom since he could walk. He was a candle snuffer and message runner when he was a boy. Later, he was a stablehand, and finally, King Balton's personal squire. This was his homecoming; the kitchen servant's bastard-turned-king of the entire realm, returning to the place where his father and mother had died.

He looked at his wife and saw that she was chewing her bottom lip. He reminded himself that this was also the place where Queen Rosa was held captive by the Dragon Queen and mutilated by the Red Priests of Kraw.

"It will be all right, my love," he told her. "This is our place now."

"You'll have that wizard's tower torn down for me?" she asked.

"Aye, my lady, I will," he agreed. "Even if I have to do it myself with Ironspike."

"And the garden yard where Pin and Hyden Hawk stopped the priest from tearing open the world."

"Aye, my lady."

"And that wicked woman's bedchamber that overlooked it all?" She was looking happy now, and her eyes showed that she was pleased he would do these drastic things for her.

"I won't have to do that, my lady." Mikahl smiled at the look on her face. "Claret took care of that when she poked her huge head in to save Phen."

She leaned into him and squeezed his arm. "I miss Pin. I would feel better if he were here."

Mikahl wasn't sure what to say to that. Phen had comforted his wife while she was imprisoned here.

"My lady." Mikahl leaned over and kissed his wife deeply. "Phen is up in the Skyler village keeping Oarly and Hyden safe." He kissed her again. "You'll just have to learn to feel safe without him."

"Oh, Mik," she purred. "You'll just have to keep my mind occupied so that the memories don't take hold of me."

"Rosa, I hope to spend our time here making new memories. Can we try to forget the rest?"

"Yes, my king. I believe that you've already caused me to forget." She kissed him. "Whatever it was," she whispered as she kissed him again, "that we were talking…" After that the words stopped and their kiss grew passionate.

A few minutes later, the royal carriage driver called a stop because of a sudden motion that made him think a wheel was busted. He was embarrassed to learn that he was mistaken.

That evening, while riding in Windfoot's saddle, King Mikahl Collum rode through the gates of Castleview City, where he had once been chased away as a murderer and thief.

The reception he received, the explosion of well-wishing people, made Crossington's excited crowd seem like an old lady's tea party. For the first time since King Balton's death, the people of Westland felt safe.

Chapter Twenty-Nine

The afternoon was brisk. Coming over the previous ridge, the icy breeze had sliced through the companions' garments as if they weren't even there. The snow had stopped, though. The sun was bright overhead and now, as they eased down into the wooded valley, they found that they were protected from the wind. After four days of constant snowfall and cold, gray skies, the rays of warm sunlight were inviting.

"Let's stop and fortify ourselves," Hyden suggested.

Talon had located Loudin's valley for them and was off searching for Borg. Hyden knew that if they ate heartily now, they could reach the cavern he was leading them to before sunset. Loudin's valley was just beyond there. The cavern would provide them good shelter from the weather. Its stony walls would hold actual warmth. The tents they had been sleeping in, even bundled in blankets, were cold and far from comfortable.

"It tt- ttts f- fargin c- c- c- cold," Oarly chattered for what was probably the two-hundredth time.

"Shut up, Oarly," a chorus of voices returned.

"It's so cold that I keep forgetting how cold I am," Telgra snapped at the dwarf. "Why do you have to keep reminding me?"

"You sound like a little girl, Master Dwarf," Lieutenant Welch said. "You're not even tall enough to feel the wind. The horse you're leading blocks it all from you."

They found a break in the trees that sheltered them from the slighter breeze in the valley. Jicks and the archers went to gather deadfall while Phen piled up kindling and, with a flaming finger, set it to blaze.

Krey, one of the archers, and Hyden had killed a tuskaboar after they ran out of shagmar meat. Hyden was finding that feeding seven mouths on this trek might prove to be challenging in the higher altitudes. The cold caused appetites to be fierce. Luckily, Phen couldn't eat because Oarly, besides whining constantly about the weather, ate like a pack of starving dogs.

Lieutenant Welch and Telgra tended to the horses while Hyden spitted a haunch of the wild hog on the fire. The elven girl had proven crucial while traversing a narrow rock ledge in a whiteout. Only she and Hyden had been able to see where they were going. By roping the group together in a line and moving the horses one at a time across the narrow path, they had accomplished it. At one point Oarly had begun complaining and for a long, tense moment Hyden thought Telgra would throw him from the ledge, but she restrained herself somehow. Every day they traveled together, Hyden's respect for her grew. They let the horses rest and fed them oats from a sack, but there were burlberry bushes that thrived around the tree trunks and the horses were soon nibbling the leaves from them.

The roasted wild pig went well with the last of the hard bread Hyden's clansfolk had sent with them. Hyden was glad they were close to the cave. Hopefully Borg would come along soon. Until he did, they would have to hunt for food and handpick greenery for the horses. He dared not lead them farther than the cavern without the Southern Guardian. After a short rest, he decided that it wouldn't matter, not if they didn't get to the cavern. Soon the procession was back on its way.

Only Lieutenant Welch and the two archers rode their horses. This was for defensive reasons, not for comfort. The elevated position allowed them a better shot at anything that might approach. When the mountainous terrain wouldn't allow for riding, the others had to lead their mounts so that their hands were free.

Every now and then Oarly would ride for a short time, just to rest his legs. He didn't like being out from behind his living wind-block, though, so he never rode long.

They crossed another ridge and, instead of cutting down and up through the valley it sided, they skirted around it. The next valley was deep and, even though the temperature seemed well below freezing, the stream that ran through it flowed with an audible gurgling force. The top of the ridge opposite the valley from them sported the cave where Hyden, Vaegon, and Loudin had once waited for Borg to find them.

As Hyden led the group down from the heights through the knee-deep snow he saw something that didn't alarm him as much as it discouraged him. Animal tracks, big ones, left by a four-legged creature, most likely a bear. Using his keen vision, Hyden saw that they led from the cavern mouth down the rock-strewn slope into the thickly forested streambed and back up again. Apparently the cavern wasn't empty anymore. If they had to, he decided, they could easily kill the bear and use its meat to sustain themselves. Its pelt would make an excellent cover for the cavern mouth.

The problem was, it might be a female readying for hibernation, with cubs growing inside her. If it was, Hyden couldn't even run it out of the cavern. He would have to find out before they proceeded. Normally, he would just send Talon across the valley to take a peek, but the hawkling was off searching for Borg. If the bear was cubbing, they didn't dare camp in this valley. What was worse, Loudin's valley was just beyond the cavern. To get there, they either had to cross over the ridge right by the cavern mouth, or skirt around the treacherous granite cliffs that formed the knife-like ridge before them. It could take days for them to get around, and for the first time Hyden's confidence in his plan to leave the village early was faltering.

"Lieutenant," he called out. "Ease the group down by the tree line and be ready for anything. I will be back shortly."

"What is it, Hyden?" Phen asked. His curiosity was piqued by the sudden command.

"There is a big bear living in our shelter cave. If it's a male, we'll kill it and let its death give us life. If it is a female, then we will be forced to not only find new accommodation, but also a different route."

"Wh- wh- why d- do we n- need to be ready?" Oarly asked, his chattering voice full of alarm.

"The bear might not be in its cave," Hyden said simply. "It could be fattening itself up on fish or deer down there." He laughed at the dwarf. "It's just a bear, Oarly."

"Bah!" Oarly waved him off with a grumble. "J- just uh fa- fa- fargin ba- bear-"

"Come on, dwarf," Lieutenant Welch said as politely as he could manage. "We'll keep you safe. Let's get down there by the trees and out of the wind."

Phen looked at Hyden longingly. He wanted to go with him to explore the cavern. Hyden saw it in the marble-colored boy's expression. No doubt even a giant ice bear would have trouble sinking tooth or claw into Phen's skin. Hyden laughed.

"I'm not going to walk over there, Phen, or I'd let you come along."

"Aye," Phen said a little dejectedly. "I can't wait until we get somewhere. I want you to teach me some of your new spells."

"Soon," Hyden promised. Then, with the wave of his hand and a smoking, crackling, pop, he vanished.

Hyden appeared a few feet back from the mouth of the cavern. As luck would have it, a huge pregnant female bear was just emerging. Hyden barely had time to blink the smoke from his eyes and take in his surroundings when the protective mother roared out in protest. Hyden, not so used

146

to his newfound magical abilities that he instinctively went to them for defense, did what came naturally to him. He turned and ran.

His first few steps found purchase in the icy rock, but a steep, snow-drifted embankment swallowed him up as he fell into it. A moment later, with the bear lunging through the deep drift as if it weren't even there, Hyden burst out of its base. Like a tumbling stone, he flipped end over end down to the tree line opposite the quest party. Far too closely behind him, the enraged mother bear charged down the hill like a cat chasing a ball of yarn.

"B- by D- Doon," Oarly said loudly as he scrambled up onto a boulder to get a better look.

"Oh my," Telgra gasped, her sharp eyes able to see more vividly what the others were looking at.

"Krey, Mort, ready your bows, and get on your horses." Lieutenant Welch scrambled to his own animal. "We have to stop that bear before it gets him."

"No!" Telgra yelled. "Do not harm the bear."

The Lieutenant looked at her as if she were daft.

"It's a female, and she's with cub," Telgra pleaded while Hyden gathered momentum. "Just look at the swell of her belly."

"Hyden looks like a snowball now," Phen interjected with a chuckle. "He'll be all right, Lieutenant. The bear won't hurt him."

Lieutenant Welch studied Phen's expression. This was one of those moments the High King had warned him about. He had heard Hyden Hawk's speech about protecting the bear if she was with cub, but by the gods, if Hyden were to die out here, what then?

"Bron Omea Hedge," Hyden's voice called out from across the valley as he somehow managed to stop his tumble. He was pointing up beyond the other companions. "Bron Omea Hedge!" he yelled again. Then, with a look over his shoulder, he half limped and half ran into the thick row of trees that lined the stream at the valley bottom. The bear was right on his heels.

"By Doon, what did he say?" Oarly asked.

"I think he said 'brown over the ledge,'" Phen answered.

"He said 'run!'" Telgra shook her head at the two of them. "Run over the ridge."

"Why would he want us to run?" Phen asked. "Hyden needs our help. I'm not going to run. I'm going to help him. That bear can't hurt me." He stalked down into the trees on a line to where Hyden and the bear had entered.

"By the gods, King Mikahl was right," Lieutenant Welch said excitedly. "You people are mad, or drunk, or both." Even as he said the words, Lady Telgra darted off into the trees at a different point and in a different direction, but parallel to Phen's route.

Oarly tried to climb onto a loaded pack horse, but only managed to pull the packs loose and fall into a heap in the snow. The loud sound of branches crunching underneath something large and heavy echoed through the afternoon. Lieutenant Welch reluctantly jumped off his horse to help Oarly. "Lead the horses up to the ridge," he snapped at his men. "Hurry, we can't stand to lose the pack horses."

Jicks and the archers did as instructed. The lieutenant was glad he gave the order when he did, because just moments later his own horse bolted in terror when Hyden and the snarling bear came tearing out of the trees straight at them.

The lieutenant froze in shock. He'd never seen such a huge creature. Its wide, round head was as big as a horse's rump, and its tiny black eyes were full of something akin to rage. Nevertheless, without hesitation, he drew his blade and stepped protectively over Oarly, who was struggling in the deep snow.

"No!" Hyden tried to change his course away from them. He knew, though, that it was too late. The lieutenant was committed to protect the dwarf. A sadness came over Hyden that nearly caused him to falter. The last thing he wanted to happen was for the bear to get hurt. He didn't understand why Oarly hadn't fled with the others like he had told him to. Now, disaster was impending as Hyden streaked past and the bear turned its attention to the other two.

It was hard to say who screamed louder: Oarly, the lieutenant, or Hyden.

"Dien," a huge, bellowing voice thundered through the valley, overpowering all of them. "Sepan Leif! Dien! Dien!" the voice continued. Then in the unmistakable common tongue, the same voice said, "Stay your sword, man!"

To everyone's amazement, the bear, which was right upon them, lurched and veered past. The lieutenant's immaculately kept steel passed only inches from the creature's skin. In fact, a tuft of fur came floating lazily down toward the wide-eyed, shock-frozen dwarf at his feet.

Hyden dodged and twisted. He had expected to hear the grunting collision of flesh on flesh, or the lieutenant's armor crunching beneath the impact of the animal's great weight, but he didn't. Instead, he heard Borg. Not sure if the creature was still on his heels, he dove to the side and tumbled to a stop.

"Bahhh," Oarly growled as he got to his feet.

Hyden shook his head, trying to clear the cobwebs brought on by his tumble. His face was hot and stinging from where branches had raked and slapped it on his flight through the trees. His body was glazed in sweat, and now he was freezing, especially from his knees down where he was soaked from running through the stream.

Suddenly, Telgra's shrill scream cut through the air. Phen called her name twice from inside the wooded area at the valley bottom and then let out a yell himself.

Just as Hyden was finally able to turn and look in that direction, a big, hot-breathed muzzle engulfed his face. There were teeth and wild eyes. For a moment he thought it was the bear, but it wasn't. A huge, slobbering tongue sloshed across his cheek. The sensation, even the smell of the creature's breath, was familiar. Huffa didn't wait for his recollection. She pounced on him and began licking him as if he were a piece of salt rock.

The low, insistent growling of another pair of great wolves held Oarly's attention. The terrified dwarf was on his feet now, his dagger in one hand, and a small hatchet in the other. The wolves weren't growling at him, though. They were growling at the huge bear they were trying to herd away from the group.

"Urge her home, Oof," Borg called from the top of a rocky precipice at the head of the valley.

Standing there, with his staff in hand, silhouetted by the clear blue sky, he looked thirty feet tall, like some dark-robed arctic god. He was only half that height, but to those who had never seen a full-blooded giant he was as imposing as could be. Even the white-furred great wolves looked huge.

Borg started striding down the slope in that long, loping gait that only giants can manage.

Telgra's shrill shriek split the valley again, only this time it was tinged with delight, instead of terror. A moment later, she and Phen came out of the trees. She was riding one of King Aldar's great wolves, while Phen was jogging along beside them. Both were grinning broadly.

Chapter Thirty

"Well met, Hyden Hawk," said Borg, with a smile. Unlike the primitive-looking breed giants, Borg looked like a thrice overgrown man. While Oarly found this frightening, Phen and Lady Telgra were intrigued by his size. The soldiers had seen Borg when he was in Dreen, so to them, he was familiar. To all of them, his presence was both encouraging and a relief at the same time.

"I hope you're being sarcastic, my old friend," Hyden said. He stood and ruffled the scruff of Huffa's neck, then began brushing the icy debris off of his soaking wet britches.

"In those furred cloaks, I thought you were a pack of gremlets," Borg laughed. "I almost let nature take its course. Only your bowman's horse bolting through the trees gave you away."

"Thank you for intervening," Lieutenant Welch said. "Come on down, lads. Hobble the horses and build us a fire. Sir Hyden Hawk will be needing some heat."

"Thank you, Lieutenant," said Hyden.

"They are beautiful." Telgra looked up at Borg from the back of a young male great wolf.

"His name is Yip," Borg replied, taking in her elven features. Her amber gaze made her look wild. "I think he likes you." Borg's eyes scanned the others but then stopped on Phen. After a moment, he burst into a deep, rumbling laugh.

Phen scowled up at him and then glared at Hyden.

"Ah, young Phen," Borg sighed through his glee. "Hyden Hawk has told me much about you and your predicament."

"It's not funny," Phen said.

"No, I suppose it's not funny to you," Borg agreed. The giant looked at the soldiers leading the hesitant horses back into the valley. Then he glanced around the area until he saw Oarly. The dwarf was staring up at him and shivering.

"Master Dwarf," Borg said, bending at the waist to extend a hand down toward him.

Oarly looked unsure as to what to do with a hand that could cover his whole head as if it were an apple. Slowly he reached up, grabbed two of Borg's fingers, and shook them in greeting.

"Let's make camp here," Hyden ordered from his place by the pile of deadfall that Jicks was trying to light. "I would like to visit my friend's resting place, and I need to speak to the Southern Guardian alone."

Just then, Spike leapt out of the saddle pack in which he had been riding. The poor lyna was trembling with terror from the scent of the wolves. It leapt to the ground toward Phen, but the little spiked cat could do no more than hop a few inches at a time through the deep, fluffy snow.

"No!" Phen yelled sharply when Yip darted his nose in to sniff the creature.

The wolf jumped back, yelping loudly. One of Spike's needle-sharp quills was sticking out of its nose and Telgra was thrown from it's back. Being elven, Telgra's reflexes and grace allowed her to land well. Rising from her cat-like crouch, she fought away a flush of embarrassment and went to pick up the frightened lyna cat.

"Get yourself dry, then go, Hyden," Lieutenant Welch said after a moment. "If you two leave a few of those wolves behind to keep the bear away, we will be all right until you return."

Huffa left Hyden Hawk's side, and after growling and nudging at Yip, she took up a position a little above the camp where she could see the bulk of the valley. Yip wagged his way over to Borg, who checked the wolf's nose and gave him a loving pat on the head. After only a few minutes by the fire, Hyden, Borg, and two of the great wolves started into the trees to cross the valley.

Hyden saw the miraculous sight long before they were upon it. A ring that was twenty paces across formed of bright blue flowers encircled the rock pile grave where Loudin was buried. Despite the fact that it was mid-autumn, the flowers were in full bloom.

The man had died saving Ironspike from Pael's evil minions. Hyden remembered watching the sword tumble through the air only to bury itself in the center, where they later buried their friend. The blade's powerful magic no doubt fueled the magical growth. It was like a droplet of spring in an otherwise snow-covered opening in the forest.

"More men like Loudin in the realm, and it would be a far better place," Hyden said as they approached the burial mound. "I didn't know him long, but I knew him well. May the goddess grant him peace eternal."

"Well said," Borg murmured softly. He moved away and stood silently at the side for a while. He only spoke when Hyden stood and starting striding out of the magical circle of flowers.

"Where did the elven woman come from?" he asked. "There's an air about her."

"She's the daughter of the Queen Mother, Borg." Hyden shrugged as if it were all beyond him. His eyes were still glazed with the memory of Loudin, but he continued speaking, glad for the change of subject. "She has lost her memory, and seeks the Leif Repline."

"Why isn't she traveling with a group of her kindred?" Borg asked.

"They died in an attack on the Isle of Salaya."

"King Mikahl touched on that subject when I was in Dreen. What will she do once you've left the fountain pool and continue north for the Verge crystal? Does she know that the Leif Repline isn't your final destination?"

"Aye, she does," Hyden said. He looked skyward and grinned broadly. Talon was approaching. The hawkling was excited about something, but Hyden could tell that the bird was tired from carrying the extra weight of its condition. Borg followed Hyden's gaze and his expression went grim.

"King Aldar will be surprised at the size and composition of your party, Hyden. Five kingdom men, a dwarf, an elf, and a living statue are going to cause quite a stir in Afdeon."

Hyden held out his arm for Talon to land on. Already he and the hawkling were communicating mentally in a way that was second nature to both of them. Talon landed, and worked his way to Hyden's shoulder. Hyden absorbed Talon's thoughts as if he were drawing a breath into his lungs.

He looked up at Borg and cringed through his sheepish grin. "Make that six humans, two elves, a dwarf and a living statue."

"What?" Borg asked, his expression incredulous. "If there were more of you in these mountains, I would know."

Hyden chuckled uneasily. "An elf and a human monk are a little over a day behind us. They are what's left of Princess Telgra's party. I have to admire their persistence."

Borg snapped a command in the old language. The great wolf, Yip, listened alertly and then went bounding away. Borg wasn't showing distrust, Hyden knew; the Southern Guardian was upset that someone was in his land without his knowledge. To Hyden's surprise, a pair of chitter birds came spiraling down. They warbled around the giant's head, whistling and chirping intensely.

"Dien!" the giant called out so loudly that the birds darted a few feet away.

Yip, who was already tearing up the far valley side at breakneck speed, heard the command and slowed himself to return. "It seems my messengers are growing lax." Borg chuckled. "It is as you say. Do we divert them, leave them behind, or do you want to wait for them?"

Hyden sighed. "I think we'll wait." He took a piece of dried meat from his pack and fed it to Talon. The hawkling ate it greedily. "I only hope King Aldar will shelter us for the winter. I never intended for the group to grow this large."

"He wouldn't refuse you anything, Hyden Hawk." Borg gave a booming laugh. "As a matter of fact, he might even surprise you."

"Surprise me?"

"I'll not say more about it." Borg turned and started leading them toward the pass where the others were. "I wish I could join your quest." Borg's voice was sincere. "I'm anxious to see how your group fares after you leave the Leif Repline and King Aldar's protection."

"Doesn't King Aldar reign over all of the Giant Mountains?" Hyden asked. A sudden worry poked in his gut, like a pinprick in a wineskin. The subtle warning in Borg's tone was unmistakable.

"He does," Borg spoke as they walked. "But not all giants are civilized. Nor are all parts of these mountains rulable, especially the northern reaches near the Wedjak. How do you reign over a band of wild mountain trolls, or an ice wyrm? King Mikahl might hold reign over the kingdoms of men, but you can't tell me he controls what the Zard or the snappers do."

"I see," Hyden said uneasily. The pinprick in his gut was now a finger hole. Confidence was flowing out of him freely. His wineskin was emptying as if it were in Oarly's hands. He'd envisioned his group making it through the Giant Mountains without having to worry about being attacked. In his mind, common animals hadn't seemed a threat. He was so worried about demon kind, the Choskas and hellcats, that he had discounted the mountains' natural inhabitants.

He would have to rethink his plan. Another random encounter, such as the one with the mother bear, could end them all, if they weren't prepared.

Borg must have seen the concern on Hyden's face. "You'll be just fine, Hyden," he said. "You can communicate with the animals through Talon. You just have to remember to listen to what they say."

From not very far away, the disgruntled bear growled out a deep, rumbling warning. Hyden looked up to see that they were passing very close to the cave mouth. Oof came bounding up out of nowhere and positioned himself between them and the opening. Nevertheless, Hyden nearly had to run to keep up with Borg's suddenly brisk pace.

After they had gotten some distance away, Borg asked if there was meat.

"Not enough for two days," Hyden replied.

"There's a large herd of elk moving in a nearby valley," Borg said before barking out more orders to the great wolves. "We'll be fine as long as there's enough meat for this night. I'm so hungry I could eat a horse."

Hyden didn't laugh. Spoken by a human it would be an exaggeration, but spoken by Borg, it was something else altogether. Lieutenant Welch had the camp erected closer to the tree line. Hyden had to smile at Mikahl's choice of commanders. The more protected location would serve them well, since they would be waiting on the other elf and the monk. As Hyden and Borg neared, the whole pack of great wolves, save for Huffa, waggled and wiggled around Oof and Yip. Then all five of them were off to hunt elk as Borg had instructed them to do. Huffa, however, waited until Hyden took a seat on a log that the young soldiers had dragged out of the trees for just that purpose. The alpha female eased up beside him and put her white fluffy head in his lap.

"She knows you?" Telgra asked curiously. She was sitting across the fire from Hyden, on a blanket with Phen. She was staring into the flames and scratching the lyna's ears lovingly. As Hyden answered, Talon fluttered down to land on Phen's shoulder.

"Aye, my lady, she does. I have to tell you, though, there's an elf and a monk following us. They tried to catch us in Dreen. I think King Mikahl might have told you about them. They were with you before you were lost in the storm."

Her look soured. She seemed embarrassed as she spoke. "I don't remember them. I apologize if I am causing trouble for you."

"It's not me who they might offend, my lady," Hyden said. "We're going to wait for them. We can't keep leading them through the giant's realm. They'll meet an ill fate for certain."

She nodded that she understood his reasoning.

"There's more," Hyden continued, trying to choose his words carefully. "I know you don't remember much about yourself, but there's one thing you should know."

Hyden looked to Borg for help. The giant's expression showed that he was offering none. Hyden took a breath and got on with it. "You are the heir of the elven realm, Princess Telgra. Your mother is the Queen Mother, and though she knows that you are alive and safe, she doesn't know where you are, or the condition of your mind."

"I knew it!" Phen blurted out excitedly. To his surprise and obvious disappointment, her yellow eyes filled with tears. She shoved him away as she jumped up and started off. After two steps, she stopped, turned around, and picked up Spike, who had tried to follow her.

"Why did she start crying? Why is she so upset?" Phen asked.

What Hyden thought was a boulder wiggled and unfolded into an over-bundled hairy dwarf.

"She's a she," Oarly said, before taking a pull from his flask. He offered it to Hyden, who refused, but Borg reached his big hand over and took it. It looked like a thimble between the giant's fingers. "Woman folk, be they dwarves, humans, or even elves are peculiar at best. Give her a while to think. I'll go talk to her for you after that." Oarly reached up to take his flask back from Borg, who had squatted down among them.

Hyden had to laugh when Oarly shook the container and found it empty, then scowled up at the huge being. Borg returned his glare with a look that caused Oarly to blanch.

"I'll fetch some more," Oarly grumbled. "And a fargin bucket for ye to drink from," he added under his breath.

Borg heard Oarly and belted out a deep belly laugh. After a moment he said to Phen, "The dwarf is right. Giant women are no different."

Lieutenant Welch sat down nearby and began whetting his sword. "Aye. Is she really the Princess of the Elves?"

"Aye," Hyden answered with a sigh.

"You've all gone mad then."

Chapter Thirty-One

News of Petar's death, Commander Lyle's reassignment, and the skeleton's attack on O'Dakahn came to King Mikahl all in the same day. Cresson had made a sending to Master Wizard Sholt, who was currently on the Isle of Salazar with Lord Spyra, tracking down the men afflicted with Pael's taint. He relayed the information to De'Rain, the young mage at Lakeside Castle.

Unlike Cresson, De'Rain wasn't afraid to add his opinion to the messages he passed. He was so brazen that, when he first spoke to his king, Mikahl almost took offense. Luckily, Lady Able was there in the throne room when the news of Petar's death was announced. Her intervention kept Mikahl from reacting rashly to the insensitive way the information was given. By the time De'Rain brought the news of the attack on O'Dakahn to the High King's ears, the two of them had come to an understanding. The mage hadn't known that Mikahl was fond of Petar, and Mikahl hadn't known that De'Rain had been humiliated by Glendar on more than one occasion. The boy had later been forced by the Zard to use his magical skills to mend pots and make collars and harnesses for their four-legged geka mounts.

A lot of Westland folk were bitter. They had been overrun and forgotten while Mikahl fought beside King Jarrek to free the slaves from Ra'Gren. The people in the streets cheered for Mikahl, but he realized it was hope, not him, that they were calling out for.

It wasn't until Mikahl finally drew Ironspike before the nobles and merchants crowded in his court that true hope began to set in. To a man, the room took a knee. No one had seen the power of the blade since King Balton sat on the throne. Due to Balton's cunning, Glendar never once possessed it, and the Dragon Queen only carried her Spectral Staff. Mikahl settled Ironspike's blade into the display sleeve that was built into the throne at the end of the right armrest. He'd seen his father do this a thousand times, and he wasn't surprised when the whole throne lit up with the blade's humming blue power. The soft glow radiated a kind of promise not seen in Westland for years.

Mikahl had been fighting evil since he left the place, but something King Balton once said came to him: "Fear of the blade, and respect of its power, are far more potent weapons than the blade itself. The more you display Ironspike's might, the less you will have to use it." He thought about his father's words as he told the people to rise.

The people in court had seemed uncertain about him, but they were swelled with confidence now.

"De'Rain," Mikahl said softly. "Make a sending to our magister in O'Dakahn. Tell him that Commander Lyle is on his way and is to have full cooperation from all involved. A count of the skeletal remains should be made and the debris stored. All witnesses should be made available to the commander so that he can make a full, detailed report for me."

Until that day, Mikahl's stay in Westland had been filled with joy. Recollections from his early childhood came to him often and left him smiling. Queen Rosa was distracted from the places in the castle that caused her grief. Lady Able was pleasant, and the most capable of castellans. Rosa spent the days with the other ladies from the area, visiting in the great ladies' hall. There, women sewed and played games, but mostly gossiped about one thing or another. Several of Westland's strongholds were vacant, having been emptied by the Zard invaders. Aspiring noble-born and notable citizens were vying for lordships, and their wives pursued Rosa's favor relentlessly. Lady Able managed to keep things civil, but rumors and dirty looks were sometimes more plentiful than smiles among the women.

Rosa loved it. She had been raised in Seaward City and was accustomed to the games the lesser nobility played. Her mother, Queen Rachel, had taught her well. She found and marked her place as queen quite easily. From there, she used all the tidbits of information Lady Trella had fed her. Knowledge of a secret affair by a lady who was portraying innocence, or the many secret rivalries and friendships that existed among the women, came in handy when judging who to trust, and in whom to only feign interest.

With Rosa busily occupied during the day, Mikahl decided to see off the Lord of Locar and his marsh patrol. The Zard who had taken the knee and chose to remain in Westland were vocal against this intrusion into their lands. King Mikahl told them quite civilly that it wasn't their land. He was the High King of the realm. That included the marshlands. Many of the Zard found no love among the Westlanders they had once conquered anyway. Most of them had either fled back to the marshes or taken up residence around Lion Lake in the growing Zard community there.

The next morning, long before dawn, Mikahl kissed Rosa goodbye, and on the wings of the bright horse, he flew to Settsted. It was a sad sight to see the place where Lady Zasha had grown up in such a state of disrepair. The familiar smell of the marsh filled his nostrils and mingled with the smell of the boats and the refuse from yesterday's catch. It all stirred up memories long forgotten.

Many a week he had been at Settsted, both as Lord Gregory's squire, and then as King Balton's. Lady Zasha's father, Big Lord Ellrich, was the lord of Settsted then. Pael and King Glendar had emptied the outpost of men. Glendar did this because Pael told him to. Pael did it so that his daughter could lead the Zard out of the swamps and take over Westland with no resistance. Mikahl found that he had a bit of respect for Pael's military planning skills. Had the wizard not gone mad with demon power, he most likely would have succeeded in conquering the realm.

Mikahl landed the bright horse near the ruined wall that faced the marshes. He was struck by a particularly fond memory.

Lady Zasha had been Mikahl's first love, and a friend since childhood. In his teen years he had fished with her from the docks while his liege and her father hunted dactyls in the marsh. By all rights, Settsted Stronghold should go to her and her new husband, Wyndall. They currently lived on the Isle of Salazar. They owned the Lost Lion Inn and were instrumental in harboring refugees during the Zard occupation. Zasha had just given birth, Mikahl had heard. He knew she would refuse the position, but he would make the offer to them anyway. They had found happiness, and Zasha did not want her husband to be duty bound to anyone but her. Mikahl had to respect that. He could make the offer to no other, though, until after she formally refused her birthright. There was no doubt that the place would have to have a lord soon. His plan to reestablish a constant marshland patrol demanded it.

Most of the damage to the stronghold had been repaired, but not the side where Queen Shaella and Claret had first attacked. Most of the wall, and a good swath of the outlying village leading up to it, had been scorched permanently black with dragon's fire.

Climbing up onto the rubble of the ruined wall, Mikahl was surprised to see nearly twenty river boats and barges gathered along the shoreline. They were tied to bollard poles, personal docks, and even grappled to the bank for nearly half a mile. The sun had lit the sky and the soldiers were breaking camp. There was no way to house that many men at the stronghold, and Mikahl was actually surprised that more than two hundred men could be mustered to duty in Westland on such short notice. As he approached the camp of breed giants, where Bzorch was conferring with a pair of sergeants and a captain, he realized that the men weren't all Westlanders. Several were Dakaneese sellswords, and a few were tattoo-covered Seawardsmen.

"You'll have to tell them to forget the heavy armor," Mikahl said to the group of bowing commanders and the breed giant. "At ease," he snapped, so that they would get back to business. "The marsh is soft and wet. A man with heavy plate will get stuck or drown. Leather, or light ring mail is all that should be allowed."

"Make it so," Bzorch growled to the captain.

The order was relayed to both sergeants, who scurried off quickly, leaving Bzorch, the captain, and the High King relatively alone among the busy soldiers.

"Captain, Lord Bzorch is going to lead the foray. I want you to advise him." Mikahl smiled up at Bzorch when the captain paled. "You'll have to be firm. He might be big and ugly, but he's quite capable. And he will listen, if you voice your concerns."

"Yes, highness," the captain said uneasily.

"I don't want you to turn this into a Zard hunt, Bzorch," Mikahl said. "If you see large groups of armed Zard, take action. If you see that fargin lightning star banner flapping over their encampments, remove it." Mikahl looked up and met the breed giant's eyes. "I do not want you attacking family groups or peaceful settlements. The Zard are not your prey."

Mikahl was glad that only a small bit of disappointment showed in the breed giant's feral expression.

"What about hellcats and wyvern?" Bzorch asked hopefully.

"Hunt them down and bring me their heads," Mikahl said coldly. "There is a Choska loose, as I told you before. Since we last spoke, it has attacked O'Dakahn with a bunch of the skeletal men. If you see any of these fleshless or rotting men, take them apart. It's the only way to make them stay dead."

Mikahl turned and looked out across the vast grassy marshland. "It's that fargin Choska demon I want, though. It attacked O'Dakahn and killed fourteen men."

Bzorch gave a slight bow. "King Mikahl, it would please me to pike the Choska's head at O'Dakahn's front gate personally for you."

"Aye," Mikahl chuckled. "That would be spectacular. The sooner the better. You'll find it around the Dragon's Tooth Spire, I'm sure. Are we understood?"

Both the captain and the breed giant nodded in agreement.

"Good," Mikahl said. "I hope to hear news of your success soon."

With that, he strode away as another memory, one of skinny dipping in the river with Zasha and other adolescents came to him. It made him think of Queen Rosa and the passionate nights they had been spending back at Lakeside. He decided that he would pick a handful of fragrant river blooms for her. He was sure they would make her smile.

The Skyler Clan hadn't welcomed Corva and Dostin very well. The two were scolded severely by Hyden's father.

"If people just followed you haughty elves around, your precious hidden forest city would be full of kingdom folk, beasts, and other unwanted intruders as well," he told them. "Here you are, hungry and cold, and not dressed for the weather, and no less than trespassing in our village, and you have the gall to ask about things that are not even our concern. Be gone from here."

The lecture had been so cold that, after they left, Dostin cried. The verbal lashing made him feel small and wrong for being there. Corva didn't let it get to him, though; he led them around the village until he found the quest party's trail. The tracks were fairly recent and this heartened

Corva. After they put some distance between themselves and the angry Skyler Clan, Corva hunted while Dostin warmed himself by the fire. He killed a doe and they ate greedily. The elf showed the monk how to line his boots with scrap cloth from the extra clothes they carried. Multiple layers of britches and shirts under the monk's robe went far to keeping him warm. Corva doubled up his clothing, but suffered the cold so that Dostin might stay warmer. They walked the horses often to keep their blood flowing. Ultimately, the two traveling alone made better time than the quest party.

One day, the frigid mountain air pummeled them for hours, and the poor monk's fingers and ears turned black with the bite. The next day, when they pressed on into the deeper snow, Corva was losing his confidence. The previous night's snowfall had all but erased the trail they were following.

Dostin didn't complain, but Corva knew that they might soon have to turn back. After they skirted a cliff trail that the elf was sure the others had used, Dostin finally faltered.

Corva picked up the exhausted monk out of the snow and built a fire. He heated snow in a tin until it boiled. After it cooled, he made Dostin soak his purple fingers in it. One of the monk's ears was already blackened at the edges. Two of his fingers looked like they would be lost. Corva had all but decided to give up. He paced to stay warm while Dostin lay bundled in all of their blankets by the fire. That night was a bitter one, but the next morning was clear and sunny. Miraculously, Corva smelled the smoke of a cook fire on the breeze.

Dostin was already awake. The monk was praying and rocking back and forth where he sat. After a time, he rose and told Corva that he was ready to travel. Corva looked at Dostin's fingers. They looked better than the night before. The monk's ear, though, was awful to behold. Corva decided that if he could smell the cook fire, it couldn't be that far away; besides that, he wasn't sure anymore if he could get them back out of the mountains.

There wasn't much choice about it: either freeze to death trying to get out, or take a chance and hope that they found the others. It was with that grim thought that he continued leading them north.

They crossed a couple of rocky ridges and skirted the run of a valley when Corva saw a pile of frozen horse dung. The smell from the cook fire had disappeared for most of the day, but as dusk stole the light from the sky he picked it up again. He didn't want to, but they camped. Fuel for burning was scarce, so their fire was small. The next morning, one of Dostin's ears tore from his scalp like a scab. He whimpered in pain, but didn't otherwise complain. Their perseverance was rewarded when they crossed the next ridge. Below them, waiting, as if they knew they were being followed, was the quest party. It was a shock when a pack of great wolves came bounding up to escort them into the camp. It was even more shocking when they finally gained the warmth of the bonfire and Princess Telgra looked at them as if they were strangers.

If he hadn't been in shock, and on the verge of freezing to death, Dostin would have cried.

The Wizard and the Warlord

Chapter Thirty-Two

The Queen Mother sat at the base of the Heart Tree in the throne formed by its tangle of roots. Behind her back, its trunk rose up hundreds of feet. It marked the center of the magical elven forest that was currently amid the trees of the Evermore. The dense woods were littered with piles of brown, russet, and gold. Most of the trees were bare, resembling grotesque bark-skinned beasts looming among the taller firs and pines that rose up proud and green like soldiers at attention. The elven court was gathered there in a long, narrow glade before the towering Father Tree. Word of Princess Telgra's appearance in the Skyler Clan village was revealed to them. The Queen Mother was worried, frightened, and angry all at once. More mother than queen at the moment, her state of distress was a concern to the family heads gathered there.

The Elmkin were concerned for the princess's safety, while the Oakhearts thought that the experience she was gaining exploring the realm would most likely help her in the future.

"Some of life's lessons are impossible to teach," they said. "Life must be lived, experiences experienced."

The Birchbloods and the smaller families, the Cherrylorns and Teakflows, all agreed with the Queen Mother, that a party must be sent to fetch Telgra at once. The Bramblers, as well as the soldiers and sentinels, held no opinion. As usual, they only stood at the ready, armed with ironwood blades and bows that could launch an arrow most of a mile. With a word, they would be off to retrieve their princess.

Some of the old and powerful members of the Hardwood Coalition voiced the idea that if Princess Telgra lost her memory, then it was clear that the humans and the new king were filling her head with nonsense. After all, it was this new High King who had personally killed a dozen innocent trees in a rage not too long ago.

Much had been whispered from ear to keen ear before the gathering. Positions were being declared, sides taken. Now, waiting for the Queen Mother to decide on what should be done, they all stood silent and waiting, save for one. One elf dared to step forward and speak; it was Dieter Willowbrow.

"Queen Mother," said Dieter nervously as he rose from his bow. "I only ask that you take a moment to read my brother's journal. Read the words Vaegon wrote about Hyden Skyler and Mikahl Collum. I ask this because Hyden Hawk is who they say the princess travels with, and Mikahl is the one they now call High King." Dieter took a knee and extended Vaegon's journal toward his queen. One of the sentinels strode forth and took the volume.

"This tome won't keep the future of elven kind safe, young Dieter," the Queen Mother said softly. "What is it you think these words will convey to me?"

Dieter swallowed hard. What he was about to say would go against the Hardwood Coalition theories. Friction with the Hardwoods was never a wise thing to cause. "It has been suggested that King Mikahl might use Princess Telgra's loss of memory to the advantage of man. The person Vaegon describes in those pages is far too honorable for that."

"Is that all?" the Queen Mother asked sharply.

"No, my queen." Dieter's voice gained a little surety as he spoke. "Once you've read what my brother had to say about Hyden Skyler, then I'm confident your heart will feel lighter for it. My princess travels with this man. She is not in as much danger as any of you fear."

The Queen Mother nodded to the sentinel and accepted the journal from him. The court stood in respectful silence as she flipped through the pages, reading them one by one, taking in the words Vaegon had written throughout his strange journey with Hyden Hawk and young Mikahl.

Several members of the Hardwood Coalition exchanged looks of concern. They represented the majority of the elven kind, at least the majority of the older elves living here in the Evermore forest.

When the Queen Mother was done reading, she handed the text back to the sentinel and gave Dieter a warm smile full of understanding and love.

Vaegon's words eased her concern, if only slightly. Still, worry for Telgra was paramount, but there was no doubt in her heart that Hyden Skyler and the High King of men were not typical humans.

"Is there anyone else who would speak to me before I seek the solitude of the Arborhaven?" she asked.

One of the Hardwoods stepped forth. Dieter was receiving his brother's journal back from the sentinel and the older elf casually shouldered him out from in front of the queen. Etiquette dictated that Dieter say nothing. The elder of the Redwoods had been alive more than four hundred years. Dieter was barely sixty. All he could do was hold his tongue, swallow his pride, and move away.

"Queen Mother," Revan Redwood said, with only the slightest of bows. Due to his age he could get away with that sort of thing. "The king of men, however honorable he may be, has already murdered in the forest. He is cocky, hot tempered, and is only as powerful as the sword he carries." The old elf frowned and shrugged. "Words written by an elf serving a life debt to a kingdom man are only words."

"What would you have me do then, Revan?" the Queen Mother asked. "Should we go to war with the kingdom folk? We are the ones who gave Ironspike its power, Revan. And don't forget that Hyden Skyler is not a kingdom man. Vaegon Willowbrow was serving a life debt to a man of the giants' realm, not the kingdoms'. This is about my daughter, the princess, and the future of our race. She is your princess, too. This isn't about your personal feelings toward the humans. How would battle help bring Telgra back from the land of the giants? That is where she has traveled."

She was growing angrier with every word she spoke. Her mate had died in the demon attack on the island. The loss, and the stress of worrying about her daughter, was pushing her to the edge.

"My daughter is seeking the Leif Repline to restore her memory. Who can fault her for that? She... she... she... doesn't even remember who she is. She... she..." With that, the Queen Mother rose and stormed off, brushing away the supporting hands of her sentinels.

"The Queen Mother will retire to the Arborhaven," the announcer spoke over the murmurs. "When she has reached a decision on the matter, we will reconvene."

A moment later, as the gathered elves were dispersing back into the forest, a statement was overheard by some. It came from the Hardwoods gathered at the clearing's edge.

"This wouldn't be happening if a Hardwood sat on the throne."

Several gasps followed, and more than one grunt of agreement.

"Ouch!" Dostin yelped as Hyden used tiny rays of magical energy to trim away the dead flesh from around the monk's earholes. "That hurts, Hyden Hawk," he whined. The sadness he felt at not being recognized by Lady Telgra was palpable. Corva was speechless. Even knowing she had lost her memory didn't prepare him for the total lack of recognition. The words of Lady Trella hadn't fully described the situation. Corva figured that Telgra might not have remembered the storm, or the horrible death of her father. He never expected her to draw a blank for her entire life.

Telgra sat at the fire not far from Dostin, studying him curiously. He had asked her a hundred questions about the time they shared at the fiery tree grove. The only thing she remembered was the dream she'd had about the red priest, the demons, and Phen.

Dostin wanted desperately to rekindle their friendship. It was clear that he was disturbed. She answered him politely and understood completely how she could have liked him so much. He was simple, but thoroughly sincere.

"How did you find the statue man?" Dostin asked.

"He's called Marble Boy," Hyden said with a chuckle.

"His name is Phen," Telgra corrected both of them. Spike let out a little growl from her lap.

"He and Master Oarly found me in the marshes." Telgra shifted herself as she answered him.

"The dwarf smells like Father Shaw's goats," Dostin observed, causing a laugh from all who heard.

Telgra had gone over the story half a dozen times, trying to ease the frightened monk's confusion. Knowing that he had nearly frozen to death, lost an ear and parts of his fingers because he was concerned for her, was unnerving. She was endeared to him, though, and she handled his questions with an enormous amount of patience.

It was getting late in the afternoon and the others were chopping and wrapping the meat from a big cow elk that the wolves had killed. They had returned earlier, all wiggling and excited, with bloody muscles and a few limps amongst them. Borg had taken Jicks, Krey, and three horses over the ridge to haul it back. Those who weren't involved in the bloody work - Phen, Oarly and Corva -were on the far side of the fire discussing the storm that had washed them into the marsh.

"What I wouldn't give for the warmth of that swamp," Oarly said. He was too drunk to stutter or shiver, and was speaking quite loudly.

Phen patted him on the shoulder. He urged Talon, who was the exact same marbly shade of white, from his shoulder to his wrist. He went over to watch Hyden work on Dostin's ear. Borg had promised a warm and dry place to study in Afdeon, but the giant hinted that they wouldn't want to sit around reading books after they got a few days' rest. The giant wouldn't elaborate, even when Phen questioned him about it. Borg had far less patience for being questioned than Princess Telgra did.

"Where is it we are going after we leave the Leif Repline, and what's this place Borg calls the Wedjak?" Phen asked Hyden as he took a seat next to Telgra.

"I'm not sure what it is," Hyden answered as he worked intently on Dostin's mangled ear. "But …" He held his tongue out the side of his mouth and did something that made Dostin wiggle and whine. "…it's called the Tokamak-Verge. The Wedjak is the old word for 'wild place'." Hyden scratched his head and looked at Phen for a moment. "My father, in his youthful roamings, once traded with a group of men from the Wedjak. He said they were brown-skinned with strange hair colored blue, red, and green. They were savage, yet willing to negotiate for furs and meat. They all agreed to gather again the next year in the same place, but the strange people never returned."

"What did they have to trade for your furs and meat?" Telgra asked.

"Wardstone," Hyden answered.

"Maybe Xwarda isn't the only place where there is Wardstone," Phen stated. "What does this Tokamak-Verge do?"

"You're done, Dostin," Hyden said with a wrinkle-faced look at his work. It wasn't pretty, but the rot was cut away, and there was still a little shape left to the mangled nub of ear that remained.

"It looks like a half-dried leaf is stuck to his head," Phen said.

"It does not," Telgra said with a sharp look. She then urged Dostin to sit on the other side of her. "It looks just fine, Dostin. Don't listen to him."

"You'll see it when we get to Afdeon," Phen said. "They'll have a reflecting glass, or at least a still bowl of water to see it in."

Dostin didn't seem to care how it looked. He appeared completely content to be warm and sitting close to his friend, Telgra.

Hyden was glad that he didn't have to answer Phen's question about the Tokamak-Verge. In the old language, the words meant power-boundary. According to the goddess, who as of late had become Hyden's confidant, the legendary artifact could channel a magical power source to create a binding or boundary. All Hyden knew was that, with enough power input, the seal of the barrier between the world of men and the world of demons could be made unbreachable. Some of the boundaries that separated the high heavens from the planes of demigods, and even some of the planes of hell, had supposedly been separated by the thing. Whether it was a sword like Ironspike, or a jewel like the dragon tear, Hyden had no clue. He only knew that he could now sense its presence far to the north of them. With it, he hoped to use Ironspike's power to seal away the thing his brother had become for good. It was the only way, the goddess had explained. It was the only chance he had to protect human kind without having to kill Gerard.

After destroying the old Abbadon, Gerard had assumed the powers of darkness. Hyden had no choice but to either kill his brother, or make certain he was imprisoned in the Nethers for good. Since he'd put Illdach's ring on his finger, the power of light had filled him. He was certain that if the balance of dark and light was tipped one way or the other, the forces would right themselves, trying to find the center quickly and harshly. Hyden figured that he and Gerard could coexist in their separate worlds, or that they would eventually be forced to kill each other. He figured that if he killed Gerard, his own demise would swiftly follow. The sole and true purpose of this expedition beyond the Leif Repline was rooted in finding a way for him and the warlord his brother had become to live on, instead of tearing apart the very fabric of existence trying to kill each other.

He knew it was selfish to try to keep himself and the Warlord of Hell alive. Keeping the balance, though, was a must.

The goddess, a wise and knowing being of the greater heavens, had been encouraging his current course of action, so he felt for now that he was doing what was right.

At least Phen, Talon, and Princess Telgra would be healed on this journey. That alone made the risks worth taking.

The next morning, Borg led them through a light flurry of fat snowflakes on a course that wound around Loudin's valley. Two of the great wolves had sped off to inform King Aldar of their approach. The trails Borg followed were easily traveled by a giant, but many obstacles forced the humans, and mainly Oarly, to have to climb over what was in the way. The horses seemed to cause the biggest delay; even with Oof and Huffa herding them, they still managed to find dead-end pockets in the rocky valleys. One horse, carrying a trunk of books Phen had brought along, slipped on a loose patch of ice while edging the canyon. He slid over, rolled and thrashed for a heartbeat, then plummeted a few hundred feet only to slam with an audible thump into a huge slab of granite. Telgra screamed in horror when she looked over the edge. Dostin retched, and Oarly almost went over the edge after it trying to look down and see the mess. Luckily, it wasn't the horse carrying Vaegon's bow. From that moment on, Hyden slung the familiar quiver over his shoulder, strung Vaegon's gift to him, and carried it at the ready.

THE WIZARD AND THE WARLORD

The weather grew worse and the terrain more treacherous the deeper into the mountains they went. Blinding wind carrying sharp, abrasive granules of ice burned and stung their flesh. After a bitter week of it, it began to seem like the journey would never end.

Up in the higher passes, breathing became next to impossible. Snow drifts that were deeper than Borg was tall filled the crags and cracks. It was hard going, and cold beyond imagining at times, but finally they topped a ridge so high that they were above the the clouds. A sea of pillowy soft whiteness spread out across a great mountain-tipped bowl. In the center of this godly creation, rising up out of the clouds like some heavenly island, was a silvery gray castle of immense proportion.

"I give you Afdeon."

"B- B- B- By D- Doon," Oarly said in awe when his eyes took it all in.

"Doon had nothing to do with this marvel," boasted Borg. "Dwarves aren't the only ones who can work steel and stone."

No one would have tried to argue, even if they could have found words, for the majesty of what was before them was truly indescribable.

THE WIZARD AND THE WARLORD

Chapter Thirty-Three

The sweltering heat that hung over the marshes was taking its toll on Bzorch and the other breed giants. They had large, bulky bodies and, though they didn't quite have fur like an animal, they did have thick tufts of hair. Bzorch's determination overpowered the fact that his body was made for colder climates. To him, it was merely an irritation, but to some of the others, the constant humidity and the stinging, biting insects were debilitating. Bzorch suffered the uncomfortable days without complaint, and with snarls and angry looks he kept his small group of breed from complaining, as well. At the moment, though, the sweaty discomfort wasn't even on their minds.

The excitement of the chase had them alert and on edge. They'd worked for two full days, skirting low-lying land masses, and negotiating channels and shallow expanses of water that were hidden under a blanket of waist-high grass. Tangly patches of drooping trees rose up out of the ground that had managed to stay above the water line. The further they went, the more dense and abundant these islands became. By the time the curvy fang-shaped spire was visible in the distance, the world around the deep channels the boats were traversing had become a full and formidable jungle.

It was late on the second day when they saw the Zard nest. There were thirty, maybe forty Zard-men, all armed and wearing studded leather armor with Queen Shaella's lightning star emblem emblazoned on their breasts. They were encamped in a clearing hidden by a densely treed tangle. Oddly, they didn't attack when they were spotted. The Zard quickly climbed up on several of the large geka lizards they favored, five and six to a mount. It was then that the chase began.

Two boatloads of soldiers stormed onto the land, followed by a pair of breed giants, one carrying a dragon gun, the other carrying the long coil of rope that made the device so treacherous to airborne creatures. Bzorch commanded the rest of the group to stay on the boats. He told the men ashore to stick with their shipmates, but to each take a different way around the island. It was a wise decision for the men chasing the Zard on foot. They found that the terrain was littered with trap after deadly trap. Thatch covers fell away, revealing staked pits. Half a dozen men were impaled on sharpened bamboo spears that jutted up from the muddy bottom. Some of those who skirted the holes found their calves and shins sliced open by poisonous brambles that had been cleverly placed. The trail the group followed led right to a large snapper nest, and when the men were finally forced to retreat, swinging branches and sandy mud slops that swallowed one man whole, took their toll as well.

The dragon gunner got off a shot at one of the fleeing geka lizards. The forearm-length barbed spear arced through the air, trailing its unwinding coil behind it like a streamer. It struck true and the rope-man had the presence of mind to quickly wrap the free end of the tether around a nearby cypress tree before it snapped taut. The geka thrashed and screamed out when it was yanked to a stop. The four Zard riding it were thrown forward into the surrounding muck. An anxious snapper snatched one of them up in its jaws and slithered away. One Zard was left twitching and sputtering in the mud after smacking hard into a tree. The other two fled into the jungle on webbed feet, disappearing quickly into their natural habitat.

Of the thirty men who had started the foot chase, only ten and the breed giants returned.

Bzorch's group was following the channel. He stood at the helm, holding one of the dragon guns like some great hunter. They didn't see much. Eventually they had to turn back because the channel dead-ended into a cacophonous cove full of big, shrieking dactyls, who apparently nested there.

The other group had found the place where the gekas had crossed from one land rise to another. A small group went after them to more carefully follow their trail. Soon, though, daylight began to fade, and they were forced to rejoin the others where they had run the barge ashore and made a camp.

The geka the breed giant had impaled on his dragon spear was being butchered and roasted. Over twenty men had died on this first encounter, and a handful of others were injured. Bzorch had the wounded put on a small boat. It would start back to Settsted in the morning. Some of the men needed to be taken back immediately, but the breed giant knew that the boat wouldn't get far traveling at night.

The returning trackers said that the geka trail led eastward, away from the Dragon's Tooth. Bzorch grunted at this news and silently munched on a meaty haunch of geka meat by one of the large campfires. He was primitive, but he was no fool. He wouldn't be tricked by the obvious misdirection. Already, the clever skeeks had bested them once.

There was no dry wood in these parts, and the grass that had been heaped on the coals created billowing clouds of smoke.

"Captain Hodge," Bzorch said as he waved the thick smoke from the front of his face. "Is it a ploy to lead us away from the fang?"

"Aye, maybe so," Hodge replied. It was clear he was beginning to respect Bzorch's instinct about things. Being an alpha breed, Bzorch's instincts were keen. He liked Hodge, because the man didn't seem to fear his presence like most humans did. Hodge licked the grease from his fingers. "What do you suggest we do?" he finally asked.

"I say we split into two forces," Bzorch said through a mouthful of geka meat. "One large group to move directly on the fang, and one smaller group to work out in flanks, just in case."

"You want to attack the Dragon Spire?"

"If we chase these bands out here around the outer marshes, we just thin our numbers," said Bzorch. "If there is a Choska roosting up in that hole, it will do what it has to do to keep us from finding it. They aren't so easy to kill, and they can control the Zard."

"You fought a Choska before then?" the captain asked.

"Killed one in the battle of Seareach," Bzorch said, pounding his fist on his chest. "Killed a few hellcats and managed to get a barb in that nasty fargin black dragon, too."

Hodge nodded respectfully. He hadn't known. A flaw in Bzorch's plan occurred to him, but it didn't seem very probable that all the outlying bands of Zard would surround them and pin them in once they got to the dragon's fang. He kept his thought to himself. Bzorch had probably already considered it. No doubt it was why he wanted to spilt the group in two.

A gasping murmur swept across the encampment. Men were pointing up at the sky and whispering nervously. Both Bzorch and Captain Hodge looked up, but nothing was immediately visible. Suddenly Bzorch growled and pointed directly above them. Hodge followed the breed giant's finger. The dark shapes only became discernible because they eclipsed the stars as they circled.

"Two small to be a Choska," Bzorch said. "And far too big to be a dactyl. Either a wyvern or a hellcat. Either way, something's brewing out here, even bigger than King Mikahl suspects."

"What should we do?" Hodge asked.

"I think we send two separate sets of messengers to inform the High King." To Hodge, Bzorch seemed pleased. "The boat carrying the wounded, and another, hastier group, to ensure our words reach him. This is going to turn into very bloody business, Captain."

THE WIZARD AND THE WARLORD

Bzorch met Hodge's gaze with a feral-looking grin that revealed the breed giant's fangs. In the firelight, he looked far less human than he ever had.

Captain Hodge shuddered involuntarily. He was glad that he wasn't one of those Zard out there, or one of those dark winged beasts. He was quite certain that Bzorch was going to enjoy killing them all.

The Abbadon left Shaella's body lying in her guarded cave, at least for the moment. Outside, several dozen Zard and the Choska demon stood watch. All of them were on edge now that the kingdom men had ventured into their territory.

In the morning, when the men didn't follow the trail he'd intended them to, the Warlord became miffed. He wasn't disappointed, though. He had other ways to stop them. In an outright battle between them and Shaella's trained Zard they would be easily eliminated. It was the reptiles' natural habitat, after all.

Standing with his dark, leathery wings spread wide in the darkness of the Nethers, he let out a long, streaking gout of dragon's fire. With the flaming pillar came a roar of summoning. In the yellow light, his elongated humanoid form glistened and reflected wetly. His plated hide was covered with a thick, glossy coat of greasy film. His legs were squat but powerful and gave way to an overly long torso. A barbed tail curled out from behind him, flicking this way and that whimsically. His hard-plated chest and well-muscled arms rippled, and the black claws on both hands and feet were as hard and sharp as steel daggers. His head still retained its humanoid shape, save for the open nose on the end of its slightly snouted maw. Long, ropy tendrils of hair hung crudely down from a face which vaguely resembled Gerard Skyler. They were still Gerard's eyes. They were the size of melons, but they were perfectly human. Only a tiny bit of the once hopeful and good-hearted boy's mentality remained inside the beast of beasts, though. The look of Gerard's determination, however, hadn't changed at all.

The yolk of the dragon egg he'd once eaten had caused the physical changes that had racked, stretched, and twisted his body into what it was now. His savage dominance over the demons and devils he'd killed and consumed changed the rest of him. He had become their master, and they would come to his call, if they were wise.

Slowly, the dark things that dwelled in the depths of the hells scurried and glided into the expanse of blackness before him. The hate, the pain, and the magnitude of the evil was rooted inside him. They could hide or flee, but he would remember and feast on them when he found them. Even the most powerful of creatures feared to face the Warlord in battle. He had bested Deezlxar, the former ruler of the hells. Now, two of Deezlxar's dragon heads sat flanking the Warlord's throne. The decorations were to remind all of how much power he wielded.

After a while, the space around Gerard was filled in all directions, and still more hellish things were arriving. Minotaurs, spidery things, six-legged cyclopeans, and all sorts of ember-eyed insectazoids had come and were now milling about, sharpening their weapons or displaying their venomous stingers.

Suddenly, another gout of fire erupted straight up from the Warlord's terrible maw. The hissing, growling, and jostling stilled to a deathly silence.

"Soon," the Abbadon boomed with a voice that shook the very ethereal substance of which the Nethers were formed. "Soon I will loose you back into the world above. Soon you will bring terror and destruction to mankind in my name. Soon!"

A murmur of excited approval spread through the crowd of hellspawn. The anticipation grew as Gerard told them what he wanted them to do. Even though he had very little power in Shaella's resurrected body, he did have absolute power in his domain. Some of these demons and devils he commanded had servants and worshipers in the world above. Now he would bring them to bear.

If the High King was sending men and beasts to hunt for him, then he had to take action. He wasn't prepared to send Shaella to Xwarda yet, and he had no other lair to retreat to. All he could do was have his minions buy him the time he needed.

He could not rush this. He would not, could not, fail. To do so would be a possibly eternal mistake. Soon, he would turn his subjects loose on the marsh invaders. He was anxious to witness just how much power he commanded. As he slid his consciousness back into Shaella's body, he decided that he would ride the Choska's back so that he might watch more closely as his influence was manifested on earth.

Chapter Thirty-Four

After gawking at King Aldar's immense and spectacular castle, and catching their breath from the long climb up, Borg led them back down a switchback ramp into the pillowy mist of clouds. After some time, they found themselves in a huge cavern. As it was late in the day, Borg suggested they camp there. The journey over to Afdeon, he explained, would take most of the morrow.

As they laid out their bed rolls, Borg built a fire. Huffa gave Hyden a farewell lick and raced off with the other wolves. Talon sped off after them, and for the first time since they'd been in the mountains, Spike yawned and stretched then roamed about the companions.

"How is it possible to get to yon castle in only a day?" Oarly asked.

"There are tunnels and passes that lead to other tunnels that will get us there," Borg shrugged. "That's about as well as I can explain it."

"Are they portals?" Phen asked excitedly. He had read about portals. His first instructor, Master Targon, had conjured one to save King Jarrek from Pael's attack on Castlemont. Phen had heard the tale from the Red Wolf, as well as from Brady Culvert. Once, on a long shipboard journey, Brady had described the portal in detail.

Phen suddenly had to shake his head to get rid of the vision that came to him. He'd seen Brady partialy melted and killed by a vicious black dragon's acidy spew. Luckily, Phen's fascination with the idea of portals was enough to ease him past the sudden well of sadness.

"I think it may be portal magic, Phen," Borg answered. "But that sort of conjuring is beyond me. I'm a mountain guardian and my ability is limited. Besides that, my visits here are few and short."

Phen deflated after finding he wasn't about to learn something.

"You'll not be staying with us, then?" asked Hyden.

"No, my friend," the giant answered. "An escort will come in the morning and take you from here. I have duties, you know."

"Aye." Hyden nodded his respectful understanding. "You have my thanks for aiding us."

"I'm not leaving you just yet." Borg grinned. "We've an evening to share before we part ways. There's plenty of meat left, and the dwarf has liquor. I say we enjoy this warm, sheltered camp by getting fat and full of drink. It may be awhile before we meet again."

"Aye," Hyden agreed. "Well said, my friend."

Hyden never passed up the chance to hear a story. Giants were the best storytellers, and he knew that after a few drinks Borg would spin a yarn. Hyden and Gerard had grown up hearing tales from a giantess named Berda. He was so hopeful that thoughts of Gerard, for once, didn't bring him down.

Oarly reluctantly donated a small keg to the affair. The soldiers set up a spit and began roasting the remaining chunks of elk meat. Dostin took a flask from the dwarf and went around the camp filling cup after cup until Oarly snatched it back from him.

Corva spoke softly to Princess Telgra, but she made an irritated face and strode over to where Phen and Hyden were sitting. The elven guard hadn't been offensive, he had merely been telling her things about herself. He was clearly trying to spark her memory, but Telgra just didn't want to know yet. She found she was starting to dislike Corva's insistence. His prodding and constant reminding of the self she didn't remember made her want to scream.

Corva was growing concerned. Telgra didn't remember anything about her childhood, nor her mother, nor her duty to her people. Corva had intentionally stayed away from the subject of her father. His death was still sharp in his own mind and he didn't want to add to Telgra's distress. The fact that she had grown fond of the marbleized human boy was an outrage, but he forced himself to hide his envy. He actually liked Phen, but when he saw them sitting close, or sometimes walking hand in hand, Corva found himself simmering with something he had to work to subdue. At those times, not even Dostin's innocent pestering could break his sullen mood. He let the monk fill his cup, though, in hopes that a few sips of the potent liquor might lift his spirits. Soon they were all feeling the effects of the dwarf's drink, save for Phen, who wasn't able to swallow, but clearly enjoyed the way the brandy loosened Telgra's tension. She was practically falling all over him after only her second cup.

"Master Dwarf," she slurred, "how do you drink so much of this fire brew? Two cups and I've lost my wits."

"You lost your wits long before you started sipping," Oarly joked. "That's why you're on this fargin journey."

Everyone laughed, except for Corva and Dostin. The worrisome elven guardsman didn't crack a smile until seconds later when Dostin spoke. "What's a wit?" the monk asked.

"I want to make a toast," Hyden said, with a pat on Dostin's shoulder. He had only sipped from his first cup of brandy. Borg, though, had commandeered a small cooking pot and had emptied it twice.

After whispering into Dostin's ruined ear what "wits" were, Hyden raised his glass. "To our giant friend, who saved us from freezing our arses off."

"Hear, hear," Lieutenant Welch added, as did a few of the others.

Everyone mumbled a fond word or two to the humble giant. Then Hyden took Borg's pot and filled it from one of the kegs piled in their gear.

"Since it might be a long while before we meet again," Hyden said as he handed the giant back his makeshift cup, "can I trouble you for a tale?"

"Yes, another story," Princess Telgra slurred with a girlish giggle.

"Tell us a tale," Jicks and the archers echoed.

Not even Lieutenant Welch's sharp look at them for speaking out of place could quell their excitement.

"Pleeease," Telgra begged.

"All right," Borg agreed. "Let me think a moment." He took a long swill from his pot and then began his telling.

"This one is for Princess Telgra, my friends," he said almost apologetically. "There will be no blood and gore in it." The young soldiers groaned their disappointment, but Borg ignored them and continued. "But since it involves a princess and a mountain troll, and you have a princess among you, I'll tell this tale. After all, the chances of you completing your journey through these mountains without meeting a hungry flesh-eating troll are thin at best."

That was enough to draw the young men's attention.

"There once was a fair princess named Karsen. She was as beautiful as a flower, and as tender as a babe. The farms around her father's kingdom were constantly being bothered by a cattle-stealing troll that was as mangy and mean as the day is long. The king had his knights, and they had their proud horses, and nearly every day they rode out to fight with the beast. At night the horses all gossiped around the stalls of the royal stable, each bragging about one feat or another that they'd performed afield." Borg resituated himself and took a sip of the dwarf's liquor.

"Well, one day, the stableman's cart-nag gave birth to a pony. It was the ugliest pony to ever be born. All black-and-white spotted like a milk cow, with a huge lump on its head between its ears. The knight's horses all made fun of the ugly pony, calling it names and teasing it to tears every day."

"Then one day the princess came to see the ugly pony she'd heard the knights talking about at her father's table. When she came into the barn, the other horses were calling the poor teary-eyed colt names like "lumpy head", and "milk horse". The princess felt so bad for the creature that she asked her father if it could stay in the garden, away from the mean old destriers.

"Her father, unable to deny Karsen her heart's desires, commanded that a single stable stall be built in the corner of the garden yard for the ugly animal.

"Every day, Princess Karsen came and visited the colt and they became fast friends. When it was big enough to ride, she rode it around the garden and inside the bailey. She treated the ugly steed as if it were the most magnificent stallion in the realm. Soon she began to see a change coming over her four-legged companion.

"While all this was going on, the savage troll was growing bigger and bolder. The knights could no longer frighten it away when it came to eat from the farmers' flocks and herds. One day the troll scared the king's men back into the castle and stood at the gate, pounding away.

"'What do you want?' the king asked from the top of a tower.

"'I want to eat the princess,' the troll replied. 'If you let me eat her, I will leave your lands alone forever more.'

"The king told his knights to make the troll go away, but even the bravest of the destriers were afraid of the huge, foul beast. As soon as they were close to the creature, they would buck and throw their riders and flee. Throughout the day and into the night, the troll kept pounding away.

"At the table that night, the princess told her father that she and her pony had heard what the troll said. To the king's surprise, she also told him that her ugly horse wasn't afraid, that it would proudly carry one of his knights out to face the troll. The knights at the table, despite their fear of what was waiting for them, couldn't help but laugh.

"'The horse is half cow,' one said.

"'It's got a melon growing on its head,' said another.

"'Maybe the troll will die laughing at it,' the first knight added."

Borg stopped to take a long drink from his pot. Everyone in the cavern was captivated, not only by his story, but by the smooth, deep voice with which he told it. The sudden lack of speech made them antsy.

"Come on," urged Jicks. "What happened?"

"Be patient, lad," Oarly said. "Let him wet his voice."

Princess Telgra was resting her head on Phen's shoulder. Her eyes were glazed and dreamy as the images the giant's words evoked slowly faded from her mind. Just when she was about to ask Borg to continue, he did.

"What the king, the knights, and the skittish destriers didn't know was how much the ugly pony had changed." Borg wiped at his mustache and went on. "While living in the garden stall, only the princess had paid the pony any attention. His black and white splotchy color had spread and blended until his coat was a shimmering silvery gray. His tail and mane, and the tuffs above his hooves had all turned snowy white. The most profound change, though, was that the lump on his head had extended into a long, curling spike of pearlescent ivory that was as sharp as a spear tip.'"

"A unicorn." Princess Telgra grinned.

"Just so," Borg continued. "The very next day, the old troll started banging on the gates again, and the king ordered his knights to drive it away. Once again, the destriers balked, unable to overcome their instinctual fear of the huge troll. Again, the knights spurred the horses in, but they refused.

"'Are you big, strong horses afraid?' a voice asked from the bailey.

"The princess sat atop her unicorn, who was chastising the terrified destriers that had once made fun of it.

"'Who are you?' one of the knights asked. 'Where did you come from?'

"'I'm the milk horse, the lump-headed pony,' he said, puffing out his chest proudly. 'I may be ugly, but I'm not afraid like these nags are. I'll go face the troll. I'm not afraid to protect my princess.'

"The other horses were clearly stunned.

"'Is this true?' Sir Jaxon, the king's bravest knight, asked the unicorn.

"'It is,' the princess answered proudly. 'He is not afraid.'

"'Then together we must make the troll go away,' Sir Jaxon told the unicorn. 'I must say,' he added, 'that only to save my princess would I dare ride a steed as beautiful as you into battle.'

"The unicorn shook its snowy mane and bashfully bowed its head. The princess slid off his back and Sir Jaxon climbed on. The other horses grew jealous and angry.

"'It's still got a horn,' one horse said.

"'He will run from the troll as soon as he sees him,' said another.

"'Your concerns are misplaced,' the cart-nag observed. 'That's no horse. You'll never be that elegant and beautiful. That's a unicorn.'

"Just then, the castle gates cranked open enough for them to ride out without letting in the troll. The filthy creature was ready and waiting. The princess couldn't help but run up the stairs to the top of the wall so she could watch. She was terrified for her brave unicorn's life.

"Sir Jaxon fought hard against the troll, but was unhorsed and smashed. He was so badly injured that he couldn't get to his feet. The unicorn danced and sprang, and ran out of the troll's range, more than a little afraid and unsure of what to do next.

"From inside the castle, through the crack in the gate, one of the destriers laughed. 'I told you he would run.'

"'He's not better than us,' another of the horses added.

"'He's not running away,' someone said, causing them all to look again.

"Seeing Sir Jaxon lying helpless, the troll bent down to grab up his meal.

"'Look,' the princess squealed to her father, who was standing protectively beside her.

"The unicorn charged with all he had. He ran as fast as any stallion had ever run, straight at the troll. He leapt with his head lowered and buried his horn deep in the beast's arse."

This caused Jicks and Phen to laugh.

"The troll screamed out in terrible pain, and when he jumped up, the horn broke from the unicorn's head. As fast as he could flee, the troll limped away. And it never returned to bother the kingdom folk again."

Borg finished off his pot, but waved off Oarly's offered flask.

Princess Telgra seemed fast asleep, but Hyden, Phen, the monk, and the younger men were waiting for more. Even Lieutenant Welch and Corva, who were both stretched out on their bedrolls with their eyes closed, were still listening.

"Is that it?" Hyden asked.

Borg chuckled. "Do you really want to know?" he asked rhetorically. "All right. The destriers were all put to plow. Sir Jaxon recovered from his wounds and was rewarded with a lordship and a thousand acres for his bravery. He also took the princess as his wife and, in return for saving his life from the troll, he gave the unicorn the run of his land."

For a long while all was silent. The tale was done.

"That was a wonderful story, Borg," Telgra said. She peeled herself off of Phen and gave the giant a big, loving hug. To everyone's surprise, the Southern Guardian blushed brightly when she kissed his cheek.

Not long after, the cavern began to reverberate with a horrible animalistic sound.

Luckily they'd all been drinking and had grown use to Oarly's snores.

Chapter Thirty-Five

"Are you not tired, Phen?" Hyden asked quietly.

Borg had just left and the sun had yet to rise. The others were all sound asleep. Phen, as usual, had spent the night lying still, staring blankly. Since his stony predicament began, true sleep had so far been impossible. Hyden noticed this and was curious.

"I just don't seem to get tired anymore," Phen said. "Nor hungry or thirsty. I sometimes wonder if I'm really alive."

"It won't be long until you're back to normal," Hyden reminded him. "We're halfway to the Leif Repline already."

"But what if it doesn't work?" Phen asked. "What if all of this time, my not being able to eat or drink makes me come back a starved-out husk." He pointed to the small but deep chip missing from his shoulder. One of the skeletons in the Serpent's Eye cavern had clipped him with a sword. "What if my wounds are fresh when I'm restored?"

"What if you worry yourself to frivels over things you can't control?" Hyden was stern. "You're not alone." He indicated the cavern full of people with a sweep of his hand. "You still wear Claret's tear. I know it will protect you, and you'll have me, the greatest wizard of all time, to help you should things go awry."

Phen laughed at Hyden's mock bravado. "Aye." He finally grinned a stony grin.

The realization of how glad he was to see Hyden alive and in the flesh, after so many months of wondering if he was dead, was enough to quell his concerns. "With you casting spells, all we have to worry about is losing our boots," Phen joked.

"Just so." Hyden nodded with a grin of his own. "Let's work on the trick of taking a man's weapon from him, until the others wake up."

Phen grew excited. He observed intently as they went about repeating the words and hand movements required to cast the spell. It wasn't that long ago that Phen was the one teaching Hyden. Now the tables were turned. Once he saw Hyden's alteration, Phen quickly mastered the variation of the spell. He was well into another trick when Oarly's snoring finally stopped. A heartbeat later the dwarf sat up and the others began to wake.

Seemingly from out of nowhere, a giant, slightly smaller and much older than Borg, but still over a dozen feet tall, strode into the cavern mouth. He had long, grayish white hair and a beard that flowed down to his ample belly. He was dressed in a fine ankle-length robe of emerald cloth that was trimmed in sky blue. An air of regality wafted off of him. He was obviously from King Aldar's castle. He looked serious, but his smile was welcoming.

"Sir Hyden Hawk, when you and the princess are ready I will lead your party to Afdeon. My name is Caden Bral, but you may call me Cade. King Aldar isn't expecting us until this evening, so there is no need to rush your morning preparations."

"Thank you, Cade," Hyden replied. "We won't keep you waiting long."

The giant nodded, as if it didn't matter. Hyden noticed the carved bone wolf's head buckle on Cade's belt. He was certain it was dragon bone. King Aldar carried a staff made of the stuff and had gifted King Mikahl with a dragon bone medallion carved like a lion. It was a long-told legend that the giants had managed to kill a full-grown dragon once, without the aid of magic. Whether they really had or not, Hyden wasn't sure, but they had given a dragon skull to Hyden's people a long time ago. It sat in the Elder's sacred burrow. The brain cavity had been opened for their fire pit. Dragon bone held some sort of magical power, he knew. He could sense it. Claret once told him that not many dragons were concerned with the ways of man, and even fewer of them were goodnatured. Properly enchanted, dragon bone was supposed to ward off living wyrms. Hyden figured that out here in the mountainous land of trolls and ice, such things were necessary.

They broke their fast on the little bit of elk that remained. After repacking their gear on the pack horses, they followed Cade out of the cavern into the mist.

They traveled a few hours without much visibility. Hyden used Talon's sight, and though he could see above the cloud of steam when he flew high, he could not seem to find a bottom to the cloud cover. Talon flew as far below the group's level as he dared but he never came out of the mist. At one point, whatever was below him grew so warm that instinctually he began to climb away from it. Hyden finally called the hawkling back to him, afraid that the curious bird would slam into a rocky floor or a hidden cliff face.

They came to another cavern; this one wasn't naturally formed like the other had been. It was a carved archway some twenty feet high and easily as wide. The floor was polished smooth, glossy and perfect. The walls were ribbed with fluted column-like protrusions that ran from the floor up to the peak of the arch and back down the other side. These supports were spaced every twenty feet or so, and gave Hyden the feeling that he was walking through the ribcage of some great beast. Spaced evenly between the ribs were large ensconced torches. They seemed high on the wall to the companions, but not so much when a giant passed by them. The stone brackets that held the flaming brands were all intricately carved dragon heads. The flames seemed to be belching out of the dragons' open mouths. The eyes of the menacing decorations had been polished so brightly that they reflected the dancing flames as real eyes might.

Oarly was clearly awestruck by the quality of the craftsmanship. The others were just impressed, and more than a little unnerved.

The long passage ended in a circular room crafted in the same manner of the long hall they had just traversed. The same fluted ribs ran up the walls, but these met in the center of the domed ceiling at an impossible upside-down pool of shimmering quicksilver.

"What keeps it from dripping out?" Jicks asked.

"Wow," Phen exclaimed when he saw the phenomena. "Look, Hyden!"

Hyden saw it, too. As curious as he was about it, though, he was even more intrigued by the strange symbol grooved into the room's floor. It was eerily familiar, and since the only symbols carved into a floor he'd ever seen were gateways into the hells, it alarmed him.

"Please," Cade urged softly. "Everyone get your bodies, and the animals, completely inside the outer ring of the mark on the floor. We wouldn't want to leave any part of you behind." The giant chuckled at this.

No one else laughed. It was clear that he hadn't meant that he would leave an individual behind, only part of one.

"Sir Hyden, Lieutenant Welch," Cade instructed. "You and the elves keep the horses calm. This process will alarm them." He looked around in the air oddly. "Is the hawkling in?"

"He is," Phen called, setting the bird from his wrist to his shoulder.

"Here we go, then."

There was a sudden smell of ozone and the air filled with static. Half a heartbeat later a whomp shook them deep in their guts. Only a flash of darkness followed, and then the horses were nickering and braying in distress. Looking around, it seemed to all of them that nothing happened. Everyone looked confused. Phen appeared disappointed.

Hyden realized that something actually had occurred. Now standing in the archway of the corridor they had come down were four giant boys, looking like man-sized ten-year-olds. They were wearing identical uniforms of emerald green balloon-sleeved shirts, trimmed in the same sky-blue as Cade's robe. They wore leather pants, probably elk hide, or some short-haired goat skin. Their boots were shin-high and they carried no weapons, or anything else for that matter. A movement came in the passageway behind them and a few of the questers suddenly realized that they weren't where they were before. A deep breath told Hyden that the quality of the air had even changed, from thin and frigid to thick and steamy.

"That was interesting," Lieutenant Welch said. "How far did we travel?"

Cade indicated that he heard the question and would explain shortly. First he gave them some instruction. "These pages will take the animals to a place where they can rest and graze. They will bring your things over to the guest quarters. Take anything you may need in the next few hours with you. We will be crossing the Cauldron. It's slow going and visibility is poor."

Cade then turned to Lieutenant Welch and spoke directly. "We have teleported from the Southern Ridgeway marker down to the Outer Moat marker. To answer your question, we have moved five miles as the crow flies, thus avoiding an estimated eighteen miles of hiking up and down the freezing rocks."

"You have my most sincere appreciation," Oarly said, before he started filling several flasks and bladder skins from another small keg he had cleverly hidden in one of the horse packs.

"It's all right, Spike," Phen was saying. The whoomp of teleporting had caused the lyna cat to puff up into a prickly ball in Phen's shagmar coat pocket. If Phen's skin hadn't been petrified, he'd have probably been picking sharp quills out of his hand.

"Oh, come to me, Spike," Telgra said, as if talking to a baby. "It's going to be all right, little one."

"Be careful," both Corva and Phen said at the same time, causing them to share an awkward look. The princess paid neither of them any attention. At her gentle touch, Spike relaxed, and already she was toting him carefully away in her arms.

Dostin seemed terrified. He was clutching the thick oak staff he'd been carrying tightly in his hands. He looked ready to fight. Corva had to urge him along as Cade led them through a passageway almost like the first one they'd traversed. The only difference Hyden noticed was that the ornate sconces mounted between the ribs on the walls were made to resemble the cupped hand of some long-clawed creature. Flames leapt and danced up out of the palm. These were the tamer flames of some sort of oil lamp, instead of the harsh, smoky torches in the other corridor.

The passage opened onto another circular chamber, but this one was a crossroads of sorts. It had no upside-down pool of quicksilver, and no strange symbol etched into the floor.

The corridor they took continued on and eventually another crossed it. They went left, and after slowly sloping downward for what might have been a full hour, the humidity became intense. The air was steamy, almost cloudy. They ended up in a vast, naturally formed cavern that opened up onto a body of slow boiling water. Steam rose in clouds, making it impossible to sense the size of what was beyond. A large, well built barge, complete with a uniformed crew of capable-looking giants, was waiting to receive them.

"Welcome to the Cauldron," said a man whose uniform wasn't green, but black trimmed in emerald. Hyden figured him to be the captain of the barge. "You're about to cross the moat of all moats."

"If the castle rises up out of the steam cloud miles above us," Hyden looked at Phen and Oarly, all three with eyes wild and full of wonder, "then the structure that lies between, hidden in the steam, must be grand indeed."

"By Doon, a thousand, thousand dwarves could live in such a place."

"I still can't believe we were teleported," Phen said to Hyden. "That's a spell I have to learn."

"How could you think about spells?" Hyden asked as they moved up the giant-sized gangplank to the barge's deck. "We're about to see... about to be inside a castle city that reaches up into the very heavens."

"I am thinking about the castle, Hyden," Phen said. "They had to use magic—probably teleportation spells—to get the upper reaches of such a place built. Just think of it." It was clear Phen was calculating and estimating in his ever quizzical mind. Figuring out how such a construction had been erected would probably keep him thinking and imagining for days.

Talon leapt from Phen's shoulder and glided to the deck rail at the front of the barge. Once he was settled he began preening himself. Telgra concentrated on scratching Spike behind the ears while Corva helped Dostin onto the boat. The lieutenant and his young men were gawking as much as the rest of them. They huddled close and spoke to themselves as the barge eased away from the cavern's dock.

As they slid across the water out into the denser cloud of steam, it became a near white-out.

"How hot is the water?" Hyden asked Cade.

"Hot enough to boil the flesh off of your bones in just a moment," he answered. "And that's just at the surface. The frigid mountain air keeps the top of the cauldron relatively cool. Just a few dozen feet down and it would boil your bones to mush."

"No serpents to worry about here, then," said Oarly, stretching up on tiptoes to look over the rail, instead of ducking to look down under it.

"That's not true, Master Dwarf," Cade said. "There are a few creatures who love these waters. Dragon kin, most assuredly. After all, what is a serpent, but a wingless water dragon."

"The serpent I cut in half was more like an eel than a dragon," Oarly said. "It smelled fishy and had suction cups on its underside, like an octanomus."

"It's an octerapus," Phen corrected with a grin at Oarly's claim of halving the serpent. "He didn't cut it in half, Cade; he just cut off the tip of its tail."

Cade, after realizing that neither the dwarf nor the marble-skinned boy were jesting, shuddered.

It was hard to imagine that these people, at least the two he was speaking to, and Hyden Hawk, had commanded dragons and killed demons.

With just a little unease showing in his normally confident voice, Cade said, "Master Oarly, I assure you that the things in this lake are nothing like you've described. These beasts could swallow this barge whole, if they were so inclined."

Oarly's gulp was audible.

The Wizard and the Warlord

Chapter Thirty-Six

Captain Hodge led his group toward the Dragon Tooth. His three flat barges were in a line gliding swiftly through the narrow channel, approaching the formation from the west. As Bzorch had commanded, they split up. Hodge's group, with two dragon gun crews and fifty of the best men, made a wide arc around the westward side of the spire.

The two groups had been separated for two days now. The plan called for them all to converge on the spire this day when the sun was at its zenith. Hodge was worried because his group was going to be late.

The maze of channels that would allow the boats passage had stymied them. Three times they had dead-ended, and once they'd spent more than an hour completely lost in vegetation so thick that they couldn't even see the fang. Now it was midday and Hodge was supposed to be converging on the formation. He hoped that Bzorch would understand. They'd done the best they could, and now they were hurrying toward the black shark fin as quickly as possible.

Gzorith, the older of the two dragon gunners on Captain Hodge's barge, noticed the captain's grim look. "Bzorch will not hold it against you," he grunted reassuringly. "It's not like we had a chart or a map." The big savage-looking breed giant paused to bat away a pest that was buzzing around his head. "The time it took to find channels that cut across the current of the river's natural flow weren't accounted for."

"True spoken," Hodge nodded. "But it's not wise to point out your commander's failures or misjudgments." He chuckled away a little of his unease. Some loud, cackling creature sounded off deep in the green density around them. "Especially when something might eat you because of them."

Gzorith boomed out a laugh. "I'll tell Bzorch we all planned badly," the breed giant boasted. "My kindred respect those who speak boldly. I don't care if it's a woman child who sees my mistakes and tells me about them. I'd rather know than not."

"Bzorch won't eat you, though," the commander joked. "He might eat me, if he had the chance."

"You're wrong, Captain," Gzorith said, growing serious. "When we were imprisoned on Coldfrost he would have eaten me quick. Do not let Lord Bzorch's civility fool you. He is the lord of my people, whether the king says so or not. He is the most savage and brutal of us, which is why he holds his command. We not only respect him, but we fear him, as well. Lord Bzorch would lose respect for me if I let his errors go unchecked. He is constantly trying to be better and smarter. Without breed like him, my people would probably revert back to our more savage nature."

Captain Hodge didn't know what to say to any of that. He walked to the side rail, leaned out, and glanced back at the two boats following in their wake. It was hot and sticky, and clouds of gnats were everywhere. All the men were still standing ready, but since they hadn't seen anything more than a few family groups of Zard they had grown bored.

The sound of someone shouting came to his ears. He froze in place, trying to make out the man's words, but an eruption of chaos from the opposite side of the barge drowned them out. He was just about to push off the rail and go see what this disturbance was when a large splash sounded alongside the craft below him. He looked down curiously, and by the time he realized what was happening, it was too late.

An arm-thick tentacle lashed up and wrapped around his neck and began pulling him over the rail. Gzorith dropped his dragon gun and grabbed the captain's feet just before they disappeared.

"Canzal! Gun! Gun! Gun!" the breed giant yelled at its kinsman.

Shouts were erupting from up and down the train of barges. A cloud of angry red finger-sized hornets were swarming out of the jungle, stinging the soldiers. The shadow of something large slowly crept by, eclipsing the sun for a moment. Gzorith ignored it and, as if he were in a rope tug contest, he yanked back savagely on the captain's legs.

Canzal leaned over the rail, aimed at where the tentacle met the water, and fired. A small cloud of red bloomed a few feet below the surface.

Gzorith was yanked to the rail. Pulling back with all he had, something suddenly gave way and he and the captain lurched backward. Hodge landed on Gzorith in a jumble on the deck.

"I thought we'd lost you, Captain," Gzorith said between breaths as he staggered to his feet.

"He's not listening, Gzor," Canzal said. He pointed at the headless corpse of Captain Hodge. Blood was still oozing out of the stump in thick pulses.

"Ahhhhgh!" one of the ropemen yelled as the line attached to the spear Canzal had fired tangled around his legs. Before anyone could even think, the breed giant was dragged across the deck and over the side of the barge. Canzal's powerful hands gripped the rail for an instant, but he was being pulled so hard that they couldn't keep hold.

Gzorith ran to his dragon gun and picked it up before it got caught in the tangle. From somewhere on their barge, men began to scream as the hornets found their flesh. Gzorith saw the dark shadow gliding across the surface of the channel at the edge of the tangled shoreline. He looked up. A Choska carrying a half-naked woman who strongly resembled the Dragon Queen passed casually over them. Gzorith was so transfixed by the sight that he didn't even see or hear the barge behind him as it came up out of the water in a twisting roll, only to smash down on the deck of the trailing boat. Men shrieked and screamed and thrashed in the water as some were dragged under and some just disappeared in swirling clouds of crimson gore.

Gzorith raised his dragon gun and took careful aim at the Choska's chest. He followed it a few feet and then fired. He knew without a doubt that his shaft was flying true, but he never had the chance to see it hit the Choska. Some bright red-winged thing the size of a small human raked his eyes with a jagged claw. He managed to bat it out of the air, but by then his eyes were full of blood and the barge was lifting askew. He would never know it, but the coil of line connected to the missile tangled on the deck. When his barbed shaft tip was only a few feet away from piercing the Choska's heart, the line pulled taut and yanked the spear back toward the ground.

Gzorith, Canzal, and the rest of Captain Hodge's group were gone. Only the corner of one barge sticking up out of the water remained to prove they'd been there. For at least a hundred yards, the water was red with death and churning thick with hungry swamp predators.

Bzorch saw the Choska flying to the west of the Dragon's Fang. It had spooked the strange green swamp troll the breed giant had been observing through the looking glass. It was obvious to him that there was a sizable presence of Zard, but he couldn't see many of them. Fire pits, trampled trails, refuse, and other signs of an encampment were everywhere, but there were no Zard. Apparently, they either let the swamp troll run amok in their encampment while they were away, or they were hiding from it. More likely, Bzorch decided, they were hiding to ambush him and his men. It was also clear that the Choska was observing Captain Hodge from above. Bzorch was almost glad that the captain was so far away and behind schedule. The plan he was now forming in his mind was even better than the other.

Since the Dragon's Tooth rose straight up out of the water at all but the southern end, access to the rocky formation was limited. If the Choska was sheltering there, Bzorch decided, it would have to be up in the old dragon hole. Bzorch ordered a man to untie the safety boat, a small four-man rower. He'd put his arm through his coil of line and hefted it over his head so that it hung across his body. He ordered his men to stay back in the relative cover. They had camouflaged their barges with branches and greenery they'd cut from the jungle. Anchored in the right location, they would be hard to find.

Bzorch was going to climb the fang. Its curved shape made the western face look easy to ascend. He ordered his ropeman to stay back. He wanted to take this risk alone.

"If I do not return, tell my cousin Gzorith that he is to take over command and work with the captain," Bzorch told his ropeman and the barge master. He then ordered the two humans in the safety boat to begin rowing him toward the fang. "Watch the wormhole, get under it, and wait for my signal."

The barge master nodded, as did the other breed. As soon as Bzorch was off, they went about putting the willow branches and swamp grass back over the place where the safety boat had been lashed.

Bzorch suddenly realized that it was far too quiet around the fang. This kind of silence was unnatural. Even the insects seemed to have fled. He began to wonder if Captain Hodge and his group hadn't drawn the whole encampment to them. A glance westward told him that the Choska was still preoccupied.

"As soon as I'm out of the boat, start rowing back," he said.

"We're coming up on the face now," one of the rowers said.

Bzorch turned and looked up at the western face of the fang. The sun was on it now; midday had come and gone. He realized that his shadow would be a long, drooping line on the rock. He would have to hurry. If the Choska came around and caught him halfway up, clinging like a lizard, he would surely be killed.

"Get me directly under that hole up there," Bzorch commanded again. When the oarsmen had him in position, he checked to see where the Choska was. It was well to the west, circling slowly over the captain's group. He didn't hesitate. Like some big, lumbering gorilla, he began moving upward. Three hundred feet was a long way to climb, but Bzorch went about it with a purpose.

About a third of the way up, a shadow sped across him and made his heart blast through his chest. Looking up and craning his neck, he saw that it was only the shadow of a big dactyl, not the Choska. Still, the creature showed him its bright pink maw and hissed at his trespass. After checking to see where the Choska was once more, he resumed his climb. Luckily, the demon was still focused on what was going on with Captain Hodge's group.

Bzorch couldn't believe it when he finally pulled himself into the wormhole of the old red dragon's layer. After he caught his breath, he pulled the looking glass from his belt and looked out westwardly to see what the Choska was so intently circling. The sun reflected back up at him in a bright coppery ray, making it hard to pick out details, but what had happened was clear. From his vantage point he could see a swath of marsh water littered with debris and stained red with blood. One of the three barges was half submerged, the others completely under water. The long, loggish shapes of several snappers eased about the pools searching for more men to eat. Bzorch swore under his breath. He saw that the Choska was now moving toward the camouflaged barges where his men were hiding. He had to move across to the eastern opening to see where they were hidden. As he went, he noticed that there was no sign of anything living in the cavernous hollow that opened up off of the wormhole. All he saw were bones from ancient meals and some hardened chunks of grizzly pelt piled in the spaces between. He wasn't sure now if the Choska was roosting here.

To his horror, and anger, a monstrous swarm of dactyls was clouding around the concealed boats. The men weren't able to stay hidden. The big, sharp-beaked birds were diving and slashing at them. The shadow of the Choska swept across the dark green collage of marsh below. Bzorch's head shot up and located it in the sky. He nearly tumbled out of the wormhole when he saw her on its back.

Was it her?

Holding his breath and willing his heart to keep beating, Bzorch put his looking glass to his eye and found her in it. He wasn't sure if he should feel relief or not when he saw the face. There was no patch of scorched flesh over her ear, no pink teardrop scar on her cheek, but he knew in his primitive heart that it was somehow Shaella.

He decided then that killing the Choska might not be as important as warning the High King of this discovery. A glance down at his men put a knot in his stomach. A plethora of life was swarming over the boats. Snakes, dactyls, and some huge, tentacled thing that was only half in the water, were all attacking. The dark channel took on a crimson sheen and, after only a few heartbeats, was only a churning mass of death.

He was alone now.

Bzorch found the Choska again and growled. He would survive, he told himself. He would wade back to Westland and tell King Mikahl of this bloody attack if he had to. The High King had to know that Shaella, or something very much like her, was alive.

He decided to use the time he had before darkness to make a plan. Alone, with no boat, it was all he could think to do.

Chapter Thirty-Seven

Once inside the huge island castle of Afdeon it was hard to judge how massive it really was. The sections of the lower floors the party was able to see were plain in appearance, other than the overproportionate size of everything. The lower floors were crude and square, and looked to be carved into the natural rock. The walls were thick and the hallways narrow. Hyden figured that this was the foundation for the towering construction above, its function obviously more important than form.

They rode up on a disk-shaped lift. The large platform had several divans and benches. One was even built for human-sized folk.

"Look, Hyden," Phen whispered as they marveled at it all. "Next to the giants and their furniture, Oarly looks like a bearded toddler."

Both Phen and Hyden were disappointed when they learned that the elevating disk was a mechanical device and not magical. Cade explained that it worked by way of a system of counter weights and pulleys powered by shafts and chambers that vented natural steam from the Cauldron.

They passed hundreds of floors on the half-day ride, but they were only given glimpses of the vast variety of things that were on them. Some lower floors held cavernous pillared rooms full of livestock, bundled bales of grain, crated vegetables, and all sorts of goods and stores. Most of the floors opened up on long hallways with doors on either side. A few held similar corridors with merchant shops. On one of these floors, about an hour into the ride, a young hawker presented them with meals of devil goat meat wrapped in flat bread. The offerings were so large that no one could manage more than half of the meal, save for Jicks, who stuffed himself full.

"How far up are we going?" Princess Telgra finally asked after they had eaten.

"The royal apartments and the quarters for distinguished guests are above the steam cloud, Your Highness," Cade answered her formally. "That is where we will exit the lift."

"You said that King Aldar is expecting us this evening?" Hyden asked, fishing for information.

"He is," Cade said.

"Will we be given time to wash the road off of us?" Hyden asked, thinking as much about Telgra as he was anyone. "And our cleanest clothes are down with our things."

"Actually, your things are already being delivered to your rooms," Cade informed them. "This isn't the only way up to the royal chambers. And yes, Sir Hyden Hawk, I believe that you will have at least a few hours to wash and recover before King Aldar summons you."

It was like sitting in a room where the open entryways changed every few moments. For a time, worked stone was all that was visible, and then an opening would seemingly slide down the wall, revealing a corridor full of closed doors, or a floor full of giants working leather, or another vast expanse of stored goods. Even though they had seen as much space as any human city offers, it was apparent that they were seeing very little of Afdeon.

Once, the giantess storyteller, Berda, had told the Skyler Clan a tale about a forest inside a castle. Hyden remembered Gerard asking, "You mean a forest inside the castle's protective wall?"

"No," she'd replied. "I mean a forest that is high above the ground, growing in a room in a great castle."

The idea of it had boggled Hyden's mind back then. He often wondered about such a forest, about where the rain and the sunlight the trees needed to grow would come from. Now, sensing an infinite largeness around him, it wasn't so unbelievable.

"Slanted holes in the walls let steam in. It condenses on the ceiling of the cavern and then drops down like rain," Cade explained when Hyden finally asked about it. The giant didn't explain how the trees got sunlight, and Hyden was too busy thinking to ask.

"I just realized that this bench wasn't made for humans," Lieutenant Welch said, as if he'd made some great revelation.

"Who else would they be for?" Phen asked.

"For the children," Princess Telgra grinned.

"True," Cade said with a smile over at Oarly whose feet dangled a good foot above the floor. "My four-year- old son is at least a hand taller than Master Oarly."

"I hope he's not as ugly," Phen joked.

"Or as hairy," added Hyden.

"Bah!" Oarly grumbled, while everyone laughed. "How much longer are we going up?"

Cade peered at the passing floor, a ribbed hallway like the one they had traversed down to the Cauldron barge. The sconces holding the lamp flames along the walls here were gauntleted fists holding knife hilts. The flames rose up like short, wavering dagger blades.

"It won't be much longer, Master Dwarf," Cade answered.

On the next floor, toting one of Phen's chests between them, two of the page boys went striding by in an adjacent passage. Hyden figured that somewhere nearby the ribbed hallway was another room with that unsettling portal symbol carved in its floor, and an unnatural pool of quicksilver suspended overhead.

The lift finally slowed to a halt at a floor far different from the others they had seen. They stepped off the platform onto a wide, short hallway tiled with glossy slabs of jade that were checkered with a lightly hued golden marble. The walls were covered in lavender silk, and several large, intricately carved, wooden doors were spaced down the length of the hall.

Small matching wooden tables, sporting clawed feet, sat between the doors. Each displayed a different work of sculpted art. Overhead, a chandelier of crystal and gold lit the area well.

"The distinguished guest quarters," Cade announced regally. "There are only seven apartments. The master suite has been reserved for Princess Telgra; it's the door at the head of the hall. The other apartments are all equipped to sleep up to three persons or couples. The first room here…" He indicated the door on the right. The carving in the door-face depicted the forging of Ironspike. Dwarves hammered the metal while elves hovered close at hand, their hands frozen in wild gestures of magical incantation. Beyond them, several giants poured melted ore into a kettle, while a lone human with terrified eyes watched it all. The scene was captivating. Hyden studied it in awe. He remembered another depiction of the same event, in stained glass high up on Queen Willa's castle wall in Xwarda. He remembered seeing the destroyed pieces of it spread across the carnage after the battle, as if the gods had thrown a handful of jewels across the battle field.

"…all of your things," Cade was saying as he opened the door and broke Hyden's concentration. Inside, most of the group's packs, their saddles, trunks, and other belongings lay spread out in neat piles.

"Across the hall, a chamber has been set up as a planning room, complete with maps and a council table."

Its door carving showed a group of giants with long spears battling a sizable dragon. Cade didn't open it. He told the others to pick from the four remaining rooms, then took Princess Telgra gently by the arm. He guided her to the door at the end of the chamber. On its face was a view of Afdeon they hadn't seen. It was looking down on the city from the top of a mountain, or maybe some point higher in the sky. Cade opened the door for her and asked her what she might need.

THE WIZARD AND THE WARLORD

To her great surprise, a beautiful gown made of some light material, that was the same yellow color of her eyes, had been laid out for her. The way its belted waist and layered shoulders were cut allowed for it to fit a woman with either a smaller, or larger, stature than her.

"A gift from Princess Gretta," Cade explained. "About an hour before you'll be escorted to the King's Gathering Hall for the night's festivities, two of her ladies will attend you with brushes and perfumes and such."

"Oh thank you, Cade," she said, so informally that it startled the giant when she hugged his waist. "Please give her my thanks."

When the giant came back out of her room his look was perplexed. Hyden motioned for him to come into the room he had chosen for himself, Oarly, and Phen. Its door showed a sailing ship climbing a huge breaking wave during a stormy night at sea. Lightning split the sky, silhouetting the giant standing on the deck of the tossed vessel. He was trying to harpoon some undefined scaly thing which was rising up out of the ocean. The detail in the depictions mystified Hyden. He couldn't fathom carving wood so well.

Once Cade was inside the room, Hyden shut the door. "You might take a moment to speak with the elven guardsman, Corva," Hyden suggested. "The princess lost her memory and doesn't seem to want to be treated as royalty. She definitely doesn't want to be reminded of her past yet."

"She wants to restore her memory to herself at the Leif Repline," Phen explained. "But she doesn't want to be influenced before then. She only learned a few days ago that she was the Queen Mother's daughter and heir."

"That brings up a most peculiar set of circumstances," Cade said. "King Aldar had intended to honor her coming this evening. His daughter wants to get acquainted with her."

"Would you tell King Aldar for me?" Hyden asked. "It would probably be better to keep our meeting private. Of course, Princess Gretta should be included. I've met her, and I will gladly explain to her Princess Telgra's predicament."

"That I can do," said Cade thankfully. "His Majesty will be glad to avoid making our lady elf any more uncomfortable than she must already be."

Later, standing near the entryway by the lift waiting for Cade, Jicks was complaining about not getting the apartment that Lieutenant Welch had chosen. Jicks had gotten the door with the hunting great wolves depicted on it. He admitted that this would have been his second choice, but he and Krey would rather have the door showing the great battle scene between giants and trolls. Huge clubs, spears, and thrown rocks rained down. Both sides had taken plenty of damage and the situation looked desperate. It was gripping.

"At least you didn't get the silly tree," one of them said.

"What about Spike?" Phen asked Hyden. It was all he could do to peel his eyes away from Telgra. Seeing her fresh and clean took his breath away.

Talon was perched proudly on Hyden's shoulder, preening himself. The bird had arrived at their apartment's windowsill after leaving them for a while.

"There might be great wolves in the hall tonight," Hyden warned.

"Spike is coming with me," Telgra said matter-of-factly. She appeared to be very nervous. "I doubt we'll stay very long. If the wolves end up with noses full of quills, it will be their own fault."

Corva sighed in distress. He was sure the princess was about to unintentionally shame her great station in front of the King of Giants and his family.

"King Aldar's daughter, Princess Gretta, wants to spend some time getting to know you," Phen said. Those were the first words he'd spoken to her after telling her how beautiful she looked in her formal gown. The time between his words had been spent gawking at her stupidly.

"Telgra," Hyden said with a comforting smile, "Gretta is only ten or eleven years old. She is very bashful, and is as big as a grown woman. She is a child. You have nothing to worry about."

This visibly eased Telgra's tension, but she still clung to Spike as tightly as she could without pricking herself.

The lift arrived and Cade beckoned them onto it. The sound of a door banging closed brought all of their attention to Oarly. Ten 'O' -shaped mouths stared at him as he scurried his little legs toward the lift. Even Cade was shocked by the dwarf's transformation.

Oarly's hair was brushed to each side of a center part. Fine black leather britches peeked out from under his multicolored silk tunic. He had on new Valleyan boots and a bejeweled leather belt sporting at least a dozen thumb-sized rubies. His normally unkempt, food-ridden beard had been brushed, shaped, and trimmed up to his chest. In his stubby-fingered hands he carried a black velvet bag and a small, finely worked silver box. When he saw the faces of his companions he sneered. Then his eyes landed on Princess Telgra and he let out a slow wolf whistle. Stepping onto the lift, he eased up next to Phen. His tone was conspiratorial, but he made sure his voice was clear to all when he spoke. "By Doon, lad, we could have painted you up so you didn't look so pale."

This got a few chuckles from the group.

Phen moved away from Oarly and stood beside Telgra.

Hyden, still taken aback by Oarly's appearance, asked, "What's in the box, stranger? I'd never in a million years expected you to clean up so well."

"That was the first hot bath and change of clothes he's had since King Mikahl's wedding," Phen said from behind them.

"That's not true, lad," Oarly said. "I took a bath at Kander Keep when we came out of the swamp."

"He did," Telgra agreed.

"Still, that was over a month ago," Phen said with a laugh at Telgra's wrinkle-nosed expression.

"Not all of us can clean ourselves with a feather duster, Marble Boy," Oarly shot back. "And at least I have the courtesy to bring gifts to the king who took us in out of the cold."

Hyden and Phen shared a look. Even Lieutenant Welch and Princess Telgra had come to know Oarly well enough to know that he was up to something with all of this grooming and gifting. Never before had he concerned himself with what others thought of him.

Just before the lift came to a halt, Dostin asked Corva, loud enough for everyone to hear him, "Do you think Phen really cleans himself with a feather duster?"

Cade boomed out a laugh that he cut short suddenly when he saw King Aldar and Princess Gretta flanked by Urp and Oof waiting on the feast hall floor for them. The look King Aldar was giving Cade was imposing, and suddenly everyone bowed. Talon broke the tense moment when he flapped himself over to Princess Gretta, landed on her wrist and cooed. Her delighted giggles seemed to please her father. He extended a hand toward Hyden, then opened his arms in a welcoming gesture.

"Rise," he commanded. "Welcome to Afdeon."

Chapter Thirty-Eight

King Aldar hadn't changed much since Hyden last saw him, but he was dressed less crudely. The previous meeting had taken place where Loudin of the Reyhall was buried. The ancient, silver-maned giant had been wearing thick furs and traveling clothes. Now he wore a sky-blue floor-length robe the hue of his own sparkling eyes.

Princess Gretta however, did not look the same. Where Hyden expected to see a child stood a beautiful, budding young woman. The definition of features on her wide, pretty face had sharpened. Framed by dark, curly ringlets, her look held the promise of long-lasting beauty. The daisy and lace layered dress she wore went well with her turquoise eyes and was of a cut similar to Telgra's. The garment enhanced the slightly curvaceous turn her growth had taken. When she saw Spike clutched in Telgra's hands, eyeing the wolves suspiciously, she came over for a closer look. As mature as she looked, the excitement that spread across her face betrayed her youth.

To Hyden's surprise, the King of Giants stepped forth, then bent down and gave him a powerful hug. Hyden felt like a little boy being clutched by his father. When the king straightened back up, he spoke to the group in a conspiratorial whisper.

"Once we get to the dining hall, and the queen has been announced, we can dispense with all the formalities. What's this?" he asked, suddenly looking down at Oarly. A sort of uneasy surprise registered on his face as the dwarf thrust up the leather pouch he had brought.

"This is for your highness, King Aldar." Oarly spoke most properly, drawing looks from Hyden and Phen. "It's a gift from the people of Doon. It's not much, but it's precious."

As soon as the king accepted the pouch, Oarly handed the silverwork box to Princess Gretta. "And this is for you and your mother, my lady."

Without opening the pouch, King Aldar beckoned the group to follow him down a series of oversized halls, all of them decorated in eye-bulging opulence. Immaculate paintings hung on the walls, and pedestals displayed carvings of dragons, elk, wolves, and various trees all fashioned from wood, ivory, and different types of stone. The walls were done in paneled burlwood and the halls were illuminated by gold-and-crystal chandeliers that hung at intervals from the ceiling.

Princess Gretta, with Talon perched on her wrist near the silver box she was clutching, and with Spike cradled lovingly in her other arm, urged Princess Telgra to open the silver box for her. Hyden watched, noting that Telgra seemed relieved after meeting the giantess. Both young ladies gasped at what lay inside the box. On a tiny pillow of black velvet lay seven pairs of sparkling ear danglers, each made of a different precious metal or gem. There were diamonds, emeralds, rubies, and sapphires, as well as silver, gold and a set made of some delicate stone that was deep gray traced with tiny veins of scarlet.

Both Corva and Lieutenant Welch caught a glimpse in the box. Corva wondered why a woman wanted to decorate herself with pieces of the earth, while Lieutenant Welch wondered how many hundreds of years he would have to work at his present salary to buy even one piece of such precious jewelry.

Princess Gretta saw Corva looking at the contents of the box and spoke to him shyly. "You look like Vaegon, somewhat," she said. Clearly, the observation took Corva's breath away. Vaegon was the closest thing to a hero the race of elves had known for his entire lifetime. Vaegon's fame came from his friendship with Hyden and Mikahl, two humans whom most of the Elder elves didn't regard highly. Princess Telgra, though, before she lost her memory, had idolized the brave archer from the Willowbrow Clan. Corva replied with a shaky, "Thank you, my lady." Then he swelled with visible pride.

Princess Gretta covered her mouth and then whispered something to Princess Telgra. Both girls giggled, and Corva flushed a light shade of blue.

"She likes you, Corva," Dostin observed loudly.

They entered a set of double doors with panels carved into something resembling a wildly split face that was hidden in the features of a mountain landscape. The room was cozy and just big enough for all of them to feel comfortable in, without feeling swallowed up. A table of glossy black marble was set for them. Chairs with higher seats, fitted so the humans could be above the surface, were set around the length of the slab. Three golden candelabras were spread down its length. The reflection of the tiny flames flickered and danced on the golden goblets and dinnerware.

Once the group were all in the room, the great wolves took up alert sitting positions just outside the dining hall. Then the heavy wooden doors swung silently shut, seemingly of their own accord. Hyden was drawn to look at them as he sensed the ozonic sensation of magic in action. His attention was drawn back to their host as King Aldar himself announced his wife.

"My honored and distinguished guests, may I present the Lady of Afdeon, Gertra Awln, Queen of the Mountains and Valleys, and the holder of my heart."

"Oh stop it, Aldar," the big woman said. She was close to thirteen feet tall and probably four feet across. A proportionately fit woman, her round face showed traces of youthful beauty. It was impossible not to notice the foot-and-a-half of cleavage her forest green dining gown revealed. With breasts the size of barrel kegs and a cheery smile, it would be hard to call her anything less than pretty. She looked easily a third of her husband's age, but such was the way of things when kings took wives.

Everyone had bowed again, and while they did, Princess Gretta hurried excitedly to her mother's side to show her the gift the dwarf had given them.

"Please rise," Queen Gertra said. "Hyden of the Skyler Clan is the only one of you who owes fealty to the Crown of Afdeon." She turned toward Princess Telgra and beamed. "I hope that after you have visited the Leif Repline you will come stay with us for a while. I would love to get to know you better, as would Gretta."

Telgra found herself taken aback at how deftly polite and well worded the queen's invitation had been. She smiled broadly at her hostess. "Thank you, Highness, that sounds pleasant. Getting to know me is also on my list of things to do."

Phen, Corva, and even Hyden Hawk laughed out loud at that.

The giant queen ignored them and looked at Oarly. The dwarf looked as serious as he'd ever been. "Master Dwarf," the queen said with a smile. "Your gift is wonderful. I'd like to speak with you more during dinner. If I wait a moment more, though, the sun will be gone and you'll miss it."

With that, she turned and clapped. Two servants appeared and moved to the center of the tapestried wall behind her. Slowly, the hanging panels of cloth slid open, the full-length curtain revealing the most spectacular view of the world that any of them had ever seen. Immediately, the bitter chill of the air swept into the room. As the group eased forward to gawk at the expanse of sun-coppered mountain peaks that extended as far as the eye could see, the servants drew back the curtains on the opposite wall, revealing a fireplace the size of a small farmhouse. No sooner was the fire raging than another curtain door slid open, filling the room with the savory smell of freshly baked bread and seasoned meat.

It didn't take long for the fire's heat to force the cold back out of the huge embrasure. And though these other things were going on around them, none of them ever stopped taking in the view. The snow-capped mountains literally looked to be formed of molten copper as the sun inched down behind them. Then as the sun's glow faded and the silvery light of the stars took over, the mountains appeared frosted in crystal. Finally, the aroma of the meal drew them to the table. A special seat had been set for Oarly to boost him up to the point that he wouldn't feel uncomfortable. As the golden goblets were filled with sweet berry wine, King Aldar peeked into the drawstring bag Oarly had given him. Hyden elbowed Phen, and both of them watched curiously as the giant's face began to split into a grin. His expression quickly went blank and he did his best to try to hide the gift under the table, but the queen had seen him and held out a snapping finger.

It was comical. The huge, powerful king of the most treacherous terrain known looked like a scolded boy handing over a frog he had kept in his pocket too long. The queen pulled from the bag a silver canteen. In her hand it looked like a boot flask. She unfastened the lid and sniffed at its contents and nearly dropped the thing. This caused both King Aldar and Oarly to lurch forward as if they could catch the container.

"What is that horrible-smelling stuff?" the queen asked.

"It's granite juice, my lady," Oarly said. "It's used to polish hard metals and etch stone… among other things." The last was mumbled so that only King Aldar and Hyden could hear it.

"It's a very precious liquid, dear," King Aldar said gingerly. "Please don't spill it. Master Oarly has carried it such a long way."

As she closed the container, King Aldar relaxed and smiled again. "What was it that the ever-so-kind dwarf gifted my ladies?" he asked.

"Oh," the queen's face suddenly beamed as she handed the flask back to her husband. "It's a wonderful gift that Gretta and I can share. Look."

She showed him the box and King Aldar nodded appreciatively at Oarly. Hyden noticed that both the king's goblet and Oarly's goblet were filled from a different flagon than everyone else's. With a hard look at the king, Dostin managed to get a refill out of that particular flagon once, as well. Hyden got a whiff of the stuff they were drinking and nearly vomited from the harsh smell. It reminded him of the concoction Master Amill once used to rid Queen Willa's castle of rats and other vermin. Whatever it was, it was potent. Oarly's eyes were glazed, and a slight grin stayed on his face as he feasted dreamily.

The fare was simple yet delicious. Everyone had their fill of meat, bread, vegetables, and gravy sauce. After a bit of pleasant conversation, the three women excused themselves. Only then, King Aldar sneaked a tiny sip from the canteen Oarly had given him. After he swallowed, he went completely pale. Hyden, Lieutenant Welch, and Corva shared looks of concern for a moment, but the king's color came roaring back with a vengeance. His face slowly turned as purple as a plum. His huge hands were gripping the edge of the marble table so hard that Hyden thought he might snap off chunks of it.

"It's the best, I assure you," said Oarly through a lilted stupor.

After taking a few deep breaths, King Aldar agreed. "'Tis!" he managed with a nod.

Noticing that Hyden hadn't been drinking much, Corva took the moment to ask him something that had been bothering him since he and Dostin joined them.

"Is there any way that I can escort Princess Telgra home, once she's visited the Leif Repline?" the elf asked in an unassuming manner. "I understand your purpose for going onto the Wedjak, but she is the only one of her kind. If something were to happen to her, there is no telling what the elves would do." Corva looked desperately concerned for her safety.

"I can't make her do anything," Hyden answered truthfully. "And I can't allow anyone to force her to do anything that she doesn't want to do."

King Aldar pointed at the empty space between them and shook his head as if he were about to make a point, but apparently he couldn't find the words just yet.

"It would be better if our group wasn't so large," Lieutenant Welch said. "I agree with Sir Hyden Hawk, though. I won't allow her to be coerced into doing anything she doesn't want to do."

"We've still got two weeks of journeying, and that's after winter relents. It'll be months before we can get to the Leif Repline fountain," Phen said matter-of-factly. "There will be plenty of time to figure all of that out, Corva."

"He he tweedle dee," Oarly sang out quietly. His voice sounded distant, like he was somewhere else. "Tweedle dee and tweedle do, flutter high and hammer true."

Dostin giggled girlishly for a moment then lapsed into a soft snore.

"I understand," Corva sighed. His voice and his expression showed his frustration. "I just have this sinking feeling about what my people might do in the meantime."

"You're starting to sound like Vaegon," Hyden said.

Before Corva could respond, King Aldar finally found his voice.

"Your journey to the Leif Repline won't be... so... so..." The giant sneezed hard, causing Dostin to erupt into a peal of giggling.

Corva put a hand on the monk's shoulder and calmed him. Over the interruption, the king finally blurted out what he had been trying to say.

"It will take days, not months," King Aldar said, fighting off another sneeze. "I... I... could put you a few days' journey from the Leif Repline in a heartbeat." He finally let loose his sneeze and seemed to lose focus for a few moments. When he gathered himself, he looked at Oarly appreciatively. "The best it is, dwarf." The king's eyes closed and his head lolled to the side.

"Teleporting?" Phen asked.

King Aldar nodded as he slid slowly into his chair. "You've got the Gwag to contend with, though. It guards the fountain jealously. It... it... is..." The king was out of it then, his huge face a study in bliss.

"Well that's good news," Hyden said.

"Good?" Lieutenant Welch asked. "A thing called the Gwag is guarding the fountain pool and that's good news?"

"Aye." Hyden grinned at Phen.

"Aye, it is," Oarly mumbled into his dream.

"It's good because we can find out what this Gwag is about, and get Marble Boy, Princess Telgra, and Talon back to normal in just a day or two." He grinned.

"I can hardly wait," Welch added sarcastically.

Chapter Thirty-Nine

"So what is a Gwag?" Hyden asked Phen the next morning.

Phen was sitting at a huge desk, looking like a whitewashed child on the giant-sized furniture. The desktop was cluttered with books, most opened, but some in crude stacks. Unable to sleep in his petrified state, Phen had spent the night searching for information about the Gwag, the Leif Repline, and anything else he could think of.

"Here, read this." Phen pointed to an open text. "It's the only mention of the fountain pool's guardian, but it's not mentioned as a Gwag. They describe it as a long, fur-coated, four-legged serpent."

"How could it be a serpent if it has fur and legs?" Hyden asked.

"Just read the passage," Phen smarted. "It's a description given by an exploration party from before Pratchert's day. One of the men in that party went with Pratchert and his father to hunt that ice bear pelt that's in your tower's trophy room."

"It's Dahg Mahn's tower, not mine," Hyden said, taking the book. He sank down onto a divan and began to read. After a moment he sat up and looked at Phen. "It says that the fountain poisoned one of their men." He glanced at the book and found the line he was after. "'Shriveled him to a husk in a matter of moments, after just one sip,'" he quoted.

"Aye." Phen faced Hyden and made a strange face, as if he were contemplating deeply. "I've read a lot here, but I'm hoping King Aldar will allow me into the giants' library, if they have one. I think there are probably traps and other deterrents, as well as this Gwag protecting the fountain. Something that powerful couldn't be left accessible to just anyone who wanted to exploit it. Some of the accounts I've read speak of the fountain's waters as if they were the elixir of eternity or something." He sighed. "As eager as I am to be returned to normal, I think we should study as much as we can before we go."

"Aye," Hyden agreed. "I'll see if Cade or His Majesty will take you to the Hall of Chronicles. Berda once told me that they keep all the stories and legends of the giant folk there."

Phen nodded with a pleased smile on his bland face. After a moment he said, "Did you notice last night that Orly didn't snore?"

"Where is he?"

"He's still sleeping," Phen said incredulously. "I wonder what they were drinking last night? It smelled awful."

"You noticed it, too, then?"

"Aye," Phen said. "Deep earth granite juice? What was that stuff?"

"I don't know." Hyden made a grinning cringe. "But whatever it is, it's so potent that a thimbleful put King Aldar down."

"It's called Malagma Cobbless," Oarly said in a rough, wheezy voice from the doorway to his bedchamber. "Concentrated to a syrup and then quantified." Only the top of his now wildly tangled hair could be seen over the back of the divan as he shuffled into the room. He had to dive up to the seat on his belly and wallow around on the soft cushions to get upright. He grunted and growled at the humbling, almost embarrassing effort he had to make just to get situated.

"The giants like to dilute the stuff into their wine," he finally continued. "That canteen should treat a half dozen kegs properly."

"What were you drinking?" Phen asked.

"Oh, that." Oarly rubbed his sunken eyes. "Liquified lotus blossom. It's a gargantuan specialty." He yawned. "I think I drank too much of it."

"The stuff you gave King Aldar is supposed to be diluted in six kegs?" Hyden asked.

Oarly nodded.

"No wonder just one sip put him down."

Oarly's eyes snapped open and he looked up with all the alertness he could muster. "He sipped it right from the flask?"

"Just a little nip," Hyden said. He couldn't help but be alarmed.

"By Doon, someone should check on him. In its concentrated state that stuff will eat a hole in a steel plate."

"I'll go," said Hyden. Before he could get up, an insistent banging came from the door.

Phen quickly went and opened it.

It was Corva and he looked worried. "Dostin's not waking up. I'm worried."

"He'll be fine," Oarly said. "He only had one goblet of liquefied lotus last night. He should come around sometime later today."

After Hyden hurried out to check on King Aldar, Phen sat back at the desk and turned toward Oarly. "If one cup of that stuff will put Dostin down for a day and night, why doesn't it do that to you?"

"I've got a drinker's constitution," Oarly said proudly. "Besides, I'm a dwarf."

Corva took a seat where Hyden had been sitting and looked at Phen. "Have you found anything useful in all of that?" He indicated the books piled on the desk.

"Not enough," he answered.

An awkward silence took over for a moment. Oarly slipped off the divan and returned to his room.

"You're really lucky, Phen," said Corva. "It's rare for one of the Arbor's Blood to take a liking to an elven man, much less a human."

"You're speaking of Telgra?" Phen asked.

Corva nodded.

"I like her, too," Phen said. "Very much."

"She will live four hundred years, if no harm comes to her, Phen," Corva said softly. "How many more years will you live?"

Phen looked away, but there was heat in his voice when he responded. "In my current state, I could live forever, Corva, but a life not feeling the warmth of a touch or the taste of a meal seems like no life at all."

Corva hadn't considered that Phen's condition might affect his lifespan. The elf, now that he thought about it, couldn't remember Phen needing food or drink, or even to sleep since they had been traveling together. The gravity of the boy's situation, and the weight of the choices he would soon have to make, became clearer to him. Phen would have to decide if he wanted to spend hundreds of years enjoying Telgra's company without feeling her touch, or tasting her kiss, or being able to couple with her. The alternative was what? Maybe forty or fifty years of enjoying the full sensations of love and life. Corva didn't envy Phen, and was finding that he had a deep respect for him.

Corva read the descriptions of the guardian of the Leif Repline and some of the other passages Phen had marked. He remembered the elven lore of the furry Gwag creature, and recalled thinking how, if it were up to him, a more formidable thing would be guarding a fountain that could allow the humans to outlive the elves. He was in the process of showing Phen a simple healing spell when Cade came to the door. He told them that King Aldar was dazed, but recovering from the dangerous dose of Oarly's brew. Then he led Phen and Corva to the Hall of Chronicles.

The majority of the giants' history was kept in the old language, Cade explained as they rode the lift down to the proper level. Phen and the elf were pleased when Cade offered to stay and help translate for them. Though both of them had a crude understanding of the old language, neither could read passages without stumbling on words or phrases that they didn't understand. It took only a few hours to find what they needed to know. Whether it was good information or bad, it was hard to say. The Gwag was a formidable beast that they would probably have to kill to access the Leif Repline. From the more detailed descriptions of the creature, which spoke of its speed and ferocity, this would be no easy task.

High King Mikahl sat on his throne listening to the Westland mage, De'Rain, convey Commander Lyle's report of the attack on O'Dakahn. Ironspike was not inserted into the sleeve in the throne arm. A display wasn't necessary; they were alone. The day's court had been dismissed after a vehement argument over the restored property lines between a pair of farms turned hateful. During the occupation the Zard had removed most of three rail cattle fences, because the splintered wooden beams and poles were perfect height for tearing open a running geka. Now one returned land owner was inching the fence into the neighboring property, trying to gain a bit more for his own.

Mikahl was stretched. One family's teenage son had challenged the old neighbor, a man of at least sixty summers, to an honor duel. Mikahl had to raise his voice and went as far as drawing Ironspike from its sleeve. He blasted a soup bowl-sized divot out of the court room's floor. Ultimately, a formal investigation was ordered. King Mikahl's' constable would try to locate the old fence line and restore it.

The disruption had caused Mikahl to send the rest of the petitioners away. Already, Master Wizard Sholt and Lord Spyra had reported from Salazar. They'd tracked down quite a few of the tainted sailors and dispelled Pael's curse. They'd also spent time at the Lost Lion Inn with Lady Zasha, her husband Wyndall, and the newborn baby, Ellrich.

As King Mikahl expected, they'd refused to move into Settsted Stronghold and take over its lordship. Zasha's request to have a smaller, safer holding set aside for her son to inherit was one that Mikahl couldn't possibly deny. But now he would have to pick a lord to take over Settsted.

Lord Spyra was his first choice. The man had spent years as the general of Queen Willa's Blacksword army. He was qualified. The only problem was, he wasn't a Westlander.

Spyra and Sholt were on the way back to Westland trying to beat the stormy cold fronts that were threatening to rile the sea gods. Mikahl sighed and indicated for De'Rain to begin. Commander Lyle's view of what happened would either ease his mind, or worry him further. It was time to find out which.

From his seat at the court scribe's desk, the mage began with his condensed version of the report.

"All three dozen skeletons that carried out the attack in the port merchant district were destroyed. No skeletons have been seen in the city since that night." De'Rain paused and took a sip of water from a goblet. "Several descriptions concurred that it was a Choska seen in the sky. A few people reported seeing the demon flying westward. Commander Lyle traveled to Nahka, on the riverbank at the marshes' edge. A group of farmers saw the Choska attack a herdsman and his flock just outside of the village. This was after it left O'Dakahn. The Choska killed the herder and fed on his flock, then flew away west again, they say heading directly toward the Dragon's Tooth Spire. It hasn't been seen since."

"Also, a marsh mage who reportedly dabbles in small animal resurrections and potions has disappeared from the village."

De'Rain took another drink. "Commander Lyle is in Nahka now, awaiting orders. He wanted me to tell you that he was prepared to go into the marsh after the Choska, if necessary.

"No," King Mikahl said flatly. "I want him to meet with the soldiers King Jarrek sent to help establish the eastern marsh patrol. Strongholds and outposts will need building. I want his assessment of that situation. Tell him that the threat at the Dragon Tooth's Spire is being handled."

"Is that all, King Mikahl?" De'Rain asked.

"Aye," Mikahl said with a smile. "I think it is."

The High King stood and glanced down at the chunk missing from the floor. "If you would, ask Lady Able to find a mason who can repair that. The queen was ill this morning and I must check on her."

"As you command, Majesty," De'Rain said. Then, as Mikahl was leaving, the mage added, "Congratulations."

Chapter Forty

Bzorch was getting hungry. The huge flock of dactyls that had roosted on the side of the Dragon's Tooth Spire made it almost impossible for him to leave his place up in the wormhole. He tried to climb back down in daylight but they tried to give him away. If he stayed where he was, he would starve to death. Already, he was contemplating using his dragon gun to kill one of the pesky swamp birds for food. He was so hungry he would risk setting the flock off to get one. He was just waiting for the sun to sink below the western horizon to do it.

The eastern side of the fang was bathed in evening shadow and would be perfect for him to get a clear shot at a dactyl, but the shape of the tooth made it almost impossible. The wormhole on that side opened up on thin air. The face of the rock below the opening scalloped inward in an inverted curve. His hunt, as well as any attempt to descend, would have to be carried out on the western face.

Bzorch decided to try to feed in the night, then climb down in the early morning shadows. The last two mornings, the dactyls had woken at dawn with a cacophony of shrieks and screeches. He hoped to be able to hurry down amid the noise. He didn't feel hopeful, though. Even if he defied the flock of dactyls, he had hundreds of miles of snapper-filled marshes to traverse. Even if he could find and salvage one of the safety boats from the barges, he would have little chance of making it to Westland to warn the High King. Bzorch was determined, though. He was a survivor. He didn't understand the concept of giving up, and he didn't acknowledge fear. He was half beast, and that primal side of him was starting to take over.

He'd been observing the Zard encampment below and knew that the Choska's lair was somewhere at the southern base of the island. Every bit of movement indicated that much. Whether it was the Choska or the Dragon Queen running things, he couldn't say. He was half determined to take matters into his own hands and try to kill them all before they started moving toward Westland. He figured that it was too soon to think about that. He still had to climb down without getting shredded by the dactyls.

As the sun finally crept down from the sky, Bzorch took up a position lying with his upper torso hanging out of the wormhole. He carefully placed the coil of line at the edge so that it would unravel easily. He tied the loose end securely around a chunk of broken rock. He lay as still as he could manage and held the dragon gun aimed and ready to fire. The nearest nest he could see was too far down to shoot at accurately. So he lay there for a long while hoping that one of the restless creatures would fly within his range. None did.

He pulled himself back into the wormhole, brimming with frustrated anger and feeling the fatigue of not eating for several days. With a growl of determination he gathered up a pile of fist-sized pieces of rock, placed them near the edge of the wormhole and resumed his position. He held the dragon gun loosely with one hand and with the other threw one of the rocks down into the nearest flock. Just as he hoped, the dactyl roosting there leapt from the cliff face into panicked flight. Three of them flapped out away from the rock, squawking in distress, then after circling around a moment, they returned to their nest. None of them flew close enough for Bzorch to loose a shaft at, but it gave him hope. After all, he had quite a few rocks to throw, and sooner or later one of the agitated dactyls would make the mistake of getting too close.

After he threw the third rock, several of the creatures went fluttering away. They all came extremely close and Bzorch took a chance. His arms had grown tired and he missed, but the prospect of a well-needed meal, and the rush of nearly having one on the end of his line, kept him from giving up. Finally, about halfway through his second pile of rocks, when the moon was high overhead and bathing the fang in an eerie yellow light, Bzorch shafted one of them. Like hauling down a kite in a gale, he pulled the loud, screaming swamp bird into the wormhole. Once the flopping, flapping creature was inside, Bzorch got hold of its neck and snapped it. During the struggle the dactyl managed to slice Bzorch's chest open with its razor-sharp beak. At that moment the breed giant didn't care. Using his bare hands, he ripped open the reptilian bird's leathery hide and devoured its bloody flesh. When his hunger was sated, he recoiled his rope, and rewound the dragon gun. After that, he leaned back against the rocky wall and waited for the moon to get low so that he could start his climb down through the dactyl roosts.

When the time came, it was as black as pitch outside. The sun would reach the horizon in the east soon and set the dactyls off on their morning tirade of noise. Bzorch hoped to be well among them when it started.

He put the coil of line over one shoulder, instead of across his body, and he used a bit of the line to sling the dragon gun over the other. The wound on his chest had stopped bleeding, but he knew the freshness of it would attract predators once he was in the water. Since there was land at the southern base of the fang, he decided to ease that way as he descended. He still hadn't decided whether he would try to kill the Choska or not. He remembered vowing to pike its head at the gates of O'Dakahn where it had killed all of those people. He didn't want to break his word, but the short-haired Dragon Queen down there was probably a greater issue. Since he had a wound that would make him little more than bait in the marshes, he was weighing the matter in his head as he started down the rock face in the dark.

He climbed to his right as much as possible while moving down the rock face. As he went, he considered his chances of surviving the swamp. He wasn't afraid of pain or death, only of failing his people and his king. What would King Mikahl do when Bzorch told him about the Choska and its rider? Probably send another party into the marshes to hunt them down. The way his men had been devoured by the denizens of this fiend-infested swamp was something he would never forget. In a matter of moments, the entire party of three hundred men had been eliminated. Even the barges were gone, either resting at the bottom of the swamp, or being overgrown by the thick vegetation. The next group would meet the same sort of fate. The Choska, or the woman who so eerily resembled that bitch Shaella, had retaken control of the life out here.

A thunder of wings, accompanied by a horrendous screech, startled Bzorch out of his reverie. He had descended into the roost and a glance upward told him that he had made thrice the progress easing to the south that he had downward. Clinging to the rock face, he held still, waiting to see if the dactyls would become aggressive toward his trespass. He was glad to find that, while they screeched and flapped in protest, they didn't attack.

As he continued downward, still easing to the south as he went, a few of the bigger dactyls did become aggressive. He was forced to hold himself to the wall like an insect traveling the trunk of a tree full of hungry birds. As big as the dactyls were, even a larger one with a twelve- or thirteen-foot wingspan couldn't hope to pull him off the wall. He was just too big. They could, however, pick and lash at his exposed back with their long, sharp beaks. And they did.

The harassment didn't last long, and didn't do any serious damage, but Bzorch felt fresh blood trickling down his back and knew that he had no chance in the water. The sky was lightening and the dactyls were filling the morning with a fever-pitched racket. Bzorch had to hurry and he knew it. He kept moving as much to his right as he did down. Another dactyl pecked at him as he found a shelf wide enough for him to stand and rest on. He threw a wild, battering blow at its head and connected. The stunned creature went semi-limp and half-glided, half-twirled down into the swamp. Its fall reminded Bzorch of a big leaf floating to the forest floor. In the light of early morning, yet still in the shadow of the fang, he watched the swamp bird splash down into a grassy shallow. He wasn't surprised a moment later when an explosion of water erupted around the flailing form. After that, it was gone.

Seeing that he'd moved far enough south that he could climb down the rock face and step off onto land, he began to gather hope. When he started the descent, he didn't see the Choska and its beautiful rider as it swept down at him from above.

The Warlord was disturbed by the size of the raid on his lair. Since the demons he called on had their minions devour the two groups with such cold and brutal efficiency, he was pleased, though. The fact that men had come in such a force meant that they knew how serious a threat was here. He had to act.

He decided that he didn't need to wait out the winter. The spies and informants who served his hell-bound horde had informed them about the realm's lax state. No one was afraid, no one was on guard, save for at the city of Xwarda where the precious Wardstone was. He knew he didn't have to take the whole city to get it. The destruction would come after he used Shaella's form to access the stuff and tear down the boundary.

To open the remaining seals, all he needed was for Shaella to place her hand on the Wardstone. All he had to do was to get her into Xwarda and before the stuff. He knew that the city's forces were guarding it against armies and demons, not flawlessly beautiful women. Once, he had used her to open the seals, then he, and as many demons that could fit through, would come into the world and show the defenders of Xwarda just how foolish they were to believe that they could stave off the might of the Warlord and his legions. He wouldn't be able to render the boundaries between the world of men and the Nethers impotent, though, until he gained access to the Wardstone in his own form. With an army of demons to distract the foolish people of Xwarda, he didn't figure it would be hard. It would be as easy as killing the foolish Wedjakin that he was watching climb down toward his lair. Shaella's head shook as the Warlord was in full control of her body. Had the half-beast not realized that he had been spotted long ago? The Warlord's thoughts were disdainful. Men were ignorant and arrogant, and though these man-beasts were brutal, they were driven by instinct, and easily distracted.

The Choska needed food for the long flight to Xwarda they were about to undertake. What a perfect meal, the Warlord decided.

He told the Choska to feed on the Wedjakin. He'd waited for it to get where it was so that when the Choska knocked it from the wall, it wouldn't plummet into the water. If that happened, the snappers would devour it before the Choska even had a chance. Now, though, it would land in the shallows, and the Master of Hell was excited to make him fall.

A sudden, jerking pain, so sharp that it nearly made Bzorch back off the ledge he was resting on, seared across his back. Instinctively, he clutched to the wall to keep from falling, but he craned his neck to see what had caused the horrible heat. What he saw was her.

Shaella's short, spiky hair and her scar-free complexion couldn't change her eyes, or the smug scowl of superiority.

Bzorch's blood turned to ice as he realized his predicament. He was about to be killed, and he knew it without a doubt.

A crimson pulse shot forth from the Choska's ember eyes and shattered an overhanging chunk of rock up above him. The hard, sharp pieces rained down on him like hammer blows, but he continued to hold tight. As soon as the debris stopped falling he shrugged the coil of line from his shoulder. The free end was tied to his wrist so that, in case it fell while he was climbing, he could pull it all back in.

The footing he was on was narrow, but he spun with animal grace so that his back was against the rock face. Then, as the Choska circled back around, he took the dragon gun from his other shoulder and aimed it. He knew to shoot high because of the weight of the line.

Neither the Choska, nor its beautiful rider, saw the weapon as they closed in for the kill. The demon was far bigger and stronger than a dactyl. It was too late for it to dodge the barbed spear when Bzorch fired. It screamed out a shrill, ear-piercing yell and dove sharply to the south as it was punctured. Shaella was nearly thrown from its back, but managed to hang on.

Moments later, Bzorch was yanked by his wrist from the rock face. He fell slowly at first, in a long, arcing swing, but as the speed of his descent increased, the Choska began to fall toward the ground, too. To his surprise, he suddenly rose, and quickly. He went up and over the southern edge of the shark-fin formation.

For a time the Choska carried him east, out over the open marsh. The beast was smart and swept low to the ground, forcing Bzorch to go dragging through the tangles of vegetation. The demon lifted back up, and the shaft eventually pulled free of it.

Bzorch went tumbling through the air. His big body crashed to a violent stop in the vast, predator-filled jungle, somewhere east of the Dragon's Tooth.

Chapter Forty-One

With ten people in the party, the particular teleportation room they were about to use was overcrowded. It looked as if a herd of shaggy, two-legged creatures was trying to huddle together with a marble statue. There was no room for horses on this leg of the journey. Dostin and the two archers were forced to argue just to get included. The need for supply haulers won out, and they were issued cloaks made from the hide of some thickly furred beast, and then given shoulder packs full of food, oiled canvases, and chunks of a substance called everburn, which the giants favored for their fires.

Lieutenant Welch, Jicks, and Corva already had packs to carry. The group wouldn't fail for want of supplies. Hyden Hawk was determined to make sure that there would be enough food and heat to sustain so many bodies if something went wrong.

According to the maps, horses wouldn't have done them much good anyway. The day-and-a-half hike to the Leif Repline cavern was all rocky ledge and scree-littered ridgeway. It would be treacherous enough on foot. Horses would just slow them down.

Hyden wished the giants' lore revealed more about what lay inside the cavern. Only a few human explorers had made it to the cave and into the first fountain chamber. All accounts agreed it was full of poison, probably to trick the greedy. A handful had ventured farther in and met the Gwag, but no one who made it beyond the creature bothered to tell his tale, save for an ancient wanderer called Olden. Olden lived for several hundred years, but in a time long before Pavreal, Dahg Mahn, and Shokin. He might have lived longer had he not openly predicted the fall of King Dar'Grav, thus earning him a trip to the Dakaneese ruler's chopping block. Luckily the old man kept detailed journals. Phen had procured a copy for the quest. Hyden hoped that the reason there were no newer stories about the place was because people wanted to protect its integrity. By the way Oldin wrote about the explorers he filched, he never gave away all he knew about the fountain. Thirteen times, over the course of three centuries, he wrote entries about people finding him with questions about the Leif Repline. He said that they purchased maps and information from him for unbelievable prices, and then went off seeking immortality. Only one group had earned a second paragraph. They'd come back from the Giant Mountains telling of the ferocious Gwag, the poisoned entry fountain, and trolls so ornery that they had to be killed without hesitation.

Princess Telgra was clearly nervous. She seemed terrified about getting her memory back. Hyden didn't worry too much about her. Dostin and Phen stayed close to her, and Corva was doing a good job of soothing her with words. Hyden could sense that the three beings who cared so much for her were all that was keeping her from drowning in anxiety.

Hyden wasn't comfortable that they might have to kill the Gwag, but by all descriptions the creature was too dangerous to be tricked or trapped. An agile and exceptionally fast wolfish thing, it had survived the centuries. As recently as three years ago some guardians had used the outer part of the cavern for shelter and had seen it. According to Durge, a guardian assigned to aid them in their preparations, the infamous water that flowed warm from the depths of the earth had no effect on the giants. He said the water in the first fountain wasn't poisonous to them either.

Hyden didn't really care about the fountain's power, beyond its ability to save Phen and Talon from the miserable condition in which they'd ended up. He was worried about the Gwag, though. If they killed the thing, the Leif Repline would sit unguarded from exploitation after they left. The powers contained in those waters were so great that, if the rumors were even half true, the place should be eternally protected from those with questionable intent. Hyden had spoken with King Aldar about it, but the king of the giants was still a groggy mess from the granite juice he'd drunk. Cade understood the predicament and promised to explain it to the king as soon as he was coherent. Cade told Hyden that the mountains themselves protected the Leif Repline. Giants could be posted if there was a real need for them. Cade's reasoning was hard to argue with, for he wouldn't stay still to argue. It was all Cade could do to keep the queen from tossing Oarly in the dungeon under suspicion of poisoning her husband.

King Aldar's chamberlain spent a whole afternoon teaching Hyden the commands of the teleportation rooms. Hyden would have to control the portal to get them where they were going and back. He hoped he had the inflections of the strange words remembered correctly. Since he'd retrieved the ring from Gerard in the Nethers, things like that were coming naturally to him. Spells he'd never heard of sometimes leapt to the forefront of his mind as if he'd known them forever. If he didn't remember the words correctly, they would know shortly, and it would be too late to do anything about it.

Lieutenant Welch was flustered and scowling. They were already gathering in the teleportal. His men had a duty to protect the group, but with the heavy packs they were carrying, they could only grunt and groan.

"What if some mad trolls attack?" he pleaded with Hyden. "Or worse, an ice dragon. By the gods, I would have trouble drawing my blade, and my men couldn't hit a barn with their arrows if they have to hurry and loose. These packs are cumbersome at best."

"I've got my bow at the ready, Lieutenant," Hyden proudly showed him the elven longbow Vaegon had given him. Corva gasped, seeing it for the first time for what it was. "If it will make you feel better," Hyden went on, "I'll have Phen carry that pack and we can have your sword at the ready, as well."

The lieutenant nodded, unshouldered his pack, and then handed it to Phen. Phen took it, but smirked at Hyden. He didn't dare complain, though. After all, these people were here to help him. Talon dind't need them. The hawkling could have flown to the Lief Repline on his own.

"Why don't you have Talon explore the cavern before we go in?" Phen suggested.

Hyden narrowed his eyebrows and shook his head at the boy. "You've been hanging around Oarly too long. You're supposed to be coming up with creative ideas, not ones I thought of weeks ago."

"I'm just worried, I guess," Phen admitted. He said his body had grown used to feeling heavy and hard. He was concerned that when he drank from the fountain he might revert to his previous form and be grievously wounded where his hardened skin had been gouged. He pointed out the place on his shoulder where a chip was missing, as well. Hyden offered no advice, for he didn't have any. Even though the weather didn't have much of an effect on Phen, Hyden did make sure his young friend was wearing a heavy furred coat for this part of the quest. Once he was cured, the boy would have to stay warm. Spike had been riding in a big pocket that was sewn into the garment. The lyna despised the cold almost as much as Oarly. His prickly little head only peeked out occasionally.

"Worried or not, Phen, the time has come for us to go." Hyden raised his voice over the murmur of the group and gave Cade a nod. "Everyone inside the rune circle, all of you now."

The giant smiled. "The kingdom of Afdeon wishes that the gods grace your quest with naught but good fortune."

"Thank you. If we are not heard from in ten days, send a search party," Hyden said. "One or more of us will most likely survive even the worst of possibilities."

"We pray that won't be necessary," Cade said, "but rest assured, it will be done if you don't return on time."

Hyden forced a smile. He had a feeling that this wasn't going to be easy. "Give King Aldar my best, when he has recovered."

Oarly sensed twenty eyes looking down at him and tried to become smaller than he already felt. A moment later, Hyden spoke a word. The air filled with static, and after a deep "whoomp!" that shook the fabric of reality around them, they were suddenly somewhere else.

A roughly chiseled version of the teleportation symbol was now beneath their booted feet, and unlike the smooth-floored chamber they'd just left, the ground here was gray and uneven. A bitter wind cut through their furs and whistled in the shallow recess in which they found themselves. They were in a scallop on an icy granite cliff, and even the layered clothes under the shagmar coats they wore couldn't keep the frigid chill from finding them.

"B- b- b- bah!" Oarly blurted, then shrunk back into his furred hood and adjusted his pack.

"Let's get moving." Hyden nocked an arrow to his bowstring and took the lead. "Moving'll keep us warm. Since you've got a blade and no pack to haul, Lieutenant, you take the rear."

Lieutenant Welch nodded and drew his sword. He leaned it against the rock face and buttoned his coat over his scabbard. He put on some gloves he'd gotten from one of the giant page boys and took up an alert position at the rear of the procession.

The rocky ledge was wide enough for a small horse cart, but beyond its lip was a thousand-foot free fall into a jagged gorge. It wasn't snowing at the moment, but the powerful wind carried granulated ice crystals that scoured the travelers. Ice and snow was piled in all the crevices along the way, making each step a slippery chore.

Around midday they found a shallow recess, similar to the one they'd appeared in. It wasn't enclosed enough to hold warmth, but it was mostly out of the wind, so they were able to enjoy a meal in relative comfort.

It was harder starting again than it had been the first time. The harsh, bone-chilling climate seemed to sap the life right out of them. No one spoke. They couldn't have heard each other over the wind anyway. Not one of them heard Lieutenant Welch's muffled scream behind them. The man was snatched off of the trail by a huge rock troll that was hiding in a crevice. It wasn't until a few hours later, when Hyden was debating making a camp in a narrow fissure, that they realized he was gone. The sudden alarm that swept over the group clinched the decision to make a camp. The fissure was out of the wind. While the group huddled around a couple of small everburn fires, Hyden, Jicks, and Phen looked for the lieutenant.

They searched into the night, using Phen's orb spells and Talon's superior vision, but they found nothing. There was no trace, not even a hint of what had happened. When they were finally forced to settle in and get warm, Jicks was in tears. Princess Telgra and Dostin both cried, as well. Hyden, Phen, and Oarly had lost several people close to them while warring and adventuring in the past. They were a little more hardened to such happenings. It was a sad affair, but it was part of the journey.

Hyden recalled his Uncle Condlin's words, right after one of his cousins fell from the sacred nesting cliffs during the annual egg harvest. "Every gain has a price, and sometimes loss is the cost of that gain."

Lieutenant Welch paid the price for Phen, Princess Telgra, and Talon to find healing. At least Welch made the first payment, Hyden thought to himself. He could tell by the look on Phen's stoney face that the boy understood this, too. Talon knew, as well. The persistent hawkling was still out in the night, riding the icy winds in search of their lost companion.

By the look on the wild-eyed faces of both elves it was clear that they understood the magnitude of the loss, as well. Elves, Hyden knew, lived far longer than men and had a peculiar view of death. They cherished life, and the fact that the lieutenant had lost his helping one of them seemed to be weighing heavily. Sleep, for some of the group, was hard to come by.

The afternoon of the next day they came to the Leif Repline cavern. To everyone's relief, it was no natural formation. The stonework was ancient, the opening worked into a perfect arch just big enough for a giant to walk under without stooping. A few icicles, as long as a man is tall, hung down into the entrance. With a marble-hard arm, Phen knocked them out of the way and ushered the others in out of the bitter wind.

Once inside it was obvious that, though much stone work had been done here, the cavern was indeed naturally formed. Talon cawed from overhead and winged off cautiously into the darkness. A few hundred feet into the gray tunnel the scree-covered cavern bottom became smoother. A semiflat carved floor led deeper into the mountain. Both Hyden and Phen cast their orb lights into existence so that each had a fist-sized glow of magical illumination hovering a few feet overhead.

"You can do that, too, my lady," Corva told Princess Telgra. "Soon you'll be yourself again."

She gave a nervous laugh that was tinged with sadness. "You seem as if you can't wait to get rid of this me for the other."

"I hope the other you likes me as much as you do," Phen said, saving Corva from an awkward response.

"I'm sure I will, Phen," she chuckled dryly. "But I might not like the other you." The last was said teasingly.

"Bah!" Oarly barked and shrugged off his pack. "We're finally out of the fargin cold and safe underground. Do I have to listen to the banter of daft folk thrice my age?" He gave all of them a good, hard stare. "You can change a person's skin, and you can erase some memories, but you can't change the nature of who someone is."

"That was profound, Oarly," Phen said seriously. "That liquefied lotus bud you've been drinking seems to have unclouded your head."

"Bah!" Oarly barked again. He pulled a little flask from inside his coat and took a long pull. Then he unbuckled his battle axe and started off ahead of Phen, letting the boy's orb light his path.

"He's right," Hyden observed from behind them. He'd had the archers and Jicks put down their gear and ready their weapons. Jicks was moving to the front of the procession near Oarly, as Hyden indicated for him to do.

"It does make sense," Phen said. "We are who we are."

"It's kind of warm in here," observed Hyden randomly. "Let Jicks and Oarly take the lead. If something attacks, those in the middle drop down so that we can loose our arrows over you. This passage is tall and there might be openings up high, as well as low. Keep an eye out for pitfalls, Oarly."

Corva let his pack drop to the floor and drew his longsword. He told Dostin to lose his burden and be ready with his staff. The monk nodded, his face a mask of silent fear.

"There will probably be nothing until after the poisoned fountain," Phen said knowingly. "Up ahead it will open into that chamber. There's no mention of branching tunnels or halls."

"Old caverns crack and shift, lad," Oarly said, using his jeweled axe to point at just such a fracture, which was big enough for a man to squeeze into. "A thin wall might have crumbled through, or such, since then."

"Aye." Phen nodded and prepared a spell, up until its final command word.

No more than a thousand feet from where the cavern bottom turned to carven floor, the passage opened into a beautifully detailed room with a ceiling done in a pattern that resembled a woven reed basket. In the center of the floor was a wonderful triple-level fountain. The water flowing through it was burbling and tinkling away. There was a pyramid formed of life-sized stone mermaids spouting crystal clear water from their pursed lips. They looked to be frolicking inside a rippling, knee-high walled pool. An ancient mound of bones sat amid a pile of rotted clothes against the retainer wall. It had been there so long that some of the bones had begun to crumble. Beyond the fountain, the passage continued into the darkness. Out of the shaft, Talon came fluttering in and landed on Hyden's shoulder excitedly.

"Not this one, Talon," Hyden said. "Fly ahead and once your eyes adjust, see if you can find another fountain, or anything else." The hawkling cooed his understanding and took back to the air.

"I doubt it needs to be said, but no one drink the water here. Jicks, you and the boys go fetch our packs while we set up camp. We will explore deeper into the passage after we have gotten out of these heavy clothes."

Jicks had Phen light a torch with his fire finger then led the two archers back up the tunnel for their gear.

No sooner had they gotten out of earshot than Talon come shrieking back into the chamber. Hyden felt his familiar's alarm flashing in his brain and saw the reflection of firelight in a distant pair of big, glassy eyes. He was about to warn the others, but it wasn't necessary. The long, low rumbling of an angry growl filled the chamber.

Oarly started toward the dark opening from where the sound was originating. Corva left Princess Telgra with Phen, and he and Hyden both hurried to the dwarf's side. Hyden nocked his bow as Talon flew past them and wisely landed on Phen's shoulder.

Spike jumped from Phen's pocket when the Gwag growled again. The lyna cat hunched its back and hissed at the sound, then scampered off toward it.

"This is bad," Oarly said.

"What?" Hyden asked. He wondered if Oarly was having some sort of dark premonition.

The Gwag growled again and the sound was massive. It was getting closer.

"What is it, dwarf?" Corva asked through his fear.

"It's a terrible thing to have to face that fargin Gwag," Oarly cursed. "I haven't even had a chance to get good and drunk yet today."

Just then, a horrible scream erupted from behind them. It came from one of the archers. The sound was accompanied by a different kind of roar. It didn't sound like another Gwag, but whatever it was, it sounded just as big.

M. R. Mathias

Chapter Forty-Two

Phen turned to see what he could behind them. Jicks and one of the archers were scrambling back toward the fountain chamber, each carrying a couple of supply packs. Their torch was nowhere to be seen. Both were pale, wide-eyed, and moving very swiftly.

"Beware!" Jicks called ahead of them. "A troll got Mort." He fought a sob and the power of his emotion carried in his voice. "Got him good, it did." He stopped speaking when he saw that Hyden, Oarly, and Corva were in readied battle stances facing the other direction. As he glanced over his shoulder, Mort's wailing cry caused him to shudder. Throwing the packs down, he drew his blade and turned to face the way he had come. "I don't think it followed us, but we have to be ready."

"It's fargin eating Mort," the archer sobbed as he nocked his bow.

"Cover that passage," Hyden commanded over the Gwag's approaching rumble.

Spike growled back at the sound and ran between Oarly's legs toward it. It took only a few heartbeats for the lyna cat to disappear into the darkness beyond the range of Hyden's magical light.

"Guard Telgra with your life," Phen told Dostin. "I'll be right back." Talon flapped from Phen's shoulder as he moved away. Telgra nearly didn't let go of him when he started toward Jicks and Krey. Phen walked right past them. The sudden lack of his orb light in the larger chamber dimmed the space considerably. Talon landed on Telgra's shoulder and settled as she and Dostin watched Phen and his light fade toward the entry.

Not sure what to do, Jicks and Krey eased in behind Phen and followed him.

Suddenly, a snarling, toothy head shot into the light of Hyden's orb. It was big and furry, like some giant fox or wolverine. It was lightning quick, for it attacked so fast that it caught them all by surprise. Corva was caught in the retreating beast's mouth and screamed. Hyden instinctually tried to call out to the beast, but in its enraged state the effort was wasted. Oarly darted toward it and, with a leaping swipe of his axe, caught the monster with a glancing blow. It wasn't much, but it was enough to cause the Gwag to let go of Corva before it pulled back completely into the darkness. Oarly went to help the elf to his feet while Hyden loosed arrow after arrow, hoping to keep it off of them.

"It's a giant snaker," Oarly announced fearfully. "A mongoose, I think. Big bastard."

Corva had been punctured by several dagger-sized teeth and was bleeding profusely. He managed to stand upright and limp toward the others. Oarly, helping to steady him, didn't see the Gwag lunging back at them.

Hyden saw it, though, and he put an arrow right in the creature's melon-sized eye, but not before it had its teeth around the dwarf.

Oarly tried to yell, but a sickening crunch of bones cut the sound into a grunting wheeze. The creature shook its head violently from side to side as it backed away, but it didn't let go. Its eye looked ruined. Thick, milky fluid slung from the wound as the Gwag shook its dwarven morsel. Bright red blood, lots of it, sprayed and splashed from its mouth. Through eyes welling with tears, Hyden loosed more shafts at the beast. They found flesh again and again, but the creature didn't slow down. Within the span of a dozen heartbeats it had taken Oarly and disappeared back into the darkness. Hyden started to chase after it, but when he saw a long, bushy, squirrel-like tail whip around and bound out of sight, he realized it was pointless. The crunch he'd just heard was still reverberating through his head.

Phen was oblivious to the action taking place behind him. He could hear it all, but chose not to pay it any mind. He was on the attack.

He came upon the troll. It was slightly bigger than a giant and covered in dark, mangy fur, with long, pointed ears, and a black hog-like snout. Its chin and chest were matted with slick dark blood, and it held Mort's leg as if it were the drumstick of some giant bird. Its big brown eyes were eerily human-like, and they stayed glued to Phen's strange appearance.

"I'm going to distract it," Phen said to the two soldiers behind him. "Get the other packs, and then get away."

The creature took a big bite of Mort's thigh. It pulled away from the bone, stretching the bloody meat until it tore. Krey sniffled and sobbed but nodded that he understood his orders. Jicks was already shouldering one of the two packs closest to him.

Once Krey had the final pack, Phen spoke again. "Get well behind me. I'm not sure how this will turn out."

The troll took another bite out of Mort and curiously studied the stone man with the light hovering over his head. Phen was glad it didn't seem to care about the other two creeping away with the group's food and gear.

Phen knew that the dragon tear medallion would amplify his spell's potency. Just how much, he wasn't sure. His intent was to wall off the passage with thorny growth. It was a spell he had once used to entangle one of Spike's giant kindred in a black dragon's lair. He hadn't had the dragon's tear medallion then, and his spell hadn't created enough growth to block a passage. Now, though, he thought he could do it.

Before the troll could take another bite of their companion, Phen cast his spell and was amazed by what happened next.

From the rocky floor and walls, tiny chips and flakes of stone broke free. Little green worm-like tendrils pushed outward. They turned and twisted and thickened. A season's worth of growth took place with every passing moment. The branches twisted and twined, and long, finger-sized thorns pushed out of them.

Suddenly, the troll darted at him, reaching out a bloody claw. It never found its mark as it was lifted by the growth that dug into it. It contorted as it squirmed in confusion and fear. It howled out terribly as merciless thorns bit in and held it in place. Phen was alarmed when the growth grew toward the ceiling and started spreading toward him. He had to back up quickly to keep from getting caught in his own tangle. The troll was mewling, its feet and legs splayed at an abstract upward angle. It was bleeding and whimpering between fits of wild shaking as it tried to thrash around, but it couldn't get free.

Phen hurried back to where Jicks and Krey stood open-mouthed and teary-eyed. A glance back made him mutter a curse. Oarly would have to hack them a way out now, but at least nothing else could come in behind them.

"Oarly," Hyden's voice came to them from down the passage. The reverberation off of the stone made it sound as if a dozen people had called out at once. Phen wasn't alarmed by Hyden's call. Oarly had probably chased after the creature. It wasn't until he heard Hyden call out again that his heart sank and his stomach knotted up. The emptiness and hopelessness in Hyden's voice was clear.

"By the gods, no," Phen said. He took off running, his heavy, stone footfalls pounding back toward the open chamber like hammer blows. Jicks and Krey hurried after him as best they could with the packs they were carrying. They arrived in the fountain chamber to see Hyden holding

Phen back in a great bear hug as the stoney boy tried to follow the bloody trail of gore into the darkness.

Corva lay under Telgra and Dostin, who were crouched over him protectively. The elven princess was running her hand over deep wounds and murmuring something. A soft yellow glow radiated from her palm into the elf's skin. All the while, the distraught monk was repeating a prayer over and over again.

Hyden and the cavern floor beyond him were bright with blood. The double light of both his and Phen's magical orbs was stark. There was far too much blood for it all to have come from Corva. At the reaches of the illumination, Oarly's jeweled axe lay glittering and still in a glossy crimson pool.

"NOOO!" Phen screamed into Hyden's shoulder. "No, no, no!"

Hyden wanted to comfort his young friend, but he was fighting back his own sobs.

"He might not be dead, Hyden," Phen managed as he pushed away. "I'm going after him."

Hyden took a deep breath and nodded. He could tell there was no stopping Phen. "Spike is down there somewhere, Phen. Use his eyes. Don't be foolish. Use his stealth." To the others he said: "Build an everburn fire. We will be back shortly, and no matter what you do, don't drink that water." When he pointed at the fountain, Talon came fluttering down to land on his forearm.

Phen was standing stock-still, looking as much like a statue as he ever had. In his mind's eye he was seeing what Spike saw. The sight wasn't normal, but a sort of orange-tinted spectral vision. It was like looking at the world through thick amber lenses. Darkness and light were well separated, though, and the details of things were easy to make out.

The lyna was low to the ground, so it seemed to Phen that he was looking up from a bobbing point just above the floor. Ahead lay empty corridor as far as Spike could see. Behind was the bend in the tunnel, where just beyond, Phen and Hyden stood. With his mind, Phen urged Spike to move further down the passage. He looked back, with his own eyes, and saw that Jicks had ignited a couple of chunks of everburn. Telgra was tending to Corva. Without another thought, he found Spike's vision again and started into the tunnel.

"Is he around the bend?" Hyden asked. Phen nodded and kept going.

Hyden took a trembling breath and followed. He was stricken by what he had just seen happen to his dwarven companion, but that's not why he was shaking. A rage was building inside him. Ultimately, all of this madness and death led back to his brother and him, and to the ring. An old soothsayer had once read their bones and foretold their futures. Most of what she had predicted had come to pass. All save for the end of it.

Hyden held no illusions about Oarly's fate. Far too much blood had been spilled for him to have survived. He still heard the crunch of bone, and the muffled gurgle of Oarly's yell. His blood was aboil with anger. The oracle had told him that he would some day destroy he who was closest to him. After learning of his brother's transformation, he thought for a very long time that it was Gerard he would have to end. What is closer to a young man than his brother? Now he saw a different truth to her words. His quest to banish his brother's evil, and his desire to help his friend and familiar recover from that evil touch, had just killed one of his closest friends. He was so consumed by his rage at Gerard, and maybe himself, that he walked right into Phen.

They were in another open chamber now. It was similar to the first one. A fountain, nearly identical to the other, tinkled and gurgled at the center of the room. Spike stood with an arched back and raised hackles on the retaining wall that encircled the flowing water. Beyond the aquatic display the Gwag lay rasping. A bloody misshapen lump lay a few feet from its mouth in a pool of dark blood.

Oarly.

Phen wailed out in anguish and started toward his friend's corpse. The Gwag rasped again and a mist of pink, frothy blood sprayed from its mouth. Thicker strands of thickening gore dangled like rope from its open maw as it reared up. There was no continuing passage from this chamber. This was the Gwag's lair. This was the Leif Repline fountain. The chamber smelled of rot and urine and was littered with the bones of a thousand meals. The Gwag was obviously injured. Several arrows protruded from blood-matted fur around its neck and shoulders.

Talon took flight from Hyden's shoulder and drew the creature's attention for a heartbeat. Phen ignored it and stalked over to Oarly. A low, moaning sound came from deep within him as he went.

Hyden nocked an arrow and took aim at the beast's good eye. It opened its mouth wide and tried to roar. The sound that came was an intimidating spew of bright scarlet. In the back of the creature's throat, Hyden saw Oarly's dagger. It was buried to the hilt in the roof of the beast's mouth. The Gwag was in pain. Hyden's rage was leaking away because the long, strange-bodied creature had only been doing its duty guarding the fountain. This creature wasn't responsible for Oarly's death. Hyden spoke calmingly to it. Whatever spell had bound it to guard the fountain was most likely broken. This was just a scared, dying animal.

A sudden sensation of a heavy burden being lifted from his soul swept over Hyden. He turned to see that Talon had landed on the chin of one of the mermaids and was bathing in the flow it was spitting forth. Hyden could feel Talon's relief. The lingering effects of the red priest's spell were being cleansed away from the hawkling like mud.

Phen would have retched if he could have. Oarly was mangled beyond recognition. Only the old boots he wore were recognizable. They were the same boots that had one time been the root of a hundred jests over Hyden's poor spellcasting ability. Phen wanted to cry but wouldn't allow himself the emotion. He wanted to curl himself up into a ball and scream, but knew he couldn't let himself succumb to grief. Instead, he let out a primal roar of his own. The sound was so harrowing that the Gwag shrank back against the wall and began to shiver.

His expression blank, and his movements mechanical, Phen picked the bloody, half-chewed body of his friend up in his arms and hurriedly staggered toward the fountain pool. Spike kept his eyes on the Gwag, but relaxed his hackles and mewled sadly at his familial master. The creature could feel Phen's grief.

Phen stepped over the low retaining wall and sat down with his friend's body in his lap. Only after Brady Culvert had been melted by the black dragon had he ever felt as much loss.

Hyden was afraid to drop his guard. His arrow might be the only thing to keep the trembling beast from panicking and attacking Phen. His eyes were filling with tears of anguish. He couldn't believe the wily old dwarven prankster was gone, but he was. As grief-stricken as he was, though, he couldn't help but smile when he saw fresh tears streaming down Phen's brightly pinkening cheeks. The Leif Repline was restoring the boy.

"Put Oarly in," he called out, hoping against hope that there was life still left in the dwarf.

Phen did, but all that happened was the release of his pent-up emotion. Oarly was beyond saving.

Chapter Forty-Three

The Choska had been mortally wounded. Being a demon, only its body was going to die. Its malignant soul would be pulled back into the Nethers where it would rally and ready the others of its kind to prepare them for the breaching of the seal. Even as it died, it served the Warlord, carrying Shaella's body out of the marshes and over Dakahn. The dead Choska glided to a crash near Lokahna, at the edge of a farm. Shaella's body survived the tumble and she ended up stumbling, bruised and bloody, toward a little cottage.

The farmer's son, a young man of seventeen years, saw her clinging to a fence post. She was half-naked, shaven-headed, and trembling in the early winter chill. He gave her his cloak. He put her on his horse and led her back to the warm safety of the farmhouse. She wouldn't speak, so the boy's mother tended her wounds, bathed her, and put her in some ill-fitting clothes while the boy and his father rode out to see from where she had come. They found the Choska twisted and broken. Clutched in one of its claws was a piece of the strange girl's clothes.

"What is it, Da?"

"Can't say, Tarren." He scratched his stubbly chin. "Naught good, I'd guess. She's a lucky lass."

"Can I have her for a wife, then?" Tarren asked seriously. "She's far more prettier than Mara Swain."

"That she is, lad, but she might be married already. She might be trouble, too."

"A roll with that might be worth a little trouble, huh?" Tarren joked with his father.

"Most likely," the older man grinned. "Once she gets her wits back she will probably want to return to her kinfolk. I suppose, since winter is on us, you could help her home and find out."

Later that evening at the supper table, Tarren and his parents slowly ate their meal while staring at the strange, stubble-haired girl who wouldn't speak. They had asked her a hundred questions. Her only response was to look at them with helpless doe eyes and to clutch at herself as if she were freezing.

In truth, the Warlord had left her mind for a time. She was thoughtless. Back in his domain he was commanding his legions to bring forth all their earthy influence and ensure that Shaella's body made it safely to Xwarda.

The Lord of the Hells learned that one of his devils had a following in the Valleyan town of Strond. Among the worshipers was a wagon master who was more than willing to appease his chosen deity. Already, a carriage was being readied to meet Shaella in Kastill. All the Warlord needed now was to get Shaella's body across the river into Valleya. It was a three-hour hike at worst, but without warm clothes or shoes, it could be impossible.

Coming back into Shaella's consciousness, the Warlord had to be mindful of the voice he used when he spoke. It wouldn't do for the bewildered stranger at the farmhouse to speak out in the voice of the Dark One. The Warlord chose not to speak for a while. He sized up the family before entering the conversation.

"Maybe she's from O'Dakahn, Dran," the wife said to her husband. "Wildra Swain said there's a barrelful of loonies running around there who drink that fire brew and smoke frog skins and such." She leaned forward and continued in a whisper, as if Shaella couldn't hear her. "Maybe she's one of them."

"She was carried here by some winged beast, Ma," Terran said defensively. "You think them loonies from the city fly around in the claws of beasts?"

The mother dropped her eyes and shook her head, making her chubby cheeks jiggle. Her husband whacked Terran with the back of his hand. "Speak to your ma with respect, boy," he growled.

"I'm from Southron," Shaella said sheepishly. She sounded as if she were a scared girl of only ten summers. "My ma shaved my head 'cause I got the lice. Where am I? I'm so afraid." She burst into tears then and buried her face in her hands.

"See there, Ma," Terran said, rubbing the knot on his head. "She's not some loony from the city."

"What's your name, child?" the farmer's wife asked. "There's nothing to fear here. We're simple folk. So come on now, tell me your name."

"Shae," the Warlord answered, peeking through Shaella's tears at Terran. "Thank you for bringing me in from the cold."

"My da says I can help you get home," Terran said excitedly. His expression abruptly changed to a look of concern. "You ain't got no husband, do ya?"

The Warlord wanted to take the carving knife from the meat plate and jab it into this oaf's eye. That, or just lean forth and take a bite out of his face. Instead, he let a grin show on Shaella's face. "Not yet," she blushed, partially from the anger of having to partake in this farce, partly because she was working to restrain herself. The Warlord knew from that moment on that the boy would be smitten with Shaella.

That night, Terran and his mother went into the attic and found some warm clothes, some boots, and a cloak for Shae. The father dug up his jar of coins and shook out a handful of coppers for his son to use on his journey to Southron. He couldn't spare them horses to ride, but since the snow decided to start coming down that evening, he could at least make sure they could afford a stall, or a loft to sleep in, and a hot meal or two on their journey.

Southron was several days, most of a week, away, but many a farm dotted the road. Secretly, the father hoped the girl had parents well off enough to offer a bit of a dowry. He had heard Southron was an uppity place—all horse traders and cattlemen, people whose only interest in farming was feeding their herds.

The next morning, Terran and Shae set out across the white-blanketed farm toward Lokahn. From there they would cross the river into Valleya. The hopeful young farmboy had no idea that his journey would end there. Shaella's wagoneer was waiting in Kastill, just on the other side of the bridge.

Hyden used his ability to converse with animals to try to stay the Gwag while Dostin and the two soldiers pried Phen away from Oarly. The creature was skittish enough to hear his soothing tones, but hesitant to comply, especially since it was in pain.

Princess Telgra healed her mind in the fountain's water. When they were done with the pool, Hyden cast the same spell he'd used to snatch Lieutenant Welch's sword from him when they met in the foothills, only this time he removed Oarly's dagger from the roof of the Gwag's throat. He made the strange creature drink from the fountain and then hummed a ballad until it slipped into slumber.

Jicks came and helped drag Oarly's body out of the cave. They rolled the mangled dwarf's remains into one of the waterproof canvases they'd brought along for shelter, then carried him back to the first fountain. The whole while, Hyden's not-so-melodic voice echoed through the cavern.

THE WIZARD AND THE WARLORD

Corva wasn't doing well. While Princess Telgra and Phen huddled with Dostin in sorrowful mourning and prayer, Jicks and Krey helped the elven man to the Leif Repline. As soon as he drank of the water he began to heal. The deep punctures in his body slowly sealed themselves and then puckered into fat purple scars.

"Why didn't it heal Master Oarly?" Jicks asked Hyden as he wiped away a stray tear.

"I think Oarly was already dead when his body found the water." Hyden answered, ending his mourning lullaby.

The young swordsman glared at the sleeping Gwag, letting his anger overpower his sorrow. "Why would you save the beast that killed your friend?"

"The beast was bound to guard this place from trespass." Hyden sat at the edge of the fountain's retaining wall and cupped a handful of the water. He let it drain between his fingers as he continued. "If we left the fountain unguarded, and some dark sentient beast or a power-hungry man were allowed to abuse it, where would we be?" He looked Jicks directly in the eye. "That creature was only doing its duty."

Jicks nodded that he understood. "What if it had been you or the princess that had gotten killed?"

"Unlike me, or Oarly, you are here because of duty, so this might be harder for you to understand." Hyden watched Corva climb out of the pool studying his healed flesh with curious yellow eyes. "I am more than willing to die for my friends, Jicks. Oarly was, too. He died an honorable death. His life was given to heal Phen and Talon, and I suppose the princess, too. If I knew my death would bring peace and long life to those I love, I would welcome it." He had to chuckle ironically at his own words. He meant them, but here he was doing everything except trying to kill Gerard, or the Demon Lord he'd become. He was dead set on banishing his brother to the hells for good instead. Was it because he knew that when Gerard died, he would, too? Was he afraid to die? No, he decided, as he fought back tears of sorrow. If he could trade places with Oarly that moment, he would have. It was something else.

If it was truly as simple as facing death, he thought, he would have the courage to meet his fate. He wasn't sure that it wasn't coming to exactly that anyway. If he failed to banish his warlord brother, he would have to kill him. According to the goddess, his duty was to maintain the balance. Hyden contemplated this long after the group had rejoined in the first chamber where they had made some semblance of a camp.

The princess had her memory back and was worried about her mother and what her arrogant people might have done in her absence. She was also saddened beyond measure, not only because of Oarly's death, but because of the deaths of the others in her life, particularly her father, and the elven party back on Salaya.

Phen looked bad, but only because his body was starving for sustenance. His hair and robes were still bleached white, but his skin was mottled pink with color from his blood resuming its flow. Telgra, between bouts of sobbing, forced Phen to eat cheese, meat and dried fruit. He took more than one piece of the nutrient-rich herb bread that Princess Gretta had slipped her before they left Afdeon. After Dostin fell asleep, Phen kissed Telgra on the cheek and lay down in his bedroll. She lay down next to him and soon joined his slumber.

Hyden, with Spike scampering along beside him, went back to the Leif Repline fountain and sat cross-legged on the retaining wall around it. He sank into a trance and sought his goddess.

His choices, and the price they were demanding of his companions, were weighing heavily on his soul. He wasn't sure what he would ask her for, or if he would seek her guidance at all. All he knew was that after losing his brother to the darkness, and friend after friend to war and quest, he needed to feel her ethereal presence. Losing Oarly was as hard a loss as any he had ever felt. The end of his brother, Vaegon Willowbrow and Brady Culvert, just to name a few, had pained him deeply. Now, with the ornery dwarf added to the list, the weight of the dead was threatening to drag him down. He couldn't allow that to happen. Hopefully, the goddess would lighten his burden somehow.

Long after the others had gone still, Phen found a restless sleep. He dreamt at first of toothy trolls and savage demons. He was being chased through a long, dark cavern. Whatever the things were behind him, they were right on his heels. They wanted to eat his flesh, to tear it from his bones like the troll had done Mort. The cavern turned narrower and graduated into a tunnel. He had to scrabble for every inch of his retreat. His nose filled with the smell of dirt and stale air. Buzzing, clicking insects crawled over his skin, and the ripe breath of what was behind him warmed his neck. He couldn't seem to gain any distance from the fiends, but ahead, he saw a light, an opening out of the depths, where he was crawling.

Phen's breath came in ragged gasps. His lungs felt weak and tired. His body was giving up on him. The opening was right there and yet he couldn't get to it. With all he had left, he reached for the light. Oddly, an invisible hand grasped his and hauled him up through the hole. Standing now on a wooden plank floor, he looked up to see a long oak table laden with delicacies and crowded with feasters.

The room was plain, yet warm and homey. Torches rested in plain brass sconces along the walls. The floor was littered with straw and rushes. A pair of stealthy dogs moved among the feet, hunting for scraps.

As Phen watched the dogs, he saw a pair of boots that dangled from the chair, but stopped a foot from the floor. He looked above the table and found Oarly there. The dwarf was chewing a mouthful of meat while downing a mug of ale. Master Wizard Targon sat at the head of the table. To his right sat Master Wizard Amill. To his left was a young man in red enamel plate armor. It was Brady Culvert, and he was smiling broadly. There were a few dozen other faces that Phen recognized. Some he knew well, but others only vaguely. All of them, though, had died battling evil.

Oarly banged his mug with the young Red Wolf fighter's in toast. The dwarf suddenly jumped up on the table and rested his boot on the head of the glazed pig. They all turned to face Phen. There was a lot of love, but a tinge of jealous longing in their eyes.

Oarly downed his drink and wiped the froth from his tangled beard. "Your almost a grown man now, lad." Oarly's tone was fatherly. "This war of Hyden Hawk's is not yours. When it is done, the realm will need you. Keep to your books, and follow your heart." Oarly reached out his mug to a beautiful serving girl and let her refill it. After he took a deep swill he went on. "There's got to be a ray of hope in all of this. Plant that seed! Heal the old wounds." Oarly grinned. "Do it for Doon, lad."

Telgra's arm wrapped around him in the sleepy chamber and Phen's dreams wavered away from him. When he awoke, he remembered Oarly's words, but wasn't sure what they meant. The first thing he did was give Hyden Hawk back his dragon tear medallion. Phen found he didn't want it anymore.

Hyden nodded and took the dragon tear in respectful understanding. The White Goddess had given him a message, as well. He knew he would have to face on his own most of what was left to be done. Hyden couldn't ask anyone to follow him further, especially those he held dear.

The Wizard and the Warlord

Chapter Forty-Four

"Oh, it's beautiful, Mikahl," Queen Rosa said. The two of them stood atop a tower facing the southeast. The High King was draped in the golden lion's mane cloak Queen Willa had gifted him. Queen Rosa was wrapped in a thick, silver-furred long coat. The view was pristine. Lion's Lake might have been a sheet of glass; only the arrow-shaped wakes of a small flock of swimming geese shimmered along to indicate that it wasn't frozen solid. To the west of the lake, the pine- and fir-scattered hills were a winter green wonderland of rolling drifts. A light snow fell lazily from the sky. In the near ground, what bit of the southern castle yard they could see was a bustle of adolescent youth. They were taking turns riding shields they had looted from one of the armories down a long, lazy slope. From above the sledders, but below the king and queen, the turret patrol heaved shovelfuls of snow down upon the youngsters as they cleaned the walkways atop their wall. Some of the children had built a snow fort to protect them from the assault. A few braver boys were firing back snowballs of their own. Every now and then one of them would manage to hit a guard. When that happened, a chorus of cheers went up from below. Mikahl had been one of those young warriors once, and silently urged the youth on.

Mikahl had recently suggested a feast as a way to boost morale for the folk in and around the castle. They'd had a rough time over the past few years, with Glendar's failing and the Dragon Queen's occupation.

He was pleased that his wife liked the idea. To his surprise, she and Lady Able took command of the preparations, saying that it was important that, while the event be grand and uplifting, it shouldn't be too much so. It would be improper to eclipse the Yule Day festival with a lesser affair. And even though Yule Day was a few months off, Mikahl agreed and let the women have their way.

Shouts from the ground to the north caught their attention and they strode to the parapet hand in hand to see what the ruckus was about. A group of riders escorting a carriage were coming in. The carriage flew the High King's lion, the Red Wolf of Wildermont's flag, and another banner boasting an axe crossing a hammer. It trundled through the North Road gate and slowed to a stop. Mikahl let out a bellowing cloud of breath and laughed. He turned to his wife with a face-splitting grin.

"I think King Jarrek has accepted our invitation to feast," he said hopefully. "And it looks as if General Diamondeen and some of his dwarves have come, too."

"Oh no, Mik," Rosa said with a fluster. "What's the proper setting for a dwarf?" She blew into her hands with a look of utter despair on her face. "Would children's tables offend them? Oh, by the setting sun, Mikahl, Spyra and Sholt are due back any day now. The feast tables are already set and waiting. What do I do?"

"Be calm, my lady," Mikahl soothed, and pulled her into his arms with a deep kiss.

She kissed him back, but he could sense that her concern over the matter was genuine.

"I'll find out from Jarrek what is proper as soon as I can, my love." Mikahl kissed her forehead. "But as long as you put out an open keg or two, they'll not be offended at all."

As Mikahl ushered the queen back inside, he made sure that she didn't look at the west side of the castle grounds, where the Dragon Queen's garden yard had once been. Though the new construction was almost done, the place where the red priest had burned the symbol into the ground and opened the portal was completely, and unnaturally, void of snow. Some dark taint remained in the earth there. It was Mikahl's hope that Master Sholt could remove the curse, or whatever it was. With the ground covered in white, save for that one circular area, it was getting harder and harder to keep it from coming to Rosa's attention. Mikahl didn't want that to happen.

"Any word from Hyden Hawk and Master Oarly?" King Jarrek asked Mikahl later in one of Lakeside Castle's luxurious gathering rooms.

General Diamondeen was there, as well. All of them had been drinking from a keg of King Balton's brandy wine. The stuff was sweet and potent. A fire roared in the hearth and a couple of oil lamps lit the mahogany-paneled room well. The furnishings were plush and covered in golden velvet. The three men and the dwarf sat in a semicircle facing the fire. The men's stockinged feet rested in the thick fur of an old bear pelt. Diamondeen's feet dangled from his divan a good handspan above it. He had pulled off his socks after the last goblet and was now curling and uncurling his stubby, hairy toes while extending his feet toward the fire.

"Last we heard," Mikahl said, falling back into his oversized chair, "they had reached Afdeon and were considering going on to the Leif Repline fountain. Though how they'd do such a thing up in those frigid mountains this time of year, I'd never know."

"At least they made it that far," King Jarrek smiled. "I suppose it's time you spilled your news to the High King, General," Jarrek said. "The dwarves have been busy doing more than rebuilding our realm, it seems."

General Diamondeen let out a huff. "Picking a new king en't no easy work."

"They've chosen, then?" Mikahl asked.

"They have," the dwarf answered as he sat up. His demeanor grew a bit more serious. He was too drunk to keep his balance, though, and ended up falling back into the cushioned divan. As intoxicated as he was, he didn't spill a drop from his goblet. He managed to sit up enough to take another sip before continuing. "A Cragbert, they say. They have a distant blood claim to the throne and no one is protesting." He belched and wiped his beard with the back of his hand. "Supposed to be crowned in Xwarda sometime betwixt now and your Yule Day. It's a blasphemy to Doon, I tell ya. You can't crown the king of the rock-dwellers above ground."

"King Cragbert," Mikahl said quietly.

"Of course, you and Queen Rosa will be invited to the coronation," King Jarrek explained. "Willa is all in a worry about it now. She wanted the dwarves to wait until spring, at least, but try explaining the seasons to all the dwarves who haven't yet come out of the earth in centuries."

"What does it matter?" Diamondeen barked. "The High King and Queen can fly to Xwarda on that flaming pegasaurus."

Mikahl and Jarrek laughed deeply.

"Aye," Mikahl managed. "I can do just that, but by the gods of man and beast, it would be a blasted cold ride."

The trek back to the teleportal cave that would carry the companions to Afdeon was slow and somber. Dostin and Corva took turns with Jicks carrying Oarly's body. Nothing happened in the two days it took to traverse the cliff ledge back.

The hardest part of that jaunt was getting started. Phen's thorn wall was quite a barrier. Corva tried using Oarly's axe to cut a path through, but the progress was far too slow.

The troll had bled to death, and stank to begin with, but now with hundreds of scavengers in the tangle feeding on its flesh, the smell was somewhat worse. They tried fire next, but the vines and branches of the growth were so green that they wouldn't catch. Finally, Hyden warned off all the creatures feeding in the tangle and blasted most of the stuff out of the passage with a fist of kinetic energy. He hadn't intended to use such force, but the power of his ring was amplified by the dragon tear medallion and proved to be far more potent than he expected.

Afdeon wasn't the same glorious place it had seemed to be a few days before. The loss of their companions eclipsed the awe-inspiring wonder of it. King Aldar was back to himself, though. After hearing the news of success, and the cost of it, a feast of honor was held. The deeds of the dead were glorified in tales told by the living. It was giant tradition and did a bit of good by bleeding the bleakness from the surviving companions.

After the feast, Hyden spoke to the others. King Aldar, his wife, and Princess Gretta were all still at the table when he did. Cade was there, as well, though he was the serving master, not a table guest. The giant emissary kept the room clear of interruption once the nature of Hyden's words became clear.

"I must not dally." Hyden stood as he spoke. "I cannot ask any of you to continue this quest with me. The powers of the elements themselves conspire against success. Yet I cannot wait until after winter. The goddess who guides me has warned me of dark days to come. Dark days for all of us, not just the kingdom folk, but here in the Giant Mountains and in the Evermore, where the elves live. I wish I knew more, but that is all the knowledge she allowed me." He looked at Phen then. "Phen, Princess Telgra, three men died so that your futures would be pure and clean. I cannot allow those deaths to be in vain."

Princess Telgra stood and faced Hyden. "Do not presume to command me, Sir Hyden Hawk," she said in a tone that caused Phen to look at her strangely. Since she recovered her memory she had been bolder and more assertive, but not like this.

"A delegation of elves is coming to get me as we speak, and eventually I must return to my people. I must warn them of this dark premonition you speak of. But be clear, if I chose to accompany you, I would do so." She turned and set her gaze on Corva. "I shan't continue with you though. Corva will go in my stead. If this dark threat you speak of will affect us all, then my people will not be denied a chance to face it with you."

"Well spoken," King Aldar said, rising to his feet and now towering over the table. "The Wedjak holds many threats, young Skyler, and there are ways we giants can hasten your travel to these lands. As the king of your clan, I command you to allow one of my guardians to travel with you, and at least a few of my wolves to watch over your way."

"I'm going, too," Jicks blurted out boldly. "There's always room for a bladesman on a quest such as this, and I'm not afraid to die for the good of the realm, either."

Phen started to demand his place on the list of those going, as well, but Oarly's warning voice echoed through his head and he held his tongue.

Hyden bowed his head to King Aldar before scowling Jicks back into his seat. Jicks blushed scarlet, but felt his demand wouldn't be ignored.

Hyden scanned the faces at the table and started to speak, but was cut off by a hesitant interruption.

"I'm… a… I'm going, as well." Dostin said.

"I thought you were coming with me, Dostin?" Princess Telgra said sweetly. "With Corva going with Sir Hyden Hawk, who will protect me?"

The monk shrugged boyishly and looked at his plate. "Nevermind." He managed to glance at Hyden. Even though he was sad, Hyden couldn't help but chuckle.

"Corva, you and Jicks spend the evening getting your gear ready," Hyden said to them. Then to King Aldar, who had given Cade a nod before sitting back down, "I hope to leave on the morrow, if it pleases."

"Cade is going to fetch your guardian. I'll have him meet you in the map room across from your quarters within the hour." The King of Giant's took a long, deep breath then settled forward with his elbows on the table and his chin on his hands. "Now tell me everything you can about this dark threat."

"All I can really tell you, King Aldar, is that it's coming," Hyden said grimly. "That's all I really know."

The mirror glass in the room in which Shaella was waiting out the snowstorm captivated the puny part of her mind that was still Gerard. He had loved Shaella dearly, and she him. Only this likeness of her held no knowledge of her past. He suppressed the dark side of his demonic power and let his fiery dragon blood heat his desire as he slowly undressed her.

It was a strange sensation, looking out of one's eyes and watching that person follow your every whim. Especially when that person was someone you loved beyond the constrictions of time and space, someone you knew loved you from beyond the grave.

The last button of the farm mother's gifted shirt came loose and Shaella's heavy breasts became visible. A dark brown stain was crusted on her chest between her large nipples, down into her cleavage. It was the farm boy's blood. Seeing it ruined the mood of the moment. When she tasted the sticky gore, the coppery flavor woke up the Warlord. Gerard's consciousness was no match for the powerful evil thriving in his mind, and he was soon forced back into a lonely, empty place where a rare memory of love and life was all that remained. The glimpsing of his past was so far removed from his reality, and so shadowed in pain and hatred, that it was madness anyway. He was trapped, a tiny, insignificant bit of consciousness drowning in a sea of pure malevolence.

The Warlord, the Abbadon, the Master of the Hells, was reveling in the memory of the dying farm boy's gasping pleas. The confusion in his eyes when his flesh tore, and the way he had so foolishly expected her to let him bed her, was savory. Shaella rubbed and squeezed at her breasts feverishly. Flakes of dried blood and gore fell away or crumbled to powder in her kneading hands. A knock at the door was the wagon master. She let him in and pulled him to her bed. He was far more smitten than the farm boy had been, but as much as the Warlord lusted for his blood, he needed the man. As soon as the snow lessened enough to travel through, the wagon master's personal carriage would carry her all the way to Xwarda.

Here in this shabby little inn, though, she would satisfy his every desire. First with her hot mouth, then with her body. Then she would command him to hire an armed escort, and if need be, chart a more southerly route across the continent that would be less affected by the snow. They could go through Weir and Seaward City, if they had to, then cut north.

From some deep, dark place within the Warlord's mind, that tiny bit of Gerard watched helplessly through his lover's eyes and a looking glass as she gave herself to the old wagon master. The jealousy and rage he felt added only to the sea of hate he swam in. The Warlord's pleasure of using both her body and this man's lust was palpable.

The Warlord moaned with Shaella's delight. What better way to wait out a storm than by draining the life from an idiot in a warm bed?

Chapter Forty-Five

Though he didn't yet have a section of King Aldar's kingdom to guard, Durge had earned the title of guardian well. When he was chosen from the rest of his peers to venture into the Wedjak with Hyden Hawk and Huffa, he was elated. At twenty-four years of age, Durge had room yet to grow. At fourteen feet tall, and nearly six hundred pounds, it didn't seem possible that he could get any bigger. He was superbly fit and had walked the boundaries of his king's land more than a dozen times as part of his training. He knew the locations and the commands to activate all of the teleportation symbols, and the rudimentary spells required to get them through the deep of the mountains. He carried a strange staff. The butt was booted in iron, while the head had a small yet wicked-looking blade attached to it. It was pointed like a spear tip, yet as long as a human forearm. One side of its edge was curved like an axe. It was an intimidating weapon, for the staff was as big around as Hyden's leg and stood twice as tall as he did.

Durge was confident, cordial, and somewhat imposing. His smooth confidence was quickly welcomed into the group.

They were camped at the mouth of a deep cave, sitting around a roaring fire. Huffa lay with her big, fluffy head on Hyden's lap. The other two great wolves, Urp and Oof, were standing vigilant, one at the cavern mouth, the other a few yards into the depth of the cave beyond the camp. The repetitive scraping ring of Jicks sharpening his sword blade could be heard over the crackling of the flames.

According to Durge they had one more day of travel to get to a portal called the Shoovway. It was different from the teleportation symbols. It was a permanent gateway, a time-tunnel, Durge called it. It would take them hundreds of miles to the north. So far north, Durge said, that it wasn't north anymore; it was south again. He said that when they emerged from the unfathomable passage they would be in the Wedjak, far beyond the borders of King Aldar's realm.

They'd come far in the two days since they left the last teleportation symbol. On the backs of the great wolves, the miles flew by. Amazingly, the giant kept up with a steady, loping gait. His huge strides ate up the miles like a hungry maw. The wolves were seemingly tireless. Hyden had ridden them before, when he, Vaegon, and Mikahl had to get to Xwarda to thwart Pael.

He'd been reminded of that trek earlier in the day when he and Huffa stopped on a ridge to watch Talon soar on the frigid breeze. Corva and the ever confident young Jicks had looked so much like Vaegon and Mikahl that Hyden shivered in his shagmar coat. He hoped this journey turned out better than the last. Grrr and Vaegon hadn't survived that one, and Mikahl had nearly died from the terrible bite of a Choska.

In Hyden's lap, Huffa stirred. She raised her big head and licked his cheek, as if to ease his heavy thoughts. She was the pack leader now, and only when she took a mate would a male lead them again. Like Hyden, she was slow to forget the losses of the past, and her standards were quite high. She might never find a wolf that could fill Grrr's fur.

Corva was admiring Vaegon's bow. Hyden had placed it in his hands before leaving Afdeon. "If I live through this, I want it back, my friend," Hyden said. "But with it in my hands, my instincts are to use it. I have the powers of the goddess and Claret's teardrop now. I hope to learn to turn to those when I'm in need."

Corva took the bow, though he clearly didn't grasp what Hyden was saying. The elf carried it reverently, so much so that Hyden had to chide him into stringing it that first day.

"It's just a bow, Corva," Hyden told him. "It's only special because it was once Vaegon's. Don't be afraid to use it. It's not a trophy, and I think Vaegon would be proud that an elf as persistent as you was carrying it. I have a great respect for how you tracked down your princess and followed your duty."

Since then, Corva had been beaming.

The next day was blizzard-like. Powerful wind blasted snow and ice at them, but they forged on. The storm made the first part of the day miserable. By the afternoon the wind had lessened, but still the passage was rough. The continuous snowfall made the drifts deeper and the rocky ledges that much more treacherous. Having the smaller party, and the great wolves to ride, helped them tremendously. They were covering five times as much ground as they had been with the full group.

Something terrible greeted them at the cavern leading to the Shoovway. With only a long hour of daylight left to them, they found a band of trolls dwelling in the cave. They couldn't see into the darkened area well enough to tell how many trolls there were. There was no other shelter about, and the nights were deathly cold. If they turned back, they would freeze to death before they got anywhere. They knew they had to fight for the shelter of the place. The aggressively defensive trolls were more than willing to put up a battle.

It started when a barrage of head-sized rocks came flying out at the companions. Luckily, the slope immediately behind them was gentle. Had it been a steep cliff edge, they would have been forced over it.

Hyden rode Huffa to the edge of the cavern mouth, while Durge and Jicks chose to dodge the rocks and charge in on foot. To Hyden's great satisfaction, Corva slid gracefully from Oof's back and covered the others' entry with a quick flurry of arrows fired from Vaegon's bow. A howling yelp confirmed that at least one of them had hit a troll.

Hyden wanted to cast a spell but he had to slow Jicks and the giant so that they didn't get caught up in it. "Make way!" he yelled and pointed.

The two swordsmen darted toward the cavern wall just fast enough for Hyden to cast his spell.

With a shoulder-wide stance and open arms, Hyden swirled his hand around and a ball of flame appeared. The sphere swiftly churned and spun and grew to the size of a summer melon.

"Watch out, Hyden!" Jicks yelled.

Without losing his concentration, Hyden sidestepped a flying rock big enough to smash his bones. He made a mental note to thank Jicks for the warning and then threw his fireball right into the cavern mouth.

The trolls went wide-eyed and were shocked still when the bright fireball came flying at them. There were five of them. One was yanking on the arrow sprouting from its belly. Just before the wizard's fire exploded into them, Hyden saw another arrow go streaking by. Corva hit his mark. The unsuspecting troll went mad as the arrow struck deeply into its throat.

The fireball flash-blinded most of the companions when it exploded. One of the trolls caught fire, and the one with the arrow in its stomach took severe damage, as well.

Outside the cavern, the great wolves howled and barked at the trolls that had survived. The wolves were smart enough not to charge in. They didn't like not being able to fight, but they had no problem ripping out the throats of the fallen when they could.

Suddenly, a far larger piece of stone went past and shattered into the cavern wall right beside Durge. The giant roared out in pain and anger as he was showered with sharp fragments of stone. The biggest of the trolls roared right back at him.

THE WIZARD AND THE WARLORD

The troll that had caught fire was sputtering on the floor. These trolls were huge, bigger than Durge by a few feet, and all sinewy muscle. In the dying light of the fireball, Hyden saw one of them charging at Jicks.

Hyden started to cast another fireball, but decided it would probably kill the young man, too. Instead, he cast his orb light into being. He didn't let it come to rest in its natural position over his head. Instead, he sent it hovering further into the cavern so that the others could see the trolls. As it went by the lanky creature coming for the young swordsman, Hyden bounced it off the troll's forehead.

Jicks took advantage of the beast's blinded confusion and charged through its legs. He jabbed upward, deep into its groin, as he passed. He must have hit an artery, for he was rewarded with a steaming shower of crimson muck. The cavern stank of burned hair and scorched meat. The thrum of Vaegon's bow came from behind Hyden through the din. The screaming troll Jicks had gelded made it an easy target for the elf.

Durge was bleeding from half a dozen places where chips of stone had pierced through his thick elkhide coat into his skin. His staff was broken into two pieces and the giant looked none too pleased about it. He raged into a pair of the trolls, one of which was about to throw another rock at him. He swung the bladed half of his weapon like it was a battle axe and caught the unarmed troll in the neck. As its head lolled to the side and a thick fountain of blood sprayed across the cavern, Durge planted his furred boot in the other troll's gut and knocked it over backward. The huge rock it was holding over its head fell and smashed into its shins. Two seconds later, one of the wolves was pulling away with half of that troll's face in its teeth.

Jicks swung at the back of the troll nearest him. His blade sliced clean through the calf meat, causing the troll to fall to a knee. The young swordsman was trying to back away when the troll turned and swung a roundhouse blow. Jicks was brutally batted across the floor by an anvil-like fist.

With all but one of the trolls down, the great wolves stormed into the cavern and joined the battle with tooth and claw. Their savage attack saved Jicks, for he was lying limp and unconscious from the massive blow he had taken.

Durge took a claw across the face as he stepped in and cut the legs out from under the last of the trolls. He yelled out a thunderous roar of victory, though, when it was done. The sound scared the great wolves and Corva as much as it did the dying trolls. Hyden didn't hear it. He was lost in a casting, and the rest of the world could have been a thousand miles away.

A crackling ray of yellowish healing magic flared from Hyden's hands and went swirling into Jicks's body. Using such magic was taxing, and Hyden was washed over with relief when Jicks sat up and looked around.

After Durge and Corva had finished killing the trolls, they built a fire. Hyden attempted to heal Durge, but the giant refused. His face had three deep furrows running from his left ear across and under his eye to his nose and mouth. The giant said he wanted the scars, wanted the pain to keep him sharp so that he didn't forget. Once they were warm, the giant gutted the trolls and fed their livers to the great wolves. He took their huge hearts and spitted them on the butt end of the staff and set them to roast over the fire.

"I can't believe you're going to eat those," Jicks said incredulously. "Yuck!"

"I've never eaten troll heart before," Hyden said. "But an old giantess named Berda used to tell my people tales when she was around. She said it was a delicacy."

"It is!" Durge boomed through his grizzly appearance. Even with his face gashed and bloody, his grin was wide and white. "It's only proper to eat from your kill, anyway, but troll heart is something spectacular. Only the tongue meat from a bark lizard has a better flavor."

"Mikahl's told me how good that is," said Hyden.

"I'll try it," Corva said. "The Elders say that troll heart is good for the spirit."

"Are you going to eat it?" Jicks asked Hyden. "Those trolls are so unclean."

"Aye, I will," Hyden laughed. He directed Jicks's attention back to Corva.

"If you think on it, Jicks," Corva said, "the troll eats better than any other creature alive. It hunts the mountains for elk, moose, and bear. It drinks from the purest of melt streams. It's only filthy on the outside. A pig, now there's a beast that should seem to have filthy meat, yet doesn't roasted pig beat anything you've ever eaten?"

"It does when it's drenched in honey," Jicks nodded and glanced at the sizzling hearts spitted on the fire. "So what does it do to your spirit?"

Before Corva could answer, Talon came sweeping down out of the darkened sky into the cavern mouth. The hawkling fluttered to a stop and landed on Hyden's outstretched arm. After sidestepping his way up Hyden's shoulder, he settled and began preening himself. His beak was bloody from a freshly killed meal.

Corva continued. "A spirit is something that every living thing has about it. Some predators, some men, as well…" Corva nodded toward Hyden. "…some can see it around you. It's like a glow that indicates the nature of who it belongs to."

"Can you see mine?" Jicks asked, looking at himself uncomfortably.

"I can sense it more than see it," said Corva. "It's an ability that will sharpen as I age. Most elves can't see the spirit aura until they are well over a hundred years old."

"How old are you?" Jicks asked.

"I'm seventy-seven," Corva replied, as if he were ashamed of being so young.

"Very young for the responsibilities of a royal guard," Durge observed. The giant brought the shish kebab of troll hearts to his face and pinched one. He seemed pleased, and inhaled their aroma deeply. The dark, scabbing lines across his face gave him a menacing look.

"It was my grandfather's place on the Hardwood council that got me a place on the expedition to Salaya," Corva explained. "Even had I not some skill with the blade and bow, I would have been allowed to go. My grandfather shamelessly used his position in my favor." Corva let his gaze fall to the fire with shame. "Several better elves, more qualified and more deserving, were passed over in the matter."

"You've proved your rightful place and position, Corva," Hyden said. "As I said before, very few would have gone as far as you have in the name of duty. Most would have run straight to the Queen Mother."

Corva nodded his thanks for the encouragement.

"They're done!" Durge announced. The meat was chewy, yet savory, not tough and ever so succulent.

Jicks didn't shut up about how good the hearts tasted. The others were thankful when sleep finally silenced him. With the great wolves standing guard, everyone else slept, as well.

In the morning, they entered the tunnel-like Shoovway. Hyden was anxious and excited about what the Wedjak had in store for them. Its wonders and dangers were now but a few dozen paces away.

Chapter Forty-Six

In a small, snow-covered clearing somewhere in the Evermore Forest, the senior members of the coalition of Hardwoods were gathered. Revan, Lord of the Redwoods, presided over the group of old elves. Some heads of other families outside the coalition were in attendance, as well. What they were about to attempt required more power and ability than the coalition could manage on its own. The Cherrywoods, the Teaks, and one rebellious old Birchblood stood in a spell circle with the others. From the center, Lord Revan spoke.

"The time of the Queen Mother has passed. It is known that a daughter's heart will follow her mother's closely. Are we ready? Are we going to stand by and suffer four hundred more years of reclusive mediocrity?"

A murmur ran through the circle. "No."

"We once hunted this land from the southern sea to the giants' borders. All of that land was once pure and untainted by the stench of men. The time has come for us to call from the earth a new leader, someone who will guide our race back to its former glory. We need someone who will not bow down and hide from the likes of man."

"Who?" the old Birchblood asked.

"Yes, who?" someone else said.

"The unborn daughter of Milea Redwood. Her father is of the purest Redwood stock, and Milea is the epitome of the Cherrywood lineage. The child will be strong and proud."

Revan reached out a hand to a slip of an elven girl wrapped in a shimmering cloak. Her belly was well rounded with child. Her luminous golden eyes were a bright contrast to her pale, almost blue-colored skin. There was no doubt that she was one of the purest of elves. "If we call forth the Arbor Heart into this child, then once she is born, we will suffer the fearful leadership of the Queen Mother no longer. We will…"

"All of you are fools!" Dieter Willowbrow yelled down from the trees. He had been out rounding up winter spore for his father's herbal works and accidentally overheard the meeting. He'd intended to hide in the trees and remain silent until they were done. Now he regretted speaking, for he might not make it to warn the Queen Mother. "It's you that are afraid of the humans, you who are even now guilty of blasphemy against the Heart of Arbor. You shame yourselves. You shame me with this… this…" He was so angry and scared that, instead of finishing, he leapt through the trees like a startled squirrel. Only a light cascade of loosened snow marked where he had been. Dieter knew that he had to get away from them. If he was caught they would have to kill him. It was never spoken openly, but all elves knew what happened if you crossed the Hardwood coalition. Luckily, Dieter was young and fleet of foot. None of the older elves, he hoped, could catch him.

Lord Revan harrumphed, regaining everyone's attention. "Our course is set! We must act before he can ruin our plans."

"What if he is right?" one of the wizards of Teak said. "You are awfully determined to connect your own son's child to the Arbor Heart. Is it the good of our race you are truly after, or is it family glory?"

"I will not argue with you, Varial," Revan said. "Stay or go, but do not get in our way." He turned slowly around, looking into the eyes of the others. "The time is at hand. We can afford to wait no longer."

Most of the elves were nodding in agreement. They had begun clasping hands, forming a powerful spell circle. Revan left Milea shivering in the middle of the ring and took his place.

Varial Teak and one of Revan's own cousins eased away from the gathering. Before they were out of earshot, Varial turned and said, "I fear you are misinterpreting the invocation, Lord Revan. The Heart of Arbor won't quicken in the unborn child. The spell is meant to be cast on a woman not yet conceived. You are risking your grandchild for naught."

"Go away, Varial. You and Matern are traitors to your own blood," Revan growled. "Leave us."

The two unsure elves turned and moved quickly away.

The sun was starting to set and the forest was growing colder. The members of the spell circle began to chant, following Revan's lead. Slowly, the rhythmic repetition of words turned into an eerily powerful melody.

Milea stood inside the circle. She was clearly terrified. The air around her began to charge with static, and the hot, clean smell of ozone assailed them all. The ground under her feet shimmered in a mosaic of pastel reds and blues. Then, slowly, it gathered into a steady emerald glow. The snow inside the circle melted away. Suddenly, Milea's chest lurched and her arms went wide. She lay back slightly, but didn't fall. Her robe and hair flowed strangely up and away from her, as if the wind were blasting her from below. All of the elves, and even the earth around them, began to pulse lightly with the beat of the Arbor Heart.

Milea's expression was ecstatic, as if she were feeling great pleasure. Slowly, she pulled her arms in and hugged herself. Her eyes shot open but her expression went blank. The pulse was hammering into her, and some of the elves realized, as she had, that what they'd just summoned wasn't what they had intended.

The clean, ozonic smell grew hot and sulfurous, and as the emerald glow darkened to crimson, the smell of the air turned to brimstone.

Milea heaved, clutching at her swollen belly. For a moment it looked as if she would collapse. Then she stood and strode quickly away, shouldering herself out of the circle. When she separated the hands of the elves she passed between, the spell was broken. The ground inside the circumference was smoldering and rank. The elves were gasping in dismay, all of them pale and sickened.

"What have we done?" one of them asked.

"Lord Revan," another started, with terrified amber eyes. "This is not the will of the Arbor Heart."

"The Willowbrow boy was right," another one added, backing away from them. "This is blasphemy."

Lord Revan stood trembling from both rage and fear alike. It had not been the Heart of Arbor they had summoned, and that angered him. For thousands of years his family had served the forest. They were owed a reward for that service. What terrified him, though, was that he felt something happen inside the girl, something unwholesome. The Arbor Heart, in his mind, had betrayed him.

The gathering disbanded, all of them feeling ill and deeply concerned with what they had just done. Revan went straight to the dwellings of his people and ordered the sentinels who served his bloodline to hunt down Dieter Willowbrow, Varial Teak, and Matern Redwood. He was certain, and he made his point to several of the elves in the circle, that those three elves had somehow conspired to taint their spell. He convinced enough of them, and then swore that he wouldn't rest until they paid for their treachery with their lives.

THE WIZARD AND THE WARLORD

In Westland, the feast was just getting underway. In the huge, torchlit gathering hall, the High King and Queen Rosa welcomed their guests to the tables in full regal splendor. Though the lords and nobles of Westland would feast before a roaring fire in the great hall, even the common folk were enjoying the hospitality of the High King's plentitude. All the lesser halls, and even some of the more open courtyards, were open for all who wished to fill a plate or draw a mug or two of watered ale.

Lines of people from Castleview City formed and led out beyond the North Road gate. There was plenty of fare. Lady Able, who'd suffered the Zard occupation with them, made sure that no one would be without. Fifty fat pigs had been roasted for the affair. Two cows, an elk, and more chickens than they could count had been prepared. Outside the castle there wasn't much in the way of vegetables or bread, but there was meat and ale aplenty.

When Queen Rosa asked Lady Able what would happen to the food left over, she was answered with a smile. "What the orphanages don't get will go to fatten the pigs for the upcoming Yule feast." Lady Able thought she was clever for not being wasteful. Even now, as the feasters took their seats in the Great Hall, she was clucking about it to the noble ladies around her.

The king's long table was loaded with bread, vegetables, and the side of a bull elk that might have weighed as much as three men. Baked swan, glazed pigs, and steaming bowls of cabbage and stewed carrots filled the places in between. There were silver trays covered with iced pastries, candied yams, cookies, pies and cakes, as well.

The end of the royal table was wide, and both the king and queen sat there side by side. Sitting in the first seat on the king's right was Master Wizard Sholt, then Lord Spyra, King Jarrek, and the captain of the castle guard. On Rosa's left was Lady Lavona, the queen's newest friend and confidant. Next was Lady Able, who had been determined to sit across from Lord Spyra, even though she had to crane her neck up and and around the ribcage of the roasted elk to see him.

The dwarves had a table of their own; they were all drinking merrily and getting their fill. The mood was wonderfully carefree, and it seemed as if the wounds of the past few years were finally healing over.

Queen Rosa stood and whistled like a salty deck girl. As the people hushed to hear her words, she whistled again, enjoying the looks she was getting for doing so. The royal herald caught on and began banging his staff on the stone floor. The dwarves thought it was the beginning of a song and began banging their goblets and silverware on the table in time. Mikahl and Jarrek thought this was hilarious, and after a bit of shouting and shushing, it grew quiet enough that the crackle and pop of the roaring fire could be heard.

"The queen wishes to speak," the herald called out. "Silence for the words of our wonderful hostess."

Suddenly, Rosa was speechless and flustered. A silly grin of delight spread across her face. Amazingly, she could hear the roar of the flames themselves. She had never been as happy. All eyes were on her now, especially Mikahl's. She smiled radiantly. Her skin was peachy and her eyes twinkled brightly. She finally started to speak, but the loud pop of a smoldering knot in the hearth made her jump and giggle. Everyone in the room was smiling. She put her left hand over her mouth to hide her embarrassment and reached her other hand for Mikahl. He took it and let her guide him to his feet beside her.

"Are you drunk, my love?" he asked in a whisper.

Both Lady Able and Lady Lavona heard this and erupted in a peal of excited giggling.

Queen Rosa squeezed Mikahl's hand and finally found the courage to speak.

Mikahl heard her words, but she had spoken them so quickly that he was left reeling in confusion.

"I'm with child." Queen Rosa said proudly. "Westland, our king will have an heir."

As the words slowly sank in, the crowd cheered. Mikahl's head swam with worry and elation alike. He couldn't imagine being a father yet, but he also couldn't wait. The rest of his night went by in a blur of congratulations and windy toasts. The news eventually made its way out to the common folk on the castle grounds, and on to Castleview City.

Later, Master Sholt received a sending from Phen. The wizard took the news of Master Oarly's death hard. He didn't allow the information to ruin the night, though. The king and queen hadn't been that close to the wily dwarf, but he, Lord Spyra, King Jarrek, and most of the dwarves had fought wars with him. Long after the feasters were settled, while the remains were being cleared, he wheeled out a small keg of Harthgarian whiska. He filled their cups with the potent, fiery liquid and then told them how Master Oarly gave his life to save Marble Boy and Hyden Hawk for the good of the realm. None of them slept that night, and by the time the sun came up they had drunk themselves sober.

Just after Phen made the sending to Master Sholt, Princess Telgra entered his room. She didn't knock. She shut the door behind her and bolted it. She was wearing the sheerest of gowns, and seemed determined to win her way through Phen's grim mood.

The sight of her nearly naked body in the candlelight caught Phen's attention, but it didn't stop the tears he was crying for his old grumpy friend. Breaking the news to Master Sholt had been one of the hardest things he had ever done. Telgra stepped up to him and pulled his head against her breast. She shushed him softly. Eventually, her soft kisses, and the feel of her fingers gliding through his hair, quelled his sorrow.

When she kissed him, a spark flared. Passion replaced his misery. They kissed hungrily. Into an already potent flame of love erupted a blazing bonfire.

Sweaty and alive with contradicting emotions, she pulled away and whispered to him. "My people will be here on the morrow. Though you will be traveling with Dostin and me, there will not be much time for us to be alone together."

"Will you tell your people how you feel about me?"

"Only after I confer with my Queen Mother," she answered honestly.

He would have protested, but her hand slipped into his britches and gripped him tightly.

Phen's words died into the kiss that followed. Soon she peeled away her gown, revealing her perfect apple-sized breasts. She took her time undressing him, then climbed up onto him. Their passion overtook him so quickly that he almost felt shame, but she took her time, and they ended up making love throughout the night.

There was no way for anyone to know such a thing, but the casting made by the elven circle did summon the Arbor Heart. Altered by dragon magic and the water of the Leif Repline fountain, Phen was now something more than human. The Arbor Heart, awakened by the meddling old elves, decided that not only would Princess Telgra follow her mother as leader of the race of elves, but her child would lead them after that. A child that was as much human as it was elf.

Phen's child.

Chapter Forty-Seven

The tunnel seemed like any other rocky cave at first, but after a half hour of traversing it, it became something else altogether: a Shoovway. The dizzying sensation of spinning and spiraling made it hard to walk. The great wolves, who were padding along beside the group, grew timid. More than one whine of worry escaped them. Talon didn't fly. The hawkling rode on Huffa's back, gripping her fur and flapping his wings for balance every so often.

"The sensation will pass," Durge said, but the unease in his own voice was unmistakable.

Hyden's magical orb light stayed a constant above his head, and Corva showed Jicks how to keep it in his field of vision so that the powerful feeling of vertigo didn't make him stumble and fall. For a short time, even that didn't help. The very walls around them, and the roughly-hewn ceiling and floor, seemed to become misty. It was like the surface of a tubular lake reflecting a storm racing past them. Then, all of a sudden, they were standing in an ordinary cave again.

The first thing they noticed was that the air was considerably warmer, but it was still cold by any standards. When they finally saw daylight ahead of them, they were more than relieved. Talon went flying out of the opening to explore, and Hyden sought out the hawkling's vision. As soon as he saw the world beyond the cave, he knew they were no longer in the Giant Mountains, yet it was still late morning.

As Talon soared, Hyden saw in his mind's eye an expanse of tree-littered plains. The morning frost was still reflecting from the leaf-strewn grass as if it were all covered in a sparkling pastry glaze. Hyden also noticed that the leafless trees seemed wrong somehow. They were tall and thick, yet the branches were gnarled and twisted. They reminded Hyden of the dying tree he'd sat under while trying to pass Dahg Mahn's trials. He sensed the presence of what they were after, though. It wasn't very far; either that, or its power reached farther than Hyden could imagine. The Tokamac Verge lay to the east of them, or was it west now? Hyden wasn't sure where north was at the moment. If north was now south, as everyone said it would be, then east was now west. He shook his head and chuckled. It didn't matter. With the great wolves carrying them, they would be able to follow their own scent trail back to the Shoovway's entrance.

Talon circled back toward the cavern they were in. It opened a few dozen feet above the plain in a large granite formation that seemed to have just pushed up out of the otherwise flat expanse of land. Getting down would be easy enough. Through Talon's eyes, he could make out plenty of hand and toe holds. For him, it would be like climbing down a stairway.

He urged Talon to circle higher and take in what lay in the direction he sensed the artifact.

"Before we exit, let's eat a hearty meal," Hyden suggested. "It will allow Talon and me enough time to explore our course and search out dangers."

Durge and two of the great wolves had eased up to the cavern mouth and were looking out at the strange, malformed trees that dotted the landscape. Huffa stuck her head out into the sun and sniffed tentatively.

"This might be the last true shelter we see for a while," Durge said. "Since we are not heading back into the mountains until our return, I think we should cache some of our cold weather gear here."

"That'll lighten our load," Hyden said. "From what Talon can see, the terrain isn't going to change much, if at all."

Corva and Jicks took a peek out.

"If we continue to wear these shagmar cloaks, we'll look like hairy creatures, not civilized folk," said Corva. "That could work both for us or against us, depending on what we come across."

"The people from here my father traded with were dark-skinned men with crude animal-hide cloaks, and wild, bushy hair that was dyed blue, green, and red." Hyden told them. "We will remain cautious, but I don't think they will be a threat."

Corva nodded and began removing things from the pack he deemed no longer necessary. Jicks did the same, while Hyden focused on his familiar's sight and was intrigued, more than alarmed, by what he saw.

From the heights the hawkling reached, the earth below resembled an archer's target. The solitary rock formation where they currently stood was at the edge of a brownish circle that would have been the queen's ring, just outside the king's ring that encircled a curious sapphire wizard's eye. The scale of the would-be-target was enormous. The strange, sapphire-blue center was easily half a dozen miles across, and the tan ring around it was just as wide. The sharp definition of the different rings was obviously unnatural. Hyden had to assume that the Tokamac Verge was at the heart of the Wizard's Eye. He decided that maybe its radiant power had caused the anomaly. After all, the words Tokamac Verge translated as "Powered Boundary." Hyden couldn't help but laugh at the situation. It seemed that, since he was old enough to draw a bow, he'd been searching for the center of the Wizard's Eye. Now here he was again.

Hyden had Talon circle down toward the center of the strange phenomenon. As the hawkling grew near, Hyden saw that there was some semblance of life near the edge of the shimmering center circle. Closer observation revealed that the center was a huge, translucent blue dome that sizzled and crackled with static. It was what made up the Wizard's Eye of his comparative target. Hyden estimated it now at closer to ten miles in diameter. If it was a radiant field from the Verge, it was probably spherical, not just a dome.

The man-made structures outside the magical shell were low-built and crude. A few crop fields and an animal pen could be seen between the huddled structures. Strangely, nothing was more than a few hundred paces from the edge of the dome. Even stranger than that, not a single man or beast could be seen. The faint tendrils of smoke trailing up out of a few of the hovels could be made out, though. Faintly visible in the depths of the glassine sapphire field was a castle. It didn't look like much more than a trio of towers jutting up out of the gloom. It was inside there, at the base of those towers, that Hyden sensed the Tokamac Verge.

As Talon winged his way back to the group, Hyden observed that there were no trees at all in the flat ring of featureless dead grass that surrounded the dome. He decided that traveling might be easy and worry free. Getting into the sphere might prove troublesome, but then again they might be able to walk right through it. They had to get there before they could find out.

He told the others what he had seen, as best as he could describe it. Since the air was still crisp and wintery, they chose to keep the shagmar coats with them. There was no way to tell how cold it would be at night, or inside the magical sphere. After eating, and hiding their stash of ropes, hand axes, ice divots, and spiked boots, they climbed down to the tree-scattered plain, and all of them, save for Durge, mounted the wolves. With the giant trotting along beside them, they started toward the Tokamac Verge. It didn't take long for them to leave the company of the deformed trees and the dark ground in which they were rooted. They were then crossing terrain that was nothing but yellowed grass with no trees at all. By early evening, they could see the shining sapphire dome in the distance, but something else presented itself as they moved through the open field.

Alarm shot through Hyden. It was Talon's alarm.

A dark, winged thing swept by overhead, its huge shadow giving it away to the hawkling. Talon came racing back, and the wolves began to growl and whine.

"Dragon!" Corva said, looking up into the sun behind them. "A good-sized one at that."

"No wonder the people live so close to that thing," Jicks said as he slid off of Urp and drew his sword. "Out here there's no cover at all."

"Put the sword away," Hyden said. "Your blade is useless against a dragon." He turned to Corva. "What color was the wyrm? Could you tell?"

"It was dark in shadow, but not black. Deep green, I think."

Corva strung Vaegon's bow as he spoke. It amazed Hyden that the elf did this without taking his feral eyes off of the dragon. When he was done, he slid gracefully from Oof's back. "It's circling back to us," he said as he nocked an arrow.

"It probably thinks we're a herd of young trolls," said Jicks nervously. "In these coats, we look like supper."

"Get back on the wolves," Hyden said. "That wyrm will get more than a mouthful, if it won't listen to reason. I want all of you to ride like the wind to those structures."

"What about you?" Durge asked in a deep whisper, as if speaking quietly might keep the dragon from hearing him.

"Huffa and I will be along shortly," Hyden said. "Now go."

The dragon had circled around and was already getting close enough that it eclipsed most of the sun from them. Like any high predator, it knew that using the sun would allow it to get closer before being detected. Hyden could tell that it wasn't an adult dragon. It was maybe fifty feet long from nose to tail. He used Talon's vision and his own at the same time, a trick he had learned from Dahg Mahn. By doing so, he could see the dragon more clearly, and its spirit aura as well. The creature wasn't evil, or even dark natured. It was just hungry.

Hyden didn't want to kill the wyrm so he tried to use his ability to comunicate with animals and the power of Claret's crystalized tear to speak with it. Before he spoke, he checked to see that the others were fleeing. They were already a good distance away and moving so quickly that he had to laugh at them. Dragons were extremely scary creatures, but he had met more than one of them and survived to tell the tale. He would never forget what happened to Brady Culvert, though, so he checked his confidence.

We are not a proper meal for you, young draca, Hyden said with as much authority he could muster in his ethereal voice. Go feed elsewhere.

The dragon swooped down lower and established its diving course down toward Hyden's position. Its chosen target was clear. Hyden had to pat Huffa's neck to ease her fear. She wanted to bolt after the others, but she had the deepest trust in Hyden Hawk and steadied herself.

From nearly a half mile away, Corva stopped his retreating great wolf mount and looked back.

"Oh, by the Heart of Arbor," he muttered as the dragon shot out of the sky straight at Hyden.

The others heard him and stopped to look, as well. The dragon swooped like an eagle on a baby rabbit. Urp let out a whimper upon seeing that Hyden and Huffa were about to be snatched away. At the very last moment, when the dragon was about to pluck Hyden and the wolf from the earth with its claws, Hyden threw up his hands and screamed out a single word. Talon shrieked from somewhere overhead. Oof raised onto his hind legs so that he could see better and nearly threw Jicks from his back. Durge sucked in a deep, bellow-like breath in anticipation.

To everyone's great surprise, even Hyden's, the dragon threw out its wings and stalled its dive to a dead stop right before them. As if it were stepping down off an invisible pedestal, the dragon sat its hind claws on the ground, pulled in its leathery wings, and fell to its foreclaws.

Its scales shimmered like wet emeralds. It turned toward the group and let out a long, low, gut-shaking roar. It seemed satisfied that they were afraid and not going to come to their friend's aid. It turned to Hyden, its lower lids sliding up to blink over bright amber eyes, and then spoke. "Your meat is no worse than any other. Why shouldn't I eat you?"

The dragon's slitted eyes were the size of pumpkins, and its nostrils were as big around as a rabbit's hole. Behind its prideful gaze was a pair of sharp, white horns, not yet yellowed with age. They were the girth and length of a man's arm. Its snarling mouth was full of dagger teeth with incisor fangs the size of short swords. It didn't seem impressed with Hyden or his great wolf mount.

"If you try to eat me or my companions, young drake," Hyden warned with no trace of fear in his voice. "I'll kill you, and that's not bravado."

The dragon cocked its head curiously. Its eyes went to the medallion hanging at Hyden's neck. With narrow brows, it asked, "How did the likes of you come across a treasure such as you wear?"

The powerful ring on Hyden's finger wasn't visible to the dragon's eyes, but dragons, he knew, could sense magic. He was fairly certain the wyrm was speaking about Claret's teardrop, though, not the ring. The young wyrm's eyes were now fixed on the shower of tiny sparkles fountaining from the medallion.

"A friend and I shared a tear once," Hyden answered. "She gave me hers because she cares for me." Hyden snarled then. "If you'd like, I'll call her. She's fiery red and you would fit nicely in her jaws."

The glittering green dragon withdrew its head and took a half-step back. Instinctively, Huffa took the same step forward.

Hyden was just relieved that he had the dragon's attention.

"What do you think they're talking about?" Jicks asked Corva and Durge.

"I'll swim the Cauldron if I know," said Durge.

"Phen wasn't lying when he told me Hyden was the most powerful wizard in the realm, was he?" asked Corva. "Not even the greatest of elven masters would dare to do such a thing as stand before a dragon."

"Just because he has the stones, or lacks the sense to avoid standing in front of a dragon, doesn't mean he's powerful, elf," Durge said. "Your old masters probably place a lot more value on their lives than Hyden Hawk seems to."

"By the gods, he's not even afraid," Jicks said. "Here we are, nearly a mile away from the beast, and I'm trembling in my boots."

"See there, man," Durge said. "You've got more sense than Hyden Hawk, too. Only a fool wouldn't be afraid of such a creature."

The sound of Hyden Hawk's laughter came to them on the breeze and they all shared a look of utter disbelief.

A few moments later, the dragon leapt back into the sky and winged away toward the setting sun. Huffa carried Hyden to them quickly, and when they arrived, even the humans could sense the pride she showed at having faced the wyrm with her rider. The man on her back was grinning ear to ear. He looked like a kid who just had a cherry pie placed on his plate.

Hyden didn't say what he and the dragon had spoken of, and no one asked as they closed on the huddle of dwellings at the sapphire sphere's edge.

"What if we can't get in there?" Jicks asked.

"We'll get in," Hyden answered.

"How can you be so sure?" Durge asked.

"Look." Hyden pointed ahead of them.

Looking as if the gods themselves had arrived to greet them, a crowd of brightly dressed, dark-skinned people started streaming out of the huts. As the companions grew even closer, the people began falling to their knees and bowing their heads to the ground. Not only was their hair dyed every color imaginable, so were their clothes. Through his link with Talon, Hyden suddenly understood why they would do such a thing.

"I'm the greatest wizard that ever lived," Hyden chuckled sarcastically. "They just saw me send away one of the dragons they are so afraid of. Do you think you were the only goofs gawking at me out there?"

Inside, Hyden was still feeling the exhilaration of being so close to, and speaking with, such a wildly powerful creature. "These people must think we are the gods."

At the moment, Hyden felt like he was one. But even the incredible encounter with the dragon and the ecstatic glee he was feeling couldn't eclipse the dire warning his goddess had recently given him. Even though they'd avoided a confrontation with the dragon, and these people were no threat, he knew somehow that this wasn't going to be as easy as he hoped.

Chapter Forty-Eight

The strange people spoke in a language that none of them could understand. While the women went about preparing a feast for the wolf-riding gods and the giant, Hyden tried to communicate with an orange-haired shaman by drawing pictures in the dirt beside the cook fire. The others were ushered into a community building made of sun-baked mud and straw bricks. It had a thatch roof that was just high enough for Durge to sit under comfortably. It smelled of sweat and spices. Flaming wicks floated in big pots of oil at the room's corners.

"Why did Hyden say they were dressed so strangely?" Jicks asked Corva as a topless young woman with jiggling breasts and green hair poured them cups of some brown pungent tea.

"When they venture away from the big blue thing, the dragons that fly over the plains feeding don't see them as food," the elf answered.

"When they see a dragon they sit down and stay still," Durge added. "Hyden said that, from a dragon's eye view, they look like flower bushes or shrubs."

"That's what they look like from right here," Jicks said in a whisper.

"You don't have to whisper, Jicks. They don't understand you," Corva laughed at the boy.

"Aye." Jicks nodded.

Just then the room darkened slightly, and several of the women buzzing around the long table yelped in fright. Durge chuckled and shrugged at the others. The giant had blown out the flaming wick in the pot nearest him because the smoke was rising and collecting around his head. Seeing that the gods weren't bringing down their wrath on them, the women calmed themselves and went back to readying the table.

Outside, Hyden and the shaman weren't doing well communicating until Talon and Urp began to help. The wolf and the hawkling enlisted the aid of a curious sparrow and a terrified goat that seemed to understand the shamans' dialect. Through the animals' strange translations, Hyden learned that for hundreds of years, on each full moon, a sacrifice to the dragons had been sent out from the dome. Since the changing of the seasons, almost two years ago, no one had come forth. Hyden contemplated the timing. It was almost two years earlier, at the Summer's Day festival, that the pact that bound Claret to guard Pavreal's seal had been broken. Hyden was certain that it wasn't a coincidence.

All he could do at this point was nod his understanding to the shaman. The animals couldn't speak back to the excited man. Hyden still had to convey his questions with stick drawings.

He did learn that the people who lived around the magical field were descendants of, or the actual people, who had been cast out of the world inside. They could go back in, but would be killed by some evil beast called the Saki if they did. No one had been brave enough to try. None of them wanted to. The Saki's master, a devil god the shamans called Bavzreal, or something similar, lived in the towers with a tribe of black-scaled guardians. The shaman said that all of the humans inside were slaves. They had been born and bred only to serve Bavzreal. Being sent out to feed the dragon as a sacrifice was the only hope they had for freedom. Luckily for them, the dragon didn't venture too close to the powerful barrier, and a lot of the sacrifices were never killed.

Hyden took all this in. Amazingly, he was starting to understand the excited man's words without the help of the animals. Under his shirt, he could still feel the warm tingling of Claret's tear as it fountained out its magic. The shaman went on, now speaking in a feverish tone full of hope and conviction, with more than a little fear showing in his eyes.

"It was foretold that you would come to us, Beast Master," the shaman said, pointing an almost accusatory finger at Hyden. "We have waited and prayed to you with all our hearts and hopes. Is it true you will take this wall down and give us the citadel inside? It was built with the sweat and blood of our ancestors. It is our destiny to inherit the fruit of their labors."

"Do the beast and the devil god still reside within?" Hyden asked.

The shaman's eyes grew wide, hearing his own language learned and spoken back to him so quickly.

"Some were seen fleeing in the night shortly after the sacrifices stopped," the shaman shrugged. "The rest of them are surely inside. Once there were many dragons in our sky, now only a few."

"Are there other places, villages near here?" Hyden asked.

"There are giants and people like us across the mountains, or so the stories say. We were brought from across the sea to be here. We are few, and out there," he indicated the expanse of barren land around them, "only dragons, and other beasts, and the roaming tribes of Wedjakin."

When asked who the Wedjakin were, the shaman described a large race of people, not quite as big as Durge, and only partially human. Hyden pictured Bzorch, the Lord of Locar, as the man described them. He was pretty sure that the Wedjakin were breed giants. That's what King Aldar had hinted at, too.

Figuring that they would have to face down this Bavzreal and his Saki beast to retrieve the Tokamac Verge, Hyden reassured the shaman that they would at least attempt to fulfill the prophecy of which he spoke. With that, the shaman led him to the others and the feast began.

Huffa and the great wolves were given the goat that had helped the sparrow translate for the shaman. As hungry as the wolves were, they gave the goat a reprieve. Worried that they had offended the mounts of the gods, a different goat was brought to them. This one was older and fatter. The terrified, bleating beast didn't fare as well as its fellow. Huffa's generosity only went so far.

Over roasted goat and a strange sweet stew, the companions learned from Hyden what he had gathered. They could do nothing but accept the fact that they might have to face beasts and devils on the morrow. They were all firmly committed to the task.

They slept well enough. Then another feast-like ceremony, where the colorful women fed them boiled eggs and an energizing fruit drink while bowing and singing a repetitious chant, was held for them. When that was done, the shaman showed them where the sacrificial slaves came out of the glassine barrier.

Hyden touched the energy field tentatively at first, then abruptly he stepped into it. Talon followed, flying right through. Huffa was next, and the others weren't far behind.

The magical substance was warm, but seemed otherwise harmless. Once inside, the world took on an aqua-colored tint, like being under the surface of water on a bright, sunny day. Outside the sphere, the chants and cheers of the outcast people were at a crescendo, but as the last of them came through, it disappeared altogether.

No devils or frightening creatures awaited them. In fact, the area inside the dome seemed to be devoid of life entirely. The terrain was flat, just like outside, but this expanse was covered with twisted, thorny bushes that looked to have been scorched to a fragile crisp. Just rubbing against them caused them to powder and fall away. There was no trace of wind blowing. The ground rose slightly up to the blocky base of the trio of towers that sat in the distance. Like long, glossy black spears, each one taller than the last, the towers reached up in a triangular pattern from the squat building at their bottom.

The nearly five-mile trek revealed nothing but desolation. It was like some great flash fire or magical incendiary had burned everything to ash so swiftly that it never had a chance to fall from its place. The ground between the ashy semblance of thorn shrubs and garden roses was cracked and deeply parched. Not a bird or a mouse, or even a single insect, stirred as they passed.

The castle's grand oaken doors were like the foliage, eradicated to cinders, yet still in place. Durge took a deep breath and blew the door away as if it were dust. When he was done, only the long iron hinge bands remained.

"What could have happened here?" asked Jicks.

"I don't think I want to know," Durge answered.

"Whatever happened, I think it happened at the exact same time the Dragon Queen broke Pavreal's seal," Hyden said as he eased inside the smooth, black-walled structure.

"Maybe the demons Peal summoned, like the one who killed Vaegon, came here," Corva suggested.

"It's possible," Hyden told them as they took in the entryway. "Several wyvern, and the hellcat that took Vaegon's eye, came around long before he opened the seal with my brother's blood." Hyden cast his orb light into being. The torches in the tarnished sconces were cindered like the rest of the flammable materials under the dome.

Even with all of them exploring, it took most of the day to find what they were after, and the whole time not even a breath of air stirred, save for that of their own passing.

They found it sitting proudly on a pedestal on the top floor of the squat base of the castle in an open room. It was a chunk of crystal, bright and vivid, with prismatic shades. From the dark color of a stormy sea to the lightest pastel of the sky, three multifaceted shards the size of scroll cases jutted out of a jagged base. The crystal gleamed majestically, but Hyden could sense its idleness. He could also sense its massive power. It might have caused the dome of magical energy around them, and affected the rings of earth beyond it, but it wasn't sustaining anything.

That made sense to Hyden. If the goddess had told him true, that it had somehow caused the barriers between the heavens and hells, and the separation of the layers within, the device wasn't required to sustain its creations.

"It's amazing," Corva observed, peering his keen eyes close to the object to get a better look. "It's like fish oil on water, but inside the surface."

Durge looked casually at the crystal then eased out of the room to explore the rest of the floor they were on. They had passed a few rooms along the corridor leading to the prize and apparently he was curious as to what else might be displayed in them.

Huffa, at Hyden's silent instruction, sniffed at the air. She sensed no danger, nor did Talon. The hawkling was outside, circling the towers and watching for danger. Hyden studied the incredible artifact. He was pretty certain that it had caused all of the destruction around them.

Suddenly, Oof growled from a dark corner of the room. Just as quickly as the wolf sensed the danger, he whined, then wagged his body in a show of embarrassment. Hyden strode over to the corner, and before he got there he heard first Corva's fine elven blade, then Jicks's standard-issue sword come out of their sheaths. His orb light showed him why.

Slumped in the corner, with claw hands held out in a defensive gesture, was the charred corpse of some grotesque partially human beast that was easily half again as big as a giant. Hyden kicked at its head and most of its upper torso whirled away in a cloud of ash.

"Well met, Bavzreal," Hyden jested coldly. "I hope the Saki beast met the same fate."

"He must have tried something with the Verge," Corva said.

"Let's hope he didn't try to move it," Hyden replied.

"It was more than that, Sir Hyden Hawk," Jicks said as he slid his sword back in place. The boy had a pleased look about himself as he went on. "Didn't he have to put it there in the first place?"

"Aye," Hyden grinned. "Just call me Hyden, Jicks. Save the formalities for Mik."

"Aye," Jicks nodded.

Hyden was about to pick up the Tokamac crystal when Durge called out from another of the rooms. His voice was so deep and loud that it was impossible to tell if it was pain, fear, or just excitement that his tone inflected. Either way, it was an insistent call, and all of them started toward it.

After crossing on the ferry barge into the Highwander city of Weir, the Warlord, using Shaella's body, told her wagon master to seek out Lord Vidian. The dark-natured lord had made a pact with the demon Cazlear in exchange for some granted powers of charm and influence. Xwarda was but a few short days away. The Warlord planned on using the man's credentials, or the man himself, if necessary, to get Shaella into Xwarda.

A knock at the carriage door drew Shaella's attention. With the hood of her cloak pulled over her spiky-haired head, Shaella opened the door and looked out sheepishly. Seeing that it was just the wagon master, she sneered and urged him in.

"Did you find him?" It was the deep, multi-timbral voice of the Warlord speaking through her now.

After seeing her leave a trail of young men's corpses behind them, the wagon master had lost his desire for her body. Shaella didn't care because he still served her out of fear.

"No, mastress," he groveled from the carriage's open doorway. "He was arrested and taken to the queen's dungeon in Xwarda over a week ago." The wagon master trembled and sniffed apologetically, as if it were his fault Lord Vidian was arrested. "There was some sort of corruption. Too many rumors to say which ones are true."

The Warlord growled deeply. It was a sound impossible for Shaella's vocal chords to reproduce, and it came out of her like a throat-tearing gurgle. The bringer of death was enraged by this development, yet his destination was still the same. When he got to Xwarda, he would have to find a way to get into the palace.

"Take me to Xwarda." Shaella's torn throat brought the words out in a raspy hiss.

"Yes, mastress."

A moment later the carriage lurched forward and began rocking and swaying its way north along the Pixie River.

The Warlord retreated from his hostess's body, leaving her whimpering and mindless from the pain his outburst had caused. Once back in the Nethers, he found the demon Cazlear and spent a long while feasting on his flesh. Sated with demon meat and power, Gerard closed his eyes and rested. Soon after, the solution to his problem came to him. A simple idea, so simple it made the Warlord laugh out manically. Getting into the palace of Xwarda, he decided, would be as easy as killing a child.

Chapter Forty-Nine

When Durge pulled the fancy jewel-hilted sword from its place atop a pyramid of skulls, something happened. Outside the window, the blue haze of light went away, replaced by the golden light of the unfiltered sun. Talon's shrieking alarm pulsed through Hyden's mind like a whip crack. The magical dome had disappeared, the hawkling conveyed, and a light wind from the plains was sweeping away the ashy foliage. Because Hyden had lingered behind the others long enough to grab the Tokamac Verge, he was the last one in the room. Durge was examining what looked like a glorified ice pick in his huge hands. Before the giant, a knee-high pyramid of strange humanoid skulls had been piled. The elf, Jicks, and the great wolves were spread about the room with tense, but easing, expressions on their faces.

"Be careful, friend," Hyden warned. "It might be a weapon of demon construct."

"It's of no use to me," Durge said, handing the weapon hilt out toward Jicks. "I only called out because it looked important."

The young swordsman's hesitation gave Hyden the chance he needed to snatch the long sword from the giant.

Jicks looked as relieved as he did disappointed when Hyden took it. He'd heard many a tale of a magical sword turning a man mad, or worse, so he didn't say anything.

Hyden gripped the hilt, closed his eyes, and felt for the nature of the blade. Finding what he was after was easy. The large sapphire set in the pommel was still dissipating the energy of its prolonged use, like a coal slowly cooling after a fire is put out. When he opened his eyes, Hyden examined the skulls that made up the weapon's reliquary. He was curious as to why they hadn't been scorched away like everything else. He found he was glad that this portion of the castle was all made of stone. Had these rooms been like some of the others, with beam and plank floors, everything that didn't burn up would have fallen to a pile somewhere below. For a long moment he thought about why the skulls were still intact.

"The sword must have a shielding spell on it," Hyden spoke his thoughts out loud. He was amazed that it made such sense to him. "When in close proximity to the marrow in the skulls its shield is activated. It's a demon sword, so there must be demon blood or demon matter present for it to work beyond normal. The Tokamac Verge magnified the sword shield's power to make the dome we entered to get here. The shield, though, only protected what was close to it. Once the radiant power was magnified, it lost its density, but the power expanded and held because of the Tokamac crystal's influence."

"By the Heart of Arbor," Corva said in exasperation. "What are you trying to say?"

Jicks's answer didn't sound sure, but he spoke up just the same. "The skulls aren't charred because they are demon skulls and the sword protected them as it would the person wielding it."

"Aye," Hyden nodded. "Explain the rest of it, if you can."

"The blue energy shield we went through was like a fishing net, but the holes in it were stretched so big that only a gigantic fish could get caught in it."

"Not a fish, a dragon," Durge said as his mind grasped the concept.

"Its old elven magic, Corva," Hyden said. "But the sword was made for a man. The shield protects the man when he was fighting a demon, that's why demon matter activates it." He turned to Jicks, gave a half-formal nod, and presented him with the blade. "You get the honors. Don't waste your time sharpening it by the fire. This is spell-forged steel. It will never dull."

Jicks was speechless as he took it.

Hyden shook his head and started out of the room. Huffa sensed his sudden urgency and yipped at the other two wolves as she padded out behind him.

Corva skip-stepped to catch up with Hyden. The others lagged behind, moving at a normal pace. They had been climbing the accessible levels of the towers throughout the day, and Hyden's desire to hurry wasn't shared by all of them at the moment.

"If that blade was made by my people's magic for a human, it must be ancient," Corva said to Hyden Hawk as he gained his side. "Is it from the time of Pavreal and Ironspike?"

"Strangely, Corva, I sense that it is thousands of years older than Errion Spightre. Its existence implies far more than I want to consider at the moment. Whether it's the Verge crystal magnifying my concern, or a feeling it is trying to send me, all I can think about is getting to Xwarda. I have a feeling…" He didn't finish the sentence out loud. He could see no reason to get the others alarmed and overly excited. The balance of things had just been tipped so far toward the side of the light, that the backswing of the scales might be catastrophic. He had a strange feeling that by doing his goddess's bidding, he had done something terrible.

Hyden ignored the praises from the strange villagers that night. Their prophecy had come to pass. His business here was done and things were weighing heavy on his mind. Durge, Corva, and Jicks, though, reveled in the glory the colorfully haired people were bestowing on them.

Over the next day, they made their way back across the empty plain, past the twisting trees and through the Shoovway. When they emerged back into the Giant Mountains they were in the midst of a blizzard. The whole way, Hyden pondered the intentions of his goddess, and his own more personal conflict with Gerard. To cause evil, in order to defeat evil, was a strange concept to him. He couldn't be certain that what they had done would result in anything terrible, but the feeling of dread hung in his guts like a fist of ice. The urge to hurry grew inside him with every step he took. He was certain that each moment they dallied now carried the weight of lives with it. Even the animals in the mountains acted as if they expected something bad to happen. The hardest part of the sensation for Hyden was the fact that he knew beyond the shadow of a doubt that it was the powerful thing his brother had become who would be the bringer of death and pain.

The only thought that relieved Hyden of the strange anxiety and guilt he felt was that the goddess knew these dark days were coming before he and his companions had gathered the powerful artifact.

By the time they neared the circular symbol carved into the floor that would teleport them back to Afdeon, Hyden's fear and worry had all but consumed him. Not only in his waking thoughts, but now in his dreams, he saw blood and pain manifested in every way fathomable. From lethal battle wounds and destroyed cities, to wailing mothers huddled over mangled children. Visions of tortured friends and enslaved families plagued his mind feverishly. Finally, with Afdeon only a half day of hard travel away, Hyden crumbled under the weight of the darkness that was pressing down on him. He fell from Huffa's back, face first into the icy track and lay there unconscious.

The wigmaker's orbs bulged as Shaella's dagger jerked up from between her sagging breasts. The Warlord stared through Shaella's eyes into the old crone's, and trembled with delight. Watching the sparkle of life fade from his victims was thrilling. In that moment, the Warlord was privy to the mind of the life he was extinguishing. The terrible things some of the good folk had done were surprising.

This particular soul intrigued him. In her younger days, this dying wench had poisoned her first husband to inherit his wealth. While trying to seduce a younger, more vigorous man, she had killed her unborn child to avoid motherhood. Later in life, guilt consumed her. She donated much of the profits she made from making wigs and reading the cards of fortune. This made the Warlord laugh. Humans were so foolish. The gods of light cared even less for regretful groveling than he did. A dark soul was a dark soul. And no amount of coin or regret could take that away.

The joy of this kill now extinguished, the Warlord shoved the old woman's corpse away and disrobed.

Standing before a full-length looking glass, Shaella tried on wig after wig, finally settling on one of long, raven-black hair. Her hair had been that way in life, but without the dragon's fire scar across her temple, or the dagger scar under her eye, the Warlord doubted she would be recognized.

She had attacked Xwarda before, on the back of the great red dragon she'd tricked into service. No one there would recognize her, for she had been wearing battle gear, not a noble woman's dress. She straightened the bodice of the blue garment. The dressmaker's life light had irritated the Warlord with the kindness it contained. The only thing about the death of her that pleased him was that her kindness was no longer in the world. Satisfied that Shaella looked like any other privileged young lady in the realm, he motioned for the wagon master to lead her back to the carriage.

The large trading town of Platt, where they were, was only a half-day's ride to Xwarda. The excited Warlord had to remind himself that getting to the Wardstone and breaching the minor boundaries was only the first step in his plan. He wasn't in his own body, therefore he wouldn't be placing his own hands on the Wardstone yet. Through Shaella, he could cause a breach. After he left the Nethers in his own body through that opening and embraced the Wardstone himself, he could destroy the boundary altogether. Some of his legions would leave with him by way of the breach Shaella created, enough to take the city before him. The rest of his horde would have to wait until he got there.

A few hours later the carriage stopped. The Warlord heard, through Shaella's ears, the wagon master speaking with a stern-voiced man. A quick look out of the curtained window showed him that they had reached Xwarda's southern gate. The confident urge to unleash his power, to try to battle for success, had to be suppressed. A soft knock on the carriage door helped push the thought aside, but did little to calm the Lord of the Darkness. Hands trembling with anticipation, Shaella reached and opened the door.

"My lady," the guardsman said as he peeked into the carriage, "just a precaution." He smiled at her. "We're sorry to intrude." With that, the door closed softly.

"Let them pass," the man called out, and the sound of rattling chains and creaking gates followed.

If the castle gate is as easy to pass through, then I will be feasting on the terror of men by nightfall, the Warlord said to himself. He worked fervently to stay calm. His minions had worshipers here to aid him. They wouldn't dare misstep as Lord Vidian's patron devil had. He had made a clear example of the price he demanded for failure. He also made sure that the rewards for success were so great that none of the banished would leave anything they could control to chance.

From deep inside the Warlord stirred the tiny bit of Gerard Skyler that remained. He'd crawled into the depths of the Nethers seeking power. Now he had so much of it that it wasn't him anymore. He'd been among the hellborn so long that he was like them now. Only, he had eaten the yolk of a dragon's egg and had become something greater than all of them. He was the Warlord, the Abbadon, the Lord Master of Hell and Darkness and only one more gate, and a leisurely stroll into Queen Willa's palace, was all that stood between him and his dominance of the mortal world.

For a moment, Gerard remembered Hyden and his cousins. He remembered the joy he had felt climbing the cliffs and dreaming of what he'd spend the money on that he earned for his harvest. But that memory was fleeting, for even the part of the Warlord that was still Gerard Skyler was lusting to bring the terror as much as the rest of the Warlord.

The guard at the palace gate was more cautious than the first. His steely eyes and the stripes on his shoulder showed he held some authority. Beyond him, on the wall the gate was set into, the Warlord saw the most peculiar sight. One of the Wedjakin was cursing angrily at a device made out of wood and steel that was mounted at the edge of the parapet.

"Don't be alarmed, my lady," the guard said gruffly, but in an obvious attempt to soothe her. "They are frightening creatures to look upon, but they fight for Queen Willa and the High King now."

She nodded and made an expression of distaste. When she met his eyes, she dropped hers and smiled.

"Sir Hyden Hawk had Queen Willa put the wall guard on full alert. Unless you have legitimate business at the palace, my lady, I cannot let you pass." He shrugged apologetically. "If you tell me why you've come, I'll have a runner see if the castellan will let you in."

Shaella smiled sadly and hugged herself in a somewhat ashamed manner. "My uncle, Lord Vidian, was arrested in Weir some days ago," she said with her eyes focused on the soldier's boots. "I must see him. As distasteful as his betrayal of the queen's law is, I... I..." she stifled a tear and hid her face. "This is so embarrassing, so demeaning, sir. I'm ashamed." After a long pause filled with sniffling and whining, she finished. "There are family matters, responsibilities both legal and personal, that his arrest has left unattended. I must speak with him to see what arrangements can be made."

The sergeant was speechless. It was clear he felt Shaella's embarrassment. The news of the Lord of Weir's betrayal and arrest was common knowledge.

"Do you not have a husband to attend these matters?" he asked.

She shook her head in the negative and started to cry that much harder.

"You're a strong and beautiful lady. I will see Master Dugak about the issue myself." He reached into the carriage and patted her reassuringly. "If you will stay in your carriage, I will have your driver pull in and find somewhere out of the way for you to wait."

"You are too kind, good sir," the Warlord replied through Shaella's roughened vocal chords. "Would you please be discreet? I... I..." She broke into another sob. "I can't stand the embarrassment. If people know who I am, they will stare and whisper about my uncle. I just can't."

"On my sword, my lady," the solider promised. "And Master Dugak may be an old, grumpy dwarf, but he is kind and wise. I'm sure he and I can help you put this nastiness behind you as quickly as possible."

With an evil grin that was hidden by a down-turned head and Shaella's long black wig, the Warlord sniffled and nodded. She softly sobbed until the sergeant closed the carriage door. The Master of Hell had to laugh, because the driver pulled the carriage through the portal into an open area of lawn. The Warlord was inside.

Soon, so very soon, all hell would come breaking loose.

Chapter Fifty

Hyden opened his eyes and blinked away the dizziness. A glance around told him that he was back in bed in the Afdeon apartment. As the memory of the dwarf's death, the young green dragon, and the finding of the Tokamac Verge all came crashing back into his head, he jumped up in alarm. It was a mistake. A thunder clap of pain exploded behind his eyes, taking his breath from him.

Now sitting on the side of the bed, he held his head in his hands and gasped for air. The feelings of darkness and imminent destruction that plagued him on the trail were mostly gone. Only a deep clot of unease remained; that and pain.

"Take it easy," Corva said from a chair in the corner of the room.

"How long have we been here?" Hyden asked with wincing concern.

"Only a few hours," Corva said. "The sun has only recently set."

"Where's the crystal?"

"There." Corva pointed to a small table along the wall. The crystal sat shimmering next to a single candle that flickered there.

"It magnifies more than magical energy," Hyden said. "It took my fears and worries and compounded them until I was overcome."

"When I took it from your pack at the teleportal, it did the same to me," Corva said. "It showed me a hundred possible ill fates that Princess Telgra, Dostin, and Phen might have shared on their way to the Evermore. Luckily, I let Jicks take it from my hands."

"Who took it from his?"

"Well, it seems that Jicks has a more positive outlook. He's not worried about much. The crystal magnifies his pride and his hunger. He hurried the Verge in here then marched through the kitchens to find some food."

"We've got... I've got to get it to Xwarda." The pain behind Hyden's eyes was ebbing away. "I've got to get the High King to Xwarda, too. It will take him, Ironspike, and the power of the Wardstone, along with that crystal, to do what I must do." The thought of all that raw magical energy in one place made him shudder.

A low, rumbling sound, a tremor of vibration, shook the room. Hyden looked up with alarm all over his face. "It's coming," he warned. He wasn't sure how he knew, but he did. He could feel the nauseating presence of demon kind. Through the open door, Talon came gliding in from the apartment's common room. The hawkling felt it, too.

Shouts of concern came from beyond the door, then a long, loud scream came from outside the shuttered window.

"By the Heart of Arbor! What is it?" Corva asked as the structure shook again.

The low, popping sound of fracturing rock threatened to drown out the elf's voice.

Hyden began pulling his over clothes on in a frantic rush. "Corva, find Cade, or Durge!" he yelled. "We must teleport as close to Xwarda as we can and then ride like the wind. The fate of all the races depends on us defending the Wardstone."

Corva darted out. After getting both boots on his feet, Hyden grabbed the Tokamac Verge and cast a sending spell to Master Sholt. The magnifying power of the Verge amplified the message so that it exploded into the mind of every wizard and mage who was anywhere near Master Sholt. When he was done, he spoke a few words to Talon and opened the window shutters. The hawkling cooed a quick goodbye then took to the air in a flutter of wings and determination.

The lift moved so slowly that it made Hyden angry. When he stopped on the floor where the teleport symbols were, he was in a determined rage. Afdeon shook again, only this time the movement was jarring. A pair of stoneworked sconces fell from the wall, and part of an arched doorway cracked and crumbled apart. There were a dozen giant soldiers gathered near the teleport symbols. One of them stumbled and fell into it like it was a gaping hole. Hyden reddened into an anger bordering on disgust and contempt.

"Put down the crystal, Hyden!" Corva yelled.

The elf and Jicks came rushing over from the void of blackness where the teleport symbol used to be.

Jicks took the crystal from Hyden's hands and almost instantly Hyden's anger began to abate.

"If you're going to carry this thing, Hyden," Corva said, "you must calm your mind and focus on what emotion is most beneficial to us."

"If we cannot get to Xwarda anytime soon, there is no need for that thing anyway," Hyden said. His rapidly decreasing anger carried him into a state of confusion for the moment. He tried to think of what he could do, but his mind was a swirling blank.

Suddenly, a chittering roar, like nothing any of them had ever heard before, erupted from the hole in the floor. A long, black tentacle lashed up out of the blackness and wrapped around one of the giants' legs. It yanked him away from them, then in the span of three heartbeats, a grotesque insectoid head peeked up from the hole. A pincer, not unlike that of a lobster, shot out and snipped the entangled giant in half.

Hyden realized that the teleportals were useless. Already another demon beast was crawling out to join the first in its attack. Xwarda had never seemed so far away from him, and no matter how hard he tried, he couldn't seem to form a complete thought.

Weapons were drawn. Shouts and commands erupted, and Jicks thrust the crystal back into Hyden's grasp. The young solider was charging toward the first demon beast while drawing his weapon. Corva began loosing arrows at it, but they did nothing. In that brief instant, the clouds in Hyden's mind parted. He had a moment of helpless and terrified clarity. Another giant was snatched and torn to pieces before his eyes. With his free hand, he reached for the medallion hanging around his neck, and with all his concentrated power he called out to Claret.

Lord Revan kicked his cousin Matern's head across the snowless area in the clearing. Where it rolled to a stop in the moonlit snow beyond the circle, a small black stain spread below it. A thin cloud of steam rose from the fresh, warm blood. The old elf's body fell forward and Dieter Willowbrow was forced to watch the almost purple life fluid pump from the stump only a few feet away.

Dieter's hands were bound behind his back, and a dozen Redwood sentinels stood around him alertly with swords and bows drawn. They were ready to kill him at Lord Revan's command. The head of the Hardwood Coalition had gone mad after his grandchild was born prematurely. A dead black thing that vaguely resembled a baby had taken its mother's life when it came out. Lord Revan's son had cursed his blasphemy and then taken his own life in the Arbor Heart. The entire Evermore, and the outlying groups of elves around it, had all gone half mad it seemed. The Queen Mother's orders were followed by most, but ignored by others, and in a matter of hours a civil war among the elves had begun.

Lord Revan slung his cousin's blood from his blade and took up a swinging stance before Dieter. Dieter hoped that his father would come to save him; he was due back from his hunt anytime now. He would put a stop to this madness. Willowbrows might only be archers and hunters, but they were respected among the older elves.

Seeing that his time was now, Dieter closed his eyes and prayed to the Arbor Heart that Revan's blade would kill him instantly. He didn't want to suffer. Once the prayer was finished, he did what he could to make certain that the stroke was well swung.

"You've already killed your grandchild and your son, you old fool," Dieter said with defiance in his voice. "You're a kin killer, lower than the roots of the festering. You may take my head, but worm rot and drought have already plagued your soul."

"Die!" Lord Revan spat as he began his swing.

"Stop it now!" the Queen Mother yelled from the tree line.

As if to punctuate the powerful anger she felt over what she was witnessing, the ground and the trees around them shook for an instant. Only the swift action of a young sentinel who had listened closely to Dieter's words stopped the blade that was swinging at him.

The raging elven lord spun his deflected blade around and squared off, facing the Queen Mother's approach. He was standing in the dead center of the lifeless circle, and the forest clearing had gone suddenly silent.

"You'd kill me, too?" the Queen Mother asked. Pointing at Dieter she ordered, "Unbind him now." Dieter saw that, a few paces behind her, Varial Teak was leading a group of Willowbrow archers into the clearing. Dieter's father wasn't one of them, but he was nonetheless glad to see his cousins and uncles.

The Redwood sentinels untied Dieter and he ran stumbling toward his family. He was careful not to get into their lines of fire. All of them had their arrows trained on Lord Revan.

As the Queen Mother stepped into the blackened circle with the Redwood lord, the ground shook again, only harder. Several of the Redwood sentinels stumbled, and a few of them took a knee, bowing to the power of the Queen Mother's wrath.

The Queen Mother hesitated. Dieter could tell by her expression that she hadn't caused the quaking boom. Lord Revan started his swing, swift and sure, but it never found her flesh. Below them, the ground fell away into an empty nothingness. Four sentinel guards, the Queen Mother, and Lord Revan fell tumbling into a hole.

The next thing Dieter knew, a Choska demon came shooting up out of the hole. In its claw was the broken form of the Queen Mother. In its jaws was half of Lord Revan. Behind it, like a swarm of ants coming out of a disturbed mound, was an army of hellspawn. Malformed humanoid things, part beast, part insect, began to attack. They were armed with tooth and claw, stinger and talon. A pair of hellcats came flapping out, all scale-covered blackness, like panthers with thumping leathery wings.

Unlike the other slack-jawed elves around him, Dieter snatched a bow from one of his cousins and put an arrow into the breast of a wyvern. The beast came crashing down out of the sky. The battle for the Evermore was underway.

Princess Telgra's heartfelt wail was accompanied by the gasps and moans of the elven members of her escort. Only moments ago, Phen had told them that Hyden Hawk had made a sending so powerful that it rattled his skull.

"Defend the Wardstone with all you have, Mikahl! Go, do it now!" Phen told them. The message, when he'd repeated it, got snickers and snorts of disgust from the haughty elves of the delegation. Now, Phen saw that something was affecting them, too. He only cared about Telgra, though, and her saddened, tear-streaked face tore at his heart.

"What is it?" he asked carefully.

"The Queen Mother, my mother, just died." She paused her step and looked up at the sky for a moment. "I am the Queen Mother now." Her voice was full of regret.

A power she had only been told about began filling Telgra. The love and pain of all the hearts of the elves in Arbor were transferring from her mother's wonderful soul to hers. Phen was left as an afterthought, as not only the spirit world of the Arbor went through the changes, but the physical as well. Telgra shuddered and wailed as the power filled her. A breeze picked up, whipping snow from the branches of the evergreens that stood among the leafless oaks and elms. The wind carried a moaning sound. The elves of the escort took a knee and bowed to Telgra, but she didn't notice. Her wild yellow eyes were full of love and fear. Both terror and triumph manifested in her gaze, but then a different emotion took reign and her brows narrowed fiercely. In a voice full of menace she spoke.

"Get up! We must move like the wind."

She started into a brisk jog. Arf, the great wolf Phen was riding so that his malnourished legs wouldn't slow them down, took off after her, as did the other elves of the escort. Dostin's great wolf mount, Yip, kept a steady, padding pace with them, too.

"For all of you who disregarded Phen's warning as human folly," she said with contempt in her voice, "you should feel ashamed. For if the elven mages who heard the warning had listened to Hyden Hawk's words, the Queen Mother might still be alive." She paused only to see that all of her escort could hear her words. "The demons we chose to let the humans battle alone are back in force. Elven arrogance just might be the cause of our own uprooting. The Evermore is under attack."

In her mind, Telgra sent the command to gather and fight to those elves closer to the Arbor Heart. The few anguished responses she received told her that the enemy had already overwhelmed them. Through their eyes and emotions, she was nearly stopped in her tracks. The elves of the Evermore were being cut down like wheat before a scythe.

THE WIZARD AND THE WARLORD

Chapter Fifty-One

The sun had yet to set in Westland when Hyden Hawk's powerful call rang through the aether. King Jarrek and the dwarven delegation had long since made their way back to Castlemont, and both Lord Spyra and Master Wizard Sholt were preparing for their newly appointed positions. The carefree spirit of the feast was all but a memory.

Lord Spyra was off braving the snow and touring Settsted Stronghold and its many outposts. He insisted on doing it now, so that when the southern weather worsened he could spend that idle time planning and preparing his command over the garrisons.

Master Wizard Sholt was now instructing De'Rain and a few other promising students, and had resumed his role as the High King's Master Wizard.

It was in the capacity of both positions, teacher and royal wizard, that Sholt, De'Rain and a young girl of seven, named Suza, were all out in the strange bailey yard this evening. This particular bailey had once been Queen Shaella's garden. The Master Wizard and his apprentices were studying the qualities of the circle the red priests of Kraw had burned into the grass there the previous year. Sholt had tried all of the obvious banishing and replenishing spells to try to make the dead spot hold life again, but none had worked. King Mikahl had ordered the anomaly removed, destroyed or even built over if necessary. Sholt and his students wanted to understand why no snow would stick there when the ground was no colder or warmer than that around it, and why no vegetation had grown there all last summer.

Sholt secretly hoped that the youngsters would notice something he'd overlooked, or maybe come up with some new angle of approach to the problem. Master Sholt was contemplating these things when Hyden Hawk's sending blasted into his mind like a war drum. De'Rain and Suza heard it, too. The sound was so harsh in Suza's little head that it made her cry out in fear and pain.

"Defend the Wardstone with all you have, Mikahl! Go, do it now!"

Once Master Sholt realized the sending was from Sir Hyden Skyler, he went into immediate action.

"Stay with her, De'Rain," Sholt said. With a flourish and a sizzling crackle, he disappeared.

The High King was on his way to meet his queen, her handmaiden Allysan, and Lady Lavona. The women had a concern about something or another and wanted him to hear it out so that it wouldn't alarm anyone else in the castle. Mikahl had no idea what the issue was, but since he couldn't seem to refuse his wife anything, he was about to find out; at least until Master Sholt came rushing down the corridor pushing servants and workers aside like a madman.

"King Mikahl!" Sholt yelled. "King Mikahl, there is urgent word from Hyden Hawk!"

Mikahl glanced around, saw a closed door, and ushered the wizard into the room. It was a pantry full of linens. Shelves full of gleaming brass chamber pots and a few stored oil lanterns lined the walls. As soon as Sholt was in, Mikahl shut the door. The total darkness, after being in the bright, lamplit hallway, was sudden, but Sholt immediately cast an orb light into being.

"My lord, Hyden says Xwarda must be defended at once!" He sounded distraught and out of breath. Master Sholt had spent most of his life in Xwarda training under the late Wizard Targon. It was the closest thing to a home the serious-looking middle-aged wizard had ever known, and he cared for the place and the people there deeply. "I can only assume they are under attack or something drastic...."

His voice trailed off as the entire foundation of Lakeside castle slowly shook and rumbled. Yells, screams, and the sound of crashing dishes could be heard from nearby. Mikahl and the wizard shared a wide-eyed look.

"You must go protect the Wardstone, King Mikahl! That's what Hyden said."

"Aye," Mikahl agreed. "I will go after I find Rosa, but what's happening here?" He looked into the wizard's eyes for an answer.

Sholt waved him off, for De'Rain was sending a message into his head. "The gateway has opened. Out there in the garden yard," Sholt repeated the young mage's warning, but he left off the pain-filled scream that extinguished the spell. "Something's crawled out of there," he finished in a panic.

"By the gods, sound the alarm," Mikahl said as he bolted out the door and down the hallway to find his wife. Before he even rounded the corner, the frantic clanging of the alarm bells rang out from the guard towers outside.

Mikahl charged up a stairway and down a short passage full of huddled, terrified castle staff. He found the room where he was supposed to meet his wife and his friends, but only the handmaiden, Allysan, was there, and she was a teary-eyed wreck.

"Where's my queen?" Mikahl asked sharply. It was enough to bring her into focus.

"She and Lady Lavona went off to the building supply lot." She sniffed and continued. "I was told to wait until you arrived and tell you to meet them there, my king." She wiped away a tear and looked at Mikahl pleadingly. "Are we under attack? What was that sound?"

The sudden lurching of the floor as the ground shook again caused the young Valleyan servant girl to cry out. From outside the window, Mikahl heard another scream. It was Rosa's voice, and with the sound came a grumbling roar, and the realization that the supply lot the girl had been speaking of was where the gateway had just opened up. Without another thought, Mikahl drew Ironspike and charged through the shuttered window.

He burst into the cold evening air four stories above the earth, and as he started to fall he called forth the bright horse. The flaming pegasus flared to life between his legs and, on magical wings, it carried him toward the garden yard.

A bright explosion of crimson and lavender energy sent bricks and broken stone fountaining into the air ahead of him. A gut-shaking demonic roar followed. The new construction built where the Dragon Queen's apartment had once been blocked his view, but the yells and commands from his guards told him he would find the worst when he got there.

The only thing on his mind at that moment was the queen and his unborn child's safety, but as he caught sight of the thing ravaging the soldiers in the supply lot, even they became secondary. The demon beast's eyes locked on Mikahl's, and the High King shuddered seeing the resemblance of his friend Hyden Hawk in them again. This was the Lord of Darkness himself, the thing Hyden's brother had become, and even now it was barking out orders to the swarm of demons that were climbing up out of the earth behind it.

When their eyes met, the part of the Dark Lord that was once Gerard Skyler recognized Mikahl, too. The last time the Warlord had stood in this courtyard Mikahl had lopped off the Dragon Queen's head.

The beast roared in anger, sending a searing gout of dragon fire at Mikahl. The High King managed to call forth a shield from the symphony of magic his sword blasted through his mind. Had he been on a real horse, he would have perished in the flames. Mikahl could smell his burnt hair and could feel the tightening skin where the dragon flames had touched his face before Ironspike's power could divert them.

He scanned the courtyard for Queen Rosa and nearly crumbled from the air in a heap of despair when he saw her. She was mauled and bloody, lying in an impossibly twisted position near the open hole in the earth. A little black-robed girl was trying desperately to drag the queen's body away from the Demon Lord. If she wasn't dead, she would be within moments. The horrid way in which her slippered feet faced upward, but her torso lay limp and facing the dirt, said it all. Mikahl had fought in enough bloody wars and had seen enough carnage to keep from fooling himself. The emerald dress she had been wearing earlier, when she asked him to meet her, was now blackened with blood and left him no room to doubt that it was Queen Rosa the girl was trying to protect.

Mikahl gave a savage war cry that rivaled the call of the Dark One. His sword blazed white hot and sent a streaking beam of destructive energy into the Warlord's plated chest. Gerard screamed out in pain and went tumbling over backward. Only a last-second leap gave him enough altitude to throw out his wings and catch air. Mikahl urged the bright horse onward and made to attack again, but a violent fist of crimson energy slammed him sideways, so that the magical mount carried him crashing into the corner of a newly built wall.

A hellcat and a Choska demon rained blast after magical blast down and around where he'd crashed. Then the entire wall structure collapsed over him. The last thing Mikahl heard before blackness swept through his mind was the Warlord's horrible laughter and the pleading cries of the little girl in the black robe.

After eating the girl's squirming body, the Warlord ordered his horde east. As much as he would have loved to stay and terrorize Westland more, he had an agenda. Xwarda, and the Wardstone bedrock upon which the palace was built, was waiting for him. By taking control of its power in his own form he could do more than rip open the boundaries. He could create an impenetrable protective shield, behind which he and his hordes could gather, plan, and rest behind between attacks. He could use the powerful Wardstone to blight crops and burn the forests. He could poison the lakes and streams and summon all the beasts of the earthly plane into his service. From Xwarda he could slowly, painfully bleed the hope and life from the world of men. On powerful wing beats he and those who could fly moved swiftly eastward. The wingless, the walkers and lopers, the slithery, scaly things, of his horde followed on the ground.

In the back of the Hell Master's head a voice was screaming out a warning, but the Warlord paid it no heed. The voice was that of a demon called Shokin, who had been ripped apart long ago by Pael. Shokin was part of the evil against which Ironspike was created to defend, and he knew its powers. When the High King went down, even now, while he was buried under that pile of rubble, Shokin screamed for the Warlord to take the time to utterly destroy him. Once that was done, the blade would be dead, too.

The Warlord ignored Shokin's advice. So loud and intense in his head were the calls and murmurs of all the demons the Hell Master had consumed, the rambling of a single voice was lost in the jumble. The surge of hatred and malice toward the world they had all been banished from, and the desire to feed upon its terror, made it hard enough for the thing Gerard had become to keep its focus on Xwarda. So intense was the desire to wreak havoc that the Warlord himself couldn't resist the urge to bathe in the blood of men.

The city of Castlemont's lantern lights became visible in the cold, dark night, and the Warlord chose that place to land first. Dozens of breaches had opened up across the land, and his army needed a place to gather. What better place, the Warlord decided, than a city full of struggling people trying to salvage a life after war? If crushing hopes and dreams would fortify his legions, then in Castlemont they would feast like gods.

In the city of O'Dakahn chaos reigned. Demons tore through the streets and neighborhoods with wild abandon, killing and destroying anything they could. Along the river and the marshland villages of the south, those witches and dabblers who served the Dark Lord were finding the bloody rewards of their loyalty. From their sacrificial circles, from the rune-marked altars, and from other places where certain magical symbols were etched, breaches between the Nethers and the world had opened. Across the entire realm, etchings on medallions or small statues were spilling forth demon kind. Buzzing black hornets and long, venomous things slithered out of the darkness, while imps and devil dogs shimmied out of the places they could fit through. In the marshlands, the circle where the red priest of Kraw had preformed the ceremony that let the Warlord into Shaella's resurrected body was a gaping gateway. All sorts of dark things were escaping their banishment.

Legions of them.

On the Isle of Borina, where the same priest had resurrected Shaella's body in the first place, there was a larger hole. In the Giant Mountains, more than a dozen teleportals had opened for the Dark Lord, and in the sacred heart of the Evermore forest, already the earth was soaked blue with blood. In King Jarrek's lands, though, the nightmare was only beginning, because all of the denizens of hell that had come to the land of mortals were now moving toward Castlemont to answer the Warlord's summons.

King Mikahl opened his eyes to see the shield he'd called forth. It was holding several chunks of rubble up off of his body. Ironspike was still in his grasp, he realized. Had he let go during his brief stint of unconsciousness, he would have been crushed. He blinked away tears from his eyes. He loved Rosa dearly, and with all of his heart. To lose her and his unborn child was deeply painful, but he was the High King and couldn't let his own emotion come between him and his duty.

A deep, loving voice echoed in his head from the past. "Think, then act," it said, and Mikahl did just that. He had to get to Xwarda to defend the Wardstone from the thing Hyden's brother had become. That he knew for certain. If he didn't, if he took even another moment to mourn Rosa and the baby, then maybe a dozen more mothers could die. Hyden would be waiting in Xwarda and, according to his missives, the would-be wizard had some sort of plan. Mikahl wiped away one last tear and then let his anguish fuel the symphony of Pavreal's blade. In an explosion of brick, fractured stone and dust, he emerged from the mound.

The bright horse whinnied and pranced, eager to be of service. All around Mikahl in the torchlit garden yard, men yelled and dove for the ground as more terrible things crawled from the hole and took to the sky.

Along the walls the alert soldiers cheered when they saw their king come flying out of a cloud of dust and debris.

Mikahl took the bright horse up into the frigid sky so high that all he could see below were the tops of the clouds. He hated to abandon Westland, but there was no choice in the matter. He set into a streaking course due east and hoped with all he had that he could get to Queen Willa's palace to meet Hyden Hawk before the Warlord got there first.

Chapter Fifty-Two

For a long night the elves battled the demon horde in the Evermore. The arrogant Hardwood Coalition set their wizards on the attack, but found out quickly that most normal spells were useless against the hellborn. Blades and arrows weren't much better, but even the greater of the devils were bound to a body of flesh while in the world of man. They fell and writhed and died just like the elves they were so mercilessly slaughtering.

The elven defensive forces had been split, and while one force, the Hardwoods and their sentinels, raged in to meet the demons like madmen, the other force, led unofficially by Dieter Willowbrow and a few of the Queen Mother's soldiers, was helping to protect the rest of the elves as they fled.

The crafters and healers, the mothers and children, and the outlying gatherers were grouped together and herded toward the only place Dieter thought might be safe. In the south there were dense tangles of forest. It was no easy task keeping so many elves safe and together while fighting off the attacking hellspawn as they went.

A group of eight young elves, both boy and girl, and their ancient herbology teacher, were trapped in a dense thicket between an acid-mouthed wyvern and a pack of devil dogs. Three of Dieter's scouts came upon them and were doing what they could to keep the demon kin at bay with their bows. Now they were growing short of arrows. They sent one of their number to get reinforcements, but as one of the devil dogs charged in and latched its teeth on the old instructor, the situation demanded action. Charging like the barbarian berserkers of old, one of the elven archers raced into the group of youngsters, screaming and yelling and waving his arms around madly. His brazen approach startled the devil dogs back.

One of the other elves charged and used the ground the dogs had given to snatch up a few of the errant arrows from the trees and undergrowth. It was then that the wyvern struck.

A boy of perhaps twenty-five years bravely shoved two of the female students out of harm's way and took the attack of the man-sized wyvern himself. Corrosive saliva and blue elven blood sprayed the group like a shower of warm rain. The wyvern's teeth were clamped on the boy's neck, and it shook its head furiously. The violent motion tore a chunk from the young elf's body and the wyvern chugged it down.

A few of the children began swatting away at their stinging flesh where the monster's saliva had touched their skin. A cloud of steam rose up from the warm blood pulsing out of the body in the snow.

The thrum of a soldier's bow and the thump of his arrow impacting into the wyvern's scaly hide was lost in the shouts and cries of the terrified group.

The wyvern flapped awkwardly into the trees and crashed, going into a sputtering death rage. Large clumps of snow and ice fell down on top of the beast, shaken loose from the branches above.

The devil dogs had the group surrounded in a rough circle. The sudden cry of the old herbologist caught everyone's attention. A pair of the red-eyed, toothy beasts had gotten hold of her again and this time they quickly dragged her away from the others.

One of the soldiers charged out of the huddle to help her, but even as the other black wolf-like beast finished tearing her apart, she commanded him back. "Save the children!" she shrieked. "Do what you must to save the…" her voice trailed away as her throat was ripped out. The elven students whimpered and moaned in horror as their beloved teacher was devoured like a fallen deer before their eyes.

With the devil dogs busy, the archers cautiously urged the young elves toward the bulk of their retreating kin. They were met in a small clearing by Dieter and a handful of sentinels who were coming to their aid. As the children were calmed and ushered away, a winged panther-like beast the size of a horse came crashing down upon them. Luckily, the youngsters had gotten out of the clearing and into the trees. The forest was too dense for the creature to give chase, but since it had just crushed one elf, and lashed another senseless with its spiked tail, it had plenty to occupy its attention.

The beast's snarling maw opened only a foot from Dieter's face. A brimstone-tainted roar blasted at his long, golden hair and filled his eyes with blurring tears. The elf with whom he had been conferring was now lying in a steaming heap of entrails at his feet. Another elf stumbled aimlessly toward the unprotected middle of the clearing, his head a bloody mess.

From Dieter's left an arrow loosed at the beast. From his right, one of the Queen Mother's elves plunged his black-blood-stained sword deep into the creature's guts. When the soldier's sword hit its vitals, the demon twisted toward the attacker and snapped out at him. Dieter had no sword, but as calmly as if he were about to peel an apple, he pulled out his dagger and laid open the beast's throat. A spew of hot crimson gore covered him, and an unseen hand yanked him clear of the demon's death throes.

As surely as he had killed the monster before him, a certain dread filled Dieter's heart. The Heart of Arbor had helped spare him, just as it had in the clearing before. He knew why he had been spared. He was the only elf who had a chance of getting them into Xwarda. The humans would surely leave them to their own fate, just as the elves had done to humans not so long ago. But Vaegon had fought to the death with the men of Xwarda. If he told them who he was, they would listen. Even though it went against the new Queen Mother's order to stand and fight, Dieter decided what he was going to do. If she didn't understand, then so be it.

Once he was back among the main group of elves, Dieter leapt gracefully to a low-hanging branch and whistled for silence. The eyes that fell on him grew wide. He was covered in blood and looked half-demon himself.

"We must flee the forest!" he yelled. "It will be here for our return, but if we stay, we will surely be destroyed by this unearthly force. If you wish to live to see your homes again, then follow me. If you wish to stay and die, then at least do so to stall their pursuit of us. Grant the children and the untrained a chance. We have a long way to run, but we are fleet and we know the forest." He paused, feeling the Heart of Arbor pounding in his chest. "Come, children of the Evermore, our future lies even farther south."

Most gathered there could feel the Arbor Heart speaking through Dieter and didn't question the young elf, but some of the older males, who'd long forgotten the dreams of youth, lagged behind. Whether by the will of the forest, or by the stubbornness of their ways, they gave their lives for those who followed Dieter.

Through that night and all throughout the next day the elves continued their run toward Xwarda. The first night the demons harried them, but then as if some magical force began to protect them, the pursuit seemed to break off.

When the group reached Xwarda, hungry and exhausted after two nights and two days of continuous retreat, they found the gate to the city open, but the alert troop of soldiers guarding the portal was unwilling to let them inside.

Most of the elves had never seen a human city, and Xwarda was one of the grandest to look upon. Reaching towers and hundreds of arched windows could be seen over the city's outer wall. The roofs were beaten copper, or brightly colored tiles. Banners showing Queen Willa's black sword on white and the High King's golden lion fluttered proudly from a hundred poles. It was as strange as it was awe-inspiring to a people who made their lives living amongst the trees.

Dieter had sweated most of the blood and gore from himself. He looked more than battle-worn when he demanded to speak with Queen Willa. The elves, tattered and dejected, watched as human folk from outlying towns were let inside for protection. The guards gave Dieter a cold shoulder and a small force was marched out to ensure that the elves stayed where they were.

It was clear that the people of Xwarda had been warned. From his position huddled on the roadside, he could see no threat yet. Dieter couldn't tell if Xwarda had been attacked or not. It didn't look like it had, but they were ready for it. On the towering white stone walls at well-spaced intervals, half-giants were loading huge, pivoting crossbows. Barrels of what Dieter assumed to be oil or pitch were being rolled into positions near dark-stained murder holes. The hundreds of archers lining the wall top could be seen between the square teeth-like crenelations. It was also obvious to Dieter that part of the wall here had been rebuilt recently. A lot of the stone was unweathered, and the mortar was rough and unrubbed. Dieter knew that his brother had died on these very walls, and it irked him that the men wouldn't listen to his pleas.

A passage from his brother's journal came to him. It pertained to Queen Willa's strange choice of advisors. There was a pixie named Starkle, if he remembered correctly.

Dieter smiled. He knew how to get to the queen then. He found an older elven woman who was wise in the ways of the Evermore's little folk. The fae folk lived among the elves sometimes in the spring, and there were ways to call upon them.

"A pixie? Here?" the old elven crone nodded her disbelief. "Are you sure?"

"I am," Dieter answered. "Can you summon a pixie, Lady Poplar? It's most important that you try, if you can."

"I can try, Master Willowbrow," she said with a look of doubt. "I've managed to summon a sparrow rider and some glitter wings in my day, but have never called a pixie yet."

Dieter gave the old woman room, but was distracted from her murmuring incantations when a ranking officer broke formation by the gate and started toward them with a strange, almost frighteningly pale look about him. The look only grew more intense the closer the man got, but a sigh and a fast flutter of eyelids when he was upon Dieter seemed to break the trance. "You look so much like Vaegon that there has to be a relation."

"There is." Dieter looked at the bar on the man's collar and the colorful medals pinned to his breast but didn't know what level of service they indicated. Dieter smiled. "Vaegon was my brother. We, my people, have been decimated. Our forest homes were overrun by demon kind."

"Demon kind?" the soldier asked. "By the gods, is that what's coming?"

"I don't know, sir, but most of my people were killed." He indicated the haggard women and children who had run for days without food and water to get there. "We've been afoot for days and have nowhere to go."

"I see bows and swords among your people. Can those able lend their strength to our defense?"

"Of course," Dieter answered, feeling the first bit of hope he had felt in days.

"I cannot make that decision myself," the lieutenant said. "But I'm sure my captain would welcome any who followed Vaegon's kin to our side."

"If I can die half as bravely as Vaegon lived," Dieter said with a proud bow, "then I have done much."

They exchanged names and Lieutenant Torkav gave the order for some barrels of fresh water and hard biscuits to be carried out for the elves while he located his superiors.

While they waited, a tiny, blue-skinned pixie came fluttering out of nowhere, complaining about the cold in a voice far too deep for his hand-sized body. Before a dialogue could be established, a collective gasp of awe erupted from men and elves alike. For now, swooping down out of the sky, looking as haggard and worn as the elves felt, was the High King on his magical winged steed.

Normally Mikahl would have landed by the huge fountain in front of the palace, or even flown into the structure through one of the large rectangular holes left when Pael destroyed the glorious stained-glass depictions that once filled them. The presence of the elves, though, and the collective sorrow and concern his sword picked up from the group, brought him down between them and the soldiers. He nearly cursed when he saw Dieter. So much did the elf resemble Vaegon, and so weary and travel-drained was Mikahl, that he almost believed he was seeing a ghost.

Every human in sight had fallen to a knee, leaving the elves standing with uncertainty and utter astonishment showing in their wild-looking yellow eyes.

Dieter made a half-bow and the rest of his people followed. Mikahl stepped from the bright horse and placed his palm against Dieter's heart, in the old elven gesture of greeting. Dieter smiled broadly as he returned it.

"You're Dieter, then," Mikahl asked, following Starkle's buzzing path back to the palace with his eyes.

Dieter nodded. "You're King Mikahl."

"Aye." Mikahl's voice was soft and full of sadness. "Is this all of you who survived the demons?"

Again Dieter nodded. "The new Queen Mother and her escort still live, as well," he said grimly. "We can feel her life force, but we know not where she is."

"The demons are gathering to attack," Mikahl said, wondering if Hyden Hawk was here. For some reason he knew his friend wasn't. If he had been, these elven refugees would have long since been admitted to the city. "Come, Dieter, bring your people. I'm too weary to think about the past failings of our races." Mikahl sighed heavily. "We will be lucky if we can win ourselves a future."

Chapter Fifty-Three

In the halls of Afdeon, near King Aldar's personal teleportal, battle raged. The giants had contained most of the demons that emerged inside the tower city, but there was more than one teleportal built into the castle. Some demons had escaped, and now several bloody skirmishes were taking place on a number of floors. The demons and devils wanted out, but the giants fought them with fearless intensity. The hellborn creatures were either destroyed or driven back into the holes from which they were trying to escape.

Corva and Jicks fought madly at first, but had been forced out of the way by the giants and their wild-swinging axes and wide-bladed swords. At the moment they were shuttling spears and pole axes up from an armory on a lower floor.

After battling alongside the guardians with the Tokamac's magic that first night, Hyden had gotten a grasp of how to manipulate the power of the crystal Verge. He'd accidentally blown a hole the size of a farmhouse into the side of the castle's wall. Near that particular teleportal the icy air bit almost as sharply as steel, and the warriors had to fight in shifts to keep from exhausting themselves in the thin air. Hyden, now asserting his will over the Tokamac Verge instead of the other way around, was trying to clear the guardians back from the bottomless portal hole in the floor so that he could cast his next spell.

A Choska demon had broken free and was awkwardly fighting its way toward the blast hole Hyden had made in the castle. In the close confines, it couldn't open its wings and gain the advantage of flight, but still its toothy maw and razor claws did formidable damage. More than one giant lay dead or dying.

A shout from Durge relaying the human wizard's intentions gave Hyden the opening he needed. Some insectoid creature with beetle-like pincers on its antennaed head was half in, half out of the hole. It took the sudden pause in the giants' attack as a chance to skitter all the way out of the breach. It almost made it.

Using the power of the ring he wore, and the magnifying crystal Verge, Hyden conjured up a sheet of ice slightly larger than the hole in the floor and easily a foot thick. Why he hadn't thought of such a simple thing earlier was beyond him. The creature coming out of the hole was suddenly stuck. The lower quarter of its fat, slime-filled body was crunched and pinned in place by the massive slab. The big bug twisted and clicked and hissed, impaling a staggering swordsman through the chest with one of its pincers, and lashing the hand off of another with its flailing barbed forearms. The fit was quelled quickly, though, as other guardians carrying long poleaxes reached in and filled the bug's exoskeleton with holes.

A sudden roar, so loud and powerful that even the Choska stopped battling for a moment, came from outside the castle. The Choska recovered its wits first and darted for the jagged opening to make its escape.

Hyden charged into a room where the door frame had been turned into an archway by the rumbling quakes earlier. He threw open the wooden shutters and climbed onto the enormous sill. When he looked out he expected to see the massive red dragon Claret. What he saw was as baffling as it was terrifying.

Two blue-scaled dragons, both more than a hundred feet from snout to tail, were spiraling through the pillowy steam. Both wyrms were drakes, and they seemed to be challenging one another to battle. Hyden sensed the territorial instincts roiling within them, almost as clearly as if he were thinking the thoughts himself. One of the blues came streaking by close, its sapphire scales glittering like sun-bathed jewels in the afternoon sun.

The Choska demon won free of the guardians and shot into Hyden's view. It flapped its leathery wings frantically to carry it away from the giants' castle. Then, seeing the dragons, it dove like a rock into the steam. Instantly, like a pair of winged canines chasing a thrown ball, the two blue dragons dove after it. The steam closed over their passage so quickly that the sky was now empty, as if they had never been there.

A distant roar came from below, followed by another and a short, high-pitched shriek. Suddenly, almost half a mile away, one of the blues shot up out of the steamy cloud with the limp, bloody Choska barely protruding from its mouth. The other dragon was right on its tail.

Brothers, Hyden decided. The two blue dragons were brothers, but why were they here? Where did they come from? The hope of riding one of them to Xwarda came and went as he probed their minds. These were wild wyrms that lacked the compassion and intelligence of a creature such as Claret. A yell full of pain came from inside the castle, drawing Hyden's attention. Quickly, he ran back to the teleportal chamber and began healing those that he could. Most of those who were uninjured had gone on the lift to join one of the other battles still raging in the castle. When Hyden was finished healing, he went after them. Not far from another skirmish, he saw Cade talking to one of the captains of the guardians.

"Will you ice over this one, like before?" Cade asked.

"It won't work here," Hyden answered.

"Why not?" the giant asked, as if all of his hope escaped with his sighing breath.

"The hole I made in the castle up there keeps the cold air flowing over the ice slab," Hyden explained. "Down here, the ice will just melt away. The closer to the cauldron we get, the faster it will melt."

"Is there nothing else you can do?"

"I have an idea," Hyden said, pondering cause and effect. Judging how much the Tokamac crystal's power would exaggerate spell-formed stone, versus frozen water, was impossible to say. "You'll have to clear the level below the teleportal just in case. Better yet, two levels, immediately under where the symbols are carved."

Cade nodded and strode off to pass the order. The guardian captain led Hyden to the battle. Hyden wasn't surprised by the amount of damage he could see as they approached. The loud clang of steel and beast, and the yells of excited giants filled the air. What looked to have once been a floor full of walled storage rooms was now nothing more than a rubble-filled expanse.

"We need a healer, wizard," someone yelled. "Durge has taken…"

Hyden tuned out the rest of the words. It didn't matter who it was. Knowing that it was one of his friends could only distract him from his efforts.

More than one giant needed healing. Hyden moved around them, and Jicks came staggering up only to collapse on the floor at his feet. Through the dusty chaos, Hyden saw Corva darting gracefully among the giants. The elf loosed an arrow here and there at a massive, tentacled creature that was destroying everything it came across. After making the healing gestures and speaking the words over Jicks, Hyden stood and started toward the hellborn monster with a purpose.

Hyden's hopes were plummeting. Not about Afdeon or the battles raging around him, but about Xwarda and the Wardstone, and the fact that his brother had found his legions. The old bone reader had told them he would. She told them a lot of things. Without the teleportals, Hyden's hope of getting to Xwarda in time to keep the Warlord from the Wardstone seemed nonexistent.

A wave of anger passed over him and he focused the emotion on the demon beast with all he had. He held out the Tokamac crystal and unleashed a crackling bolt of energy that charred nearly half of the creature's flailing tentacles to ash. This allowed several giants the chance to charge in and attack. A heartbeat later, the creature used its own reserves of magical power and pummeled Hyden backward through the rubble as if he were a leaf in a storm. Hyden landed well, almost cat-like. The power of the crystalized dragon tear dangling at his neck added to his agility and kept him from crashing. Then, out of nowhere, a hot, concussive blast sent all of his thoughts from his brain. The Tokamac Verge fell to the floor with a clunk as Hyden went stumbling down with it. He tried to stand up and get air back into his lungs, but stumbled back over. A pair of guardians rushed past him to divert the powerful devil's attention. Then Jicks grabbed Hyden and the crystal from the rubble and dragged him behind a partially fallen wall.

Blackness flooded Hyden's vision, save for a single white swirl that found the center and forced the darkness back. He heard Jicks's voice cry out in fear, and the deep, gasping sound of someone as they suddenly sucked air. Cade's voice spoke out, but the words spun away to the edges of Hyden's sanity.

Slowly, a misty shape began to form. In his mind's eye, a curvaceous woman appeared. Her arms beckoned him closer, and her eyes softened in welcome.

The goddess.

Bathed in her presence, Hyden's thoughts regathered themselves. She was there for him; there was reason to hope, but still, something about her was changing. It was like he was with her instead of just envisioning her in his mind's eye. For a moment, Hyden panicked. He felt his body somewhere in the distance as it slowly let go of his soul. Then all he could feel was a frigid mist and the goddess's loving embrace.

The Warlord's hordes found no easy victims in Castlemont, but that didn't stop the slaughter. The breed giants of Locar spotted the demons from their watchtowers and came to King Jarrek's aid in force. With tree trunk clubs, spear-launching dragon guns, and savage intent, they raged into the hellborn like the half-primal beasts they were.

King Jarrek's soldiers had become builders. Neither they, nor the dwarves helping them, were prepared for the sudden attack. Using tools and anything else they could find, they defended themselves with all they had. Eventually, the weapons that had been cached were found and distributed, but even with their axes, swords, and crossbows they were no match for the ever-growing number of hellspawn. The breed giants' attack brought them time, though.

The dwarves led the Red Wolf king and as many innocents as they could save into the caves and mine tunnels under the city. The Warlord's horde turned toward Locar and the wild half-breeds' attack. Even with the effective dragon guns, and the brute force the breed brought to battle with them, they were overrun. Dark magic, and violent acts so mindless and brutal that they could only be called evil, ripped through the breed before the sun rose to end that first night. By the next night, the whole city of Castlemont, and Locar as well, was alive and crawling with devils, demons, and skittering, slithering hellspawn.

Only the most well-hidden groups of refugees survived them. The rest were rooted out and devoured.

The Warlord felt wholly confident with his amassed army. To wait for more of his minions would only delay his conquest. There were more wingless creatures and far fewer flying ones than he had hoped. The march across the continent would be slow but pleasurable, for the huge city of Dreen was just over the mountains and directly in his path. The hellborn that hadn't joined him yet could catch up or not. He didn't care. Knowing he had an army that could chew through the land to Xwarda unscathed was all that mattered to the Hell Master.

Just before dawn of the third day, he gave the order to start east toward Dreen. Like a slow, oozing puddle of spilled sludge, the horde made its way over the Wilder Mountains and into Valleya.

The Red City was half empty, and those remaining were in the process of trying to flee with the horse lords. Lord Gregory had refused to allow livestock leave the city before the women and children. Now, herd masters fought each other, and their terrified horses, to win free of the city gates as the demon spawn swarmed over the walls in a hungry fury.

Cresson had heard Hyden Hawk's warning, and Master Wizard Sholt had followed it up with news of what was happening in Westland. Other wizards from Castlemont had warned those in Dreen, as well. Lord Gregory had issued the order to evacuate as soon as he learned they were gathering in Castlemont. To him it was obvious where the horde was going. His command to flee the Red City saved thousands and thousands of lives, and almost as many horses. Those who didn't get out were swallowed in the bloodthirsty black maw of the Warlord's army.

Lord Gregory, with Lady Trella and her two young Westland-born handmaidens, steered their carriage toward Oktin. From there, the Lion Lord planned to cut back west and north. He was beyond his fighting days now. All he wanted was to get his wife safely home to Lakebottom Stronghold. He was no coward, by any means. In his day he had fought enough battles and brawls for any dozen men. If he and the High King somehow survived this horrendous foe, he swore to himself that he would beg Mikahl to release him from his duties. His days as a hero were done.

Chapter Fifty-Four

"Oh, Hyden," the misty form of the goddess spoke in a voice of tinkling chimes. "Don't you understand?"

Hyden shrugged. He was still trying to figure out why this audience with his goddess felt so different to the others.

She smiled, seeing his confusion. "You've died," she said simply. "At least your mortal body has." She put her hand on his bicep. Oddly, he noticed that her touch on his skin felt solid and cool, even though she seemed to be made out of mist. "You cannot afford to get caught up in the moment. It's the very traits that caused the greater gods to choose you that keep drawing you from your purpose. You must weigh your loyalty to friends and family, and your sense of honor, against the balance of the whole. What are you fighting for here?"

"What does it matter, if I've already died?" Hyden asked.

"You've powerful friends, Hyden Hawk. You cannot waste your efforts battling a single demon in Afdeon when your brother is leading thousands of them toward Xwarda. What do you hope to achieve?"

Hyden dropped his gaze shamefully. "Must I kill Gerard?" he asked. "If I do, I will surely die, too."

"The Abbadon is not Gerard," she said a little more forcefully. "And you've already died, Hyden. Your brother chose his own path. He was consumed by that thing, and you should be battling it this very moment. The idea that the brother you remember is still somewhere inside the beast is foolish. Gerard is gone. If any bit of him still lingers, it is that corrupt, jealous part of him, and it must be destroyed or banished with the rest. The very people you love will fall victim if you fail."

"But how do I get to Xwarda?" Hyden asked. "The teleportals all open into the Nethers now. I… I don't…"

"If you had been exploring your god-given powers, instead of planning unnecessary adventures to find trinkets you could retrieve in minutes, you'd know." her voice had a hard edge to it. She was angry. "Where did you send Talon? Your familiar's place is with you." Her voice softened and she touched his cheek. "Lucky for us all that you have made some mighty friends along the way. Without one of them, we'd all be doomed." She smiled and touched his nose lovingly with a fingertip. She drew her face very near his and it seemed as if she might kiss him, but she stopped and whispered, "Always remember who your true friends are, Hyden. Never forget them." Then her lips moved to his cheek and he was drifting.

"Is he dead?" Durge asked.

"I think he is," Jicks replied with a sniffle.

A trio of roars erupted like thunder outside the walls of Afdeon, one after the other. They were angry sounds, low and guttural, and from something absolutely massive. Suddenly, Durge's eyes glazed over and his movements became mechanical. He bent down to pick up Hyden's limp body and carried it back to the lift. Jicks wiped away his tears and followed dutifully. A moment later they were rising up onto the cold floor where Hyden accidentally blasted away the outer wall.

"By the gods, what are you doing?" Jicks asked as the giant stalked over to the open hole.

The young swordsman suddenly froze.

"Durge!" Jicks yelled out in a loud whisper as a huge, split yellow eye the size of a wagon wheel pressed against the hole from the outside. The eye was hooded by a dark green-scaled brow. The whole orb gently rose up and down with the huge wyrm's wing beats. A lower lid blinked up once and then the dragon's head pulled away from the opening. Jicks's heart was thundering. The green dragon was so big and terrible-looking that he couldn't move his legs for fear of it. He began to tremble as his mind registered what he was seeing. Another roar sounded, this one far louder and more menacing than any of the others had been. This roar shook Jicks in the guts and vibrated the very walls of Afdeon.

Durge, seemingly oblivious to what was going on outside the castle, walked straight up to the opening and stood there. It took Jicks a few heartbeats to pull himself away from the spot he was standing in, but he finally did. He eased across the rubble-strewn room to the giants' side and looked out. The voice of another giant speaking excitedly came from an open window or a balcony a few levels below them.

Jicks scanned the sky, looking for the giant green dragon, but he didn't see it. He saw two blue dragons, slightly smaller than the green. They were circling high above in the open air. And there was a distant speck, no, two of them, winging closer from the east. They grew in size with every breath he took. Suddenly, the green dragon came shooting up before them out of the steam. It passed barely an arrow shot away. The green's worn ivory-colored underscales followed its sleek horned head past the opening. Then came its long body and even longer tail. Its wicked-clawed hind legs were tucked tight against its body and its wings were spread wide. The sight was breathtaking, but Durge acted as if he had seen nothing.

"By the Heart of Arbor, it's three times the size of the one we saw in the Wedjak," Corva said as he came up behind them. "Its roar scared that devil back into the portal."

Neither Durge nor Jicks replied, but Jicks glanced at Hyden still lying limp in the giant's arms. Corva saw the tears flowing down the young swordsman's cheeks and sucked in a breath. He started to say something, but a roar louder than all the others combined, that lasted nearly a full minute, ripped through the world around them. Afdeon shook again and pieces of stone and mortar vibrated loose.

"By the gods," Jicks mumbled softly as the roar ended.

Corva stepped up beside him and looked out. A ruby-scaled dragon, which was easily twice the size of the green wyrm, was winging its way directly toward them. It was darting its angry head to and fro as if it expected a challenge from one of the other dragons in the sky. They stayed clear, giving it a wide berth; all save for a smaller red that was barely ten feet long and flying under the other, in her shadow.

The monstrous red let out a blasting gout of flame ahead, and downward, of its path. The raw heat of its breath evaporated the steam for at least five hundred feet in all directions. Satisfied that no threat was hiding in the mist below, it closed its maw and banked around so that it was facing the hole in the castle directly. With a thump of wings that made Jicks's knees buckle and Corva take two steps back, it threw its wings out wide and stalled itself less than a hundred feet from them. The dragon's body lifted and lowered in time with its massive wing strokes. Its huge head eased forth with narrow brows on a long, glittering, serpentine neck.

Durge, as if presenting a small child to its parent, held Hyden's limp body out before him. Jicks's heart hammered through his chest in both fear and awe. He had heard tales of how Hyden and the High King had defeated the demon wizard Pael, and he was most certain that this was the dragon that had helped save the realm.

Jicks glanced at Durge. The giant still showed no expression on his face. He was entranced, Jicks decided. The medallion on Hyden's chest was fountaining sparks as bright as diamond chips in the sun. He swallowed hard, then looked back at the dragon. Its elongated snout scrunched up as if it were sniffing the air. Beyond it, the smaller red wyrm looped and banked around, chasing the other's tail as a kitten chases a yarn ball. Jicks saw that the little wyrm's wing scales were long and resembled feathers, some of them had shed, revealing a thin membrane of wing skin underneath.

A loud whooshing sound filled the moment. Jicks could feel himself being sucked forward toward the dragon. It was drawing air into its cavernous lungs.

"J- J- Jicks!" Corva managed. "D- Dragon's fire!"

The dragon's mouth opened, revealing sharp, yellowed teeth as long as a man is tall. Its forked tongue drew back, and its throat opened up. Durge, still holding Hyden out as if in offering, took a knee and lowered his head.

Both Jicks and the elf bolted away from the hole in the wall as fast as they could.

Claret couldn't help but chuckle at their foolishness. Then she let out a roar that was loud enough to wake the dead. And the blast was laced with more than enough dragon magic to do exactly that.

Talon found Phen, Dostin, and Queen Mother Telgra as they and the elven escort came upon the bodies of the fallen elves in the Evermore forest. The hellspawned horde had long since abandoned the carnage to answer their master's call. Arf whined under Phen, sensing the sadness of the elves around him. Phen, too, could feel the almost palpable emotion oozing from them. Dostin cried openly as his mount, Yip, padded along closely beside the new Queen Mother. All around them, littered in the forest undergrowth, near the few hulking demon corpses, lay the decimated bodies of elven archers and swordsmen. Some women and a few children lay here and there, as well, but not nearly as many as there could have been. The lack of innocent corpses was clearly heartening to Telgra.

"They fled like cowards, south to the human city," an older elf said as he stepped out of the woods. He had a large gore stain on his tunic and haunted amber eyes.

Telgra stopped and glared at him. Dostin's hands clenched his staff, and the wolf beneath him growled silently.

"Better than to die like fools fighting an enemy far greater than you can defend against," Phen replied. The ease with which he moved now was still surprising. He'd been petrified so long that his muscles weren't used to doing anything.

"Where's your wife, Bandear Cottonwood?" Telgra asked the elf. "Where's your daughter?"

"Mind your manners when speaking to the Queen Mother," one of Telgra's escorts said when Bandear started to reply harshly. His expression shifted to a sneer and the old elf turned and ran away.

"Should I chase him?" the elven guard asked.

"No, leave him," Telgra replied. "He's obviously distraught. He's seen our people killed and is probably terrified. Leave him be." She wiped away her tears. "I must go into the Arbor Heart alone."

"We will follow you to the Heart Tree, Queen Mother," the guards insisted. "There's no telling what beasts or scavengers might still be lingering."

She nodded and wiped her face again. Phen wanted nothing more than to go to her and hold her in his arms, but he knew it wasn't proper. She was a queen. He forced the impulse away and mastered his emotion. She must have sensed his inner struggle because she caught his eyes with her own and let a faint smile of understanding curl the corner of her mouth. It disappeared quickly when she had to step over half of a young elven boy. He was clutching a bow in his left hand and his face was a grimace of pain. It looked like his legs had been bitten off. The appendages were nowhere to be seen.

Talon observed them from the trees without letting his presence be known. The familiar link between him and his wizard had been broken. The hawkling understood that Hyden had passed from the world of life, but he wasn't sure yet what to do. Since his hatching, Hyden had been there for him. Hyden was Talon's mother, father, and sibling, all in one. The hawkling was too confused to go to Phen yet, and Spike was in Phen's coat pocket sleeping. Talon thought to communicate with the lyna first, but he couldn't until it awoke. He flew from limb to limb and watched Hyden's friends from a distance while trying to sort through his avian instincts and familial emotion.

Luckily, the goddess called upon him. Talon was pleased to be needed by such an esteemed being. He didn't hesitate to do as she asked.

The escort came to a stop in a long, oval-shaped clearing. At one end of it there was a towering tree. Its trunk was as big around as some of the smaller castle towers Phen had seen. It stood majestically among the other trees like a king among peasants. At its base, a tangle of roots twisted their way into the ground. Phen slid off of Arf and made Dostin give Yip's back a rest, as well. The two great wolves immediately bounded into the forest to snatch a meal.

Queen Mother Telgra disappeared through an archway formed by the roots of the Heart Tree. Phen saw her hair reflect off a shaft of golden sunlight as she continued past the Heart Tree trunk to disappear into the forest beyond. Phen took a breath and was about to ask one of the guards if there was any food about when half of the elven escort gasped in unison.

Phen turned to see Dostin sitting in the throne-like seat formed by the tree's roots. The elves seemed shocked, or afraid to say anything, and a few of them exchanged disturbed looks. Phen understood that the simple-minded monk was sitting in Telgra's throne.

"By the Heart of Arbor," one of the elves said. "I never thought I'd see such a thing."

"It's the prophecy, I'm sure of it," said another.

"What prophecy?" Phen asked. Before the elves could answer he spoke kindly to Dostin. "Get out of the Queen Mother's throne. By the gods, do you have no manners?" Dostin jumped up quickly. His face reddened and he looked around sheepishly.

"I didn't know," he said. Then to Phen, "I'm hungry."

"I'm hungry, too, Dostin." Phen forced a smile. "After they tell me about their prophecy, maybe they can find us something to eat."

One of the elves barked an order in the old language and two of their number moved off into the forest. The elf who issued the command looked at Phen sadly. Phen thought his name was Gaveon, but he wasn't sure.

"The prophecy says that when a human sits upon the throne of Arbor the time of elves in this land has begun its end. Those who survive this darkness might return here only to find that the Heart of Arbor has moved on without them."

"But isn't the Arbor Heart somewhere else already?" Phen asked. "I read that the heart of the forest is not truly where it is, that it can sort of be moved to another forest if a need arises."

"It is so," the elf answered. "But if it were to move without us, then we would be left behind. It could take us a thousand years of searching forest after forest until we found it again."

"The Arbor Heart could appear in a forest we've already searched after we have moved on," another elf added.

"Then so be it," Queen Mother Telgra said as she stepped back through the root-formed arch.

Two elves stepped out of the forest looking bloody and tired, then another, and another. From behind them, a small group of seven or eight became visible as they moved through the trees.

"We will go to the human city and fight beside them, if not for any other reason than to restore our honor." Telgra's voice rose as she spoke. She leapt gracefully up onto a root, and climbed even higher on the tangle of roots as she continued. "We have let ourselves down. We have let the Heart of Arbor down. Already our demonic foe has tainted the soil here. The fiery trees of Salaya were all but ruined, and the Heart of Arbor struggles to beat while the blood of demons chokes up in its roots."

More elves came out of the forest as she spoke, not many, not nearly enough, but the ones who came were soldiers, freshly proven on the black blood of hellspawn. Swordsmen, hunters, archers, and a few of the older magi came out of the woods, too. By the time the Queen Mother was ending her speech there were two hundred battle-ready elves gathered around her. At some point, while she spoke, the great wolves returned.

"…if the Arbor Heart has moved on by the time we return, then that is the price we pay for our arrogance and betrayal of those who sought our aid before." She hardened her look. "I am not ordering any of you, but those who do not march with me to defend the Wardstone from our enemies are nothing to me."

Phen was swollen with the pride her words inspired, and the determined look on her face was unyielding.

"I'm the Queen Mother, and as long as the Arbor Heart pulses through my veins I will remain such. Those who wish to rise above our past should gather the rations and weapons you'll need. It is a long run to Xwarda. I can only hope we get there in time."

The Wizard and the Warlord

Chapter Fifty-Five

Gerard's legions devoured the farming and trading community of Kastia like a plague. Lord Gregory's decision to send Dreen's city guard and as many soldiers as could be mustered ahead to defend Xwarda saved most of the common folk between the two cities. Some, though, thought to defend their homes. The foresters of Tip sent their women and children to Southron, and then stood in defiance. They lasted about as long as it takes to draw a breath, but unlike many, they died defending the life they loved, not running and afraid.

The people of Tarn and the Pixie River fisher folk weren't as bold. Two years before, Pael's army had marched through and now there was an obvious lack of young, hearty men willing to fight. Most of them made the day-long ride to the safety of Xwarda's walls, hurrying along behind the Valleyan soldiers Lord Gregory sent. Those who waited too long were consumed by the Warlord's horde.

The large city of Platt acted as Xwarda's main trade center. Queen Willa didn't allow mercantile activity outside and along the city walls. This prevented the chaotic and often unclean huddle towns from forming around Xwarda's main gates. People either traded inside the walls in an establishment, or in the open market that Platt had become. The people of Platt acted in a completely different manner than those who lived in Xwarda. Though the Queen had opened the gates for all who sought protection, there were many merchants with warehouses full of stores. Most of them hired sellswords to guard their goods. Platt, after all, had a solid wall around it, too. These men were just starting to recuperate from the devastation Pael had brought. Having rebuilt their inventories of goods, and stockpiled grain, oats and other staples for the long winter months, they were reluctant to abandon everything a second time.

They should have.

Platt's wall stood twelve feet tall and was built of solid stone blocks. Though it did a superb job deterring bandits and thieves, it fell over like a picket fence under a stampede.

The Warlord's legions left nothing but blood, death, and destruction in their wake as they rolled through the place like a bloody tidal wave.

Queen Rosa's mother, Queen Rachel, had sent the bulk of Seaward's soldiers to help defend the Wardstone. She did this of her own accord, after her mage told her of Sir Hyden Hawk Skyler's warning. They had taken too long to muster. Now, as the head of the five-thousand-man column was approaching Xwarda's southern gate, the rear of the procession was falling prey to some of the Warlord's winged beasts.

The hellspawn and demon kind bound to travel by hoof, claw, and undulating slither were closing in on the city's western gate. At both places, swarms of Blacksword soldiers were pouring out to meet the dark enemy. Accompanying Queen Willa's elite troops were a few thousand dwarven axemen. Along the top of the sixty-foot-high granite walls, both human and elven archers, a few dozen breed giant dragon gunners, and small groups of robed wizards hurried into position to lend their spells and shafts to the defense of the powerful bedrock. Above the shouts and commands, alarm bells and short horn bursts shrilled and gonged the armies of the realm into position.

The High King stood atop a blocky crenelated tower at the southwestern corner of the city, watching it all unfold. He could see the Seaward men being decimated by lavender and crimson blasts of dark magic. They fought hard, but swooping clawed monsters snatched men from their mounts and hurled them like so much fodder. He shook his head. They would have been a welcome addition to the defense had they arrived in time to enter the city and organize. Maybe only half of them were going to get the chance to form ranks and make a stand, and those only because of the Blacksword troops pouring out to aid them.

The idea of sending dwarves and swordsmen out to meet the hellspawn army bothered Mikahl. General Wisikman, Queen Willa's newest commander, had explained that, with the addition of the elves and all the human refugees to the overcrowded city's numbers, they had no choice. The streets, alleys, and even the long, wide tunnels that led east under the walls toward Jenkanta were already packed full of refugees.

"It's just as well," Mikahl said to himself. "Against a foe like this it might be better to die sooner."

He glanced down at the western gate to his right. The heavy banded portal was closing. Dwarves, a few elven swordsmen and most of the soldiers Lord Gregory had sent were forming up in lines to meet the cloud of evil that was closing on them.

The sun was low in the western sky, giving the approaching beasts long, imposing shadows.

Having learned about night fighting in the long battles that were fought right here, four-keg pyramids of flammable oil, three in a triangle with one on top, had been stacked at intervals out beyond the walls. Flaming spears would be launched into them later to give the archers light by which to aim.

Mikahl wished Hyden were here. He expected him to be. Even young Phen would have been a great boon. The boy would have already researched what there is to know about the dark army. He would know the weaknesses and strengths of each particular creature, and be full of suggestions that might tilt the battle in the right direction. As it was, Mikahl held little hope of surviving the night. His plan was to seek out the leader of this foul army and end it. He and Ironspike would cleanse themselves of the rage he felt over Rosa's death. He would do his very best to avenge her and his unborn child. It was all he knew to do. Since the day he took the king's sword from Father Petri and started into the Giant Mountains, the realm had been fighting one war or another. He was no king; he was a swordsman, and he had every intention of finding the limits of his skill as such. He resolved to die fighting, for that's what fighters do.

None of the wizards could reach Hyden Hawk, the giants in Afdeon, or even Phen. Learning from Dieter Willowbrow that most of the elves had perished in the Evermore gave Mikahl little reason to hope for his friends.

If he had known that Queen Mother Telgra's arboreal magic was shielding out the attempts to contact Phen, and that they and a few hundred elven soldiers were quickly approaching from the north, he might have felt the need for some restraint. As it was, he was resigned to kill or be killed by the dark, malignant thing that had taken his wife and child from the world. Even now, as he scanned the battleground and the disheveled ranks of the enemy's charge, he couldn't help but search for the Warlord. He was anxious to get on with it, no matter what the outcome might be.

Queen Willa took the news of Queen Rosa's death hard. She had been instrumental in arranging the marriage and had a strong maternal affection for Mikahl. She'd welcomed him into her arms earlier, in her private chambers, and let him cry out his sorrow against her bosom. She smothered his hair and rocked him as his own mother might have done long ago. After he recovered, she got the sense that he was in a reckless mood. This frightened her. She understood the power of the enemy and knew that if Mikahl were lost, then so was Ironspike's might. Without Ironspike's power to defend the Wardstone, the Warlord would soon do more than a open few doorways into the Nethers; he would tear the boundary wide open.

After consoling Mikahl, she gathered her wizards and commanders and explained that the heroes of the previous years couldn't be found. Sir Hyden Hawk Skyler was unaccounted for, his powerful warning sent from somewhere deep in the Giant Mountains. King Jarrek, the old Red Wolf warrior, was being held prisoner by his own men in a mine shaft in the Wilder Mountains. They were holding him to keep him from raging into the Dark Lord's host with no army behind him.

Queen Willa smiled internaly at the thought of him. She loved King Jarrek. They'd grown closer over the last few visits. She was pleased that his men had the sense to keep his temper and his fierce pride from getting him killed. His bravery had always outweighed his good sense.

She went on to explain that Phen was off with Hyden Hawk. She called him Marble Boy instead of using his name, because no one knew who Phen was, but everyone from Portsmouth to Jenkanta knew who Marble Boy was.

General Spyra was now Lord Spyra, and too far away to be of any assistance. The dwarven general who had so cleverly orchestrated the sinking of Seareach to save Castlemont from King Ra'Gren's assault was in the Wilder Mountains with King Jarrek.

"The High King stands with us," she told them. "But he has lost his wife and unborn heir to this evil foe. He is distraught and may prove unpredictable. He will be prone to vengeance." She paused and took a deep breath. "It will be no easy task, but he and Ironspike must be protected at all times."

"This is the time for new heroes," she said. "We must not falter against the darkness, for if we do, we may never see the light again. Rally your men. The creatures they will face are terrifying to look upon. They are unnatural things that should never have found the light of day. If nothing else, you must give your men encouragement and hope. Master Wizard Feist says that the Warlord leading this host is most formidable, but without him the creatures that make up this horde will lose the power of purpose. This thing that commands the others must be our main target. Outside of defending the city and protecting the High King, killing the Dark Lord is what must be done." She raised her hands and smiled as if she knew they could win. "I say rally your men. Prepare them well, for the dark host will be upon us this night."

As the commanders and wizards left her to carry out her orders, the alarm bells sounded. The harrumph of dwarven battle horns filled the air, as did the ringing of bells in the towers. The city was so crowded with panicked people and herd animals that most of the commanders couldn't get back to their troops in time to command them. The more powerful of the wizards teleported to the wall top and began spreading the word, but already the battle had begun in earnest.

Queen Willa returned to her private chamber hoping to have a word with Mikahl before the battle began, but he was already gone. In his place was Master Wizard Sholt, all the way from Westland, and lying on the divan was Queen Rosa. The rise and fall of her chest was obvious and the soft snore that accompanied the movement left no room to doubt that she was alive and whole.

"She's alive," Queen Willa gushed, feeling a tidal wave of relief wash over her. She turned to Sholt, "But how?"

Master Wizard Sholt shook his head in confusion. "What do you mean? Was her safety ever in doubt?"

Queen Willa gasped, covering her open mouth with her hand. "Mik thinks the Warlord killed her when he came out of the Nethers."

Sholt was silent for a few long moments. From outside, the distinct clanging of bells and the tiny shouts of men came to the room. As soon as Mikahl had given him the order to sound the alarm, Sholt had teleported to the garden yard to try to save young Suza from the same fate

De'Rain met. The sounding of alarms was a simple kinetic spell. He didn't tell a man to ring the bells. He rang them magically and went directly to his students. He found Queen Rosa frozen in shock. She had blood spattered across her chest and was so close to the hellborn beast that was crawling out of the gateway that Sholt had no other choice but to protect the queen. He grabbed her and teleported them from the garden yard to an empty, snow-covered field just south of Lord Able's abandoned stronghold. The casting had cost him most of his strength. Spell weary and somewhat in shock himself, he checked and found that the queen wasn't wounded and led them through the snow to the crumbled tower. A few rooms were still intact, and with the rest of his strength he set a magical fire to blaze and slipped into a deep slumber.

"I don't know why he would think such a thing," Sholt finally said to Queen Willa. "There was a small girl there in the yard, and Rosa's handmaiden was down. Maybe he…"

"She was wearing my green dress," Rosa whispered. Neither the wizard nor Queen Willa had noticed that her snoring had stopped. "That thing crushed her and nearly twisted her in two. I was wearing that dress when Mikahl saw me that morning." Rosa got to her feet and ran the few steps from the divan into Queen Willa's arms. "She was just trying it on so we could get the hem the right length," she cried. "He must be horribly sad. He was so pleased about the baby, and now he thinks…"

"He's more than sad, dear," Queen Willa said. She was relieved. Mikahl wouldn't rage off into an unsurvivable situation if he knew that his wife and child were still alive.

"Master Wizard Sholt." Even though Queen Willa was no longer his liege, she commanded him with total authority. "As soon as you have told the High King that his wife and child are here safe, that he must fight with some restraint, then you should rest." She gave her old castle wizard a look that was insistent. "Those magi serving on the wall will want and need your guidance now, but your strength will be more valuable when they have grown weary and you have recouped. King Mikahl, though, must be told this news immediately."

Queen Rosa lifted her head from Willa's shoulder and sobbed. Sholt had teleported the two of them more than a dozen times. He had only enough constitution to move them so far at a time, and each effort was all the more taxing. He had seen what the demon horde left behind in Locar and Dreen. His assessment of the enemy left him anything but optimistic, and he wanted to converse with the High King anyway, before this battle became all-consuming.

King Mikahl had sworn him to the duty of protecting Pavreal's bloodline, no matter the cost. If things grew dire, he wouldn't hesitate to take Ironspike and Rosa and sail to Harthgar, or seek protection in Afdeon. He felt the High King should be aware of these things. Even though it would take all the strength left in him to find his king, he nodded his understanding to Queen Willa and then disappeared from the room with a crackling pop.

Outside Xwarda's western-facing gate, the setting sun's rays painted the horizon beautiful shades of pastel blue and peach. The wingless faction of the demon horde engaged the ranks of defenders in a violent clash. It was a disheartening sight for the High King to look upon. The relatively white field of trampled snow turned quickly into a steaming mush of gore. Mikahl decided that defeating this army with swords, axes, and bows might prove impossible. Already, streaking bolts of lightning and scarlet blasts of hellborn magic were scattering body parts. Mikahl held his position and continued his search for the vaguely human form baring those familiar Skyler eyes. It was all he could do to keep from drawing Ironspike and raging mindlessly into the fray. He might clear a path through the enemy's ranks, or kill a handful of the monstrous creatures, but that would serve no real purpose.

To the south he could see the flying beasts going high over the wall, out of the archers' range. They were coming down in the crowded streets now. A Choska demon was flapping wildly like a kite in a gale. Its vain attempt to get away from the barbed tether one of the breed giants had stuck into it was futile. It would die as soon as they could reel the line in, but it was only one of a thousand foes swarming the sky.

"Mikahl! High King Mikahl," Sholt's voice called weakly from the roof below and behind the High King's position. Mikahl barely heard him over the shouts of the archers and the roar of the beasts. He turned and nodded to the wizard, but quickly put his attention back on the enemy. "You made it," he said simply.

"We must speak," said Sholt, but he was so exhausted that the words barely made a sound as they came out of his mouth. Sholt closed his eyes and summoned what was left inside him. "My lord," he said a little more loudly. Seeing that Mikahl had heard him, the wizard continued. "The bloodline must be protected."

Mikahl assumed that Sholt meant that he shouldn't enter the battle and risk dying. As far as he knew, he was the last of Pavreal's kin. "I'll only fight the Hell Master himself, wizard," he snapped his response. "Now leave me," he commanded as he saw a gout of flame shooting skyward, reflected in the wizard's eyes. He turned to find the source of it, hoping it was the beast Hyden's brother had become. "Do not return until you have rested."

Before Sholt could respond Mikahl leapt to the next merlon, then the next.

Sholt found that he was so tired he could barely move, yet he screamed out, "My Lord, listen to me! Queen Rosa is…"

"Dead!" Mikahl finished for him as Ironspike came out of its scabbard with a rasping metallic ring. The normally passive blue radiance the sword emitted was white hot with Mikahl's rage and was nearly as bright as the sun. Sholt was temporarily blinded by it, and by the time he could see again, King Mikahl was gone.

The over-fatigued wizard could barely make out the bright horse as it went streaking madly toward a distant eruption of flame. Ironspike lit the carnage immediately below the High King as if it were midday.

Sholt managed to get to his feet, and the amount of bloody death he could see in the field was sickening. He started to cast one last spell before consciousness left him, but he was yanked off the wall by the claws of a swooping hellcat. He didn't have the strength to fight back, and the creature wasn't strong enough to carry him far. Both of them went sinking toward the battle below, until the hellcat dropped him right into a knot of swarming demon kin and banked away.

M. R. Mathias

Chapter Fifty-Six

At the west gate, the wingless horde outnumbered the soldiers so greatly that some of the Dark Lord's force broke away from the battle and circled the wall toward the city's little-used northern gate. It was called the forest gate because it opened onto the southern edge of the Evermore Forest. It was guarded, but not nearly as much as the other gates. Queen Willa's rangers used the horse door and the barracks there. With their constant presence it had never needed guarding before.

The demon spawn were surprised when, about two-thirds of the way around, an entanglement of thorny growth sprouted around them. It engulfing most of the front of their charge. They were even more surprised when scores of elven archers began loosing arrows at them from afar. The entangled demons were easy targets as they struggled to tear themselves free.

Phen was leading Telgra and the elven group toward a hidden tunnel entrance he knew of. It was still a good way east. The elves had waited until after sunset. They and the great wolves could see well enough in the dark to follow Phen's direction. Yet, oddly, it was Phen's human senses that picked up the demons first. He felt more than saw or heard them. His thorny growth spell was cast in the best place it could have been. Most of the dark things leading the pack were caught up. Those following didn't have a chance to slow as they ran into the stuff. The elves engaged them freely.

Under Phen, Arf growled and shivered, waiting desperately to have a go at the evil creatures that were offending his senses. Phen wouldn't allow it. He spoke soothingly to the great wolf, though, trying to calm him. "You'll get your chance, pup, I promise."

Torches flared on the walls above them, followed by the shouts of the forest gate guards. Dostin let Yip charge into the fray and used his staff in the torchlight with deft ferocity. He had an intense look, narrow-browed and scowling, with his tongue sticking out of the side of his mouth. The heavyset monk whacked and jabbed everything around him. Crack! Crack! A heartbeat of pause. Crack! again. Then a flurry of chak-chak-chaks as he spun the heavy wooden pole. Yip snarled and growled, then bit into a hell boar's flank. A piece of the beast tore free and Dostin clobbered it as it turned to attack.

"Leave them!" Queen Mother Telgra yelled to her fighters.

Phen cast an orb light into being and sent it to hover over the dark host. Already some of the Xwardian rangers were gathering archers on the wall and loosing into the group. It was all the elves could do to break free before a kettle of boiling oil was poured over the wall. A moment later, a flaming arrow streaked down and the whoomping sound of the oil igniting thundered through the night. With only a handful of hellspawn on their heels, the elves followed Phen and his great wolf mount away from the blaze and back into the darkness.

Inside the wall, almost a dozen hellcats had landed and taken to the streets. Innocent folk, farmers, seamstresses, and leathermen were thrashed by tooth and claw. Women and children were torn to shreds, and refugees trampled by their own townsfolk trying to get away.

But there was no place to go.

A series of streaking blasts sent a wagon full of chicken cages spinning over into a small, roped-in herd of sheep. The herd broke loose. A piece of the blazing wagon set a young girl's hair on fire. She flailed and screamed in terror and pain. Her mother ran to help but both were mangled to bloody chunks by the more powerful kinetic blast of a Choska demon that was perched atop a chapel nearby.

A huge, smoldering hole was left in the street were the woman and girl had just been. A blackened leg, smaller than a man's arm, with a shiny red shoe on its foot, twitched once, then again. People screamed and still tried to flee, only to find a pair of wyverns slinging acidic slobber over the crowd like rain.

A bat-like Choska glided down over the crowd and snatched a fat, shrieking farm wife.

A block over, an angry young plow boy swung a dirt rake into one of the wyverns. The tines caught in the beast's black, scaly hide and the boy pulled it out of the air. A half-dozen men with hoes and shovels beat the thing to a pulp only to find their feet and lower legs sizzling and dissolving from the wyvern's acid blood.

While the Choska sat on its perch busying itself by tearing apart the huge meal it had caught, a young mage attacked. The boy sent a thin little crackle of lightning at the Choska from the rooftop of a nearby inn. The bolt would have been insignificant had it not finished its jagged streak directly into one of the Choska's ember eyes. The mangled farm wife fell from its jaws and landed half in, half out of an abandoned pot maker's cart that still had a terrified horse harnessed to it. As the demon screeched a terrible, ear-splitting cry, the horse charged through the crowd, leaping and lurching over huddled people until the wagon finally hung on something.

From under the broken wagon an old man wailed. The horse fell as a pair of arrows pierced its vitals.

Half a mile away, a row of shops owned by tapestry weavers and tailors was fully ablaze. Around the fire, two imps, a wyvern, and a blood-lusting thing that looked half insect, half reptile were decimating the people, causing them to stampede like cattle, trampling their neighbors and kin into the bloody snow.

Closer to the city gate a terrible creature as big as a two-story tavern lashed and destroyed everything within reach of its many tentacles. Already a dozen people had been grabbed up and dashed against the rubble, then tossed away by the evil monster.

While all of this was happening, fat, lazy snowflakes drifted down out of the night sky.

Inside the city, even where hellspawn weren't attacking, the conditions were miserable. It was freezing cold and blankets were scarce. No one dared brave a fire, not even to cook. To attract one of the dark-winged beasts was to attract death in quantity. Even atop the smaller thirty-foot high wall that surrounded the palace grounds, the soldiers and archers crowded there didn't light the torches yet. They would have to soon enough. Already a pair of hellcats were ravaging through the reserve troops who were waiting in the forested park near Whitten Loch.

And above them all, searching for the place it would unleash its evil magic, was an angry, one-eyed Choska.

Along the rooftops of the eastern portion of Xwarda, a dark creature skittered to and fro. It was seen here, then there. It was pointed at and whispered about, but it didn't stay still long enough to be identified. Whatever it was, it was terrifyingly fast and left behind long streamers of glittery dust that glistened in the moonlight.

King Mikahl found the Warlord. The Hell Master had cleared a large circle around himself with dragon's fire and ordered his minions to leave the human king to him. The young Westlander had chopped off his lover's head. Even the parts of the Dark Lord that had long forgotten Gerard knew that much. After all, it was the Dragon Queen who had tried so hard to help him break free of the Nethers before. This pesky little man and his sword were nothing but fodder to him. The Warlord wasn't a mere demon, nor was he susceptible to being drawn into Pavreal's blade, but it was the satisfaction of avenging her death that caused the Warlord to fight the High King alone.

The two of them exchanged blows with both steel and claw. They blasted powerful magics at each other and circled cautiously in ever defensive patterns. Both took wounds, but both found the shielding spells that thwarted the other's magic. Neither of them had the advantage, and neither of them was backing down.

Mikahl was frustrated beyond rational thinking. Nothing he seemed to do more than nicked the powerful thing Hyden's brother had become. He was dodging and defending himself fairly well, but he knew that if the Warlord let his minions into the fight, it was over. The only reason he was still alive was because this malformed monster was determined to kill him itself.

Mikahl fought the Warlord most of the night and accomplished nothing more than keeping it out of Xwarda. He wondered if it wasn't the other way around. Was this thing with Skyler eyes toying with him to keep him from defending the city?

Like spectators at the Summer's Day brawl, a few dozen greater demons lingered, watching their master fight the human king. Mikahl was determined to kill this powerful, dark beast that was somehow able to avoid the bite of his blade, but he was wary of the others. If they started at him, he would try to break away and regroup. Until then, he would fight on, thinking that if he could just get Ironspike through his foe's plated hide it would be over in an instant. Deep inside, he knew that if he didn't, it was over for the world of men.

The idea came to him that Ironspike's power had never been enough to conquer all this evil, but the thought of his unborn child and wife being torn apart by the thing before him wouldn't let him succumb.

Without faltering, Mikahl ground his jaw and fought on.

Phen led the elves through the same tunnel that Vaegon and Dugak, once used to rejuvenate Ironspike while King Mikahl lay dying. That's how Phen knew about it. Once he'd heard the tale, he pestered everyone until he was shown the location, but that was before all of this madness, even before he and Hyden sailed after the silver skull. To Phen's surprise, when he climbed up the ladder at the end of the tunnel and lifted a floor section that opened into an old wine cellar, Dugak and a pair of young castle-born dwarves were huddled there. A candle stood in a teacup and lit the room enough to see that they'd tapped a small keg and were getting drunk.

"Ah, Phen," Dugak said in a slurring stupor, as if the boy popped his head up out of the castle floor every day. "Good to see you, lad."

Phen grinned for an instant, but the memory of Oarly's death shattered his mood. "I've got company," he said.

"Good lad," Dugak slurred. "The queen will be glad to hear it. There is already a handful of demons outside in the park. They're trying to get into the castle now."

Phen shook his head, climbed out, and then helped Dostin and Gaveon shove the two great wolfs gracelessly up through the square hole. The Queen Mother came next, and Dugak stumbled to his feet so that he could bow with reverence. Even a drunken castellan knew royalty by sight, and Dugak was most capable at his job. "I'll go announce you to Queen Willa," Dugak said as more elves streamed into the room.

"Just open the door," Telgra snapped. "We need room. There are more than two hundred elven warriors with me, and we're already out of space."

Dugak shook his head to clear it; luckily the other two elves were already exiting the cellar. The corridor beyond was torchlit, and a long rectangle of light shined on the group. Dugak backed out into the hall and bowed again. "What should I tell Queen Willa?" he asked, glancing first at Telgra, then at Phen.

Phen shrugged.

"Tell her I'm sending my blades and my bows to greet the evil things at her doorstep," Telgra said. "Please have someone show the archers to a rooftop or a set of windows that will allow them the opportunity to loose on the enemy."

"Come on," Phen said. "Archers, follow me. Dugak, have someone show the swordsmen to the gate, and then present Queen Mother Telgra and this monk to Queen Willa."

Phen didn't wait for a reply. He began herding the elves carrying bows out into the hall. Arf gave him a quizzical look and whined. "Go with Yip and the swordsmen," Phen told the wolf.

Arf barked his agreement and wagged his tail briefly. Their eyes met and the feeling that they might never see each other again passed between them.

Phen wasn't sure which of them was going to die, and he didn't have time to ponder it. If the castle's protective walls were already breached, then it would probably be both of them. He intended to get the archers situated then round up both Queen Willa and Telgra back here where they had a way to escape, if it came to it. As an afterthought, he ordered several of the elves to go back and guard the opening that led to the tunnel. Then he led the others to a stairway and started climbing up. Since they were four floors below ground level, an elevated position for the archers was at least half a dozen flights above them.

The sun was just starting to rise in the east when an explosion shook the entire battlefield. A huddle of devils, led by a long, serpent-like creature with a dozen legs on each side of its body, had concentrated their magic and blasted a whole section of the wall inward. Now, the wingless horde swarmed over the rubble to join the rest of the Dark Lord's legions on the already blood-soaked city cobbles. Outside the walls, barely a quarter of the men and dwarves who started the battle still lived, and most of them were exhausted and injured. They didn't stop fighting, and they found the fortitude to attempt to fill the gap in the wall while breed giant dragon gunners and spell-weary mages did their best to protect them from above.

The gatesmen in the northern and eastern sections of the city threw the gates open so that the people trapped inside could flee. Only those who exited at the forest gate made it very far. Most of the eastern part of the city had been turned into a massive spider web overnight. Dozens of man-sized, bulbous-bodied arachnids scurried along the web lines that spanned from building to building. The streets and alleyways were closed off by wild, kaleidoscopic patterns. The people who got caught up in the sticky mess were quickly stung and wrapped in webbing. When the sun topped the hills to the east, a few hundred cocooned corpses dangled from the higher strands like laundry.

Phen saw it all from atop the main palace building's pebbly roof. Directly below him, battle raged around the freezing waters of the huge fountain pond called Whitten Loch.

Beyond the palace's protective wall, nearly a full quarter of the city was also covered in shimmering webs. Elsewhere, people huddled, chattering and terrified, in ragged groups. It was so cold that wispy clouds formed by their breath rose from them and gave them away. A dozen huge fires raged across the city and twice as many were now only smoldering piles. Entire blocks lay in ruins, and bodies littered the crimson slush-covered streets.

Hundreds upon hundreds of demon kind could be seen oozing through the distant breach in the outer wall. They flowed toward the castle as if they were a spill of molasses. Hundreds more dark, evil things circled overhead like carrion birds waiting for something to die. And below Phen, now under a steady rain of elven arrows, more men, dwarves, and elves fought with the creatures that had come down inside the barrier.

The Wizard and the Warlord

Shouts from the defenders below told him that the castle itself had been busted open. Phen looked up to see that the palace walls beyond the fountain pond were being overrun as well.

King Mikahl heard a sound over the din; a mighty sound. The Warlord seemed to recognize it, and so did the greater devils and demons encircling their battle. All of them went tense and seemed more alert. Mikahl pressed harder at the Warlord and managed to get a powerful fist of kinetic magic past the Hell Master's guard. The Warlord went staggering back a few steps and nearly buckled a wing as it tried to catch its balance. Then the Warlord let out a roar of pain and anger and suddenly Mikahl was the one being pressed.

Raking foreclaws, fiery breath, and then a blast of red-hot sizzling power sent Mikahl and his bright horse reeling up and backward. Ironspike's shields took the brunt of the damage, but Mikahl was left off-kilter and forced to flail about to keep himself mounted.

With a snapping whip crack, the tip of the Dark Lord's tail pierced through Ironspike's shielding. It shattered the protective field as if it were the thinnest layer of glass. Then a quick, cartwheeling spin had the Warlord's hind claws raking across Mikahl's face.

The High King twisted away in time to save his eyes, but his forehead was gashed wide, and blood poured over his vision in a crimson sheet. It was all he could do to stay on the bright horse while the magical pegasus fought to right itself.

The sound he'd heard came again. It was a roar, a gut-shaking roar, full of contempt. The sound caused an involuntary shudder of fear to pass through Mikahl. The Warlord paused, too. Then he answered with a flame-spewing roar of his own. The Master of Hell's call was a full-out challenge. Mikahl started to attack in that instant, but a shadow completely engulfed the overhead light and made him pause. In that same heartbeat, the Warlord unleashed a hissing blast of freezing cold magical power. Mikahl, with Ironspike held in his hand at the ready, and the bright horse pulsing between his legs, froze instantly solid and began tumbling toward the ground.

M. R. Mathias

The Wizard and the Warlord

Chapter Fifty-Seven

After using his dragon's fire and his kinetic blast over and over again against the human king, the Warlord decided to do something different. When he heard the depth of the roar that drowned everything out, he decided to end this skirmish right here. Sending out a pulse of freezing energy, the Warlord's magic froze Mikahl and left him dropping like a stone. The roar meant that there were dragons about, and the Dark Lord didn't hesitate. It would be foolish to restrain the greater demons any longer.

As the High King tumbled toward the ground, the helborn that were gathered around took to the sky and engaged the approaching dragons. The Warlord tucked his wings into a streaking dive at the palace. Now that Shaella's death was avenged, only the Wardstone mattered to him. He could smell the power it radiated. It was beckoning him, and he was coming as fast as he could.

Falling, an unexpected warming sensation hit Mikahl like a blast from a furnace. It held steady on him as he tumbled, until he could feel his skin starting to blister. Suddenly he could move, but as he went to call the bright horse back into place he saw the frozen earth racing up into his face. He squeezed his eyes shut and threw out his hands to protect himself from the impact. Ironspike went spinning away. He slammed to a stop, expecting to either feel his body shattering on the icy ground or feel the blackness of death take him. He felt neither. In fact, he felt nothing at all.

He opened his eyes to see his sword lying on the ground only a reach away. He was hovering about a foot over the frozen earth. He tried to move but couldn't. Then suddenly, as if he were being released from some invisible grasp, he fell the last foot. He impacted no harder than if he had fallen from a tree stump. Sensation raced back through his nerves and his body felt as if he had swum through the frozen sea then walked across a desert. His bones were still frozen, but his skin was burned.

It took him a moment to catch his breath and regain his wits. When he did, he grabbed his sword and felt its magical symphony blare into his mind. The amount of tingly healing magic it exuded through him was distracting. He turned quickly to defend against an attack, but he saw that he was well away from the wild new battle taking place above.

Dragons - red, blue, green, and even a white one - some with riders and some without, were in the sky fighting the demon spawn. He saw Hyden Hawk on the back of a massive red-scaled beast that could only have been Claret. He couldn't remember his name, but he recognized the determined elf that was riding the shoulders of a smaller blue wyrm, too. Half a dozen others were engaged in the sky. Some of the dragons were viciously attacking the greater demons. They were doing some damage.

A large piece of something that was writhing and flapping came spiraling down and crashed into the snow. A great bellowing cloud of steam rose from it as hot brimstone blood met the frozen earth. Above, Claret spat the rest of it out of her mouth and roared. Mikahl took in what had landed before him and saw that it was nothing more than a single wing with a scallop of meat the size of a wagon cart attached to it.

Mikahl called forth the bright horse and took back to the air. He went after Hyden and Claret. Trying to catch up to the huge red dragon was akin to trying to catch a stallion while riding a mule. Mikahl was too torn over Rosa's death to actually feel real hope, but he felt like they might be able to save some lives. Hyden looked like a child's doll on a destrier's back. His long black hair was flapping wildly out behind him, and his face was set in a determined grimace. The boney, triangular plates that ran down Claret's spine were as tall as he was. Mikahl couldn't see how Hyden stayed on as they banked and then dove, racing toward the castle, in direct pursuit of the Warlord.

Corva could do little more than hold on to the ridges in the fin-plate on the blue dragon's back. The massive, yet quick, wyrm swept down across the demon horde and blasted huge swaths away with its liquid lightning spew. It dragged its razor-sharp, sword-long claws through the ranks of hellspawn as they went. Another blast of breath at a Choska sent the demon flailing into the face of the wall with a sickening smack.

Durge, on the back of the mighty green dragon, was big enough to use his leg muscles to hold on to the sinuous neck of his mount. He and the wyrm had landed in the wall breach and were deftly fighting back those dark, wingless things trying to enter the city. Lashing teeth and claws, and misty, poisonous dragon breath made most of them stall their invasion. Those that survived to get through met their end at the tip of Durge's bladed staff.

Cheers resounded from the walls and in the streets as dragons came from everywhere, swooping, blasting and lashing the dark horde away from the refugees. Even though the streets were littered with the dead and dying, the dragons brought hope to those willing to take hold of it.

Claret veered off to snatch one of the greater demons out of the air. She did so effortlessly, like a mother dog picking up her puppy, only followed by a savage crunch of teeth and a blast of flame as she spat the ruined thing away. Edging back on course, the whole assault took maybe five heartbeats to complete, but it allowed Mikahl to catch up so that Hyden could hear him yelling.

"What's your plan?" he called over the bitter wind.

Hyden had expected a friendlier greeting. He took in the stricken look on the High King's face. He hadn't seen his friend look that sad since they found Vaegon, or what was left of him, lying in the rubble of this very wall. He immediately figured that something had happened to either Lord Gregory or Queen Rosa. No others could affect Mikahl so strongly. He didn't have time to dwell on what his senses picked up about Mik, though. Gerard was almost to Whitten Loch, and there was no time for emotion.

"Remember when you unleashed all of Ironspike's power at once." Hyden paused to adjust himself on the dragon's back. Then he cast a spell so that his voice found Mikahl's ears as if they were just standing and speaking to one another. "You made that thunder storm appear to drive the black dragon away from King Jarrek's men. Do you remember?"

"Aye!" Mikahl screamed back unnecessarily. "I remember."

"I'm going to face off with Gerard, or whatever that blasted thing is now." Hyden had to fight back a tear as he thought about the horrors his little brother must have been put through. "When I raise both of my hands over my head like so, do that again, but unleash all that power at me."

"Are you mad?" Mikahl yelled. "Why not at that thing? You'll be killed."

"Just do it, Mikahl," Hyden commanded. "Swear to me you will."

Mikahl didn't want to blast his friend, but Hyden was insistent and looked as if there was some sort of method to his madness. He remembered thinking he was leaving Hyden to die once before. It was the last time he had seen him, yet here he was again. He had no choice but to trust him, so he gave his word. He tasted regret as soon as the oath was given because he couldn't help but remember Hyden miscasting the simplest of spells and losing one of Oarly's boots. There was still a goat somewhere that could no longer grow hair, too.

"Where?" he asked Hyden.

"Whitten Loch," Hyden returned. "Right now." Then Claret dove down like a streaking arrow, leaving the bright horse once again struggling to keep up.

Mikahl heard Hyden's next words, too, even though Hyden hadn't intended him to.

Hyden's voice grew full of concern, and then anguish. "Oh, Phen, no," Hyden said. "No, don't, Phen."

Mikahl focused his gaze ahead and down into the castle's courtyard. There, running from the palace steps toward the fountain pond, was Phen. Around him, elves and dwarven axe men were battling back the dark host, but Phen's intention was obvious. The Warlord was wading into Whitten Loch, trying to find the place where the Wardstone was exposed. Phen was weaving his arms, casting a spell. Seeing him first, the Warlord sent a huge crimson pulse at the boy, then quickly turned and blasted another up at Hyden and Claret. Hyden nearly fell from Claret's neck when he met the Warlord's eyes—Gerard's eyes.

Hearing the cries of "Dragon!" and "Hyden Hawk!" and the hope that filled those voices, Queen Willa rushed to her balcony and peeked out of the heavy oak sliding door to see what was happening. The last time she had chanced a look, her soldiers, the dwarves, and the Queen Mother's elves had all been caught up in a brutal battle on her doorstep. She was surprised at how much ground her fighters had gained, but they were already losing it back to the fierce, evil creatures. When the palace's entry was caved in, her personal guards, along with Telgra's dozen guardians, had bolted the three of them in with a few of the most proficient sword masters. One of these men harrumphed at Queen Willa's breach of security. She wasn't supposed to be opening the doors.

"Hush your mouth, you big thug," Queen Rosa said to him. "The queen has a right to see what's going on outside."

Queen Willa sucked in a breath and turned away from the sliver of daylight she had revealed. Rosa darted over to see what was going on. "Oh my," she gasped.

A great, black-skinned beast stood with its leathery wings half open and stepped off into the fountain pond. Slick plate-covered flesh reflected in the rippling liquid. It strode, human-like, into the deeper water as if it were searching for something. It was a terrifying thing and it had eyes just like Hyden Skyler's. It flicked its tail back and forth behind it, and its muscles rippled and flexed authoritatively. The Warlord towered over the men fighting around Whitten Loch. Easily twenty-five feet tall, it was only waist deep in the water as it neared the middle of the pond.

Rosa was glued to the scene until the top of a familiar head bobbed into view. She hadn't seen Phen since he had recovered from his petrified state, but she recognized him immediately. Fear shook her to the very core as he charged out heedlessly to attack the massive demon beast.

Without thinking, she threw open the sliding door and charged out to the balcony rail. "No, Pin! NOOOO!"

Queen Willa's guard and an elven swordsman roughly pulled her back inside.

The Warlord's powerful blast rocked Claret's body and she roared out in surprise. The blow was so heavy that Hyden feared it to be fatal. Claret tried to hold her path toward the palace but faltered. She was determined to help Hyden, though, so she let their crashing fall carry them over the fountain.

Hyden leapt from Claret's back in mid-flight. He knew, and regretted the fact, that he could do nothing to help her or Phen. He had to stop the Warlord, no matter the cost. Why the fool boy was still trying to act like a hero after the last time, he couldn't understand. This was the Lord of

Hell, not a Zard ship. With only a flick of its wrist it had just knocked the biggest dragon in the realm from the sky. Hyden didn't know what Phen hoped to accomplish. He'd hoped that Oarly's death, and the events that had transpired at the Leif Repline, would have put some sense into the boy, but apparently not.

As he prepared his levitating spell to halt his fall, Hyden saw Mikahl swooping in on the bright horse to help Phen. The Warlord saw him, too, though, and in a sudden flash of realization, Hyden saw it all falling apart before his eyes. He wanted to shout out a warning but it was already too late.

Mikahl saw the swath of sapphire energy leap from Phen's hands toward the Warlord. An instant after, the Dark One's clawed fingers sent ten jagged bolts of lightning directly toward Phen's chest. Mikahl forced the bright horse down and dove streaking like a crossbow bolt toward Phen. He had to knock Phen out of the way or he would be charred to a smoldering husk. He didn't see the Warlord's thick tail whipping around to greet him. The sound of his dead wife calling out Phen's name in her unmistakably peculiar way distracted him from it. "Pin!" He turned to see her being pulled back into an upper room by Queen Willa's guards, then tried to refocus his flight to save the boy.

He was utterly stunned. How could it be? Rosa alive and here in Xwarda? It was the last thought he had before the Warlord's tail smashed into his face. His momentum saved Phen when he and the bright horse crashed into him, knocking him clear of the Hell Master's lightning. In the process, though, Mikahl lost Ironspike, and consciousness, and was then blasted across the courtyard when the Warlord's lightning hit him full on.

Hyden came falling feet first out of the sky with his arms held high for balance. The Tokamac Verge was in his right hand. He was ready for Mikahl to loose Ironspike's power at him so that he could magnify it with the crystal and banish Gerard to the Nethers for good. But Mikahl was nothing but a heap of charred flesh, and Ironspike was still spinning to a stop on the blood-slicked cobble walkway near Phen. Hyden halted his fall with his levitation spell and came to a hover a few feet above Phen.

"Hurry! Put Ironspike in the High King's hand!" he said as he turned to fight the Warlord. "Hurry, before it's too late!"

Phen understood. The healing power of the sword could restore Mikahl if he was still alive. Phen grabbed the weapon by its hilt. It was so heavy that he could barely drag it, but he did so as quickly as he could.

The wizard and the Warlord met each other eye to eye, Hyden hovering a few feet above the surface of Whitten Loch, the thing that still had his brother's eyes standing waist-deep in the pond. It was those eyes that arrested Hyden's attack. In that brief instant of hesitation, the Warlord swatted him across the air like he was no more than a pesky insect.

Using the thrust of his levitation spell, Hyden recovered swiftly. He held forth the Tokamac Verge and cast a spell through it. Three sizzling rays, one crimson, one lavender, and one bright blue swirled out and into the Warlord. The powerful magic held him there nearly half a minute, sending violent shudders through his plated form. When the spell exhausted itself, the Warlord still stood. He was snarling, and a few curls of smoke were rolling up from his flesh. He turned and roared at the wizard, defiantly bathing him in a searing gout of dragon's fire.

The crystalized tear drop hanging around Hyden's neck protected him from the blast, but by the time the flames were gone, the Warlord had dived under the surface and was swimming toward the Wardstone.

Chapter Fifty-Eight

As Phen dragged Ironspike's blade across the bloody cobbles toward King Mikahl's roasted body, something extraordinary happened. The blade became as light as a feather and a throbbing buzz filled his ears. Slowly, like the sound of an approaching bandwagon in a parade, the murmur turned into a melody. Then, all at once a full cacophony exploded into Phen's head. The sensation was staggering and nearly brought him to his knees. The sound sorted itself out, leaving an angelic chorus shimmering over a powerful and rhythmic melody. Phen's blood was hot. It tingled and pulsed in time with the music.

Phen couldn't believe what was happening. Ironspike's blade was blazing bright blue, just as if the High King were holding it. It was impossible. Ironspike's magic only worked for those of Pavreal's bloodline.

Phen forced the confusing thoughts out of his mind and ran the last few steps to High King Mikahl's side. Instinctively, he knew what to do. He'd seen Mikahl heal people with the sword a few times. He touched Mikahl's blackened flesh with the glowing blade and separated out the melody of healing from the rest of the symphony in his head. The blade answered by fading from blue to a bright green, then yellow. Phen could feel Mikahl's life pulsing away before Ironspike's magic took effect. Slowly, the High King's heartbeat strengthened, but not much. An untuned note, sour and mis-struck, sounded in Ironspike's music. Like a bad taste in an otherwise delicious stew, the tone offended the rest of the music horribly. A feeling of warning came to Phen. Ironspike's power was dwindling. He was suddenly worried that if he used the sword's power any longer to save the High King, it wouldn't be strong enough to help Hyden Hawk banish Gerard.

Torn, Phen didn't know what to do. Rosa would never forgive him, and he would never be able to forgive himself, if he let the High King die.

The rotten note in the symphony grew more prominent, and Phen could feel the sword's might ebbing away. He clenched his eyes shut, and tears started flowing down his face. He felt he didn't have a choice. He pulled the blade away from Mikahl's flesh. The sword reverted to its normal bright blue color and the music in his head became beautiful again, but when he opened his eyes he saw King Mikahl still dying in the bloody snow.

Hyden's insistent voice, and the sudden darkening of the entire sky, brought his mind back to the battle. He whipped around to see the waters of Whitten Loch frothy and boiling. Hyden was hovering just above them, wild-eyed and frantically trying to get Phen's attention. Behind Hyden, the Warlord rose slowly up out of the boil, his jagged mouth split into a smug, self-satisfied grin. Dark purple emissions of smoke jetted out of his clawed hands into the sky. Phen saw the Verge crystal in Hyden's hand and remembered with perfect clarity what Hyden had told him about it at their camp in the Giant Mountains. He knew what had to be done.

"At you or at the crystal?" he asked with a shout.

Hyden, confused beyond all rationality that Phen was holding Mik's blade while it still glowed with power, saw the uncertainty fade from Phen's face. The boy's expression grew deathly serious. Hyden could feel the dark power radiating behind him. Gerard had found the Wardstone and already was working his newfound power to blot out the light of the sun.

The meaning of Phen's question became clear. "All of it, Phen!" Hyden called out with more than a little fear and uncertainty in his voice. "All of it at me!"

The wizard spun around to face the Warlord. The beast was ecstatic and marveling in wicked delight as the power of the Wardstone came funneling through him. He looked at Hyden and Hyden saw plainly his little brother's innocent joy in the expression. He missed Gerard so much.

His brother hadn't been evil; he'd just wanted to be a mage, or something other than a cliff-climbing clansman. Now he had to be destroyed.

Beyond the Warlord, at the edge of his vision, Hyden could see the limp hind quarters and tail of Claret's body lying across a section of broken palace wall. She had crushed it when she fell. Above her, her young hatchling flapped and screeched in confusion and sorrow because his consistent pestering refused to rouse his mother.

Hyden felt Ironspike's white hot swath of power hit him in the back. In the span of a heartbeat, he saw in his mind's eye Vaegon Willowbrow shredded and broken in the rubble; Brady Culvert being eroded in his tracks by a black dragon's acidic spew. He saw Oarly's pulverized body, and the smoldering form of the High King lying in the bloody slush like a roasted animal. When he looked back up at the Warlord and started channeling Ironspike's power through Claret's tear drop, all he saw before him was evil. When he directed that tremendous flow into the Tokamac Verge, he knew that even though none of Gerard's goodness remained in the thing before him, it would remain in his own heart, where it would always be.

Durge and his fellow dragon-riding guardians had herded the bulk of the common folk fleeing the gates into a snowy, horseshoe-shaped valley in the hills north of the city. One of the cocky red-scaled wyrms had set a good portion of the trees on fire to keep them warm and the others had taken up positions to defend them.

Jicks, on his long, sapphire dragon, and the two white wyrms that seemed to obey his blue's every command, found themselves in trouble. Most of the imps and wyvern had fled the sky out of fear of the dragons, but the hellcats, Choska demons, and the larger beasts still fought with ferocious intensity. Just when it seemed that the young swordsman's mount had gotten the best of the dark flock, a noxious purple radiance filled the sky. One of the ice dragons began sneezing out shards and circles of frozen spew as the stuff irritated its nostrils. A Choska hit it hard and raked a claw down its back. White scales opened wide, exposing pink muscles and cartilage that were soon flooded with crimson. Blood streaked across the dragon's scales in thick rivulets. Before it could recover, it was set upon again, this time by two hellcats that savaged the wounded wyrm's wings until they folded back, broken. Finally, with a shriek of horror, the proud white wyrm went spiraling down to the earth like an autumn leaf falling from a tree.

Jicks's blue and the other ice dragon fought with all they had in them. Now they were fighting to get out of the choking purple cloud, instead of being on the attack. With half a hundred hellspawn still in the sky, all of them unaffected by the miasma, the situation was suddenly grim.

Corva could feel the pulse of the Arbor's Heart coming from his Queen Mother. He urged the sparkling blue he rode toward her. He found the battle on the palace's front steps. The horrid stench that was permeating the sky wasn't as bad down low. He found it was bearable, but for how long, he didn't know.

Hyden Hawk and Phen were battling a beast so malignant that it actually pained Corva to look upon it. A patch of golden green on a blackened Westland coat caught his eyes. A ruined man, whose chainmail armor had been melted to his torso, fought in vain to survive. Corva might have been able to help him, but he doubted it. There were elves pinned down who needed him and his dragon far more desperately.

Three elven swordsmen were fighting a losing battle around a pair of wounded pikemen and a dwarf who had lost a forearm. Some two-legged, wolf-headed monster, whose claws and furred head were soaked black with the blood of its previous victims, had hemmed them in at the edge of the forested park that flanked Whitten Loch. Corva urged his dragon to the scene just in time to save one of the two uninjured defenders.

While his dragon's attention was on the attack, a hellcat attacked Corva out of nowhere. It happened so fast that the elf was ripped from the dragon's back before he even felt the claws digging into his shoulders. The blue dragon wasn't physically harmed, but feeling the proximity of the demons behind it, and with Corva's weight suddenly gone from its back, it whipped around and left the warriors to their fate. The two uninjured men joined to attack the bloody beast. The sparkling blue dragon leapt back into the air in pursuit of the hellcat that was still holding its rider in its claws. The hellcat led the blue wyrm up into the toxic cloud the Warlord had created, and then dropped the elf. Torn between chasing the demon and trying to catch Corva, the dragon followed its instinct. It could only assume that Corva was already crushed to death, so it went after the beast. It wouldn't have mattered if it had chosen to dive after its rider, though; it had been led into a trap.

From above, below, and even behind the sparkling blue, a dozen or more hellcats, and a massive red-furred apish thing converged on it all at once. The red-furred beast had a black, leathery chest and its wings were far too small to actually carry it. It flew by way of magic. It was a greater demon and it tore into the blue with its power while its minions did the same with tooth and claw. It was all the hellborn creatures could do to get away from the wyrm when it started falling from the sky.

"Put me down!" Queen Rosa screamed at the Blacksword Knight who'd just brought the Queen Mother in from the gate. He was fearfully trying to drag the queen of the realm from the balcony. "Tell him, Willa!" She thrashed and swung as she yelled. The last words she spoke very loudly and very clearly. "Mikahl is out there!"

Queen Willa gave the man a nod and he let the High Queen loose. Telgra stepped up to her quickly in order to keep her from scratching the poor man's face.

"Come," the Queen Mother of the elves said. "Both of you. Stay close to me and the Heart of Arbor will shield us from sight." With that, she shouldered away the stupefied guard.

Rosa saw Mikahl lying burned and broken in the snow, saw Phen touching him with Ironspike. The fact that the sword was responding to Phen didn't register on her. She was overcome with grief. From her vantage, Mikahl looked injured beyond hope. She barely heard the gasps of the other two women.

Queen Willa was gasping because of Phen. She remembered vividly the large Westland lord named Ellrich who'd brought the boy to Xwarda so long ago. In a single sitting he had eaten the better part of a roasted pig.

Willa hadn't been a queen then, only a princess. The expression of anguish on the boy's face as he pulled the sword away from the High King said more than words ever could. She stepped up behind Rosa and gave her gentle support.

Telgra gasped because the sight and smell, the very presence of the thing rising up out of the water before Hyden Hawk, was appalling to her senses. The Arbor's Heart hammered through her chest in disgust and she had to fight to breathe as some dark purple taint jetted up into the sky from the Warlord's outstretched hands. She didn't even notice the body Phen had been worrying over, but she saw the sword's bluish glimmer brighten to red, then orange, then pure white. She could almost feel the heat from the magic warming her skin. In her heart she cheered Phen as he strode forward purposefully and pointed the sword at Hyden. Her intense focus was broken suddenly as Corva's body came slamming down into the balcony with a sickening crunch. All of the women screamed in terror. The way the body lay across the rail, like a grain sack, limp and still, left no room to hope that he had survived.

Queen Willa, shocked to the core by the impact, pulled Rosa back into the chamber. Rosa was far too traumatized to resist.

Telgra knew immediately that it was Corva, and it crushed her emotions into a compressed knot so tightly that they exploded. She lost the spell of concealing she'd cast over them. She fell to her knees and wailed out tears of sorrow. That was when Phen sent Ironspike's magical blast into Hyden Hawk. It was the last thing she saw, for the elven guards rushed out onto the balcony and pulled the Queen Mother, and then Corva's broken body, out of the open.

The Warlord was in ecstasy, especially now that the High King was dead. That brief moment of terror when the stubborn man and his glowing pegasus came streaking back in had been enough to jolt the Warlord into action. The fact that the High King had survived his frozen fall was as infuriating as it was eye-opening. He thought he had already disposed of the man. This time, he was certain.

It was nearly as frustrating as fighting the wizard. He wasn't worried, though. In the bottom of the pond he had found the Wardstone and claimed its power as his own. This wizard might be able to survive dragon's fire, but he wouldn't survive what was coming.

The long-consumed demon Shokin's voice came calling through the glee. A distant, whispery sound, but clear enough to be heard above the rest. "Pavreal's blood still powers the blade," it said urgently. "Beware."

The Warlord disregarded the warning words while continuing to spray his toxic miasma into the sky with one hand. He conjured forth a blast of magical force powerful enough to level a mountain with the other hand. He then sent his churning destructive construct directly at Hyden.

THE WIZARD AND THE WARLORD

Chapter Fifty-Nine

It was too late when the Warlord realized his mistake. Had he heeded Shokin's warning and conjured forth a shielding, he might have had a chance. As it was, the power of Ironspike, magnified by the crystalized dragon's tear, then multiplied further by the Tokamac Verge, hit the Hell Master just before he could release at Hyden. It didn't hurt the Warlord, and it didn't immediately stop him from using the Wardstone's power, but it held him fast and confused him long enough for Hyden to do what he had to do.

Hyden had to fight to maintain control of himself as the monumental force of multiple magics exploded through his body. He was filled with sensations so pleasureful, and so gut-wrenching, that it would have been easy to lose himself in them. There was pain, too. His body jerked and trembled with it. With each passing minute he aged a month or more. He managed to tune all of it out, though, and focus on what had to be done.

With the power of the ring he'd taken from Gerard, he conjured forth a clear, glassine orb of magical energy. It was slightly larger than the Warlord, big enough to contain him. The power of Ironspike, the dragon's tear, and the Tokamac Verge suddenly let loose on the Hell Master. Inside the translucent globe, the Warlord struggled mightily to break free of the field that contained him. He began pounding and yelling and trying with all his might to summon forth the Wardstone's magic, but the field Hyden had created kept him from reaching it. Now, the glassine substance was thickening inward, stilling the Warlord's aggression as it encased him.

Hyden let the power of the crystal Verge snug the magical boundary down around the Warlord so tightly that he couldn't even move a finger. The Warlord was trapped in place, as if he were frozen; only this ice wasn't tangible, it was magical, and as bindingly solid to the Hell Master as the dividing boundaries between the heavens and the hells.

At that moment, Hyden could have killed the Warlord for good, but he couldn't bring himself to do it. He was certain that the binding would hold, and besides that, he just couldn't bring himself to kill the thing that used to be his little brother. He wasn't sure if those were the real reasons, or if he was just afraid that he would die if the Warlord did. At the moment he was too exhausted to worry much about it anymore. The fact that he felt twice his age was what confounded him as he collapsed into the water before the hovering prison he'd created.

The seemingly solid sphere settled half in and half out of the water. It appeared to be floating, but it wasn't. Hyden sat down and leaned against it, so that only his head and shoulders were above the surface. The water was cold but not frigid. Apparently, the ground or maybe the Wardstone kept it tepid.

A long, black-and-gray-flecked beard trailed away from his chin and floated on the surface. Hyden tried to laugh, but then his eyes settled on Mikahl. Across the way, his best friend was lying dead in the snowy cobbles. Hyden was too tired to stand, but not too tired to cry. The tears blurred his eyes so that he didn't see Phen hurriedly wading through the water waving Ironspike and screaming at him.

Behind Hyden, the Dark Lord had found the power of the Wardstone again. He had wiggled room to move here and there and was now thrashing frantically to get through the prison's walls. Sensing the movement, Hyden turned. Already the Warlord was wearing through the globe. Hyden's head dropped in defeat. He had failed. His fear of death, and love for his brother, had doomed them all. He should have just killed Gerard when he had the chance, but now it was too late.

More tears streaked down his face as he called to Talon. To his surprise he found that the familiar link between them had been broken.

He heard Talon's screeching call from afar just then. He was sure it was a triggered memory from somewhere in his weary mind. He glanced up as Phen closed in on him and the failing imprisonment and realized that the sky had cleared a little bit. The purple smog and the swarms of hellspawn were thin to the point that the two dragons he could see up there held reign. He heard the hawkling again, but didn't see him. His attention was now drawn to the boy.

Phen, with Ironspike's wildly glowing blade held out before him as if it were a spear, charged right up to the magical prison and ran the sword right into it. When Ironspike's blade pierced through the barrier and buried itself to the hilt in the Warlord's chest, the explosion of blackness that engulfed him was no surprise at all. What was a surprise was that Hyden could hear the old cackling fortune teller saying, "Some day, you will watch helplessly as one you love dearly attempts to destroy what the one that sits beside you is to become."

The concussion did surprise Phen. It sent him flipping backward head over heels. The force of the impact blew the breath from his lungs, and the sudden loss of Ironspike's glorious symphony in his head left him empty and lost. When he hit the ground, he landed in a painful tangle of limbs.

Dostin raced to Corva's side. He had been sitting with the three queens, waiting and watching patiently as they fussed over the balcony rail. He'd started to wallop the guard who pulled Queen Rosa back into the chamber in such a bodily fashion, but Queen Willa had called the soldier off of her in time to save him from Dostin's staff.

The simple-minded monk had known many friends in his sheltered life, but most of them had treated him like a parent treats a child. Telgra had become dear to him during her stay at Salaya, but he and Corva had shared an adventure. Dostin loved the elf beyond measure and it showed as he urged the Queen Mother aside and began to pray fiercely over his friend's torn and broken body.

Telgra gave him room, but she didn't give up her place over the fallen hero completely. She, too, had grown fond of Corva. He was a proud young elf and loyal to a fault. She called upon the Heart of Arbor, hoping that the great guiding force of the elven people would lend strength to her healing magic. The first part of the response she received caused her to pull away sobbing and put her head in her hands. There's nothing you can do for Corva, the Arbor Heart's deep voice spoke into her mind. But you can use your restorative powers elsewhere, if you act swiftly.

No sooner did the words finish resounding than Phen ran Ironspike's blade into the Warlord. The whole palace shook with the force of the explosion. Queen Willa and Queen Rosa screamed out in fright, but Telgra felt the poison absorbing into the roots of the Arbor suddenly diluted. She knew where she was needed and without further hesitation she ordered her soldiers to come with her. After a quick glance at the High Queen, then at Queen Willa, she climbed over the rail and gracefully made for the courtyard below.

Dostin stayed behind, still chanting and praying with fevered intensity over Corva's body. Queen Willa would have stopped him, but it was clear that the man was either too simple, or too stubborn, to give up.

Dieter Willowbrow and a handful of elves had grouped outside the palace walls in the street. They had lost most of their fellows out beyond the outer wall, but now that the demon horde was fleeing, they worked their way toward their Queen Mother. They took the time to end the lives of the mortally wounded and heal those they could as they went.

When turning a corner, trying to locate the palace gate, the battle-weary group came upon a horrid creature. It was twice the size of a wolf and its fur was saturated with matted blood and gore. The beast stood over another just like it that lay still. At first, the savage thing snarled and growled angrily. It circled its fallen companion and settled into a defensive position with its blood-soaked hackles trying to rise. Dieter looked around him. The beast was walled in on three sides, and now his group of elves was blocking its only chance of escaping. A trio of dark, hulking bodies lay around the savage creature.

One of the elves drew his bow string back and started to loose at it, but Dieter's quick reflexes stopped the arrow from hitting its target.

"What gives, Dieter?" the angry archer said as his arrow bounced harmlessly off the cobbles and skittered into a drift of snow against a broken store front.

"Look at those creatures lying dead around them," Dieter said. "Those are dead hellcats."

"Two of them are," an elf said from behind them. "One is a Choska, or what's left of it."

"That isn't our enemy," Dieter said. "I think it's a great wolf. My brother wrote about them in his journal."

Yip barked and wagged his tail, slinging blood as he did. The movement aggravated a wound on the great wolf's back and caused him to yelp sharply, as if he had been kicked.

"Whatever it is, it's injured. And by the looks of those teeth marks on that hellcat's neck and throat, that wolf is what killed it." It was an older elf, one of Dieter's uncles speaking. His voice held enough confident authority that Dieter handed away his bow and started down the alley to see if he could help the wounded creature.

Yip responded by limping a few steps toward the elf and wagging his tail as slightly as he could.

"May Arbor forgive my hastiness," the archer who'd almost fired an arrow at the creature said as he started after Dieter.

Dieter put his hand out and let the huge wolf sniff it. Yip licked it immediately. As Dieter began healing Yip with his elven magic, the other elf called out to the group what the scene told him.

"This wolf was killed after it mortally wounded the first hellcat here." He pointed first at a wolf's corpse, then at one of the dead hellcats. "It looks like one of the cats tried to eat him. This one fought off the hellcat and then killed the Choska." He pointed at Yip, who was fidgeting nervously as the yellow glow of Dieter's healing power swept over his matted fur.

The other elf spoke on reverently. "He killed them both with no help at all, just to protect his fallen pack mate's body." He shook his head in wonder and strode over to Yip. When he stood face to face with the sitting wolf, he found that he had to look up to see in its eyes. "I apologize for almost loosing on you, my friend." The elf's tone showed the sincerity of his words. "Defending your fallen friend was honorable."

Yip surprised the elf by projecting a thought into his head. It was almost a command. "Carry my brother and follow me," it said.

When the elf nodded his understanding, Yip quickly opened his jaws, leaned down, and gave the startled elf a slobbery lick across the face.

Talon winged himself and his burden in a great circle downward over the courtyard before Queen Willa's palace. It was a place the hawkling knew well. Many times he had sipped from the fountain's water, or wetted his beak to better preen himself. Hyden had spent half a year in Dahg Mahn's tower studying the books with Phen, while Talon soared the sky above this place.

Talon could see Claret lying across the palace's wall, half in the city, half in the forested park. From above, her scarlet corpse looked like an open wound on the land. The dragon, all dragons, had always scared Talon badly. However, the hawkling knew how much Hyden had loved and respected this great wyrm.

Seeing the person he needed to find floating face up in the pond caused the bird to falter and nearly plummet from the sky. He recovered when he saw Phen blink his eyes open. Phen wasn't moving at the moment, but he was alive.

Talon had flown long and far carrying his heavy load. The time he had spent with his body being heavy and petrified had strengthened him. Nothing else could have prepared a bird his size to carry a skin full of water so far.

Seeing Queen Rosa burst out of the palace after Lady Telgra, Talon followed her course. As the hawkling guessed, she went straight to the one who was to receive the fruit of his labor. Hyden Hawk had once sworn his loyalty to Mikahl as a friend, not a king, and so had Talon. Just because he was no longer linked to his wizard didn't mean that the bird would forsake his vow. He'd shared too much human thought to suddenly revert to being an ordinary hawkling. The goddess had sent him on his own quest, and Talon had no desire to let down either her, or the High King; not if he could help it.

Seeing Phen twitch, Talon dove toward the boy and fluttered to a stop, perching on his chest. The sound of Rosa's wails as she reached the High King's side told Talon that he might be too late. Even if he wasn't, he still needed Phen. Queen Willa's sorrowful gasping, and the shouts of soldiers all around them, didn't seem to stir the dazed boy. For Talon, this wasn't good. He needed help.

The thought occurred to Talon to find Spike. The two of them had communicated regularly on the journeys they had undertaken with their wizards. Talon was relieved to hear the prickly little cat's mew coming from an ornamental shrub by the palace steps.

Knowing that it might be too late to finish his deed, Talon began squawking orders to the lyna cat and any other animal that might be in hearing range. Luckily for the realm, the great wolf, Yip, and the elven archers who carried Arf's tattered corpse had just come over the rubble of the broken wall. Yip heard the hawkling's instruction and was eager to help save the life of the High King. The great wolves revered Mikahl Collum above all men. Their ferocious pack leader Grrr had died to save him.

Rosa found Mikahl barely breathing. His hair was burned to a hard, crispy mess, and his left knee was a bone-splintered hole. The long chainmail shirt he always wore to battle was blackened and melted into his chest and shoulders. His arms were drawn in and his legs were curled, their skin fused together as if he had been dropped in a pan of boiling hot grease. His face was swollen and disfigured. The only thing that indicated he was alive was the nearly inaudible repetitive rasp of his lungs struggling to draw air.

Queen Mother Telgra took one look at him and went about finding another to heal. She knew there was nothing she could do for him, and the Heart of Arbor confirmed it in her mind.

Queen Willa had her hands to her mouth. "Oh, Mikahl," she sobbed at the horror of his injuries.

Around her, the guards were struggling between protecting the queens and letting them mourn. No immediate threat had presented itself until a black, wolfish thing came leaping toward them as it fled from a group of elves.

"Protect the queens!" a shout rang out.

A frantic hustle ensued as Queen Willa's guards tried to form up around them. Yip darted inside the closing ring, and with a series of loud, insistent barks, scared Queen Rosa away from Mikahl's body. A sword slashed an arcing slice at the wolf, but an elven arrow dinked off of the blade in mid-swing, saving Yip by a hair's breadth.

"Back!" Dieter yelled. Already he had another arrow nocked. "It means no harm."

Another of the guards ignored him and jabbed at Yip, but Talon came flapping down gracelessly past his face and screeched out an ear-splitting cry.

Spike braved his fear of great wolves and darted from the bushes through the trampled pink snow, between the soldier's legs, and to the High King's body.

A long, tense moment ensued, a standoff between the men and the elves. For a long while it seemed that the animosities of the past would get the better of them and they would attack each other. During that time, Queen Rosa and Queen Willa watched with wide-eyed wonder as Yip kept everyone at bay while Talon unstoppered the wineskin and Spike clumsily used his paws to direct the water Talon had carried all the way from the Leif Repline fountain into King Mikahl's mouth.

Chapter Sixty

Once again Hyden Hawk found himself before the goddess. Her misty form stood thigh-deep in a swirling cloud of steam, scowling at him. "What's wrong with you, Hyden?" she asked.

The question stupefied him. He was too saddened by his failure, and the sight of his fallen friend, Mikahl, to even try to form a reply. It didn't matter, though. The angry goddess didn't wait for an answer.

"I tell you that Gerard no longer exists inside the Abbadon, yet you falter at the critical moment!" Her voice was stern, yet loving, like a scolding mother that is as relieved as she is angry at her child. "Don't you remember dying? The dragon had to bring you back, Hyden Hawk. Don't you remember?"

"Aye," he mumbled. "It's only Hyden now. When I died, the link between Talon and me was broken."

A heavy sigh of understanding escaped the goddess. It was she who'd made the mistake. All the confidence and direction she had instilled into the hawkling hadn't reached Hyden. Her expression softened.

"You'll always be Hyden Hawk," she reassured him. "Sir Hyden Hawk Skyler, the greatest wizard the realm has ever known."

"Is that how they will remember me?" he asked.

"What?" She looked at him as if he were daft. "Why would you ask that?"

"Because of the balance," he replied. "Gerard, the Abbadon, Hell Master, Warlord, whatever he was, is gone now. When the scales balance back..." He let the sentence trail off and shrugged as if his point were clear.

"Phenilous is right, Hyden," the goddess chuckled. "Deep down, you're still just a hick. Why the greater gods ever chose you..." Shaking her head, she put her hands on her hips in exasperation. "You paid your life forward, Hyden Hawk Skyler. To keep the balance, the Warlord had to die. You already had. The Dark One is no longer alive, but there are still an army's worth of his hellspawn scattering across the lands. Mikahl hasn't died, but he's been crippled. Phen's destiny lies with his unborn child. Who else but you is there to keep the balance?"

"Mik is alive?" Hyden asked with wide-eyed hope. Out of all the things she'd said, that was the one that registered.

The goddess threw up her arms in frustration. "You're impossible," she said with a huff. She pinched the bridge of her nose with a misty finger before continuing. "When you regain consciousness, you'll be under water, fool. Try to swim up instead of down." She turned and stormed away back into the roiling steam cloud from which she'd come.

"You mean I'm not dead?" Hyden called out to her.

"Ughhh," he heard her grunt as the mist he was in quickly turned into tepid water and closed over him.

Hyden blinked, trying to take in his surroundings. Just as the goddess said, he was underwater. Instead of swimming up toward the surface, though, he glanced down and saw a shimmering glimmer. Curiosity's grip just wouldn't let go of him. He wanted to give his body the air that it was craving, but whatever he could see down there was calling out to him and he didn't think he could resist it. With a shrug at his own foolishness, he did the opposite of what she'd told him. He swam down toward whatever it was.

Somewhere in the misty heavens, the goddess chuckled to herself. Hyden, so much like Gerard, wouldn't be able to resist the temptation of what was down there. She'd told him not to swim down so that the thought of doing it would find his mind. While he struggled to hold his breath, she restored the familiar link between Hyden and Talon. It was hard not to want to reward a man who cared so little about the powers the gods had granted him. Selfless was the word. Hyden had barely scratched the surface of his capabilities. She wondered when he would spread his own wings and fly through the sky with Talon in a physical form. Maybe, she decided, Claret's young hatchling would draw the ability out of him. She had a feeling that, to repay his debt to the severely wounded red dragon, he would willingly watch over young Alizarin.

THE WIZARD AND THE WARLORD

A Year and a Half Later

Queen Mother Telgra held her baby girl in her arms and smiled proudly at Phen. As with the elven life span, their pregnancies lasted longer than a human mother's. The child was half elf, half human, the first of its kind. The child's eyes, while slitted vertically like all elven orbs, weren't yellow, nor were they feral-looking. Her eyes were lavender, and enthralling. Phen melted for them. At only a week old, Princess Tamaerra had captured the hearts of all the elves. With the Arbor's Heart gone from the Evermore, save for the faint residual protective power it left behind for the Queen Mother to use, the elves clung to the hope that the newborn would some day lead them back to the heart of the forest.

Phen, now properly known as the High King's Ambassador, couldn't wait for Mikahl and Rosa, and their son, Prince Vaegon, to arrive. Mikahl could hardly walk, even with the aid of a staff, but he could ride as well as he ever had. His knee would never be the same, but he refused to let it hinder his traveling, or his sword drills.

In the elven tradition, the whole Forest of Evermore celebrated the childbirth for a full turn of the moon. This was so that the mother might enjoy the festivities, and also to make sure that there were plenty of elves around during those critical first weeks of life.

Princess Tamaerra was strong and healthy. Both Phen and Telgra couldn't wait to show her off to the realm. A new tradition was being started with this birthing celebration. No longer would elven society hide itself away from the kingdom folk. They would embrace each other and celebrate life. After all, Tamaerra was as much human as she was elf.

Dieter Willowbrow became known throughout the Forest of Evermore as the elf who saved their whole race from annihilation. The Queen Mother offered Dieter the position of Master of Defense, but after fighting a war and reading the stories that Vaegon had written in his journal, Dieter found that the forest couldn't contain his curiosity anymore. He declined in order to join the great wizard Hyden Hawk and his band of demon hunters.

Bzorch, the mighty Lord of Locar, fought snappers, dactyls, and packs of Zard for months while struggling to get out of the marshes. The fall he took hadn't killed him. He found a rise on which to rest while he healed. He lived off of snappers and small geka until he was ready. Then he covered himself with the moss that hung from the swamp trees so he looked like one of the trolls that the typical marsh denizens seemed to avoid. He spent three long months fighting his way through the treacherous shallows and swimming the snapper-filled channels. Finally, in the heart of spring, he pulled himself out of the marshes near Settsted. It was a feat of survival that might never be repeated.

Another event was being planned, besides the elven birth ceremony. King Jarrek and Queen Willa were to be married, just before Summer's Day at the new Palace of Oktin. The wedding was to be the first of many grand events to be held in the fabulous architectural marvel the dwarves were finishing.

Not long after the Summer's Day Festival, Lady Trella's baby would be due. With his new post as the High Lord of Westland, Lord Gregory had been enjoying the free time his position gave him with his wife. He was more than happy to turn over Lake Bottom Stronghold to Zasha and her husband Wyndall. Their son would enjoy the title and benefits Lord Gregory previously held. In this new age of hope and peace, it was a grand title to have.

Mikahl Collum, the High King of the realm, sat atop his old horse Windfoot in the saddle his father had once given him. The jarring and swaying of the royal carriage aggravated his wounds. Besides that, his grunting, groaning, and complaining kept the baby from sleep.

For the most part his body was healed, but the pain of the wounds never left him. He could never forget. It was a small price to pay to be alive. He decided, when he'd opened his eyes to find a great wolf, a hawkling, a lyna cat, and the beautiful, teary eyes of his wife all staring down at him expectantly, that life was the most precious thing. He would gladly suffer the pain for the joy Rosa and Prince Vaegon gave him.

Mikahl was anxious to see Hyden Hawk and Phen, and especially Talon. After hearing the story of the brave bird's dangerous flight back to the Leif Repline, Mikahl declared that the Unified Kingdom's banner would be a green-bordered field of gold with the silhouette of a swooping hawkling centered on it. The bird had Ironspike clutched in its claws. Lord Gregory would always be the Lion of the West. He had earned the right to call that banner his own.

When Mikahl looked up at the new banner, it was flapping proudly in the wind. He remembered Hyden standing in the fountain pool wet and dripping, looking more like a wizard of old than the carefree man Mikahl knew. He was holding Ironspike high over his head like a trophy and was smiling broadly as he came wading across Whitten Loch toward them.

Mikahl had been lying in the bloody snow then, feeling the Leif Repline's power slowly rejuvenating his lightning-blasted body. Talon had lifted from his chest and flown to Hyden's shoulder, and in that moment of triumph the image of the new banner had taken in Mikahl's heart.

Hope and glory.

They had banded together: men, elves, giants and dwarves. Even dragons had joined with them, and they had beaten back impossible odds. Mikahl knew this feeling of unity wouldn't last forever, but it was his hope that it would last an age. Hopefully his son Vaegon could use Ironspike to rule men in peace, instead of having to constantly defend the realm with the blade. Mikahl glanced at the carriage carrying his wife and child. He shook away all those concerns and smiled broadly. He couldn't wait to see Hyden Hawk and Phen.

Hyden was growing accustomed to feeling older. He decided to look the role of a great wizard and kept the long beard. He started wearing fancy, high-collared cloaks too. He didn't feel all that great. Seeing Oarly die, and knowing that Gerard was gone, left him hollow. Then the process of moving Claret's huge body to a cavern hidden in the hills north of Jenkata took its toll on him and the rest of Xwarda's wizards. Claret had a ruined wing, and both her foreclaws were swollen to twice their normal size. She'd extended them to cushion her crash, but only managed to break her own bones. Queen Willa assigned a whole brigade of rangers to hunt food for the dragon. At least the old red wyrm was able to mother over Alizarin when the growing young dragon was at the lair.

Seeing Dostin cry like a babe when they buried Corva near Vaegon's Glade hadn't been easy, either. Now Dostin and Alizarin were Hyden's charges and the only interesting conversations he found were with Claret, or Talon.

Phen was a man grown, and as capable as they come, but he was in the Evermore more often than not, these days. Hyden couldn't believe the boy had fathered a child with the Queen Mother, and even though a lot had transpired, leaving the elves in a new, weaker situation, he couldn't believe they were getting along with the kingdom folk.

A great expedition into the Wedjak was looming, but Hyden worried little about it. They would hunt demons on the way. Dieter helped prepare, as did Durge, and a trio of young dwarves strived daily to live up to the drunken legend Oarly had become.

Jicks eventually became known as the Hunter. His enchanted sword, the sparkling blue wyrm he rode, and the ice dragon that did its bidding, took seriously the chore of ridding the world of hellspawn.

Hyden's body was older, and his mind was expanded so greatly that he was sometimes on the verge of getting lost in his own head. He was also struggling with the fact that all that magic passing through his body had changed him in other ways. It was likely that he wouldn't age anymore. That bothered him, too, but not because he looked older. He'd lived only twenty-one summers, but looked like he was twice that. He just didn't like the idea of living longer than a man should.

He found that the long beard, with its few gray hairs, lent to his credibility among the Xwardian wizards and scholars. There was a group of them studying, notating, and cataloguing everything they could find about the side effects of channeling so much raw, arcane power. Several times over the course of recorded history, a wizard had misspelled, or gotten a potion wrong, and ended up bathed in power. The ones who'd survived their mishap lived far beyond their expected time. Hyden had taken in and then released more than a thousand times as much as any three of the wizards they were reading about.

The births of Prince Vaegon and Princess Tamaerra were welcome distractions. Hyden was proud and happy for Mik and Phen, but on the whole he wasn't feeling anything more than content. Not even planning for the upcoming journey could pull him out of his melancholic mood. He'd been to the Wedjak already and had since learned from Claret that it wasn't much different than anywhere else men dwell.

There was something missing in his life. He thought about it often, but couldn't pin down the issue. It itched at his curiosity like one's nose does when it can't be scratched because one's hands are full. No matter how hard he pondered, he couldn't figure out what it was. Then one day he was going through some of the texts in Dahg Mahn's private study and everything changed.

He came across a volume titled: "Harthgar – Observations"

After reading only the first page, where he learned that Dahg Mahn had once visited the fabled city and had taken these notes himself, he began to feel a tingle of anticipation. After reading about some of the strange creatures and locals who waited there, he had half a mind to climb on Alizarin's back and go.

Maybe he did.

THE END

Other titles by M. R. Mathias

The Dragoneer Saga
The First Dragoneer – Free
The Royal Dragoneers – Nominated, Locus Poll 2011
Cold Hearted Son of a Witch
The Confliction
The Emerald Rider
Rise of the Dragon King
Blood and Royalty – Winner, 2015 Readers Favorite Award,
and 2015 Kindle Book Award Semifinalist

The Legend of Vanx Malic
Book One – Through the Wildwood
Book Two – Dragon Isle
Foxwise (a short story) - Free
Book Three – Saint Elm's Deep
Book Four – That Frigid Fargin' Witch
Book Five – Trigon Daze
Book Six – Paragon Dracus
Book Seven – The Far Side of Creation
Book Eight – The Long Journey Home
Collection -To Kill a Witch – Books I-IV w/bonus content
Collection –The Legend Grows Stronger – Books V-VIII
Books IX-XII coming soon!

And don't miss the huge International Bestselling epic:
The Wardstone Trilogy
Book One - The Sword and the Dragon
Book Two - Kings, Queens, Heroes, & Fools
Book Three - The Wizard & the Warlord

Short Stories:
Crimzon & Clover I - Orphaned Dragon, Lucky Girl
Crimzon & Clover II - The Tricky Wizard
Crimzon & Clover III - The Grog
Crimzon & Clover IV - The Wrath of Crimzon
Crimzon & Clover V - Killer of Giants

Crimzon & Clover Collection One (stories 1-5)

Crimzon & Clover VI – One Bad Bitch
Crimzon &Clover VII – The Fortune's Fortune

About the Author

There are few writers in the genre of fantasy that can equal the creative mind of M.R. Mathias – now acknowledged as a master in this genre of dragons and dwarves, and magic, and spells, and all aspects of fantasy. — Top 100, Hall of Fame, Vine Voice, Book Reviewer, Grady Harp

M. R. Mathias is the multiple award winning author of the huge, #1 Bestselling, epic, The Wardstone Trilogy, as well as the #1 Bestselling Dragoneer Saga, the #1 Bestselling The Legend of Vanx Malic fantasy adventure series, and the #1 Bestselling Crimzon & Clover Short Short Series.

Use these series hashtags on twitter to find maps, cover art, sales, giveaways, book reviews, upcoming releases, and contest information:

#Wardstone – #DragoneerSaga – #VanxMalic – #MRMathias

CPSIA information can be obtained
at www.ICGtesting.com
Printed in the USA
LVOW09*0516311016

510969LV00010B/82/P

9 781946 187109